The Falling Hills

THE
FALLING
HILLS

Perry Lentz

UNIVERSITY OF SOUTH CAROLINA PRESS

Published in Columbia, South Carolina, by the
University of South Carolina Press

Manufactured in the United States of America

Originally published in 1967 by Charles Scribner's Sons

Library of Congress Cataloging-in-Publication Data
Lentz, Perry, 1943–
The falling hills / Perry Lentz.
p. cm.
ISBN 0–87249–988–X
1. United States—History—Civil War, 1861–1865—Participation,
Afro-American—Fiction. 2. Fort Pillow (Tenn.), Battle of, 1864—
Fiction. 3. Afro-American soldiers—Tennessee—Fiction.
I. Title.
PS3562.E494F35 1993
813'.54—dc20 93–24496

For
PROFESSOR DENHAM SUTCLIFFE
(1913–1964)
Magnanimiter crucem sustine

Preface to the 1994 Edition

Differently titled and differently featured, and longer by virtue of some ancillary vignettes, this novel performed admirably for me as an Honors Thesis at Kenyon College; but then won no admirers at all, when it went out on its own—agentless—to seek publication. One publisher handled my best typescript of it with such carelessness that it returned to me in separate chunks, the last of which found its way back only because my name and college happened to be written on each of the pages which separated the typescript's divisions. I took that literally dismembering dismissal as final proof that the publishing world was not interested in a novel about the Fort Pillow incident; laid aside the rebundled book; and buckled down to my graduate studies at Vanderbilt.

But one of the short stories I wrote for my Master's Thesis garnered some positive responses from *The New Yorker,* and Walter Sullivan said it was time for me to get an agent. Diarmuid Russell showed interest, invited me to send him my novel as well, and—without my being much aware of the fact—set about placing it; and on a summer noon-time in Nashville I found, amidst the mail awaiting me at the end of a vacation, an offer from Charles Scribner's Sons. I can remember exactly where I was standing (the door from the garage into the house, with my left foot on the step) when I read it.

So one brilliant late-winter day I stood in front of the black-and-gold facade of the Scribner's Building at 597 Fifth Avenue, looking at a massive display of my novel (*my* novel) in one of its front windows—the one on the right-hand side. Miss Richmond, who had assembled the display, shook my hand warmly. I was with my father, Lucian Lentz, who was my best and earliest mentor in historical narratives—some of my earliest *intellectual* memories are of fresh mornings in Alabama, sitting on his bathroom hamper as he shaved, and listening to his enrapturing stories about the Civil War. We had lunch with Mr. Russell (my father, whose huge array of hobbies included wildflowers, was long- and well-acquainted with his monumental folio publications in the field), and Burroughs Mitchell, the patient and genteel man who was my editor at Scribner's. After lunch, we were welcomed by Charles Scribner, in his offices; I particularly recall his graciousness—recall finding instead of the polished seigniorial ease you surely could have expected in such surroundings, a genuine (and even somewhat shy-seeming) personal warmth.

Thus although this novel was first published in 1967, it had been substantially written some few years earlier, between the summer of 1963 and the spring of 1964. I had been writing it, then, during the years of the (fairly marmoreal) celebration of the centennial of our Civil War, during the first vivid and burgeoning years of the Civil Rights movement, and before Selma and Watts and the assassinations of Malcolm X and Dr. King; I was working on it, in fact, the day of President Kennedy's assassination.

My principal intention was to recreate, with all the vividness and the historical accuracy that I would muster, what was once the most famous racial atrocity in a war that was caused by racist beliefs and by the peculiar institutions and cultures that had been built upon them in this nation. But at the time I wrote this, the "Fort Pillow Massacre" seemed to have slipped from the American imagination. It was never portrayed at even modest length in any of the admirable current popular histories of the War, such as Bruce Catton's; granted, the incident had always been of negligible military significance—but evidently it no longer had any resonance at all. Sometimes it received a few pages of attention in narratives about the river war, such as Fletcher Pratt's; but they generally portrayed it as but another example of the satanic southern mentality. It necessarily warranted a chapter in biographies of General Forrest, such as Robert Selph Henry's; but they inevitably relied upon hoary justifications.

I wanted to get it *closer:* closer to my own eye, and imagination. Since no one else was doing this for me, I hoped in this novel to satisfy (at last, and by my own endeavor) a curiosity, a hunger, a *frisson,* a yearning—I do not know the word for it, even yet—in myself. I do know that this emotion, however it might be described, had been awakened in me by a lurid contemporary engraving of the massacre reproduced in a twentieth-century biography of Forrest—Henry's, almost surely; I clearly remember coming across that picture at a cousin's house late one afternoon, in my hometown of Anniston, Alabama. I must have been twelve or fourteen. Back beyond that motivation, I cannot go.

At the time I wrote this, the "Fort Pillow Incident" had never received substantial treatment in literature; except for a very brief incident in a novel by Frank Yerby, I do not believe that it had been depicted in fiction at all. There was a vignette in *John Brown's Body* of "A colored trooper named Woodson," on guard at Newport News prison: after bayonetting a rebel prisoner, he says that " 'They buried us alive at Fort Pillow.' " But nothing else; had there been anything at all commensurate with my curiosity, I surely would have found it, and I would not have had to write *The Falling Hills.*

Because of the contemporary notoriety of the "Fort Pillow Massacre," there was at least a good deal of raw, archival material—eye-witness testimony and the like, in *The Official Records of the War of the Rebellion* and elsewhere—about the specific incident itself.

But my motivation also compelled me to try to create a persuasive picture of African-American formations in the Federal service before the incident. And, searching for revealingly ordinary (rather than shatteringly apocalyptic) details relevant to that effort, I could find only a few historical sources, and no literary or imaginative ones. Robert Lowell's "For the Union Dead" was hardly relevant, and of course all this was at least a quarter of a century before the film *Glory* would offer its splendid and justifiably celebrated evocation—and please note that the 54th Massachusetts, the regiment commemorated in that film (and whose monument was the catalyst for Lowell's poem) was composed of African Americans who had lived freely in the North before the War. There was considerable belief that regiments composed of newly liberated slaves would be very different in character; see, in this regard, Thomas Wentworth Higginson's excellent *Army Life in a Black Regiment,* which was the very best of the few sources I could find. Certainly the 54th Massachusetts was quite different in its experience, its character, and above all in its officer-corps, from the African-American artillery companies at Fort Pillow.

Were I to write this again, thirty years later in my life and in the life of our nation and our culture, it would be a different novel; which surely just states the obvious.

Some of the specific terms and techniques I used may, nowadays, give particular but altogether unintended offense. I could not have imagined, in 1963, that the word "Negro" would be an irritant today; I was schooled, then, to believe that the term "black" was offensive; and, had I heard the term "African American," I would have—back then—assumed that *that* usage would have also been egregious to people of that heritage and descent. Part of my strategy in the novel was to reinforce its vividness by differentiating characters according to patterns of speech peculiar to their different classes, backgrounds, and ancestry. My own ear and imagination were influenced by deeply-buried literary models; among them Twain, Benet, MacKinlay Kantor, Robert Penn Warren and, of course, William Faulkner. Faulkner had been dead only a year when I began writing this; by contrast, Toni Morrison's first publication was a half-dozen years away, and *Roots* a full dozen. And I had no historical models to advise me to proceed in this area with any greater caution or subtlety. Needless to say, these are among the things in the novel which I would render very differently, today.

In the novel I did write, the major characters are two white officers, because it seemed obvious to me then to concentrate upon people of the class and race who were in command and in power, and who bore the responsibility for what happened that day in April 1864, in West Tennessee. I assumed that it would go without saying—certainly without the need to illustrate through creating an equivalent African-American character—that those who suffered so horribly during the afternoon and early evening of that day were fully as capable of suffering and of heroism, and fully as deserving of sympathy and understanding, as the white soldiers around them; and that the failure of the white soldiers, rebel and Federal alike, to recognize that humanity was the most ghastly shortcoming in their own humanity.

My father passed on in the early autumn of this year, before I ever managed to find a publisher for the novel I intended to dedicate to my parents (the novel in which the South finally wins the War); the last time that I was in New York, the Scribner's Building was a Brentano's; but just as the gilded facade still reads "Scribner's," so memory, and even more enduringly, remains.

Perry Lentz
Gambier, Ohio
Autumn 1993

Commands at Fort Pillow

Union

Thirteenth Tennessee (Federal) Cavalry (*also* "Thirteenth Tennessee Battalion"; "Bradford's Battalion")—four companies, one unmustered fifth company, Major William Bradford.
Sixth United States Colored Heavy Artillery (*formerly* "First Alabama Siege Artillery"; "Fifth United States Colored Heavy Artillery")—First Battalion, Major Lionel Booth.
Second United States Colored Light Artillery—one section, Captain Lamberg.
Battery: 2 ten-pounder Parrot rifled cannon, 2 twelve-pounder howitzers, 2 six-pounder howitzers.
Gunboat on Station: *New Era*, 157 tons; battery: 6 twenty-four-pounder howitzers. Master James Marshall.

Confederate

Second Brigade, Chalmer's Division, Colonel Robert McCulloh commanding, composed of:
Second Missouri Cavalry, Colonel McCulloh.
Willis' Texas Battalion, Lt. Colonel Willis.
First Mississippi Partisans, Major Parks (detached from Fort Pillow assault).
Fifth Mississippi Cavalry, Major Perry.
Eighteenth Mississippi Battalion, Lt. Colonel Chalmers.
Nineteenth Mississippi Battalion, Lt. Colonel Duff.
McDonald's Battalion ("Forrest's Old Regiment"), Lt. Colonel Crews.

Fourth Brigade, Buford's Division, General T. H. Bell commanding, composed of:
Second Tennessee Cavalry, Colonel Barteau.
Sixteenth Tennessee Cavalry, Colonel Wilson.
Twentieth Tennessee Cavalry, Colonel Russell.

Yet not more surely shall the Spring awake
The voice of wood and brake
Than she shall rouse, for all her tranquil charms,
A million men to arms.

There shall be deeper hues upon her plains
Than all her sunlit rains,
And every gladdening influence around,
Can summon from the ground.

Oh! standing on this desecrated mould,
Methinks that I behold,
Lifting her bloody daisies up to God,
Spring kneeling on the sod,

And calling with the voice of all her rills
Upon the ancient hills,
To fall and crush the tyrants and the slaves
Who turn her meads to graves.

HENRY TIMROD
"Spring"
(1863)

BOOK ONE

The Third Winter of the War—
Incidents and Recollections in
West Tennessee

I

THE EARLY SPRING RAIN SPLASHED AND SHUDDERED AND CAME DOWN
in driving sheets, and the trees moaned and lantern light flickered and gleamed through it, from the porch of the house. The
soldiers faded against the row of shade trees where the road entered the yard of the house. They huddled in their rubber ponchos, and the rain sluiced and poured off cap visors and hat
brims. Corporal John Arness Suttell held his Colt revolver on
half cock and stared at the sparkling porch lantern. The rain
dribbled over his face and poured down his chin, and soaked up
from the ground through his trouser leg. Corporal Suttell was
leading twelve men of the Thirteenth Tennessee Union Cavalry organizing under Major Bradford at Fort Pillow, and they
were kneeling and crouching in the shelter of the willows and
oaks in front of the house. 'Y God that nigger better have been
tellen the truth. They better be in there. They better all of 'em
be in there. Suttell was lanky and sharp-faced with high cheekbones and flat grey eyes. His skin was taut; he was sharply handsome, with sun-bleached hair.

He kept one hand over the chamber of the revolver so the
caps wouldn't get wet. Them sombitchen deLaceys better all be
in that house. I heard they was comen through, the deLacey
boys, and they was goen to come by home. Nigger tol' me, and I
heard it from Pete Luke. Ain't nobody can keep John Arness
Suttell away when the deLaceys come home, not if ol' John got
him a gun. And I got me a gun.

Another man scuttled through the line of trees to his side.
"You reckon they's in there? I ain't seen nothen."

"Just you wait. We wait another ten, twelve minutes. If they's in there, they got to be comen out pretty soon, if they just stopped in for supper and they're moven on. Just wait. We hit 'em when they come out on that little porch."

"It sure is wet. . . . I never been out in rain like this before, I don't think. Got more sense than to be out in the rain." He splattered back to the trunk of the right-hand tree. Suttell looked at the porch. The lantern was gleaming above the door, and the porch was covered with yellow light. It was a dry- and warm-looking island, with little baskets of plants hanging from the ceiling.

Them damn deLaceys in there sloppen up the food while we wait out here in this fool rain. Ol' man deLacey ain't got but one arm left, I heard tell. Ol' sombitch lost the othern up east. Them damn deLaceys with their niggers and all, don't do no lick of work between dawn and dusk. 'Yassuh, Marse deLacey, I done planted that cotton and them corn just lak you done tol' me, Marse deLacey. Yassuh, it sho is hot, Marse deLacey. Cain I hep you off with them boots, Marse deLacey?' Sombitch. It's enough to make a grown man puke the way them deLaceys carry on.

He scrubbed his face with his left hand and wiped the water off. They must have ten, twelve niggers. I work from sun-up to dark scratchin' at that poor ol' dirt up side the mountain, and down here them deLaceys is sitten back and sleepen late and visiten all over the place and hunten and carryen on fit to kill. All mornen.

And this ol' war come along and them deLaceys they all go off to fight. And we don't want no war. What we want a war for? Them deLaceys got all the niggers. We ain't got nothen to fight about. So they come, the secesh come up, and they conscript my ol' brother Henry and they take him off, and Ma's cryen and carryen on and there ain't enough of us as 'tis. They come riden up at midmornen with ol' Henry out in the field and they ketch him up and say they shoot him unless he comes. And they hawg tie him and lead him off so that the damn deLaceys can kill him one way or another. And they sure enough killed Henry, they put him up where the ol' Yankee could shoot him. They push

Henry right into the front. Hell, you wouldn't ketch any damned deLacey in the front. Nawsuh. But a Suttell, they shove him up there. Rich man's war, po' man's fight. Mister Suttle, they say, like they don't even know how to call him by his name, Mister Suttle, yore son's been killed.

Then they come back and they ketch up all the stock, our ol' hoss and the ol' mule. We need these animals, Mr. Suttle. And they give us that worthless ol' paper shitass stuff. They try to ketch me too, but I run off. And ol' Pa, he tries to get them hosses back, and they ketch him and they hang him. I wisht they come for me, come to conscript me, with ol' deLacey doen his own damn dirty work. I'd conscript them longside the head, damn if I wouldn't. I'd stomp them into the mud. With all their niggers and all their god damn fancy ways. "Mis-tuh Beau, how's yew? How's yew, Mis-tuh Chet?"

His teeth were aching and his hands were sweaty and aching. I been biten down, I hate them so much. He shifted the gun to his other hand, and squeezed his right hand on his trouser leg, and rubbed it along his thigh.

Well now by Gawd just a little more, and we'll see about ol' Mistuh Beau. Mistuh Suttle will see about him. We done seen about one of 'em. That sombitch little Bobby deLacey come riden down that road, whistlen to beat all, and we seen about him. We seen with a bitty ol' pine tree and a piece of hemp, we seen about him. And in a minute we see about the rest of 'em, with their niggers an' all. All them niggers too, they act like the deLaceys. Push you off the road, into the ditch. Black sombitches. Ol' black fiel' han', ol' black buck come along. Yo on Marse deLacey's lan', boy. Yo get offen Marse de-Lacey's lan', boy, fo' I take a hickory switch up ginst yo, fo' I tell Marse deLacey 'bout yo. I ought to had busted him up side the head. He did tell. Damned if he didn't. Mis-tuh Suttle, sir, please tell your youngest son, ahh, John, please tell John to be sure and don't cut through the corner of our north field. Not even getten off his ol' hoss, it prancen around and everything and Pa just standen there yessuh Mister deLacey yessuh.

Well Mister deLacey you can treat your niggers like dirt but you can't treat us like dirt, and your niggers they can't treat us like dirt. Not no more. And I tol' Major Bradford I tol' him the deLaceys was comen back. And hell Bradford ain't got no reason to like them deLaceys. He's licked their boots just like us, maybe more. And he wouldn't let me go after 'em. He looked at me in that funny ol' squint-eye way, and wouldn't let me and sent that damned lieutenant whose ol' man ran for govnor, sent him all jinglen out with a lot of men and tol' 'em to round up any secesh. Me I get the wagon and he tells me to take some men out on the wood detail. Hell with that. I cut and come up here with these men. We ain't sitten in this rain to cut down no wood.

A back door opened, and a splatter of light flickered over the hoof-cut spring earth. Then a shadow, and for a cold moment Suttell thought they were going out the back way, out to the barn. Then the private, McCain, came over again from his right, slipping on the mud, and said, "A nigger just went out to the barn."

"Hope them fools out that way have the sense to keep out the way."

"They will. Wilson is as good a man as there is in th' regiment."

"We see."

The Negro came back around to the front, leading four horses. His feet and the horses' hooves made sucking, splashing noises in the mud. "Lor', an' it's rainen." The Negro boy laughed to himself, and stood away to the side of the porch, his hair wet and glistening in the rain wash.

"They got to be comen in a minute."

"Remember, wait till I shoot first. We got to get 'em all out on that porch."

"Yeh— Well, I be gitten back." His poncho sucked and rustled.

John Arness Suttell's body tensed and he felt tickled inside, tickled and laughing. He felt a twist of excitement run all the way down his back, and he shivered and his lips pulled back and he grinned; the rain water still poured off his cap visor, running down his face. He brought the hammer of the Colt back with a click, muffled by his hand and the thick rubber poncho. His genitals twitched with excitement. By God and this whole country overrun with the damned secesh. Kill a man, take his hosses, burn him out. Everbody kissen ass with the deLaceys, doen what they say, getten killed for 'em, ketchen up my brother for 'em, killen my father for 'em. You got to teach these secesh. They learn hard, and you got to teach 'em. You got to grub up this country, put the torch to 'em, hang 'em, burn 'em till they learn. Caint no man go putten himself over other men 'cause he has some niggers. Niggers ain't no good for a man, give him ideas. Man with niggers has to be taught, 'y God.

Them Yankees to Memphis don't know nothen. They fight a war with maps and papers and big guns. You caint lick 'em like that. You got to come and kill 'em, and you got to remember that's what you're here for. Killen. Clean up this place. Burn 'em out. If you don't, the secesh come along and shoot you down in the door 'cause you don't want to truck with 'em and 'cause you ain't got niggers. They done called the tune, and now they got to pay the piper. I don't care one damn bit about taken orders from a damn Yankee or a big-talken politician, but I care a damn sight less 'bout taken shit off a nigger-owen secesh man. Ain't anybody in West Tennessee, owen slaves or not, goen to get away with killen my brother and my pa, and taken our cattle and our grain.

The front door of the house opened. A grinning Negro, white-headed and holding a lantern, stepped out and turned to hold the door with one hand. Voices, sing-song with affectation, came through the door and the rain-noise. The Negro's lantern threw misty clouds of shadow behind the hanging pots of plants, and split the single shadows of the railings and pillars into vees. A Confederate soldier pulling on a bulky overcoat came out, still looking back in and smiling and talking. He had a big moustache, and he was saying, "Miz deLacey, that's the best fried chicken I ever had in my whole life. It surely was." Then another soldier, clean-shaven, with a straight nose and chin, came out wearing a tattered cloak, smiling over his shoulder too.

Then Mrs. deLacey, old and small and white-haired, came out, gobbling and chattering. "Why Mr. Spence, you and Mr.

Barnard were entirely welcome. I wisht you'd come and see us more, the place is so dreary with all the young men gone. Now you must make Tommy bring you both back!" The two soldiers grinned and edged around, Spence with his back to the steps and Mrs. deLacey between them. "And Mr. Spence, you tell your mother what a fine-lookin' son she's got, and you tell her I hope she gets to feelin' better soon, hear?" Another boy came through the door with Major deLacey, wearing a short cavalry jacket trimmed with a yellow collar and carrying a poncho loose over his arm, buckling on a pistol belt.

Suttell got up then, his poncho sighing and his feet rustling. He started walking forward, toward the light but still holding the pistol under the cloak. The feeling, the tickling and the breath-catch, was mist-like, dense upon him, and he was grinning and walking straight toward them, silently now on the mud. They kept on talking and shaking hands and grinning and he was picking them out, one by one. His boots slipped over the mud and the rain splattered off his varnished cap and his rubber cape.

"Why Mr. Barnard, you're entirely welcome too, and I declare you're one of the best-mannered young men I ever did meet. You know, Tommy and Bob are so sloppy, it does me good to think they have young fellows like you and Mr. Spence to keep them cleaned and looking proper and mindful of their manners." Barnard, embarrassed, kept looking out into the rain and for a moment Suttell, stalking forward, was afraid he would see him. Barnard kept on talking and listening and gulping. "Miz deLacey, this was real kind of you—you're sweet to say that, ma'am, wisht my mother could hear it—that surely was good food, ma'am—like Jeffy says, it almost makes two months of winter campaignin' worth it—" and behind them deLacey kept on talking to his son, "Now boy, you take good care of yourself, and take good care of Bobby too. Now that I've lost this arm you're the men of the family, and you boys take care." Young deLacey was nodding and embarrassed too. "Yes Pa, yes Pa." The rebels were wanting to be off, their hands twitching and flipping their gloves against their thighs and their boot heels making small clicks on the wood.

Suttell stopped twelve feet away and raised the Navy Colt slowly, pulling the poncho aside and leveling the gun, wrist stiff and eye down the barrel. Slow, he kept on thinking, it feels so slow and good and in a minit with all their talken they're goen to be dead. DeLacey standing in his broadcloth with the empty sleeve, white-bearded, still talking to his son, all of the boys ready to leave and Mrs. deLacey saying, "Now Mr. Barnard, you check and see if Mrs. Malcolm is my cousin Sophy, 'cause I believe she is," and "Yes ma'am, I sure will and thank you again," and Mrs. deLacey saying, "What fine boys," and beaming at them both; Spence now standing on the step and Barnard turned sideways to the darkness, the deLaceys shaking hands and the old man with his arm again on his son's shoulder walking toward the horses and the rain, and the Negro with the lantern smiling and grinning. Mrs. deLacey said, "And I sure am mad that Bobby deLacey wasn't here, he talked about you so much," and Barnard saying, "I guess he couldn't get off at the last minute, ma'am, and thank you and good night," and all of them in the light, still and about to leave.

Suttell got the notch in the hammer of the Navy Colt leveled right on Barnard, right on his throat, and he kept on thinking about lying in his bed in the cabin and hearing the deLacey boys whooping and riding up the valley and the dogs barking and thinking of the nigger telling him not to cross the field and nigger women soft and black under the deLacey boys, breathing and filling himself cold-chilled with his hate; just images now and not even thoughts in the second before he pulled the trigger, the horse deLacey rode and the deLacey boys and his brother dead and the niggers and his own sweat-dark and stinking shirt and blistered body out hacking at dry flinty earth and the picket fences and the whitewashed outbuildings and nigger girls and boots and his father dead down in the next county.

The Negro boy was holding the horses and looking at him white-eyed when Suttell fired the big pistol. It blasted and jerked back in his hand and there was the smoke and the sting on his face and the dry, acrid smell. He swung the pistol back over his shoulder up in the air and cocked the hammer and swung it down again, never taking his eyes off the cluster of people on the step. Barnard, the handsome one, was punched back against the slim pillar, his eyes shocked and staring, and then he slumped to the ground with his white hands fluttering to his open cloak collar and his neck. Suttell had the notch on Spence's back, but there was blasting and gunfire on both sides of him and before he could fire Spence was kicked forward with the "pock pock" sound of the slugs hitting his back. Suttell swung the notch left along the porch looking for another rebel to shoot. Splinters were flying off the railing and the flower pots were shattering in bursts. Young deLacey swung, dropping his poncho and pulling out his pistol in one motion. He fired and moved to the end of the porch on his right, the pistol blasting and blasting, and then deLacey with his face white took one stride for the railing on the end of the porch. Suttell could hear the soldiers around him loading and clicking their Sharps and he tracked the pistol, arm straight and wrist stiff, keeping up with deLacey, waiting for the last split second, his genitals swollen. DeLacey swung his right leg up to clear the railing, putting his left hand on it and rolling to clear it in a dive, his face white and his hair fluted, and just when he was about to cross the railing into the darkness Suttell held the notch of the Navy Colt on the silhouette of his face, leading him perfectly, and then the gun fired and rocked back again and he heard the bullet hit. DeLacey didn't roll over but collapsed, his face and head bloody, and his body bounced back off the wooden railing and he landed dead on the floor, crumpling just like a hit quail, Suttell thought, with his jacket fluttering, just like a quail.

Suttell swung the revolver back along the porch and the Sharps volleyed again and Barnard, who was sitting slumped with his hands at his throat, was kicked over and chopped up. Suttell put the gun right on Major deLacey who was standing already wounded in the shoulder and open-mouthed, his mouth moving and his jaw-muscles working and his eyes still wide and trying to narrow to look out into the haze of the rain. Suttell put the notch right on Major deLacey's throat and shot him there and the man crumpled back flat against the wall, with his shirt front splashed with blood.

Mrs. deLacey was screaming little high-pitched yips; all the men were dead, even the nigger holding the lantern had pitched it into the mud and was lying dead against the wall. Suttell moved with his revolver toward them, cautiously. He was starting to think, well good, when the front door slammed inward, opening. Another boy rushed out at them, pale-faced and his eyes burning, diving down the step and out into the mud. Suttell sidestepped from instinct, and his gun went off but didn't hit anything, and then the boy was past him, down the path.

Suttell turned. "God damn." Then he heard the slapping footsteps trip and the boy splash into the mud. He pounced toward the sound of the boy's scrambling, and then McCain whooped and thudded against the boy, and they thrashed, and another Yankee caught up with him, his poncho flapping like a hawk's wings, and they both wrenched the boy up and around.

Suttell stood over him, holding the revolver up and pushing away the flailing arms with his left hand. He found the boy's cotton jacket, already wet and now mud-caked. He ripped at the jacket and heard the buttons tear free. And all the time the boy was cursing up at him, "God damn you to hell you shiteating Yankee, God damn you to hell all of you, you gonna get killed I swear it, long as I live I never forget you never gave 'em a chance, not a chance," babbling and choking and tears and hate filling the voice. Some part of Suttell thought, just like a pore little pig squealen away, and then his palm slapped over bare flesh.

"Hold him, McCain."

He shoved the pistol barrel into the squirming, thin, wet chest, and the boy suddenly gulped and choked and shouted, "Whatcha doen, whatcha . . ." and Suttell pulled the trigger, holding up the boy's head by his hair. But the cartridge missed fire and Suttell cursed and thumbed the hammer back to cock it. The rebel was yelling suddenly, "No for God's sake, NO DON'T, OH DON'T, I give up, you got me, don't oh DON'T," screaming and struggling and twisting. "Ain't no game, boy." Suttell pulled the trigger, knowing it was his last shot, and this time the gun blasted and Suttell's hand was wet and the flame muffled against the flesh. McCain and the other soldier dropped him, cursing Suttell. "God damn, John, that was messy. I got covered with blood, I swear." There was the stinking-sweet smell of burned flesh and the dank smell of blood.

All the West Tennesseans turned again toward the porch, sloshing through the mud. Suttell reached into his pouch and pulled out another pistol, walking toward the porch.

Mrs. deLacey acten like she crazy, Suttell thought, off-hand. He felt empty and he began to shiver up and down his spine. His hands were sweaty. He climbed onto the porch, taking deep breaths. It's over, it's over. By God, I done it and come through.

Mrs. deLacey kept on saying, "Oh, NO, oh NO!" She stumbled over her husband's body and bent down and kept on saying, "Oh no, oh, NO," and then she began to shriek, twisting her hands and shaking her head. She looked up from Major deLacey's body and John Suttell thought he'd never seen such a vacant look. She kept on shuddering and shrieking and her body made wrenching and gasping motions, like she couldn't keep up outside to what was inside, Suttell thought.

Suttell looked at her a minute longer. He brushed back his cap with one hand, and put up his revolver. The other men of the detail gathered around looking at the deLacey woman, who was bending now over Major deLacey and whooping, "NO NO," and shuddering, taking deep breaths.

"Lay 'em out on this here porch," Suttell said. "You can leave the nigger in the mud." He began to nose around the house, looking inside. The others stretched out the five bodies, pulling down the overcoats and jackets which had been jerked up by the bullets. They bent over them, dark, great crowbirds in their black, flapping ponchos, and pulled out the dead men's wallets and letters and watches. One of them rocked back on his haunches and began to read a letter aloud which was folded into the overcoat of the boy with the moustache.

"Dearest Myron, I hope this finds you in the best of health and thinking of me, as I think of you," he read in a loud falsetto voice. The men on the porch slouched easily and lowered their carbines, relaxing and getting the tension and the cold out of their bones. They laughed. "The Reverend Whiteside came by to our church today, Myron, and we all offered prayers for you boys. Of course, I thought only of you, and I prayed to our dear Lord in heaven to keep you safe. . . ."

"She sure did miss a bet on that one! I mean to say I never want anybody to pray for me like that!" and they all laughed, and Mrs. deLacey kept on crying. Now she was whooping, "Oww oww oww" over and over.

Well now, it's over. It's over and I done it. They's dead. Lord but I feel tired inside. Tired and dead. Been waiten in that rain too long. He leaned back against the wall of the house, breathing deeply.

Twenty minutes later the detail walked back down to their horses near the road. The rain let up slightly and a wind, dank and cold-edged, came out of the hills. They folded up their ponchos and fastened on overcoats. It sounded as though they could still hear the deLacey woman. The lantern light of the porch at the deLacey house flickered through the trees. Suttell told Farley and Overmay to ride out on point, and they started back toward Fort Pillow.

After an hour they got in past the pickets and went to the shebangs in the town, down the slope from the fort. Suttell, not thinking much any more, saw to the horses and then splashed back down the line of huts to his tent. Pennell, who was from Michigan someplace, sat up when he came in, and then went right back to sleep.

2

THE NEXT MORNING THERE WERE THICK, CURDY MISTS FROM THE
river. An orderly came down before morning muster and shook
Suttell awake. He got up, scrubbing his palms over his eyes. The
orderly grinned down at him, his face lit up by a tin lantern
shining on his cheekbones and his beard. "Git up, boy. Git up.
Old Bradford wants to see you up t' the fo't." The orderly stood
back outside the tent.

"God damn sombitch." He pulled on his blouse and sword
belt, and threw some water in his face from the tin basin. Pennell swung up, thin and ribby and tousled. "Wassa matter?
Whut time is it? . . ."

"I got to go up see Major Bradford. See you at muster."
Suttell put on his cap and went out. They walked up the slope.
The place had been cut and cleared around the fort two years
ago; there were stumps and scrub brush and fallen logs, a tangle
of branches and spring leaves deep-green below the thick mists.
"It's gonna be clear today I reckon."

"Umm," the orderly said. The mud and earth were mauve
and purple, and the sky was palely blue. White mist and fog
were everywhere. They scrambled up the path to the fort, over
thick roots crossing the red trail. Suttell looked at the ground so
as not to slip, and began to get scared. He was cold and chilled
and he felt dog-tired and he ached. Ain' no time to get a man up
in the morning. No time 'tall.

The fort rose ahead of them, a thick block of earth. He
could see gleams off the brass muzzle of the six-pounder in one
of the southern embrasures. They crossed the deep, eight-foot

ditch on rickety grey planks, and entered a sally port. The fort looked big and empty in the early morning. He could see one lone sentinel on the east face, shielding the chamber of his carbine and padding aimlessly along the firestep. They got to the little headquarters shack at the rear of the fort, above the river bluff. Suttell decided he couldn't do much one way or the other, and maybe it was good news anyhow. He stood in the pitted mud outside the door, and then they called him in.

Bradford was behind the desk, sallow and white and nervous, twisting a little penknife around in his hand. His coat was only half-buttoned, and the brass buttons gleamed in the lantern light. Suttell looked over at the man standing beside the desk. It was the new lieutenant from East Tennessee. He was young and thin and black-haired and his face was twisted up toward Suttell. He still had on his rubber poncho, and he was breathing deep and the temples stood out.

"Corporal Suttell," Bradford was saying, "what happened out at the deLacey place last night?"

Oh. So that's it. "Well sir, I was out with the wood detail, an' a nigger come 'long down the road, and tol' us that the deLacey boy was home with some friends from Forrest's brigade. So we went up there las' night." The new lieutenant was glaring at him and his eyes were solid and flat like musket balls. "An' we got there and hollered for 'em to come out, and they came out and made a fight of it. Only we were in the dark and they didn't have a chance. So I reckon we killed 'em all. . . ."

"You butchered them all, Suttell, in cold blood."

He looked over at the lieutenant, and he kept his eyes on the smooth-shaven skin along the lieutenant's chin. "You never gave those men a chance. They came out and you shot them down like animals. And then your men looted their bodies and took their money. . . ." Suttell stared at the patch of skin.

"Well now, Lieutenant . . ."

"Men like you are a disgrace to the Union Army. You butchered those men right in front of Mrs. deLacey and didn't even have the God-given grace to bury them." The lieutenant's hand slapped at his thigh. The skin was pale yellow in the gleam of the lantern.

"Well now, Lieutenant . . ." Suttell kept looking at his chin, and the little patch of skin.

"I got there, Corporal, with my patrol twenty minutes after you left. You left that poor woman there on that porch with those dead bodies, and she was out of her head by the time we got there. Corporal, you ought to be hanged, God damn you. . . ." Suttell snapped inside and, loose-mouthed, eyes flat on the spot of skin, thought, that Bradford is a yellowbelly coward. I got about as much chance of him taking up for me against this little bastard as I got of getten to Memphis tonight. Bradford ain't gonna buck the little sombitch 'cause his ol' man run for the govnor of the state. ". . . and I'm preferring charges against you right now. . . ." So I got to outshout him in front of ol' Bradford here, is that it?

He felt too the old hatred coming back: him sayen "prefer charges" and "disgrace." What the hell does he know about this here war? The little bastard.

"Look at me, Corporal! Look at me!" Well now, Lieutenant, I am looken at you as hard as ever I plan to.

"Lieutenant Cleary, maybe they do things different . . ."

"God damn it, Corporal, answer me now! Answer . . ."

"All right, all right, God damn it, you take the word of a rebel woman over me. You go ahead and you take her word against mine, and me bein' in the same regiment and a good Union man all my life. . . ."

"I know what I saw! How you going to change what I saw?"

"All right! . . ." He breathed deeply and he mastered his voice, still looking at the lieutenant's chin. "All right, Lieutenant, you gonna give me a chance to say somethen or ain't you? Ain't you? 'Cause no man can stand there and say things against me and not give me a chance to say nothen." The lieutenant quieted and kept breathing loudly through his nose. "An' you can stand there and snort at me," thinking Ol' Bradford didn't even make a move—then he's scared. So I work on him. Suttell was growing calmer and calmer. The wrinkles went out of his forehead. "You can just snort at me all you want. But you can't make out that I'm lyen. 'Cause you just listen. Like I said, I don't know how they do things out in East Tennessee an' I don't care. An' I don't care what your pap is or was or what he done. Or what rank you are. After what you said to me I don't figger you got any rank, not so as I'm concerned.

"Now let me tell you two things, an' just two things. An' you listen. I ain't got much use for you or people like you, Lieutenant. 'Cause you talk big and you say 'dis-grace' and 'ought to be hanged' and things like that. But you sure don't know what this war is about. Nosir. And you know somethen else, Lieutenant, people like you with their big words and big ideas and stuff got us in this war. People like the deLaceys with their honor and stuff and all that crap, they got us in this war. Now you let me finish, damn it! . . . Now you listen. You started this thing, your people started it, and the only good thing I got to say about you is that you had the good sense to get on the winnen side. 'Cause I caint give you much else credit. You had ever'thing else, the big houses and ever'thing. The big houses and th' niggers . . . all right, all right. I don' give a damn about the Clearys but you listen. You had ever'thing and you went on an' started this war, people like you, with ideas about dis-grace and hangen's for people like me.

"But you know whose payen for this war, Lieutenant? Me. Me and my family. 'Cause if you didn't conscript my brother then I reckon people like you on the other side did and he sure as hell is dead right now. An' my paw is dead. And they tried him and said he was a hoss thief, and he was only tryen to get his stuff back, his own truck they took from him. People like you in uniforms, they stood up and said, 'Mr. Suttell, you ain't fit for liven,' and they hung him too. People like me is starven and dyen all over this state for your war and your ideas, and we sure didn't want it and didn't ask for it. But if you don't go in the greys you go into the blues, and it don't matter which side eats up your beef cattle and drinks your cow's milk 'cause it sure ain't your folks what does. This war is a mess, 'cause people like you started it, but you ain't got the good sense to finish it."

The lieutenant started to say something. The patch of skin stretched and worked but Suttell spoke louder, the words coming easy to him now. "So people like me, we got to finish it as soon as we can. As soon as we can. 'Cause it's a pore man's fight, but it's yore war, yore big ol' fancy war. Me, I want to get this thing finished. An' to fight a war means killen, and I plan to kill an' kill till this war is over. 'Cause people like you is payen me to do it. So if I don't fight this war to your satisfaction, Lieutenant, it's because it's my fight, and I fight it like I please."

He breathed sharply and started in again. The lieutenant drew his head up and back. "Sure, Lieutenant, we're on the same side. An' that's the second thing you got to learn. The first is this war means killen and people like me do that killen and people like me do that dyen.

"An' the second thing is that you all reckon about how ever' man-jack in this state is for us, but they ain't. Nawsuh. They're secesh, all of 'em. The ones that ain't, you can shake a stick at. We down here on our own, we got to cut the mustard on our own. So, Lieutenant Cleary, you better learn which side is yours, and which people you better hang on to." He slid his hands along the side of his pants, and turned to Bradford.

Bradford had his hand in his scraggly black beard. His eyes were bloodshot and he squinted. "Now Major Bradford, sir, you know what I'm talken about." He put all the appeal he could in his voice. Behind him he heard the sergeant shift at the stove, and the orderly snuffled. Bradford nodded and Suttell thought, good, I done it. Bradford had two ways he could go and he went my way. Pore ol' Bradford.

"Now I say this. We come up to that house, and those rebels come out, and we did what we had to do. Another minute they'd have been long gone. So maybe I broke orders, but I did what I knew to do. An' ol' Forrest, he got four less men. And they were big men around here, and I reckon they were here recruiten. Forrest is comen back. I heard tell. I thought you'd want to know."

Bradford nodded and coughed. Suttell thought, Lieutenant Cleary ain't no fool, he knows not to push it. "Thank you, Corporal. I know all about Forrest." Bradford's face, shifting, while the flesh rearranged itself, looked very young. Then it set and Bradford seemed to accrete and solidify behind it. "Lieutenant, you've got quite a bit to learn about things out here. The corporal was a little loud, but he was right. You got a lot of things to learn. You can't trust these people. You can't trust them a bit. You got to show 'em we're here to stay, and we're going to stay hard." He fidgeted and then sat back and shaded his eyes. "I know about these people, Lieutenant, it's like the corporal said. You can't be fair to them. You got to hit them, or they will hit you. It's bitter work, but you will learn." Ol' Bradford, Suttell thought, he's feelen his way. He was goen to hit *me* hard, so now he's got to feel his way. The chickenshit. He braced a little more to attention, his head up in the shadows. Bradford picked up the penknife and began to work at his fingernails, talking a little more steadily.

"Corporal there's right. You got to hit these people hard. They will hit you hard if you don't. They don't care about the rules." He snuffled and wrinkled his nose, and then went on. "I don't mean to side against you, Lieutenant"—the hell you don't, Suttell thought—"but you do have a lot to learn. These secesh are traitors, after all, and they around here are as mean a set of bushwhackers and thieves as you'll find. Now that's just the truth. They understand force. Like Colonel Hurst down to Memphis said, we got to grub up the country.

"Now we gave them their chance, I reckon. We set up enlistment depots in every county. But the rebels in the secesh counties, we got to hit hard. It's really the only way they learn." While he went on, Suttell thought again, I got to watch for that lieutenant. He ain't through with me, and he'll be layen for me. He swallers hard. He'll be comen after me, so I got to be on my step. Bradford he is a spineless yellow-bellied coward, I know. He don't like people like me. I hear tell he ran for office and got beat or somethen', anyhow he never made good. Lukey tol' me that. I got to look him up. Find out. . . .

"Corporal. Corporal?"

"Yessir?"

"That's all, boy. That's all."

Suttell saluted and left, and went back down the path to the town. It was higher morning, and troopers were stirring around; there were bugle calls and wisps of smoke from breakfast fires.

Pennell was pulling on his blouse when Suttell walked into the hut. "Well?"

"Well what?"

"What happen up yonder?"

"Ahh, that sombitchen ol' Cleary, he reported me to Major Bradford. Wanted to get me hung or somethen."

"Whaffore?"

" 'Cause his ol' man was near bouts govnor of this state, as near as I can tell. He came acrosst those bodies back at the de-Lacey place. I tell you, you caint trust that little bastard. And I tell you somethen else. I ain't in this war for Cleary, nor none of his kind. An' I tol' him so."

"What'd he say?"

"Couldn't say nothen. Ol' Bradford, he's such a chickenshit coward he wasn't about to outshout me, not with Eggers and Wick there too."

"He didn't do nothen?"

"Nah. I started shouten at Cleary and carryen on, and he jus' backed off."

"Good for you."

They both walked out into the crispness and colors of fresh morning. Cavalrymen were heading up to the fort for muster, blue jackets sharply etched against the tangled greens and mauves of the hillside.

Bradford in the little headquarters room leaned back and put his hands behind his head. Cleary stared out of the door, and his lips were bloodless.

"Major, that Suttell is worse than any animal I ever came across."

"Aw, no he's not. He is not near so bad as some of 'em, and he is capable and he does his work."

"Major, I say again, you weren't there at that house." Cleary was biting down on his words. "That poor woman was more than out of her mind. She was crazy. Really crazy, wandering around over those bodies. . . ."

"Look, Bill. Now that woman was a rebel, and don't forget that. I made myself too many enemies down south of here not to know anything about rebels. They do that and worse than that to any Bradford they catch. You caint let them people come next to you, not them rebels. Now I been hard, and I stood up. You got to be hard." Bradford began to talk confidingly, softly, and he got up and buckled on his sword belt and buttoned his coat while he talked. "Now listen, Bill. You got a lot to learn. Now I don't blame you one bit, boy. I had to learn too. I set off thinking about teaching these people right, and I lost too many men doing it. So you got to just set your mind on what you think is right, and forget how you get there. Really. You forget about them being people. They were enemies, they were secesh and rebels, and don't you forget for a minute they'd do the same and worse to you and every soldier with you. You hit 'em so they learn to respect you, you hit 'em hard. You can hit 'em a lot harder than they can hit you, in the long run. Unless you let all their lies and whimpers get to you.

"Now it's not easy. No, it's not." He moved around the desk and put his hand on Cleary's shoulder, and they both walked toward the door. "I don't like to sit here and listen to people I heard of all my life get shot down, and let men like that Suttell run roughshod over the country. But it's my duty. I got to do it. I got to shut my eyes and forget everything for a while save this war. Don't ever, ever get to think I like to sit here. Nosir. But somebody's got to do it. Somebody I reckon has got to take care of this part of the state of Tennessee. And I will."

They walked out into the parade. Soldiers were forming ranks inside the horseshoe fort. Cleary, head down and still mad, walked off toward his company. Bradford smiled indulgently, his wax-white face melting softly around the lips and the scraggly beard. He cherished the brief, sliding feel of guilt smoothed by the manly thought, well I got to do it, I got to go through with it. The ranks of men were skeleton-thin, the yellow piping picking out their blue jackets against the dark earth walls. He put his sword under his left arm, fiddling with the twine on the hilt, and walked across to where the battalion was forming. No, I don't like it. I don't like to do it. But somebody's got to do it. And that somebody might as well be me.

After the muster, the troopers filed back to the huts down in the ravine, or scattered around the fort. Bradford walked back to the orderly shack. Lt. Mack Leaming, the adjutant, was seated at the desk. He stood up when Bradford walked in.

"Good morning, sir."

"Morning, Mack."

The sergeant brought them coffee. Leaming was short and solidly built, with long arms. Bradford got down to work with him at the desk, going over requisitions and filling out the forms and papers. Leaming passed him another thick sheaf of army requisition forms. "We got to get some equipment for the men enlisted two days ago. Try to get some good mounts for three of them too."

"Yeah." He filled in his name on each one. "Say, Mack."

"Yessir?"

"You heard tell Forrest is on the loose again?"

"Yessir."

"Umm . . . I wisht these niggers would get here."

"The ones Hurlbut promised?"

"Yeah . . . they ought to get here today, tomorrow, don't you think?"

Leaming put his pen down. "Yessir, I'd think so."

"You know anything about 'em?"

"Nosir . . . 'cept I heard of Major Booth. Regular army, they say."

"Yes, well . . . we caint put those nigger troops down in the town with the Tennessee boys. I don't see how we can." He got up from the desk. "Give orders they're to be sheltered in the fort, on the bluff side. They can put up some tents there, with straw and all."

"Yessir." Leaming got to work writing a note.

"I'd a whole lot rather have half a battalion of white troops than a whole battalion of niggers, I don't mind telling you. But I'll be glad when they get here. So many more bayonets to hold this place. We ain't really got enough troopers yet for a fort this size. . . . You know, Mack, I got me some enemies in this state. I sure have."

"Yessir. I'll put out the orders to bunk the nigra battalion in the fort."

"Ah hell, Mack. With them we can hol' off a dozen Forrests. This here is a strong post, Lieutenant. Niggers may not be much good, but you put any man behind a wall with a gun and some cartridges and he's bound to be of some good."

Leaming smiled. "Yessir. He ought to be." Leaming got to work again at the requisition slips. Bradford played aimlessly with his sword hilt. He began to talk again. "I don't know what they want me to do here, Mack. I swear I don't. They don't give me enough men or equipment or supplies, horses, anything. I work myself down to the bone raising a regiment here for 'em, and all they send me to hold this place is a battalion of niggers. Work-detail niggers from Memphis. Hurlbut, he sends in Major Booth to take over command, they take that away from me, they put my boys, the ones I raised, under a damned officer of black troops. I swear, Mack, I certainly don't know what they expect of me."

"Nosir." Leaming stopped writing but kept on looking down at the notes and forms on the desk.

Bradford was worried, and his face worked at the corners of his mouth. He put his hand in his beard, and looked out the window and sighed. I've given everything for the Union, every damned thing I ever had. . . . And now they send up nigger troops and take away my command and this damned Cleary comes running in, and his father's a big shot with Andy Johnson up in Nashville, and I don't know what to do, Christ I don't know. I done my level best. I made enemies, but I done my level best.

"You know, Mack, I have given more for the Union than just about any man in this state." He rocked on his heels, still looking out of the window. "I gave up a good law practice, a good law practice. I made more enemies than you can shake a stick at. I fixed myself up real fine in this state. Hell, I can't live here any more. Not now, not even after we whip the rebels. I've had to push myself hard and it's hurt me. You better believe it's hurt me. You can't see people you lived with and known all your life turned out, their homes burned, and not hurt over it. It's hurt, but I've done it, Mack. I tried to do my duty and be the best soldier I know how. . . ."

He suddenly wondered where his brother Ted was. Need to see ol' Ted. "Well, Mack, I got to be going. Just leave those forms on my desk, I'll initial 'em. If they're all right by you, they're sound enough for me, sight unseen."

"Yessir."

Bradford walked out across the parade ground. The sky was washed clean by last night's rain. It was a clear, cold day, with the strong clay odor of earth and the dark, wet smell of the Mississippi.

Against his mind trailed the recollection of columns of smoke high against the sky, crops burning and the land being ripped up; lines of sweating young Yankee soldiers and him behind them, behind the clean, sharp, long bayonets, wearing a blue coat and watching the cribs and homes and cotton gins roar hollowly with fire.

Before the war he'd been a young jackleg lawyer, a Union man, but just a jackleg lawyer. He come out of the dogtrot cabins along the flat hillsides with a mindless hot melting in his soul for power. The damned slaveowners owned the democratic party, so he had become a Union man. His personal ambition blew him like a leaf in a hot summer wind; he saw all of the fine new houses, still smelling with paint and sawdust, which men just a few years earlier—not better, no, 'y God, nor smarter, just earlier—had built for themselves from the proceeds of their personal ambition, in a wide-open and richer'n hell land. He came just too late for that, and it wasn't right nor fair and he'd get his cut or know the reason why. So he moved into the irresistible shadow-world of politics. That was where the power lay, that was how you got people from the big houses to come to you, instead of wearing out your ass drumming up paid-in-kind cases from the backwoods and dogtrots of the county.

But the ambition ran thin, now; he could feel it running out of him. He thought briefly of his campaign for the state legislature; and his fruitless, ridiculous posturing, before the planters, and his desperate swagger and energy.

He walked aimlessly across the parade, and stood against the wall, on the firestep, watching the details riding out into the clear, cold morning, the pickets on the far trenches and ditches, the smoke of breakfast fires tracing up through the grey and red of the foliage and the earth. Hell, I never ought to have wasted one red cent's worth of time on them high bastards. He had had this talk with himself so much that he almost said the phrase aloud. He seemed to be preparing the phrase for some sort of moment in some sort of argument. Hell, I ought never to have wasted one red cent's worth of time on them high bastards. They ain't the ones to learn.

But it was too late for the phrase; the argument would, he knew, never come. He bit down on his tongue, thinking of his campaign. He had ridden all over the damn county, going into the homes with his campaign arguments proffered like visiting cards. He had been a jackleg lawyer reaching out with both hands for power. "But what they don't tell you, sir. . . ." "But the way I and my party see it, sir. . . ." "But where you are wrong, sir. . . ." He could still suffer how his sweat had soaked through his shirt into the broadcloth, how he had talked and wiped furtively at the perspiration on his forehead, while boredom and annoyance played across his host's face; Bell or de-Lacey and once even Forrest, who had been a rich man in 1860; or else how the cluster of men at the bar or in the plantation office would squint their eyes and he would be talking alone, endlessly, cigar smoke stinging his eyes. And of course he had taken a hell of a beating—I shouldn't have wasted a red cent's worth of time on the high bastards, he repeated without conviction—but then the war had come.

When the war came he was spit at and cursed, and once some men even came out looking for him, riding big blooded horses around in his yard while he scrambled into the shelter of the dusty, dry trees, pale, with his scraggly beard and his tight eyes.

With the war, he had found his power, but he had lost the thirst. The Federals came down and beat hell out of the rebels on the river and the Yankee gun boats steamed into Memphis. Almost without choosing, without having had a choice to make, he was in Memphis, talking to the Federal commanders, to Hurlbut and the others, sitting again in cigar smoke, with open decanters of brandy, listening and telling about Tennessee. They sent him out to recruit with squads of troops. He set up the bureaus and did the talking, and some of his recruits were killed and the weeks plunged by, amid burning homes and torches and whinnying horses. Power had leaped to meet his hand, suddenly. He rode down hard on the land. Hurlbut had said it. "Somebody's got to do it, Mr. Bradford, and we are fortunate to have a man as dedicated as yourself."

So he kept on, now commissioned as a major and treating in Memphis with Major Hurst, who commanded another Union Tennessee regiment; living high in Memphis by the gaslights, the polished bars and the thick, warm odor of hotel corridors, walking in a blue frock coat with the streets filled with regiment after regiment of Yankees. Now it was settled, and he worked as hard learning the drill manuals as he'd worked learning law books; he worked at the cavalry depots with the recruits, malcontented, sallow men from the hills and men with hate screwing and twisting at them, and Yankees looking for a softer place than the steel-edged life of the infantry soldier. He found himself looking for solid men to come in, men handsome and sure in their convictions whom he could recommend for commissions and whom he could teach, on the hot drill fields and in the quiet moments at the tables in the hotel bars, teach and talk with about the kind of war they were fighting. But men like that did not come; he learned the simple formula, that the rebels enlisted whole towns and counties, that they had marched off together and left the ones from the piney woods, the men with anger and hatred and flat-lined faces, the men with flesh curled close over sharp bones, with flat eyes and parchment-like, pale skin, and hawk noses and cackling laughs. That a man didn't have a reason for joining a Union regiment so much as he had had a reason for not joining a Confederate regiment—farmers and crackers mad at the Confederacy and poor, holding what they called freedom with a desperate, whip-sharp arrogance and pride. "So I told him, ain't no man goen to tell a Jones what to do, nosir. . . ."

Bradford lived in a dry bitterness. He was twenty-seven years old. He took what comfort and companionship there was, the bars and hotels and the talks with the mad or embittered colonels and majors, the profiteers and the army contractors. He compared power with them. But even as he would sit enjoying his drink he would still hate and envy the dusty cavalrymen and the bedraggled infantry passing in the street far into the night hours; and especially he would hate the lean rebel prisoners, in rotting grey clothes, carrying their bundles and rags, passing between the Negro guards in the streets, the people often taking off their hats silently when the hairy-faced, weary rebels passed.

With his regiment of Tennessee Loyalists, Hurst had burned and raided the country around Memphis, turning his men loose to grub up West Tennessee and crush the secesh spirit out of the people. Hurlbut liked the results; and he had heard that there were men farther north along the river who wanted to join the Union colors. So he had sent Major Bradford, with forty men and three wagonloads of breechloading carbines, to reactivate the old rebel works at Fort Pillow and form his own loyalist regiment. Bradford had set up the outposts and tapped all the accumulated hatred and resentment against the Confederate conscription. His power was limitless, but he was alone with it, suddenly. It blew him before it as his ambition had done. He had wanted power so he could escape from the sort of men he was sent, now, to enlist; so he could live in and visit in the sort of houses he was sent, now, to burn. In the face of such bewildering change, he lost all volition, all will. He had set to the task with energy, but now he no longer wielded his power; he let it run its own course.

The ambition, draining away, took most of his character, and even personality, with it. He was steadily afraid. He just tried to do his duty, he told himself; that was all there was for him to do and he tried to do it well, but they would not understand. All those etched columns of smoke and all the talks he had made, with his troopers herding the people to the dusty square and him standing before them ceaselessly talking so as not to feel the hatred; his earnest, smiling inducements coupled with all the destruction and punishment his regiment had done, all of this had put a mark on his name. But he could not really believe it. No, he told himself, they could not hate me that much. Not Will Bradford, who used to come courting their daughters with sweat running down his flanks, and who earlier used to play with their boys in the dirt. Naw. They could not hate me. What have I done? Where in me was the burning will or the hatred, or anything? There was a desperate hollowness around him; no, it is a dream, no, they do not hate me. They will take me back saying, "What are you talking about? What on earth are you talking about?" How could they hate me so? But he knew, in the way you suddenly perceive a depth of things beyond the ongoing momentary concerns of life, he knew with a cold, hard sense of reality that they did.

He pictured death to himself. It would come out of the hollow darkness, a huge comet of pain and horror and humiliation, when they broke through and killed him. He waited within himself for the moment it would all come, and no matter what he said they would break in and kill him. The prickly feeling of fear ran up and down his back when he thought of how they hated him. I should never had wasted a red cent's worth of time on the rich bastards. . . .

He walked down to the sally port, and was told his brother was out on patrol. He liked to talk to Ted because he was grinning and innocent-eyed and did not notice the hatred congregating against their name. His brother was out on a patrol toward Killdeer Crick. They had heard of some loyalists out that way.

"Oh yes." He walked back to the orderly shack along the river bluff, to see about shelter for the Negro troops who ought to arrive today or tomorrow.

3

THEY HAD COME OUT FOR CAPTAIN HAMILTON LEROY ACOX UNDER
a yellow winter sky, with the blighted fir trees along the ridges
pointing like thin, spidery fingers into the sky. Tyree Bell, big
and red-faced, had guided his horse along the cedar-lined road
to the Acox house, and sallow Judge Morris had been with him,
and a file of twenty rebel cavalrymen. Acox had stood with his
hand on the door jamb, and watched them come with a thick
sadness inside his throat. It had been shadowy in the hall, and
the men had tethered their horses, and he had gone out to meet
them.

"Got your details raised, Lee?"

"Yes, Judge Morris . . . they are raised."

Tyree Bell had climbed up the porch steps and shaken
hands with him, and Acox made a jerky motion with his hand,
and the troopers all filed up after them into the warmth of the
house. One of his slaves clattered off after food and milk and,
with the smell of horses and woolen ponchos and gun-oil on
them, the twenty soldiers settled around the fireplace in the big
drawing room. Acox led Morris and Bell across to the library
behind the stairway, and closed the doors behind them.

Books, leather-bound and rich, banked all around them,
and a lantern fluttered at Acox's desk. They all settled down in
the room and Judge Morris pulled the enlistment and recruiting papers from his frock coat. Acox thumbed through them,
slowly and sadly. It is late, he thought, late afternoon. Somehow
I did not think they would ride out to get me before Christmas
came, or not anyhow in the late afternoon.

Bell leaned back in his chair. "We nearly missed you, Lee. We nearly did. We are about ready to move south to Mississippi, Sherman and Hurlbut and Grierson have big columns moving down on us from three sides, and General Forrest is getting all set to pull up and move. Four, five days and we would have missed you."

Damn, thought Acox. God damn. "I wish you had, Ty. I do wish you had gone and gotten away and left me." He looked at Bell solemnly. Bell fidgeted and smiled, and glanced at Morris. Morris, his flesh like paper over the thin-boned face, scowled. Bell said, "We got to have every man we can get, Lee. You know that. You will be one of the few to keep their rank. . . ." His voice trailed off. He put his hands on one of the law books along the wall beside him. His fingers came away dusty. Acox, his face lined and tired and sad, got up and paced back and forth around the room. His hands were thumb-spread around his hips. Acox was an average-sized man, with small feet and hands, and a deep chest, running a little to fat now. He was just under thirty years old, and his face looked ten years older than that. He was clean-shaven with three months of civilian life, and he had deep-set eyes and a straight, big nose. Acox's eyes had dark circles beneath them. His flesh was very thick over his skull, with white lines in the forehead and beside his nose. His mouth was small, and full-lipped; it seemed almost too small.

They could hear the troopers in the next room, laughing and talking. The lantern made fluttering noises, and the winter sky through the window darkened. Acox roused himself from blank staring.

"I don't have any choice, do I, Ty?" He was pleading with his eyes. Bell drew back the corners of his upper lip, uncomfortably.

"That's the way to take it, Lee." But Acox had asked a question. Six years of practicing law with a man, Bell was thinking, of fetching him along like a brother. I did not think Acox would hit me there, but he surely did. I did not think he would plead.

Morris cleared his throat. "This is a war, Lee. This is a war, and the law says every man between sixteen and fifty is liable for conscription. . . ."

"But I am a recruiting officer. I'm detached from Wheeler's cavalry for recruiting. . . ." His eyes were desperate. This is it, Acox thought. This is the final line of defense I have, the shadowy excuse that I have thought of and laid awake at nights worrying about. It sounds so empty now, bringing it out.

Morris, old and bitter and arrogant, stood up abruptly. Acox froze, startled and suddenly realizing completely that he had no choice, that he had to go back. "Do not be a fool, man. We have pulled in dozens of men who were hiding behind that pretext. Dozens. You have used your commission to retire from the war, to avoid the conscription and hide yourself up in these hills. The law cannot be fooled any longer. You can come as a captain or we will impress you as a private."

Bell thought he had never seen a man drain so rapidly. Acox sat down, looking out of the window. His small mouth quivered. Morris left the room, his feet striking on the thick pine floor.

"God damn it, Ty, I have had my share. You know I have. . . ." Acox shook his head vigorously, like a man trying to free a cobweb from his face. "God damn it, Ty. . . ."

Bell stood up, big-chested and vigorous. "All right, Lee. All right. Listen. We must be gone in twenty minutes. We only have twenty minutes, and we have to round up the men on your muster rolls. Go and say goodbye to Amanda. Give her my love. We will wait down here for you. . . ."

"Twenty minutes. . . ." He looked out of the window again, and shook his head. "My God, Ty. . . ." He sighed. "All right. All right." Bell slapped him on the shoulder, and then went out of the room. The house was dark and shadowy; the servants had not lit the hall candles or the lanterns yet. Bell stopped, hunched for a moment. There was a thick warm smell in the dark hall, holding the winter at arm's length. He felt very, very tired. There was an open cedar chest in the hall, and it smelled honey-sweet as he passed it. Behind him he could hear Acox crossing the hall and the stairs creaking slightly beneath his weight.

Amanda was at the top of the steps, just going down. She was patting a curl into place, and breathing deeply. Her hands were still reddened. She had been out in the back, making soap.

She had heard the horsemen, and looked quickly around the side of the house, and then had run upstairs and slipped off her working clothes and put on a cotton print dress, a blue dress with patterns of flowers on it. She kept thinking, Lee has guests, Lee has guests, and she had run from the room, brushing at her hair, and dropped the hairbrush on a table in the upstairs hall. She saw her husband. "Didn't I see Ty down there?" She smiled and started around him.

Lee came to the top of the stairs, and he put his hands on her shoulders. It was shadowy in the hall. She pressed against him, trying to pass him, thinking, men don't know how to act civil, and trying to get down to the parlor where the guests were. Lee felt the weight of her, pushing, the soft body beneath the dress, pushing against his hands gently and a little exasperated. He bent and kissed her on the neck, beneath her ear where the delicate bone rose upwards to her temple. And he folded his arms around her, and hugged her, and felt all the soft warmth of her body against him. She shoved back now, trying to look up into his face, puzzled. He felt the fear growing in her. She stiffened, and a small tremor ran through her. The flesh beneath his hands quivered and tingled. He saw she understood, and he backed away from her.

His whole world was shrunk to the tiny, narrow hall, the sounds of the troopers and the growing winter darkness, and his wife pressed against him, the realization suddenly awakening in her too. It was a precise repetition of the comprehension that had struck him when he heard the dogs bark and rose from the desk where he had been writing and looked out of the window, and saw the winding column coming down from the ridge toward the house. He drew her back to him and looked into her eyes, and she looked into his.

He saw her delicate round face, round and soft and smooth, reddened a little by the cold winter day, the deep brown hair, the full, pale lips. Her eyes were wide now with fear. Her mouth was open and poised and she leaned from the waist, away from him, her brown eyes going from one of his eyes to the other, back and forth like beats of a heart. She pulled away and made a flickering motion with her hand, and then went into the warmly lantern-lit children's room, and he followed her. He shuddered and tried to clench the moment to him, to hang on to the yellow light and the woodwork and the neat pattern of the house and the tiny room.

They came together again in the middle of the children's room, with the two small beds neatly made and the old, thin-ribbed, wheeled crib, and the round scatter rugs. He hugged her against him, folding her to him with his hands. He breathed and pulled her and while he was feeling the great wave of sorrow and concern and loss wash over him, while he was pressing her tightly to him and feeling the soft, round, full warmth of her body and the pressure of her hands on his shoulder blades, he thought, oddly, how neat the children's room was, and then thought, of course but we have no more children, they died last winter. And while he pulled her against him and buried his face in her hair, the ash-tasting sorrow of that mingled beating against the thought of leaving her, and of leaving the little valley and the house, until he thought there was so much sadness in the world that to leave the embrace of his wife would be surely to die. He rocked with her, and heard her sobbing; recollections, images, beat like birds' wings against him in the twilight. Acox thought that there was more love and more sorrow in his heart than he could stand, a great, choking, aching surge of love and sorrow and sadness that flooded like the lantern, a thin yellow light covering him and gleaming inside him.

But stray and rational thoughts still plucked at his attention: the uniform, I must pull the uniform out of the cellar closet where it is hidden, and then the weapons. I shall need the pistols that are hidden in the cellar, but I must check the powder in the cartridges. And the sword. If I am still to be a captain, I must take the sword. And where is that? The blankets, then; perhaps the brownish one from the bedroom chest. And his eyes swung guiltily around the room, probing it, seeing the matching green blankets on the neatly made children's beds, and thinking, well, those two would be useful . . . and then he was so ashamed and horrified that he buried his face in his wife's hair again, and his arms ached with holding her. Again everything momentarily flooded into the yellow light, but suddenly too he had to think of the horses and hoped he could persuade Tyree to let Amanda cling to at least one good animal, and decided to take Jenny Black, the fine, gentle mare. . . .

And this time, thinking of the horse and thinking too of the smell of powder and sword metal and of harness and holster, he was too much the intruder. He pulled away from her, and from the yellow light. When he leaned to kiss the trickling clear tears down her soft cheeks and when he saw the thin sheen of light catch in the tiny, soft white hairs of her upper lip, he felt like a great fumbling bear, a huge profane animal, suited not to the gentle delicate memories of a mother in the room of her just dead children, but to the battlefield and the shriek of gut-shot horses and the smell of blood and horror and the endless filthy staleness of camp.

She was looking again at his eyes, shifting from one to the other, back and forth. "Wouldn't they . . . didn't you tell them you were on . . . on detached . . ." she fumbled for the word, a hand flickered again ". . . on detached duty? . . ." She spoke so softly he was surprised he could hear her.

"Yes."

"And they didn't . . . they wouldn't? . . ."

He put his arms on her again. "No, they wouldn't. Perhaps they are right." Tears were in his eyes, and they were swollen.

"But . . . but . . ." she looked from side to side now, at things in the room, at the crib and the lantern and the tiny dresser, trying to grasp something. Acox was suddenly worried and he knew he had to give her something. He said, "But I will be with Forrest and, even if he is a horse-and-nigger-trader and a hellion, he is the best leader we have in the West. If I had to go back to serve after all, it could not be better." She started to say something, her mouth quivering and her eyes glistening with tears, and her hands trembling in the air. Like small, help-less birds, he thought with a sudden detached vagueness, and he went on quickly. "It could not be better, save of course here with you. But then you will take care of the place and I will come home soon. There is no danger with Forrest. Not like before, in the infantry. So you will not worry, will you?" He took her chin in his thumb and forefinger. "You will not worry or grieve, and you will be busy and, before you know it, I will be back. I will leave Sam with the instructions. Buck is a good nigra, the best I have ever seen, and he has not left by now, and I do not think he will. We can put a cot in the kitchen for him, and I will give him the old shotgun and Father's old horse pistol. But then you will not have anything to fear. Mrs. Vance and Jim Taylor's wife will come out and visit with you."

She was still slipping from him, he knew. Her face was cast suddenly in a sad and split way, and if she broke into tears he would too, and he would not be able to leave. They would take him to prison or shoot him, but in a moment, if she cried, he could not leave. He raised his voice and spoke rapidly.

"Eliza and Buck and Jennie May, they are good nigras and good people, and it is up to you to look after them, and take care of them. I will leave Buck with a list of instructions too, and you must read them to Sam and Buck. It will tell them when and where to put in the crops and what to do for the stock. There are a lot of things you must remember—where to hide the cattle from the raiders and a lot of other things. I have a list, and you must each morning read out the instructions to the nigras. . . ."

"Oh Lee, oh Lee, they can't . . ." and she sobbed and dropped her face. He pulled her against him desperately and squeezed his eyes shut and filled himself with her feel, sensing her sobs and her tears and her warmth, and he felt like dying, like closing out the world and pulling the thick warm earth over him.

"Oh no, oh no, no no. Don't, Amanda! Don't! Don't! Oh Amanda, if you cry I cannot go and I must go. You must be strong now, you must! I must go, for you, because the only strength there is left in the world is that between families and neighbors and if I do not go you will lose that. I must go, and you must stay here." When she sobbed at that, muffled into his shoulder, he said, "And you are the only strength I have and the only reason I did not die at that hospital in Georgia, and that I am not dead now. So. So." He realized that he did not know any more how long he had stood with her, or how long she had sobbed. But it seemed an eternity. And yet during that eternity part of him had been thinking of packing equipment and selecting weapons and even of making the rounds to call in his enlistments, part of him reacting with stubborn, unheated, unemotional rationality, and he realized too that his right hand was instinctively closing for the butt of a revolver, clenching and tightening.

He stood away from her again, and saw that she was quiet and self-controlled. She had lowered her head, and her large eyes were closed and her hands were clasped, the knuckles white, in front of her. Her bosom rose and fell with her heavy breathing, and she sniffled and her face was lacquered with paths of tears. She looked so lovely and pathetic and strong and weak and warm that again he felt a spark flare inside him and when it was quenched he felt like sliding into death. But he squeezed her again, this time with a sad coolness, and she put her hands on his elbows while he held her, and then he pulled away.

She looked up at him, and her eyes were burning and shining. "Lee . . . oh Lee . . . you do know how much. . . ."

He smiled and looked down at her and said "Yes, yes, of course, and you too know you are my world." While she pushed a handkerchief to her nose and mouth and sobbed and then straightened and remembered the LeRoy Acoxes had guests, he turned and went into the bedroom and lit the lantern, and began throwing some of the things that he would need into a thick cloth haversack.

He changed clothes, pulling on his warmest pants and buckling on a worn leather belt, hearing half-attentively the sudden scraping and fluttering of sounds as his wife entered the drawing room downstairs. He put on a warm cotton shirt and put three more into the haversack, and found boots and a thick blanket. He bound some more things into a loose bundle to take downstairs, and thought as he was about to leave the room how odd it was that here, when he was leaving to perhaps die, he could pack in a matter of minutes, throwing things together and binding up cords into the smell of thick clothing and oiled leather. And yet when he had gone off to college in Virginia, it had taken him two days to pack. This, this catching up of things he would need, a few strong, sturdy things, reminded him nostalgically of a hunting trip. Images came back, of living with his father in Georgia and the late autumn mornings spent hunting, of the quail rising in shocking, sudden bursts and the thrill of the blood at the sight and the smell of powder and of the dark red earth, the grey sedge grass and the fir trees and the blue winter woods, his father guiding the horses across a stream lipped with ice, late afternoon sunsets and the smell of horses and woodsmoke and canvas and gunmetal.

He stopped in the middle of the room, hefting the sack and blanket roll. He thought also, yes, I am going hunting, truthfully. For the sensations will be almost the same, with perhaps a heightened and throat-catching terror added, but almost the same. He felt the tingle of his blood, and the sensations of battle, the sights and smells and the shocks and the horrors which you knew not to look at but which you had to look at. And he faced the big bed in the middle of the room, and thought of Amanda's white, soft loveliness, how she slept with one arm folded against his side and the hand gently pressing into his ribs; then at how it had been the first year, deeply embarrassed yet deeply in love and locked on the bed with her feet twined about his, or how, the last time, affectionate and soft and melting together. He wondered why he thought about these things. Then he left the room and went downstairs, thinking rationally of last-minute necessities.

Acox went down to the cellar, hearing, as he passed the drawing room, the chatter of his wife, and a strong masculine laugh. In the cool, dank cellar, smelling of wetness and cobwebs and turned earth, he found an old chest of drawers, and pulled out the bottom drawer. While he knelt on the gritty dirt floor, pulling out his uniform, Tyree came down the steps.

Bell stood over him. "Well, Lee . . . well, I am surely sorry. God bless it, boy, I know how hard you have worked here during the winter, and about your children, but . . ."

"Let us not talk about it, about any of it." He could tell Tyree was hurt when he snapped at him, and he did not like to hurt people. But damn it, this is not anything small, this is life and death, and this is making me leave my wife out here in this godforsaken countryside with nobody to take care of her save the Yankee patrols, and there is a sick and emasculating feeling in leaving the women to the protection of the enemy, since you cannot protect them yourself. And Lord knows Amanda's had a hard winter, the hardest a woman can stand, and she has another month or two to go. She has lost both of her children and now there are no relatives any more in Georgia to refugee to, and she has had to learn to do all sorts of things that she never had to turn a hand to before. The image beat softly again, of her, lovely and delicate and standing in a warm, rug-covered and well-lighted room, talking and smiling and happy; and then came the thought of the hard iron pump and the wooden washtubs and the smell of winter backyards, of the truck garden and of stiff drying clothes. He straightened up on his knees and looked blankly straight ahead; his hands paused holding the grey coat and the leather and steel.

Bell snuffled and paced in the background. He put his hand on Acox's shoulder for a moment, but Lee flexed away. Bell stopped pacing, and then left the cellar. As soon as he was gone Acox, who had never really stopped thinking about his equipment, even while the bitter steel edge of despair and fear bit into him, put on the coat and strapped the sash and the belt around his waist. The belt with pistol and saber was heavy, and he was weak from the wounds he had gotten at Chickamauga. He looked up the flight of stairs, and the great urge came to him to not climb up them, just to stay in the cellar in the flooding darkness, listening to the water drip and the feet on the boards above his head.

But he had things to do. He had to go to his desk and get out the five pages of carefully written instructions and give them to his wife. He had written them slowly and carefully, trying to think of everything he could foresee about the winter and detailing what should be done on each day in any given circumstance. He had used an almanac and had called in Sam and Buck, since he was a lawyer and had only just this fall turned everything about his life into the soil, into farming. Since he had to. Since there was no other way to survive; administering the law or teaching or praying or the other forms of ministering to man's soul had become secondary to the functions of ministering to his body, of simply making each day a victory for the flesh over death. All over the South.

He climbed up the cellar steps into the light, knowing he still had to add a few instructions to the list, in case the spring was unusually rainy.

On the way to the library he stopped in front of the hall mirror, to smooth and shape the frock coat of his uniform across his shoulders again. He was surprised by what he saw, and a cold chill ran through him. He was a different man, clean-shaven and haggard and pale and hollow-eyed. But the uniform molded over his shoulders felt stiff and solid and comfortable. The yellow cavalry sash swung at his waist, and the big hip boots were folded above the knees. The double stripe of rank ran in curlicues up his sleeves from yellow cuffs, and the yellow collar and rank slashes stood out from the dull grey cloth. He tugged at the bottom of the coat, and, satisfied, turned for the closet. Some of the pride returned, and he pulled himself up straight and walked crisply. By God, by God, some of this is worth it, he thought for a fleeting second. After scratching out the last of the instructions, he pulled out his muster book and put it inside his coat, thinking ahead now to the men he would have to fish out of their coves and bottoms and from their farms, for service, now that they were being called in.

He kissed his wife goodbye, and Judge Morris promised to ride out three times a week to look in on her, and said he knew some women in town who would be glad to come and stay with her or put her up in town, either one. The sky was still faintly yellow when they rode back up the ridge, past the green cedar trees. And he suddenly realized he had hardly even thought of his wife after he put on the uniform. He turned in the saddle and saw her, a tiny brown-haired girl, standing alone and waving sadly to him. He raised a gloved hand, and, bitter, he waved back. 'Y God, he thought, I am going to come back to her. He bit his teeth together in determination. I am going to come back. Hear me? I am going to come back. . . .

Then the jingling rhythms of the ride enfolded him. He

pushed up beside Tyree Bell and Judge Morris. "I have the muster book, Judge Morris, for the people I have recruited. Do you want to begin to bring them in to us tonight?"

Morris looked at him, and then took the muster book and ran his thumb down the line of names. The flesh around Morris's thin-lipped, pale mouth worked stiffly, like parchment folding and cracking. "Only twenty-two names?" He looked sharply at Acox, and Acox hated him with all the bitterness and resentment he had felt at the house. He turned away, to watch the clump of hackberry trees on the knoll that marked the last of his property. Here I am riding away from everything I love, he thought, and this old bastard, sanctimonious and boot-licking and self-important, is talking to me about not doing my duty or being slack.

He looked back at Judge Morris, the flinty, cold eyes and the old, lined flesh, and rose slightly on his spread hands in the saddle. "Judge Morris, I have had a wife and family to take care of, and so do most of the men in this territory. There are federal recruiting stations and rebel recruiting stations, and they are sick of the war. Like me. They want to protect their own and live in their own little piece of the world, and they do not want old bastards like you smashing their lives. The ones I enlisted I told not to worry, that they probably would not have to be gone during the winter, that they could take care of their folks during the winter." What the hell, he thought. He sighed. His breath was making a frosty veil as the last of the winter sun spread across the earth. "You leave me alone, Judge Morris. You have done enough to me. You leave me alone."

He looked at Morris as he finished, and there was something timelessly inhuman and horrible in Morris's face. Morris closed his lips tightly together, and Bell looked from one to the other of them, and then pushed his horse up between them. And in a horrible moment, with just the blank look of hate in Morris's face, Acox recognized the double truth of what he had been saying, recognized that the judge was out to round up all the men that he could and send them off regardless, that he was obsessed by something other than justice and maybe it was revenge on the Yankees and on the Confederate states as well, because he was old and in wartime it was a young man's world. And, too, Acox realized that Amanda was there alone with only niggers and that Judge Morris held the county in the palm of his hand, combining military and judicial roles and signing passes and conscripting sixteen-year-old boys to send to the Tennessee regiments in Johnston's army. That no longer was there a house that belonged to the LeRoy Acoxes but rather a whole domain of fields and bottoms and timber and houses, all of it under the thumb of one man. And that too was war. And Judge Morris, who was either a schoolteacher or a judge by the bones and blood and flesh across his body, who could be either teacher or judge with equal dry-lipped, wrinkled brutality and who could be nothing else, that now Judge Morris would hate him and he would never come home, or if he did there would be nothing there. Acox looked at the judge, sitting calmly and pressing his dry, thin lips together and glaring at Acox, his dry, black frock coat in odd contrast to the mottled greys and browns and blues of the soldiers. Acox looked at him, and felt more fear, a great, huge sheet of fear, than he had ever felt before in his life. He was helpless there, he knew. He was utterly helpless, a man lying on his back with his arms strapped down and waiting, belly up. He had the terrible urgent fear to undo the thing, to erase saying whatever he said, like the schoolboy at the last split second when the teacher focuses on him and everything evaporates around him in a hollow fear.

But Bell was saying, "Judge, Lee here has been a good officer and the winter has so far been hard on him. After all, it is hard to find men where recruiting has been going on and on for years, Judge. . . ." What is he talking about? Oh yes, the twenty-two men, Acox thought. "And I am sure he did not mean what he said. I know him too well, Judge." He sounded like a lawyer apologizing away a junior partner's *faux pas* and he put his hand on LeRoy Acox's shoulder. Acox thought how he loved Tyree Bell.

"Yessir, Judge Morris. I . . . I am tired, sir. I am very tired. I am sorry there were so few men, but I have been busy, and since Tom and Parkie died, I have had precious little time. . . ."

"You see, you see?" Bell said, and the judge nodded coldly and went back to counting down the list. Then still painfully unforgiving, uncommitting, silent, he looked at a small hill and said clearly and precisely, with no shade of anything, "We shall probably do best to start with Van Nest, who lives on the other side of the ridge," and both the soldiers agreed with him.

4

WHEN THE WAR CAME, ACOX HAD HAD A YEAR-OLD SON, AND
Amanda was pregnant with Parkhurst LeRoy Acox, who would
turn out after all a little girl. So when he had gone off to fight,
marching away as a sergeant in the ——th Tennessee Infantry,
he left thinking of noble, heart-catching things, of his home and
family and his willingness to die for them, of Amanda and his
love for her. But from the moment he had marched away, in his
cadet-grey coat with the light-blue cuffs, thinking of self-sacrifice and of Amanda, he had entered a savage and kaleidoscopic
nightmare.

Shiloh was the battle for West Tennessee. At Shiloh the
generals stood poised and confident on knolls and in wooded
copses, gleaming and surrounded by gleaming aides, while the
shoddy, weary grey and brown ranks, poorly armed, stumbled
by, half-trained and already whittled by disease. Acox remembered thrashing helplessly and wildly through thickets with his
men all around him, rifles and knapsacks catching and hanging
on branches. All the months of waiting in the stinking camps at
Pensacola with death and desertion mounting—all of the
months of waiting while home in Tennessee the river forts fell
and there was the physical ache of helplessness—all of this led
only to lost and leg-weary marches, and armed mobs stumbling
through spring woods toward mutilation and defeat. While men
blundered and died magnificently and uselessly or missed their
lines altogether, the officers and generals commanding them
rode about splendidly and tried to bring some sort of sense out
of the carnaged haze of gunsmoke with grandiose orders and

43

splendid deaths. Shiloh was an awakening; Acox suspected no one would forget the dogwoods at Shiloh.

On the aching, wet retreat to Corinth, he tried not to think about Amanda and his world, now irrevocably behind Union lines. He had never seen the Yankees through the smoke. But the battle had been lost, and Albert Sidney Johnston was dead.

The West Point officers had been too wrapped up in the meaningless words of a trade; they had not calculated the effect of loads of canister from massed batteries smashing into lines of green men, and had not assessed the inability of raw soldiers in battle to carry out complex and difficult and often contradictory orders. Brigades fired into one another and some ranks broke completely and others charged to foolhardy near-annihilation. The soldiers had learned too. They had not realized before that hot-headed, knife-fighting courage, with violent, bared teeth and bellowing yells, could not support the flesh against the thud and tearing rip of a minie ball.

It became worse and worse, during the next two long years; endless, long periods of boredom and short, awful spates of savagery and bone-chilling destruction. The pattern remained the same: the commanding generals cut off and living in a different world from the men, the officers like Bragg talking of so many "muskets" and so many "effectives" and leading long campaigns and losing won battles; the men themselves becoming more and more capable and learning to bend with the wind, learning when to attack and when not to attack, and even learning when to desert and when to campaign. The generals never gave them one good, solid victory. They still thought in professionalized terms, still grew cautious when the forms on paper became mangled bodies of men, when a charge no longer meant a sweep of the hand across a map but a trail of shattered and screaming bodies. The generals were inhuman and vague and professional when they should have been lenient, marching the men to death and starving them to death and never clothing them properly; and then suddenly when they should have been strong and steel-willed—when at Perryville and later Murfreesboro they should have simply forgotten the momentary price like a surgeon forgets his compassion when the knife bites into the gangrenous leg—they became cautious and remembered the human cost, so that campaigns and battles and the long rows of shallow graves were meaningless. Bragg was the worst, stern and uncompromising and hated.

Nothing marked the years for Hamilton LeRoy Acox, since everything passed in an aura of terrible fear and weariness and meaningless exhilaration and despair. He knew he was watching his world breaking down. The well-clothed and -fed Yankee columns never won much but never lost a scrap of what they won; stolid and plodding and lacking the wild, savage exhilaration of the rebels, they also lacked the elaborate plans and the wild, calculated gambles. They were never beaten too badly and always there were two of them to replace one you killed. Their artillery was getting better all the time and their cavalry was improving too, and the only real advantage the South had was in its matchless infantry. And it was squandered; irreplaceable men and an irreplaceable spirit thrown away while the Yankees could, after all, always find and equip more hands to ram bullets into more rifles.

There was a melting away of the old hot spirit of patriotism and the vicious thrill of the attack. And for Acox there was always the unmanning thought of his wife and family practically alone, and dependent upon such order as the enemy could bring for her safety. That, he thought, was the ultimate indecent demand made upon them, that the men from Tennessee and Kentucky had to leave their women to the protection of the damn Yankees. Some part of you was held continually hostage.

He went home on leave twice. Amanda and the slaves and the home smells, the patterns of light in the hall when one lantern was on in the drawing room, the smell of the breakfast table on a crisp, frosty fall morning with the leaves yellow— these always ate away at his heart and at his will. Dreams tore at him, of men breaking into the house, breaking down the door and going up to her bedroom—the final hollowed space away from the world, the place where the final sweet secrets of their love and their self-sufficiency lay—breaking in and defiling his wife and killing her and destroying his world and himself.

The Third Winter of the War   45

These dreams were pumped and fed by nasty rumors and tales of such things happening.

The rumors and the tales in the Tennessee regiments, by this time away in Georgia, were told around the fires by the hairy, wide-eyed infantrymen with sallow faces and lank wrists. There were stories of bands of deserters, and of Negro uprisings; Acox sat in the dark near his own fire and overheard the fear and the hatred spill out into the clustering nighttime woods. The stories of Negro uprisings were infrequent; but they were the worst. You could tell they were probably baseless. But what worried Acox more than the stories themselves— of burning houses and rape and kitchen-knife murders and roaming slave bands—was that the soldiers were telling them, and were listening to them. He played with the tassel on his infantry sword, in the half-orange wash of the fire. They were telling and listening to stories that they would never have been desperate enough, worried enough, to tell or listen to before. That one fear, the fear of the nigra uprising, always lay at the back of their minds: but it was too obscene. It did not need to be exercised before. They all shared the fear, but they were strong enough not to admit it. Maybe they just never thought it possible, before. He looked away into the blank darkness. "Well, I heard it from a boy over t' th' Thirty-Eighth Tennessee —y'all know, Wright's Brigade—and he says he saw that the Yankees were armin' the niggers. Said he saw some of 'em up to- 'ads Paducah on his last leave. . . ." There was a moment of silence. One of his soldiers sighed, and said, "Well, I better never ketch me one of 'em. 'Y God, I'm a Christian man, but I hope to say I better never ketch me one. . . ."

Acox did not worry so directly about the Negroes and the raising of Negro regiments: he had heard of it a week ago. But they stood—the Negroes—as a dark cloud right on the border of his conscious fears. You never could tell, with niggers. He was principally afraid of bands of roaming bandits and deserters, of the terrible capriciousness of violence. The Negroes did not frighten him as much: he had always been indifferently lenient with them, and had never been interested in their women. He depended upon them, the ones that stayed, and he had called them all together on his last leave and promised them their freedom. He pleaded with them to remain and work the fields and feed his family, and protect them. He said, in turn, he would pay them from that date. Sam helped him by returning from following a Union column and reporting that things were only worse with a lot of loose niggers, and the best thing to do was set still until it was over. Of the nine slaves on his place, two had left. The rest—Sam, Buck, Tomlee and their wives and Sam's youngest son—all stayed. Acox had known them all his life; he could not apply any of the things he overheard from the next fire to them. They could not do anything like that. He could not conceive of it. But—he rubbed his hand across the ground at his side—with niggers, you never really could tell. He had heard that too, all his life.

Shiloh had been a great awakening; but it was after Chickamauga that Acox quit the war he had set out to fight. His war was over after Chickamauga. They would have to come and get him if they wanted him to fight their war any more.

On the morning of the second day at Chickamauga, a man had brought him a letter from home. Acox was a captain by then. He had put it in his frock coat, and planned to read it when he had time. He had bent over the campfires in an agony of apprehension, and shouted orders and then moved with his men through the cold, chill, spidery September woods, waiting and cursing and hearing the sounds of battle spread toward them. He prayed for the day to be over, he prayed for something to happen and then he prayed for just another minute's thought, and then the delirious shudder and pull had come down the line and he ran forward screaming with the waves of men. The sense had been upon them almost immediately; they were going through, the Yankees were breaking. They ran and ran and ran, bellowing, and the trees and saplings and brush slapped at them and sang. Acox was caught up, they all were, in the insanity of victory, and he spent all morning and all afternoon, breathless, exhausted, sobbing, leading one group after another, strangers, friends, in one rush after another.

He was leading a small, lone group against the Yankees on Snodgrass Hill, then, forty men at the most, blind with exhaustion and with the exhilaration of near-victory; they plunged in where an attacking brigade bore to the left. Massed artillery fire slapped them down. Acox remembered smashing into the ground and the heat of a shellburst and the hiss of canister; and more men surged up behind him, mouths open in soundless yells and rifles held across their chests. He thought he was dying, and all he could feel was enthusiasm, hysterical joy. This is it, we have them! They are running and we can whip them into the ground—and the earth had seemed to close over him. Everything was grey and gold and brilliant red.

A week later, he awoke in blue and purple, and everything was suffused with pain. Bragg had thrown it away. He had not followed up the victory. Finally he read the letter; it was an afterthought; he was already biting into the most terrible sense of frustration and loss he had ever experienced. It said that his two children had died, and could he come home right away, and the ink was washed into hollow circles where tears had fallen. He realized in the hospital that the victory itself would have been meaningless without Amanda. He hated himself for not reading the letter earlier, and for not being with her, and for not even having known the children beyond moments of hilarity in the garden, tossing them in the air, or quick parting glances at the delicate, curly heads in the nursery—that was the worst of all, not even having known the children, having to painfully recall every detail he could of them, trying to piece together a fitting sort of monument in his brain.

And so, sick with the whole thing and weary and wanting to get home, he had applied for leave. The four holes in the flesh of his shoulder glazed over and the long livid scar along his ribs healed, the wound they said would probably have killed him had they not found him when they did, and which as it was cost him a week of delirium from his life and may for all he knew have meant the difference between life and death for Amanda. So with pain he had walked to General Cheatam's desk and received sick leave, and had gotten a ride into Alabama and then through the lines and had finally gotten home. Amanda was alive, and that fact and the fact that she was not going to die too made the long agony of the trip through the fall forests and across the rocky-banked Tennessee worthwhile, even no more serious than a nightmare from whence the awakening was sweet and secure.

He could not leave her again, of his own choosing. He held her to him and kissed her many times in the fall afternoon sunlight, and looked at her paper-thin flesh and the redness of her eyes. She felt weak and feverish, and her hands were work-chafened, and she kept on whispering his name over and over, "Lee, oh Lee, oh Lee. . . ." She cried for two hours in the gathering twilight. He walked with her out to the family cemetery, and looked at the small headstones in the little stone square. The cemetery was flinty, barren, as if the earth had been stung by death. He could feel precious little for the two new red cuts; he had not known his own children, he had been off trying to shelter his world when it was impossible to protect it, when he should have been at home bracing it for the catastrophies and the hideous shock of defeat and desolation. He held his wife again, stroking her hair smooth while she cried into his shoulder.

She looked up, and he could barely see her in the darkness. "Oh, Lee, I tried . . . I tried to save something here for you. But the young nigras have left, and the . . ." (she sucked in her breath like a thirteen-year-old child telling something through tears) ". . . the children died. Oh Lee. Do what you must, and I will try again. But don't leave me for a while. Just stay with me a while. . . ."

He wrapped his arms around her and thought, here, here is my world, and I can put my arms around it and cherish it, and I shall never let it go. "You are my world, Amanda. You always were. . . ."

His enlistment was over that fall, and he sent in his resignation to the ——th Tennessee Infantry. He was notified almost immediately by Judge Morris in town that he might be liable for conscription once the month of sick leave was finished. It was October, and the trees were turning and the mornings were misty and chill. The sunlight and heat were no longer bronze; the world was cool and moist and green. He sat down at his desk in the heart of the big white house, and wrote off a series of letters, using all that his seven years' legal practice had instilled in him concerning the way governments and military bureaucracies ran. It began to work out simply, like a man pulling the strings and then seeing the marionette respond. He received a commission as a captain of cavalry, and was detailed as a recruiting officer, responsible for enlisting or conscripting a company of cavalry in West Tennessee. There was no time limit, and he would never have to return to the Army of Tennessee or to the infantry. He hoped he would have six months—until the spring —before he had to report anywhere. He thought he might be able to avoid returning altogether.

He got a yellow sash and repaired the rents in his frock coat and changed the lapels from light-blue to yellow. He made two or three expeditions a week, checking in town the names of the families around him and then riding out to see them. A lot of the men he visited just had not re-enlisted in the army. He told them they would have to serve anyhow, but that he did not think they would be called up until the early spring, and in any case he certainly was not going to call them out until he had to. He talked at back porches and out in the fields. He looked at the flat, empty faces, the eyes twisting with suspicion, and felt very weary. He knew which formulas he would have to apply, not to secure their trust or their affection or their enthusiasm, none of which he felt he could reach out to, but only to persuade them to sign several sheets of paper, enlistment records and receipts, carefully folding up one copy into his frock coat and giving them the other. They almost always stood on the steps or against the fence, holding the paper slightly away from them and looking steadily and suspiciously at him until he rode out of sight. Some of them did not sign, and looked at him with complete mistrust and said over and over, "Naw I ain't goen back no more, naw I got my crops to put in an' a family t' feed." He scrupulously wrote down their names on a separate page in the little muster book and then smiled and thanked them and rode off, marking them down for conscription.

One of the men from his old company in the ——th Tennessee came home, he heard, and he rode over to see the man. It was Robert Bowles, a slight young man with buck teeth and a full brown moustache and very pale skin. He had been a conscientious and efficient sergeant until his brother was killed up in Virginia, and then he had walked away from the army at Chattanooga and wandered through the lines and dodged military patrols until he had gotten home. But when Acox talked to him he saw a glimmer, a quick, reflexive shrug. Bowles was not one of the sharp-faced men who walked away with no conscience. He knew Bowles felt the pressures of being completely alone, legal prey to any armed body of men to come riding up over the ridge, rebel or Yankee, and how that merciless helplessness nagged him. So he sat down on Bowles's back porch while a grey-haired old woman stirred something in a mixing bowl through the door behind him and breathed asthmatically, and he looked out across the blue afternoon fields, and offered Bowles the lieutenancy in his company. He had no real idea about the legal or military details but, judging from seven years as a lawyer and two as a soldier, he said, it seemed reasonable that if a man were a lieutenant and was active and raising soldiers for the Confederacy then that might not only mitigate but absolve him from previous desertion. Bowles looked away with a trace of disgust around the corners of his mouth and a look of utter helplessness and weariness, and finally said yes, he would do it, if the captain was reasonably sure that they would not have to go until around the middle of spring. Acox then got up and handed Bowles the papers and looked at him while he held the pen and said the usual litany, knowing that it always worked at this point. "Robert, I can't promise you anything about that one way or the other; but I can promise you that I, personally, am not going to raise one little finger toward making this troop leave before then, and I can also promise you that when we do have to serve, they are going to have to send some men out here and make us." Then he added the single phrase he also always used, giving himself a particular, confiding expression and saying, "Between you and me, Robert, I have had enough of this war for a long time, and this seems as good a way as any to avoid it for a long, long while."

With Bowles as his lieutenant he went out even less, and instead had Bowles come in and report to him every Tuesday, entertaining him in the drawing room over peach brandy and both of them sitting in their uniforms and feeling clean and warm and secure, talking of weapons and horses and feeling a lot like they had felt, all of them, in 1860. Only both of them also knew that there would be no return to the purblind innocence of that time; both of them knew that this was a masquerade, a definite and conscious effort to insure their own freedom from the army for as long as possible, even if it meant hours every week working at enlistments and correspondence. The talk at the end always turned to crops and cattle and the weather; sometimes Acox would lend Sam or Buck or Tomlee to Bowles, to help him out for a day or two. Both of them gradually accepted the fact that their hours were probably numbered, and that as much work as possible had to be done in as little time as possible, and that Acox would not make the offer unless he had a momentary respite and could afford it. Acox and Bowles understood each other: they sat in Acox's front parlor late at night, feeling liquor working through them in the half-darkness in front of the fire, stretching out and easing their bodies from the work in the cold fields. When they were with the women, they did not say how bad it was—the war, their chances to avoid going back. Even when they were together, they still did not say how serious things were, they played at the masquerade. "Nah, I don't think they'll take us, Robert." But when they sat alone, looking into the shifting hells of the fire and feeling the heat of it touch the ridges of their faces, they made their silent prayers together—about the harsh patterns of military justice, and how the war was really going, and how safe the homes were out this way. With a crystal certainty, they both knew that they would go back soon; that the war was, if not lost, then probably unwinnable and not even worth fighting; and that they could not secure the homes in the valley, with their wills or their energies, once they were called up. Acox knew that before the winter was half over he would have to go back again.

When he walked back to the house in the afternoons, through the October fields, or over the forest carpet of fallen hackberry and oak and linden leaves, the thoughts that came to him were almost intolerable. His world had been reduced by the war to an ultimate source, and here, in this little girl who was barely twenty-four and yet had lost two children already and had managed seven Negroes and a large house, here was everything he could ever hope to find. He would spin for himself the picture of how he might hear of her death; it became so agonizingly real that it squeezed at his heart.

Lying beside her at night, her hand pressed into his side, folded like a bird's wing against him, he stared at mooncast patterns around the room, and prayed into the arching nighttime sky that he would not lose her too. There was some sin, he thought, some sin that he had committed. It was a mindless, silver-hard time. He trusted in God's mercy, God's awareness and response, for the same reason that he trusted in the Negroes on the land; because he could not afford not to. Take me then, God, if you have to have another one of us. Take me then.

For two months he was able to create a separate time and place for the two of them, in the valley, among the cedars. But it was undermined. He knew all the time that the world would again intrude, that the male vanities of warfare would again appear—knowing because he felt them inside himself, and found every now and again his hand turning, as if to grasp a saber or a pistol butt. In the middle of the week before Christmas, Tyree Bell and Judge Morris and the file of troopers came out to call him up with his company. Forrest was recruiting a full command, in West Tennessee.

5

IT TOOK TWO DECEMBER DAYS TO COLLECT THE ENLISTED MEN AND
to conscript the others. Morris and Bell left Acox with ten soldiers from McDonald's battalion. They had made a camp in the
cut of a creek, a timber-choked brown ravine with an ice-laced
stream at the bottom. They spread out blankets and tent-halves
to make shelters, and set about bringing in the men.

With the sunlight a warm, liquid feeling against the uniform and cavalry gauntlets, Acox would sit in the front yard of
the cabin and watch while the troopers closed in from the back,
and he would send in Bowles. The two days were clear and
sunny, with yellowed sedge grass and small, lonely, olive-green
fir trees dotted across the winter fields. Acox sat on his horse and
felt the good, clean, metallic feel of the winter day. The men he
had enlisted looked blankly disbelieving and then disgusted.
They cursed and muttered and their flat eyes tilted with the
strong wisdom of confirmed mistrusts and fears. Some of the
men they conscripted hid, or the womenfolk clung to them and
wailed. The ten troopers he had been assigned were from Forrest's old regiment and they were strong, clean-limbed men and
they acted with all the brutal, thoughtless certainty of dedicated
soldiers. Once they rode down a running eighteen-year-old boy
like a man riding down a stray calf, until the boy was knocked
sprawling by a lunging horse. Then they tied him up and sat
him on the family's only horse, and the boy's narrow, dark eyes
were pinched with fear and hate.

Acox sent Bowles in and sat on the horse in the yard without moving, expressionless, feeling no moral commitment or

even responsibility; just relishing and tasting over and over the thought that, well now, I have been trapped in this huge injustice and I will do my part without thinking. I have already defined the limits of my participation in this world; it is the limit of my house and my fields, and I am dedicated only to that, so that while I may be trapped in this hideous irrelevence, I will only perform my duties and nothing more. So that I may some day resume my definite and allocated and God-given responsibilities to my farm and my family and my people.

They set volunteers over the conscripts as armed guards, and some of the conscripts were bound and gagged in the tiny shelters. There were forty men now, twenty of them volunteers and the rest conscripts, and there were no revolvers except Acox's and Bowles's, and only seven good rifles. The men were lined up on the third day and, amid mist and thick underbrush and blackjack and hackberry spidery brown with winter, were read to from the Articles of War and assigned to platoons. Acox put the eight veterans, all of them volunteers who had left the ——th Tennessee and re-enlisted, as non-commissioned officers. He walked down the ranks. There was no spark or trace of feeling in the men's eyes. They were blank and expressionless and Acox figured they would fight only if they had to in order not to die. They spent four days drilling, and two of the recruits still had to be bound and gagged during the night.

The mornings were bitter cold and when you breathed the cold air snapped inside you, but it did not rain or snow and the sunlight was warm. No one left the little creek bed except for parties of troopers from MacDonald's battalion under their own sergeant, who scoured the countryside for stock. Acox had a fair idea of which local farms owned horses that would be good mounts. He spent some time each day reviewing an old manual on cavalry tactics, which in the end only convinced him that he would have to rely on his old experience in the infantry, because not only did his men not have swords and so could not deliver a mounted attack, but he doubted that they would ever find much opportunity to. So he had the sergeants work them a little among the trees and the rocky banks on the rudiments of infantry tactics, and forming a skirmish line with horseholders in the rear. The days were no longer bracing and clear; there was a mean edge in the wind, and the skies turned the color of lead.

Then Forrest pulled out of Tennessee for Mississippi, and Acox's company joined with the brigade. Due to the absence of rifles the brigade was really an unarmed and half-trained rabble slipping over ice-coated winter roads to the southwest, away from and then between thick, converging columns of federal cavalry and infantry. Acox rode hunched inside his blue-grey cloak, and watched the long lines, mud-daubed and wrapped against the cold, riding into the lead-colored December days. All of the men looked the same, hollow-eyed and listless at first and then more and more frightened. They all rode in desperate silence. The fear hovered over the column like a mist, of suddenly stumbling into a column of Yankees and not even having a ghost of a chance except to surrender and then starve to death in prison. They rode until their backs ached. The men talked quietly, about which way they were going, or about a family they knew not too far away, or how in another damn hour they would be in front of the Gayoso in Memphis didn't the damn fool generals watch out. They felt helpless, like rabbits who could not run but had to proceed at a shambling military pace.

Gradually the column heard skirmishing, sometimes to the grey east and sometimes over near Memphis where the men swore it must be just about in the center of town. Acox listened to the distant popping and noise, and wondered if they would ever get out of Tennessee with all of these unwieldy, frightened, unarmed conscripts. He watched their hollow eyes and their hands involuntarily squeezing for rifles which had been given to the flank companies, or which had never been there in the first place. He rode at the head of the company and Bowles rode at the rear, and they had the only weapons left, a pistol apiece and Acox's sword. Acox did not know whether he could shoot one of the conscripts or not, but he finally decided he would have to if the man suddenly broke in daylight where everyone saw him, and where Acox could be held reprehensible.

Officers he did not know kept coming back to tell them to

close it up or for a certain regiment to take the left fork up ahead. He did not know where they were, except that they were somewhere not too far from Memphis and probably just north of the railroad. They forded ice-chilled streams and rivers, and were avoiding the main roads, and the country was bleak and wind-blasted and cold. Since he had disclaimed moral responsibility and even concern for the fate of his company, he swung along with the winding column and wondered in a detached and theoretical way whether they had a prayer of making it or not, and reached his second decision, that if they were suddenly caught or surprised he would not be captured, but would try to slip off on his own. Whenever they were crossing a stream or riding through a narrow cut in a forest, anyplace where perhaps they might be attacked, he carefully looked for a quick way to leave the column. He steeled and tensed himself, putting his muscles in preparation and thinking, now jerk the horse toward that little fir stand, and lean to the left and try to get over where that ridge lies, and braced in case they were hit with a volley of gunfire.

But at least they were moving, at least there was none of the snarl and confusion and trapped frustration of an infantry column. He seemed for the first time to be part of an organized and purposeful and capable movement of men. The officers were mostly farmers and lawyers and planters: they dressed like the troopers except for wearing a sword or a sash or maybe a cloak, and they acted as if they knew precisely what they were doing. The small companies of attached veterans seemed cocksure and they joked and kidded and rode easily in the saddle, some of them sitting unconcernedly with a leg thrown over the pommel, talking to the men beside them. The weather grew colder and colder, and the men squatted at night around the small fires. Acox and Bowles sat and talked together aimlessly about what they were going to do after the war and about crops and how the winter was shaping up. They never talked about the company or about the war or the campaign. They rode through the coldest night any of them had ever seen, wrapped up and moaning and aching from the chill. Acox shook continually inside the cloak and jacket, and only his eyes showed above his scarf. They could hear the recruits chattering and shaking and crying in the cold.

And then the command was in front of a small Union blockhouse, a brownish cabin seen across a steep little creek among leafless winter trees. There was a trestle for the railroad and a ford and a bridge, and word came that when they crossed the creek they would be in Mississippi and safe, but that they would have to hurry. They could see rifles glinting against the rough log walls, and the Yankees had a small artillery piece in an earth embankment to the east, about twenty yards from the blockhouse. A young officer crossed the creek under a white flag, and they could see a squat, angry federal officer standing talking to him in front of the house, and other Yankee soldiers slouching with rifles in the doorway. The Confederate pointed toward the mass of troops on the far hill, and talked loudly, and finally turned and came back to them. Acox kept feeling the back of his neck quivering, and he knew the Yankee column was closing in on them. He could hear skirmishing both to the east and the west. They had about forty guns in the whole cavalry column, and he didn't see how they could get past the blockhouse. He looked at the spidery, bare hillsides and the trees and the cold, hard sky.

A young officer with a long, bony nose came riding down past Acox's company saying over and over, "We're going to bluff them out of there, boys, we're going to bluff them out of there." Acox's company shuffled and looked at each other and spit against the ground. Some of them picked up branches. Bowles came and stood next to him. "Well, Bob, try and keep them next to cover all the way." Bowles nodded and they both looked across at the blockhouse. Acox looked back at the recruits; they were talking to each other and looking blank and scared. Some of them made small movements with their hands, in front of their chests, and others scrubbed their hands back and forth across each other. Orders came to deploy the armed men in a skirmish line to the front at wide intervals, and then to move the unarmed men in thick battle lines behind them, to give the impression that the whole force was advancing armed and ready to chop into the blockhouse. Two tough-looking young troopers came through, one of them with a short carbine and the other with a rifle. They shouldered through the recruits, and Acox's men looked at them as they spaced themselves out along the steep bank. Acox's company dismounted and followed the skirmishers down toward the creek. The ground under their feet was frozen and hard; they heard the ripple of the water beneath frozen ice and they could see the sheen of the rifle barrels in the slits of the blockhouse. Acox looked at a weatherbeaten sycamore on the far side of the tracks. He was amazed at how close it was, thirty yards at the most. The line of skirmishers began to fire, their rifles and carbines making a hammering noise, and grey-blue powder smoke filled the brown creek bottom.

The whole column, dismounted and filling the slope, pushed through the pine trees and the bare winter branches and into the icy water. A bridge, the flooring removed, was to their right. Acox saw as soon as they were down in the creek itself that the federal howitzer was pointing squarely down the length of the company, enfilading it. He was walking behind the second platoon, the left of his company line, and he began telling the men, "When I give the command, break and shelter behind that little rock outcropping. Break and shelter behind the rock." An officer behind him with a major's star sewed on the collar of a brown coat said, "Forget that, Captain. Forget that." Acox turned his head a little, and splashed through the water with the rest of the command, feeling the dull, leaden sky and watching the muzzle of the cannon. He had an odd, feathery feeling, as though at any moment his head might swim away and he might fall into the water. He breathed deeply, and kept waiting for the cannon to fire. The water got into his boots, cold and chill. The creek was greenish, with flecks of ice and some piled foam next to the bank. The company got to the other side and suddenly scrambled up out of the water, nervous and anxious to get out of the line of fire of the field piece.

Don't, Acox kept telling himself. Don't break. It was a damn fool thing to do, he knew. But he kept on walking steadily through the water and then he deliberately climbed the bank, all the time the side of his face twitching furiously. He

The Third Winter of the War 59

wanted to duck so badly that his ribs hurt. Blue powder smoke was everywhere, and the armed troopers in the skirmish line were now firing their revolvers. He could see their backs and the movements of their legs as they climbed the slope. The blockhouse, new cut so you could almost see the resin in the wood, loomed silently over them at this angle. Acox looked back, and the rest of the column was walking down the slope and across the stream with the same stiff-jointed, nervous pace. He saw one trooper with faded grey pants inching down a steep fall between the pine trees, holding on to the pine trunks and twisting his face with the effort of keeping his balance.

There were no Yankees in the blockhouse. Acox's company crossed the tracks, grinning a little sheepishly and mingling behind the armed troopers who were breaking into the house and climbing over the earth parapet of the redoubt. One of Acox's soldiers, an eighteen-year-old boy named Tell, was looking seriously at a blanket he had found on a cot inside the blockhouse. It was still warm, he kept saying. "Feel of it. It's still warm." Acox climbed up on the earth parapet and holstered his gun and his saber, realizing for the first time how his hands had been sweating. Bowles came and stood next to him, and they both looked down at the cannon, a twelve-pounder which was spiked. The little redoubt was well made, with a plank floor and a trench running to the side of the blockhouse. The Yankees had left the blockhouse and run along the trench and then into the woods, or down the railroad tracks. They had taken the spongestaff and the handspike from the gun.

Bowles said, "My God, Lee, look back there." Acox turned around. The last of the column was crossing the creek, and the horseholders were bringing the horses in batches up to the bridge, where some of the troopers were relaying the planks across the two rough string timbers. The cannon had completely covered the little valley of the creek; Acox could look almost straight down, and about ten feet down and twenty yards away, at the troops still coming across through the water.

"I am certainly glad they did not choose to make a stand here."

Bowles nodded, and tugged absent-mindedly at his big

moustache. "Wonder how they knew the Yankees would quit the place?"

"They told them Forrest was over there. And we must have looked like quite a lot of men, coming through the woods."

"But hell, Bell or whoever could not have known the Yankees would not just cut us down like wheat, Lee. It was a hell of a bluff."

The whole bank was covered with grinning, gesticulating Confederate soldiers, saying, man, they were glad the Yankees pulled tail and ran. Knots of recruits were standing on the edges, shifting from one foot to the other and trying to look past the packed ranks of men at the fort and the redoubt. As soon as they made out the cannon or saw the size of the two-story blockhouse, they all made whistling noises and widened their eyes and turned to the others beside them, filled with things to say. Officers began moving among them, telling them to form ranks along the road and the railway and mount when their horses were brought across, they could still get caught milling around like cattle on these tracks, and they still had a long way to go. It took the ranks about twenty minutes to get reassembled, and then they were on the road leading southeast, away from Memphis and down into Confederate Mississippi.

Once they were on the road, Acox rode next to Bowles and the little sandy-haired sergeant, Clark. The troopers and recruits were talking about the bluff, and whistling their amazement and chuckling about it. Everyone was bouncing around in his saddle, talking to the men on all sides and adding points and embroidering. They were cocky and certain; it was even better for them than a real battle, because after all no one was killed. The Yankees had been made to look like jackasses. They all said how they and their maiden aunt or their mother-in-law could have held that damn ol' fo't against any number of damnyankees, against ol' Grant hisself. A big private who had been conscripted almost from his wedding bed was grinning and saying, "Hell, all a man's gotta do is just tech off that ol' gun, and he could clear out that ol' crick from one end to the other ever' time," and the men were all nodding and laughing. Hell, one of the quiet young boys they had conscripted said, hell it just proved it wasn't the guns or the forts that made a difference, it was the men behind them. Everyone said yes, by God, if that wasn't so. Acox listened with a faint grin, remembering that that was the boy they had had to drag out of a haystack, and Clark and Bowles looked at each other, smiling too. They listened to the boy say how ol' Bedford sure'n hell knew what he was about, ol' Bedford took care of his men, you better believe it. If Forrest had been in that blockhouse, 'y God, it would have taken the Yankees a couple divisions to get him out. "Divisions, hell. It would have taken 'em more men than they got in their army, I reckon." Well, yeah, and anyway they would still be back there tryen it.

Acox shivered, twice, hard, and he knew that that was his nerve reaction to the whole thing. It sure as hell could have been a damned fool thing to do unless you knew those Yankees were going to pull out like that. Right now he could be lying back in that ditch, spattered all over a corner of Tennessee. He remembered the grey trees and the dark-brown winter earth and the splotches of ice in the creek, and it made him shiver, thinking about the Yankees not running or even just firing their cannon once before pulling out. He for a moment thought of frightened recruits stumbling and panicking and falling into the spraying water, and blood and the stinging clatter of canister, and all of his men running and trampling him in sheer defenseless terror. But as it was, the little pale-faced boy with the receding chin kept on talking, and the others were listening and agreeing, sitting back for a while to relax inside their new sense of competence.

They kept on saying Forrest and ol' Bedford, and though Acox thought the commander of the column was a seedy, bony-faced man named White and he wasn't even sure about that, they were still giving the credit to Forrest, who was miles away.

And that was all right, certainly. That was fine with him. Forrest's aura had spread over them like a banner; it had spread all over West Tennessee. It hung in the still, cold air, its fringes touched their faces. Perhaps after all Forrest and his men knew that a place like that blockhouse would fall simply at the sight of his name, on a slip of paper, backed by forty rifles and unarmed recruits. It wasn't really a gamble; or no more of a gamble than when a brigade commander threw his lines against federal artillery. The men in his company had begun to swagger and relax like the troopers who were guarding them. " 'Y God, they'd never have gotten ol' Bedford out of that blockhouse, nawsuh. . . . " The aura that Forrest threw over them, and over the Yankees, was one of success. Success so steady, measured, often so cheap, that he seemed implacable. Acox still knew him by reputation as a man- and horse-killer; reckless, brutal. He disliked feeling that he was now joined with a man to whom success was the only goal, to whom proprieties were expendable. What, then, were they fighting for? Did they have to resort to men such as Forrest? . . . But he noticed, he reflected wryly and not unhappily, he noticed that whereas dissension and rumor were woven about defeat, legend and confidence were woven about success. "One time I hear tell, ol' Forrest tuk just ten, twe've men into a bluebelly brigade—'s trewth, I sweah—a hull brigade. . . ." "I don't doubt ye for a minute, only I heard 'twas a division. . . ."

The day slanted into evening, and they were well into Mississippi by the time the moon came up. They sat around the campfires and it was colder than last night, the coldest night ever. It was January first. But they were in fine spirits, and they wanted to get in and go to work with ol' Bedford, and whip these damnyankees and the Tories and the niggers. And whip 'em hard, so they could go back to work in the spring, go back to their farms. And Forrest was just the man to do the job.

6

... Thus it is, Mother, that we have been transferred to Fort
Pillow.

Second Lieutenant Jonathan Endicott Seabury dipped his
pen into the inkwell. The sunset, in flat colors of pink and
orange above the Arkansas shore, threw rectangles of light
across the small, scarred table he had dragged up from the deserted warehouse in the town to his tent.

I am in a small tent above the Mississippi River. There is a
Town of sorts in a ravine just to the South of the Fort, but that
is being used as quarters for the white Tennessee troops and we
are not to be quartered there. Major Bradford who commands
these Tennesseans met us at the landing below the Fort when
our steamers arrived, and, while remaining unfailingly cordial,
made it nevertheless clear that tents for our men would have to
be constructed within the Fort itself. This I find to be just as
well, Mother, since the Town is nothing more than old Quartermaster sheds and a few wooden hovels. Our men were set to
work by Major Booth constructing tents. I am sharing one of
these with Lt. Dan Van Horn. The Negroes use straw and
wood to floor the tents, and they have the prospect of being
both clean and most comfortable.

I am ashamed to say this, but of all the officers in our battalion, only Dan and myself are actually quartered among the
Negroes. The others are all in officers' tents in the ravine.

On the other hand, Mother, I wish you could have seen the
wonderful appearance of our men as they left Memphis a day
ago. They are all in the finest humor, and stoutly proclaim
their desire to "pitch into" Bedford Forrest. Forrest, they know,

used to be a slave dealer in Memphis, and I believe I have heard that some of the men in the command were actually bought and sold by the great rebel "wizard of the saddle." As you can well imagine, this only redoubles the manly and soldierly valor in their breasts, and they are eager to have a go at their former owner.

The sun was down now and his hand hurt, so he stopped for a few minutes, lit an old lantern, and settled back in the thick light. He rubbed at his right hand for a few moments, lost in thought, and then dipped the pen into the ink once more, and turned to a fresh page. Is this how Mr. Higginson would put it? His mother was saving the correspondence (he had seen the small locked box of polished wood from China, a design of trees and Chinese fishermen on the lid, that she kept his writings in), and he always remembered in the back of his mind that he was, after all, writing for generations of Seaburys. If he died in the war, he thought, they will remember me by this. They will turn the pages of my letters, and talk about the cousin they never knew. His hand felt better—he tried to write with the best, manliest style he could, even to his penmanship—so he started again.

The men all assembled on the parade ground at Fort Pickering, completely uniformed and equipped for the first time in the three months I have been with the Sixth. They all take exceeding pride in their equippage, especially in their rifles, which I suppose the poor devils feel is tangible proof at last of the white man's trust. And the Good Lord only knows too well how long they have had to wait for that trust! . . . but I digress.

That is good, he thought, and dipped the pen again. Van Horn, pallid and thin-faced, came in, glanced over his shoulder for a minute, and then began bustling around in the rear of the tent. The lamp guttered occasionally, and the pen made a peculiarly dry scratching sound, inching across the thick paper.

As only the first battalion of the Sixth was to go to Fort Pillow, along with a section of light artillery from the 2nd United States Light Artillery (Colored), the other men of the regiment clustered close around them while they waited for the orders, manly comrades bidding their friends and companions good luck, and openly envying their chance of getting to see some real action soon. We all stood in marching order, with full packs and rifles, and a wagon for each company to carry our tents and ammunition, etc. to the slip where we were to board our steamers. The Negroes made a fine sight indeed, Mother, wearing their long frock-length coats, all piped in red, light blue trousers, and forage caps. Their brass fairly shone like sunlight. They take great pride in their breastplates and buttons, and in the great shoulder scales which most white troops long ago discarded, and they spend hours shining these "brasses" to gleaming perfection.

Then the orders came, and the men all fell in, with much cheering and fine "huzza-ing" for the benefit of General Hurlbut, their officers, and the men and friends they were leaving behind. General Hurlbut, we thought, might come and see us off, but he failed our expectations. The colored troops were especially disappointed, since to their simple minds a federal general must be only a step below the Holy Trinity, and they treasure having one address them.

Behind him Van Horn was cursing and trying to buckle a clasp to his scabbard. He kept turning around and around, like a cat trying to catch its own tail. The metal struck the cot's wooden frame.

"I'll get it for you, Dan." Jonathan carefully put the pen down beside the paper, his eye running over the close-spaced words like a man's hand across a fine carving. Pivoting in the chair, he clipped the scabbard on the sling while Van Horn grumped and rocked on his heels and stared at the wall, for all the world, Jonathan thought, like a girl being laced from behind. Emily, the thought came, and he felt a feather-tickle of excitement. I must finish the letter to Mother, he thought, and then perhaps I will think of Emily. He smiled and Van Horn said something unintelligible and stamped out into the spring night. Jonathan debated, and then decided to start a fresh paragraph.

Though denied the thrill of a General's Farewell Address, the Sixth set off to the wharves with a resolute step. As soon as they descended the slope into downtown Memphis, the usual ragtaggle of small Negro children, or "pickaninnies" as they are called, danced and skipped between the marching ranks, bedazzled I suppose by the shining golden brass, the martial wink of the bayoneted rifles and the throb of the drums. But I feel I should be much amiss not to suggest perhaps another emotion than that of mere cheap military enchantment in the gay and carefree little hearts of the little . . .

Jonathan went back and changed "little hearts" to "great hearts," thoroughly blotting out the first word by scraping away at it with his pen point and adding a few camouflaging whorls and loops.

. . . fellows. After all, these were their own black brethren, their comrades and brothers and uncles and fathers, and perhaps some single Ethiop yearning, some sense of complete identity with and pride in the Sixth, made their yips a little shriller, their chuckles and chortles a little more heartfelt.

That did not make sense. He took out a penknife and meticulously cut the lower part of the page. Then he took out a fresh sheet.

. . . fellows. After all, these marching men were of their own deep-hued race, their brethren and uncles and fathers, and I am certain some great Ethiop heart of hearts was fused between the marching men and the little cavorting children, between the so-recently-freed men and the little tots (not to mention the Afric bystanders), some single sense of identity and pride which would make the cheers which resounded round our Massachusetts volunteers leaving the Commons to look childish and insincere. I am perfectly convinced the little fellows' yips were a little shriller, their chortles and gambolings a little more heartfelt, than ever before.

That had been a difficult page; now he settled back and began to write more fluently.

However, the march through the downtown of Memphis was quite a different sight. The regiment kept the step quite well, considering the irregularities of the pavement, etc., plus the presence of a half a hundred wives and sweethearts mingled among the men, clinging to their chosen ones and destined to accompany them to the new garrison. The Negroes are very proud to be allowed to march with full equipment and under arms through downtown Memphis. While the sight of Negro troops is detested by the inhabitants, but certainly not unusual (I have told you of our provost duties), the sight of a full battalion with complete equippage, all armed, with wagons and packs, is something else again.

The populace, weak and sallow people, standing before their cheap stores and small grey buildings, all turned and watched with the utmost hatred imaginable. Nor is this incomprehensible, since our battalion stood for the complete overthrow of their previous way of life, a way of life they will neither acknowledge as evil nor repent of. The people, shopkeepers and *huswifs,* a file of rebel prisoners, bankers and street sweepers, all turned and faced our marching men, some of them making insulting gesticulations and shouts. The Negro soldier, armed and capable, is the final blow to these secesh, for it is the final affirmation of their freedom, of their acceptance as citizens (for can you arm a man and then not trust him to the further limit of complete equality in the society he is to defend? as Mr. Higginson demanded so eloquently). Further, the scathing irony—that these former slaves shall be used to defeat their former masters—must be bitter and repugnant to the rebel palate, as in like measure it is refreshing and cleansing to ours.

We were forced to wait for several hours beside our steamers. The stevedores and white sailors refused to load the contents of the wagons, despite Major Booth's eloquence, and we were forced to break ranks and complete the job. The Negroes did it with equanimity, however, and that great and deep joy for which the Ethiop race is known. In a matter of ten minutes they had the boats loaded and they were back in rank. We filed aboard two stubby army river transports, and were accompanied by one of the gunboats they call "tinclads", the No. 41, I recall. The maindecks of the transports were open with removable railings, and the Negroes were packed into nothing more than the shelter of the overhead boat deck, exposed to the biting March winds on three sides. But they took their lot cheerfully (though I was greatly uneasy about the several Negro children of the Sixth's families, who were clad in hardly more than rags) and settled down in groups on the filthy deck.

The boat, we were told, had just carried a deckload of horses from the Kentucky area for Hurlbut's cavalry, and the evidence of the animals was, I am sorry to say, amply scattered about the deck. But the men did not seem to mind, and pitched in with will. I had thought the sailors would have cleaned the decks, but evidently they are not responsible and we hardly had time to wait for the proper men to do the job. With the spirit of the race, always willing to undertake any job, they worked with a will, and soon the deck was quite liveable.

The officers were shown to rather shabby little cubicles on the boat deck, and I shared one with a navy lieutenant Carpenter, and lieutenant Van Horn, whom I have already mentioned several times. We stayed awake late into the night, thrilled as we were by the huge moon and the gliding progress along the river, and each of us musing, inwardly, about the possibilities for some action in our new garrison duties. (Oh, I forgot to mention that I first sent down all the blankets in the room despite Dan's heartfelt objections, to the Negro families with children. They did not get shared about, however, and some of the smaller children had to do without, though today they seemed none the worse for wear.)

He thought for a few more minutes, rubbing away the soreness in his right hand again.

Our first glimpse of our new fort came this morning, the 28th of March. From the river Fort Pillow looks simply like a mound of red earth on the river bluff. The transports tied up at a small pier, and we marched ashore. Bradford, a sallow, black-haired man who seems very young and quite nervous, met us at the water's edge. Our men made their way to the site of their new quarters, at the rear of the Fort near the bluff. They set about building their own tents.

The Fort is shaped precisely like a horseshoe, though you must imagine a horseshoe a hundred yards or more around, with a ditch of some ten or twelve feet width. The dry moat is some six feet deep. The earth was thrown up along the inner edge to eight feet in height. If the rebel dares attack, we man a small firestep and our men can step down in the shelter of the Fort to load their pieces. There are six artillery pieces, all of them small calibre, two six-pounders and two twelve-pounder howitzers and two small ten-pounder Parrots. All in all it is a very secure and safe Fort, since the parapet is of such size as to deter any assault, I am sure. The ground has been cleared for several hundred yards in all directions, and stumps and undergrowth make it all but impassable. The Tennesseans keep the countryside well scoured and patrolled, and their picket posts extend well over five-hundred yards from the Fort. In addition, since Forrest has made his appearance, a small gunboat, the *New Era,* stands always just off shore to lend protection. If he comes to *swallow* us, I am confident the rebel will find quite enough Fort *diet* with gunboat *chaser* to satisfy his appetite for some time!

And of course, Mother, you must never forget the splendid spirit of my ebony comrades. They exude the utmost confidence and prate of what they will do to Forrest should the old bugaboo dare attempt the Fort. The Negroes are the ultimate in soldiery, for they know, as Mr. Higginson wrote, that no prison pen, but slavery, awaits them if they are captured, and as they have had ample foretaste of what *that* is like, they are more trustworthy than the best white troops, I am convinced. If there is any flaw in our situation, it must be that of the white Tennesseans, not of our Afric ranks. These men are nearly all sallow and yellow-looking, as if they were all jaundiced. Bradford is a nervous man and poor officer, from all we hear, though he has been courteous enough to us. The troops of his command, however, hardly treat us as comrades in arms. They all seem skilled veterans, though, and perhaps we have first to prove ourselves in combat before they will accept us. And I have no doubt, and neither must you, that we shall do so.

Well, Mother, I must close now. I think of you and the whole family often. Please say a good word to Aunt Roberta and dear cousin Julia, and Miss Eversham.

Your devoted son,
Jonathan Endicott Seabury.

He signed his full name, and sat back to read over the letter. Then he took out an envelope, addressed it to the house in Boston, and folded the paper into it and sealed it with wax, stamping his ring into it for a seal. He tossed it on the desk and squeezed his eyes shut with thumb and forefinger.

"Otto! Otto!"

The orderly came in, a tall and hump-shouldered young Negro, with a bony, angular face. "Yassuh?"

"Otto, take care of this letter for me. I imagine the river boats handle the mail, so place it in the proper spot, please."

"Yassuh." Otto shuffled forward, picked up the letter and turned, murmuring to himself, "Gotta go down to thet town."

"What?"

"I say I gotta go down that town, suh. . . . That's whar the mail del'vry spot is. . . . "

"Oh. . . . "

Otto bobbed and wheezed and padded out.

Jonathan sat back and wondered about all the hypocrisy and the lies. He wondered about the letter. Bitter hopelessness coursed through him like liquid. Abruptly he got up and put on his frock coat. His face was sharply cut and chiseled, fine and straight and almost too fragilely perfect, with the long blond hair and the blue eyes. He went out of the tent and walked over toward the wall of the fort. The stars were out, springtime stars; last year he had seen March stars through the lacy springtime leaves in Massachusetts.

He had enlisted straight out of college; he had been commissioned and asked specifically for a colored regiment and one in the West. The sergeant with a very scarred face and only one eye had looked up at him oddly and then began to get out the brownish forms; Mr. Higginson who commanded that colored regiment down in Carolina had helped him very much. And he had been sent out.

He had always wanted to command Negro troops. In his yellow-brown college days Jonathan had always pictured himself as an officer in a black regiment. He was always in a cabin or a raw brick garrison room, and the Negro troops were always sitting, great, huge men with the gentility and pleasant gaiety of children, sitting and leaning forward and even gaping a little and all of them watching with endless, boundless admiration as he worked to teach them English or history or geography. He was always endlessly patient too, and when they won his approval they would nod happily among themselves. Or he would see himself marching with them beside sneering, distrusting white troops; and then they would behave with transcendent bravery and heroism, unflinching and dressing the ranks while he smiled at them, before going forward into immolation.

He leaned now against the earth parapet where it ended, and he looked out over the river in the darkness and moonlight, toward the Arkansas shore. He saw line after line of shadow, grey and black and purple.

In the vision, in the mind's world, it was always so noble and straightforward, there lying the duty and there lying the path for him and for his conscience and his heart. Touching the great black men, touching their inmost hearts and soothingly erasing all of the hatred and accumulated fears, living with them and sharing their life. Dying perhaps (and he had always gotten a pleasant lump in his throat thinking of it) like Mr. Shaw had died, buried now beneath his men, mingling his body with theirs. Like a saint mingling his body and flesh in a last great sacrifice with the blasted and the downtrodden, with Ham's descendants.

He shifted within the thick frock coat, looking down at the twinkling lights in the little row of shacks they called the town. There were fires behind him, between the Negro tents, and he heard singing down along the river bluff; the thick, greasy odor of the Negroes came and floated. The light from their fires flickered on the earth walls around him. He cast a shadow, thin and faint and outlined in clay-orange, before him on the wall.

The Negro camp was much noisier and brighter than the Tennessean camp down in the ravine. He kept on staring out over the river, his feelings stirred and aroused by the shift in place and the transfer from Memphis, which seemed to draw a line across things, to seal off and fold away what was just past.

So he had elected to become a commissioned officer in a Negro regiment; and "one out in the West, please, sir," because after all Mr. Higginson had said things were much worse out there, and capable officers needed for the blacks in the worst way. For a time it had been all he had ever wanted. He would go to the parties and dances for the soldiers in Boston, wearing his new frock coat, buttons gleaming and his bright crimson sash twined around his waist, talking of the scales and the buttons which were unfamiliar to most people. He stood in the middle of parlor after parlor, holding in one gloved hand a cup of punch or a glass of brandy, folding his other hand into the small of his back, bending his head to listen politely and comment politely and learnedly about the war. "No ma'am, I never knew Colonel Shaw. But he has set an excellent example for all of us, I feel." The faces lifted to him, the eyes smiling and twinkling up at him, old gentlemen whispering of the Mexican war and what they knew or thought of this war, old ladies commenting on his handsomeness and on the wonderful "sense of purpose" he had.

He had met Emily at such a party; she was a cousin of his, demure, fragile, blonde, with straight, tiny, perfect teeth and a faint, delicate blue touch at her temples. He suddenly realized she was listening to him, devotedly. Everything vanished, time and his sense of himself, even the small, creeping, spindly doubts about the coming months. All of it folded away; he was looking at her and talking fluidly and softly and politely, aware of nothing else.

"Well you see, Miss Eversham—Emily—that it is my opinion that every man must confront this war as he must confront life. That unless he takes it upon himself to give it meaning, it will have no more sense of purpose than the butchering of hogs or the work of madmen." She would nod yes; her eyes searching his eyes.

"And, Miss Emily, I do not see how one can have any sense of real or lasting victory unless one has added that purpose into the war, and has made that war a private thing. That is what I am trying to do. This war, shameful but necessary, is the ultimate thing in our time, and I must come to deal with it. But I cannot—forgive me, I know this must be boring you—" and she shook her head, her lips softly forming the word "no" and her eyes drifting across his.

"Well, then, you are too kind."

He was lost in his eloquence. The rest of the group, the men in uniform and the elderly men and bright young ladies, the winking, glittering chandeliers and the glasses of punch, the heat and the mellow liquid light and the piled and drifted, pure, clean snow on the other side of the window, all of that melted into a corolla sparkling around her. His words, tumbling out, built a world removed from time and the glitter and sparkle of lights and the conversation and presence of others:

"I cannot bring myself to accept blind, animal-like slaughter, a fierce struggle for mere survival, battling conscript-like for purposes I do not know and ends which I cannot feel in my heart. I must have more meaning that that. And the great sin of our times is slavery. It is the great and grasping sin. The rebels do not concern me, save insofar as they perpetrate that evil upon my awareness. I cannot condone it, and to stand by and do nothing would be to condone it, would it not? So, I have chosen this course, to go out among the freed slaves, to work with them and try to teach them. They are, I understand, children anxious and willing to learn, to find a pride and a sense of themselves and of their abilities. In this way, you see, I plan that my war will have an end and a goal above pure military victory. . . ."

"Yes, yes, I see, Mr. Seabury . . . I think it is wonderful, and noble. You do have a goal and a mission, Mr. Seabury." She sought back and forth across her hands, to find the words. Tiny wrinkles formed across the pure white of her forehead. "If only everyone else . . . " she broke off, and looked up, and blushed. He was close to her, and he sensed his own maleness and competence, and he was very proud. This is the moment, this is my moment, and my course is clear. He wanted to dance and jump and fling himself at the stars.

"You are too kind, Emily," and it was almost a whisper. She had looked closely at him, trying to read something in his face. He tried then to put it there for her to read, his happiness and the wondrous sense of purpose that he felt, and the slight twinge of anxiety that all should go well, that he should indeed be worthy. His eyes wrinkled too, and he felt a slight shift of bone and flesh across bone. And he saw her suddenly read his expression and then seem to sparkle, the whole action so tiny and delicate, like a mote in the sunlight, that he did not breathe for fear it would shatter. Yes, yes, yes, yes, he kept saying to himself. The moment approached eternity, he thought; then she looked away and blushed, and it fitted so perfectly into the whole moment, the glistening look in her questioning eyes, her eyes finding the answer he put there, the delicate sense of a closed, tiny, secure place for just the two of them, the tiny tickle of power over her that came to him, then the blush. . . . And he was up and talking to other people then, while she fled in a whisper of silk. Jonathan talked to them, fluent and eloquent, his eye catching her from the midst of a group by the fireplace or near a sofa, watching and listening to him, across the crowded, glistening room.

That night in his bed he thanked God for Emily, or rather the whole thing; he heard the sounds of the city and he smelled the room and touched the sheets, and everything took on a new and deep quality; there were shadows and depths and dimensions behind every sensation, every sight and smell and taste. He felt drawn up out of himself, he held tight to the bed covers just for the sheer encompassing exhilaration of everything.

It was fully dark now, a spring night on the bluffs above the Mississippi. Seabury pulled his coat closer at his throat, still musing, and listened to the sounds of the river below, and then to the gusts of laughter and the metallic tinks and scrapes from the camp behind him. He felt a twinge of duty—I ought to go and see to the men, but of course I shall not. He began to pace back and forth, along the little section of fort wall between two artillery embrasures. His feet clacked along the wooden firestep.

The night was clear, but it smelled of rain. When Jonathan looked up he could see tongues of clouds reaching out for the moon, curving around it, lacey white where the cold, clear light came through. A pale pink and green halo spread far from the moon. He stared at the halo, trying to bring it into some kind of focus. Jonathan sucked at the night air, clear and wet and smelling hollow. He felt himself burst open inside, shadowy hands opening and spreading inside his chest, his heart thumping into a bluish, dull ache, lonely and small and wanting to touch at the moon.

Before last January, when he had reached the regiment at Memphis, he had been a different person, uninitiated, stupid, with faith in things that were clotted and repulsive; and the thought of himself then caught in his throat. "Well, Emily," he had said to her in the fire-glint of a ball and the silver and brass and trim blue of his uniform, "you see, I must serve. Yet I have never been able to. I have never been able to touch life and feel it. I feel I have much to give, but I have never been able to give it, try though I have, to my fellow man. Perhaps"—and he had let his eyes grow narrow and furrows form with the tragedy of his failure—"perhaps it was because the white men were too much like, well, grotesques of myself, masques all the more horrible, Emily, because they reminded me of the true nature of myself. That, stripped of home and wealth, I would have been as they, deformed and dirty. So, what then could I offer them?"

She shook her head, then—no, no, not deformed or dirty— and he smiled at her wearily, a man who has tried to face the world and has learned failure. Then he continued, the mauve throb of nobility filling him, willingness and urgency to believe in himself everywhere. "So I deliberately chose the Negro branch of the service. Because there, there will be none of that cloying similarity. Only the pure sense of a relationship between two human beings, as different one from another as to obliterate all but the purity of that relationship."

Late that night he had continued the speculations, walking down the pure-white, snow-covered way to his home, his feet striking down on the packed and glittering ice along the sidewalk, the banks of snow covering and molding everything into a single piece. He would embroider—I should have told her this too: That among the Negroes, I shall be reviled by the whites. But I am seeking that too. For that will be the final stamp of my triumph over pride in myself, the final reduction of the stifling sense of pride and pleasure in contemplation of myself which prevents me from touching others. That contempt will be a continuous fire (and images approached of him leading his black men down lengths of road, with white troops jeering and he only turning and smiling to his men and they smiling in reply and keeping cadence) which will burn me down until I am ready, and can learn the depths of my own abilities and of my soul. " . . . and of my soul." He would rehearse the key phrases for the next time he saw Emily, all the while smelling the tingling wetness of new-fallen snow, feeling the coldness and the purity across the bridge of his nose, his flesh fluid and warm and clean and crisp inside the thick blue overcoat, his feet clapping on the ice and exposed brick.

On the firestep, he thought about those winter days in Boston. There was a brutal satisfaction, a physical pressure on his heart, in recalling every one of his callow, brazen stupidities. He remembered one afternoon, clear and cold, while he sat watching the sunlight pour through the bay window and melt into the carpet, and Cousin Ben, a lieutenant colonel of engineers, paced and talked to him.

"Now Jonathan," he had said, "I don't believe you honestly know what you are getting into. I don't believe that you have thought all of this out, or that you really know yourself. It will be hard, Jonathan, from all I understand about such things."

He had thought, all the while, here begins the persecution. He smiled inside, answering nothing, but treasuring up his own sureness.

"Jonathan, were you not an only child, and were your father not dead, I feel you would have a better perspective on things. Now, son, do not take this amiss, but I doubt seriously that you are of age or have the temperament to join a colored regiment in the West. They are not like you think, son." He became very angry at that, a stinging anger. He had to say something. "Colored troops in the West, Jonathan, are not of the best. They are poorly officered and poorly trained, and there is little chance for them to see any fighting, since they are used as guard details, or as labor gangs."

"Sir, as much as I respect you, what you say will only make me angry. I have decided. There is a certainty about the way I feel. Here is a place where I can do necessary work, where I can be of use. As another officer in a line regiment, I would only lose myself in the concussion of battle"—Cousin Ben quit pacing: he looked sharply at Jonathan, the long, livid scar running along the side of his face into his hairline—"but there, with the Negroes, I can teach and work with men that need my talents."

Cousin Ben had sat down, then, painfully: he was recuperating from the rebel shellburst which had scarred his forehead, and from the fevers he had contracted in the seige lines outside Charleston. "Jonathan, Jonathan . . . " Seabury had decided that Cousin Ben would not understand: his eloquence was wasted. He had grown impatient. He turned down a position on Gillmore's Judge Advocate staff at Beaufort, quickly, and tried to change the subject. I was a fool. Outside, he remembered, there had been a blinding glare across the snow.

Three days later, amidst the steam and confusion of a train station, a battalion of conscripts boarding for the South under guard, baggage and steam and the smell of oil and grease, he had said goodbye to his mother and his relatives. Emily had come with them. Her face was soft, her body balanced on tiny feet, the slight weight of her flesh and her roundness making his arms itch and his face grow red. He had gotten very excited looking at her, and was embarrassed and glad when he could hide his excitement and sit down, more embarrassed and confused than ever, but glad and thinking it must be of a piece, it is just my body confirming my choice, there is nothing evil about it. He had not mentioned writing to her, though the thought had played against his mind, a slight, delicious "if I did ask her, she would." But he had not, he had preferred the thing wrapped up and put away on the shelf, perfectly and neatly, thinking as the train left Boston in the darkness, well I will write, I did everything perfectly, and she will be waiting for me. He had almost drummed his feet against the floor of the train, his face stiff and sore from smiling rapturously, endlessly. A weatherbeaten soldier across from him struck up a conversation, and said he was from the Army of the Cumberland—where was Jonathan bound? He had told him, the man leaning forward, smiling and lonely, until he said, "My orders read the Sixth Colored Heavy Artillery at Memphis." Oh yes. Well. The man made an odd curve with his mouth, and then leaned back to sleep. There was coldness and hostility palpable among the troops around him, sleeping and waiting to rejoin their regiments, and a sergeant behind him said, "nigger troops," and he heard someone spit.

Jonathan had never known Negroes before he went south. He had passed them a few times on the streets of Boston, speaking politely and feeling noble, magnanimous. And there had been breath-catching moments when his father was still alive, stumbling in later at night with Negroes new-freed from the South, big, breathless black men and women, wearing borrowed clothes and smelling of sweat and mothballs and nervousness all at once, the bricks on the cellar steps standing out in the lantern light, and hot buttered rum spicing the air and the Negroes grinning and showing teeth and hardly intelligible in their chatter; with Jonathan standing just to one side, feeling a delicious spark of getting away with something, like hiding beneath the covers from imaginary giants.

And on the trip down, he had spent his time not looking out of the train windows or at the passing shoreline but showing himself off, writing letters and pacing across decks looking worried and intense, talking with men and women in the riverboats. He had memorized drill patterns and evolutions in his cabin, pacing out the steps across the deck, doing the turns and facing movements and occasionally sketching an evolution so that he could grasp the way it worked.

Then he had stumbed off the steamer into the greyness of winter Memphis, with crusts and rimes of discolored snow and ice, and teams plowing up the streets, blue-brown columns of troops marching through the mud and cavalry details splattering around corners. He had watched sections of ragged Negroes hefting and shouldering bundles of equipment and leather goods from steamboats, wrestling artillery pieces to the shore, stacking lumber and coal and crates of uniforms, manhandling great bales of cotton to the ships for passage upstream. He had stood on the landing and watched the Negroes, the gangs of them, plodding and scuffling with their work, and white soldiers cursing and shouting at them. The Negroes moved with colorless eyes, and blew out plumes of steam-breath, and huddled around small fires when they were waiting for another boat to begin unloading.

Jonathan had gone up to Fort Pickering, a long, sprawling cantonment with huts and wooden sheds for barracks for the Negro troops, sentinels on self-conscious parade across the earth parapets and great artillery pieces glaring over ditches and moats. He went across a sally port, his red sash swinging with his stride and his feet clattering on the wood. A Negro sentinel challenged him, a great hulking man in a blue frock coat and red chevrons. He had shown the man his sheaf of orders, and the man looked at them bear-like. Jonathan realized that he had expected the man to read them and of course he couldn't read, so he had said, "I am Second Lieutenant Jonathan Seabury, reporting for duty with the Sixth Colored Heavy Artillery."

The bear-like man, stinking of sweat through the thick coat, said, "Ovuh det bluff, yonduh," and turned away, slopping, back through the mud. Jonathan had entered the orderly office, and a thin-faced man with pale-blue eyes looked up from the desk at him. He was reading a newspaper. A Negro stood hunched over by the stove in a corner, warming himself. Inside it was stinking and fetid with sweat and woodsmoke and the odor of close-packed bodies. There had been no sense of potency or challenge or climax.

The pale-eyed man said he was Captain Donaldson, of Company I. He looked over Jonathan's orders and wrote a few lines across a ruled page, and then said, "You're in Captain Smith's Company, B. Go over and see Smith."

"Thank you." The man looked back at the page of the paper in his lap, and said nothing. Jonathan stood holding a salute. He felt the Negro looking at him. Donaldson did not return it, and he dropped his hand self-consciously, and walked out. He went through the mud the length of the lower part of the fort, down the Negro lines. The tents looked orderly and white, but there was the grey smell of woodsmoke everywhere. Negroes in pieces of blue uniforms and rags stood in the company streets, forming vague lines and drilling in some places and talking around the thick gleam of fires in others. There was a strong, musty odor, of earth and manure and meat and grease, and it washed from the tents and shacks and seemed to spread all over the ground. Jonathan walked along above the river bluff, and stopped for a few minutes at a gun embrasure, trying to smell the river and clear his nostrils. Shacks and trails and paths cluttered the river bluff below the fort, and Negro women and children and old men slouched among them, like ants, Jonathan thought, when you've ripped open the ant nest. Some women clambered through a gun port near him, past a

huge, fat-bodied Parrot, laughing and saying, "lawse, lawse."
One of the women was fat and old, and her hair was grizzled
and tied in greasy pigtails; her flesh jiggled under the cheap
print dress as she walked.

Jonathan reported to the headquarters tent of Company B.
Captain Smith was a fat, squat man with a tiny mouth and long
sideburns. The tent stank of sweat and the smell of an oil lantern. Two Negroes stood in one of the corners, talking low to
themselves, and another sat on the ground at the door of the
tent, head hanging.

"Seabury, eh? Welcome." They shook hands. Smith
grinned conspiratorily. "Where from?"

"Boston."

"Oh? . . . Well, we don't get many from Boston. Mostly
from up th' river, Cincinnati, so forth." He looked at the yellow-
brown sheaf of orders on the camp desk in front of him. "Boston, hunh?" He seemed to be musing. He shook his head. Then
he looked up.

"Where's your gear and truck?"

"I left it down in the town, sir. The man at the dockyard
guardhouse said he would keep it for me. I . . . I wanted to
see the regiment, as fast as possible," and the moment he said it
he knew he had said the wrong thing. You did not talk like that
here. Not here. Smith drew back up in his chair. He looked at
Seabury curiously. His small eyes clouded over, and he sighed
deeply.

"Well, grab yourself a nigger and get your stuff. Lieutenant Marlowe is home sick, so you'll get a tent to yourself. I'll
point it out." He walked over to the door of the tent. Behind a
traverse of huge, basket-like gabions stood a row of whitewashed
shacks. Fifth from the end, number 17, he was told. Smith
turned and went back to the desk.

"Uhh . . . " Jonathan felt like a fool. Smith looked up.
"Which Negro should I get?"

"Anyone of 'em, it don't make no difference." He went
back to filling out a report. The Negroes in the tent were looking at him. He motioned hurriedly to the skinny one near the
wall, with a wide, flat nose. "Private, how about . . . "

"No, no, Lieutenant," Smith said, "these are headquarters niggers. You go down to the lines and get one."

Jonathan had not. He had walked past the lines, looking at the Negroes' tents. They were small and filled with splintered and greying furniture. The Negroes were gathered around, talking to the women who had climbed through the embrasure. They were laughing, and when Jonathan saw them laugh and their faces split, he felt the old surge of purpose and goodness and nobility come back, but then he breathed in the smell above the wet mud, the warm and greasy odor, and he withdrew and went back down the lines, and out the sally port. He wrestled with himself, but he could not walk up to them, he could not approach them and ask for one of them to help him. They were another people, the closed circle around the fire. They were black. He noticed in confusion that their faces were not black-colored white men's faces; they were caricatures, it seemed to him. Their noses were big and flat and their arms swung loose, with thick big wrists and pink palms. The fire gleamed from their flesh, as they laughed, and their lips were wide. There seemed a smell hanging to them, that musty smell, and their faces seemed chopped out of something other than flesh. They were not like children. They were not like white men who were only a little gayer. They were different, completely. He could recall looking around in desperation. There was nothing to reach out to.

He could recall even trying to find one that was light-colored, to get him. And he saw one, a yellow-faced Negro with liver spots purplish upon his cheeks. Yet that had somehow seemed all the worse; all the more ghastly. He had turned away, hearing their blurred chatter, and he could not even understand what they were saying. He walked out of the sally port down to the town, sick and wishing above all else that that day could be over, could be closed and all the introductions and the new things to learn could be over and done with. He felt cheated and trapped. No one had ever told him this, that the faces were big-boned and the flesh was dark clear through. That phrase repeated itself in his mind. Dark clear through.

In the town he had gotten an old, hunched Negro porter to

carry his things. The man, his hair white like dirty snow, had wrestled the steamer trunk up to the fort. At the gate the sentinel came down and began to curse at the man, "Whufo you come heah? Whufo you take dis white man's money? Whufo you ain' stayed in de town?" He had raised his musket angrily, brandishing the butt end, and the old Negro had cowered and stumbled out down toward Memphis. The sentinel stood cursing him, and then turned to Seabury. He smiled at him, bad teeth, yellow and blotched, set in a yellowish face. "Yo ain' got to get no wuthless town nigger to fetch yo stuff. We done hit. Dint you know we done hit? Didncha know?"

"No."

The Negro sentinel turned and shouted up toward the line, and a thin, loose Negro had come running.

"This heah is Otto. He take care of yo."

"Thanks."

Otto saluted and Seabury returned the salute. Otto grabbed at the big steamer trunk, and got it set on his shoulder. Filled with infinite relief, Jonathan walked into the fort. There was a small crowd of off-duty Negro soldiers, watching and talking about the scene at the gate. Jonathan's back and neck prickled as he walked past them. They were in the area of the Third Artillery, and he was glad when they got behind a mud traverse into his own lines. It felt, oddly, like coming home. The warmth and greasiness of the odors wrapped around him. He felt less naked.

Otto, behind him, grunted and strained and talked all the time to himself, "He dint have to get no town nigger fetch his stuff. Ol' white man, he knew. He ought to know he dint have to pay no fool town nigger." Jonathan listened vacantly to the shuffling and the grunting monologue. They walked down the lines again, but he did not look at the Negro huts. A party of Negroes from the Second Light passed in their shell jackets, grinning and laughing, a tall, gangling one horsing around, pushing and shoving at the others. They all stopped laughing and snapped into a crooked double rank, and the tall, gangling one, a corporal, snapped off a salute, and Jonathan saluted back, and then they were gone. Again, there was that momentary glimpse of what could be, of him in the classroom and the friendly colored faces looking toward him like a teacher. But it shifted past in the flood of the odors of the Negro lines, and a scattering of laughter from around the campfire.

They had walked through the gabion wall and Jonathan had paused with relief. The faces like carved grotesques, the light shining off the black skin, the smell and the splintered furniture. That was gone. Behind him, Otto stopped his monologue, and shuffled in silence.

They had come to the little hut, a square white-painted box with a big number beside the door. He saw some other white officers inside one of the nearby huts, and caught a glimpse of a red beard and parts of a pistol, open for cleaning on a table. The little hut had seemed fresh and clean, with a grainy smell of vacancy. There was a cot, and a table made from a barrel, and a chair. Pegs for hanging clothes were along the walls. There was a brick fireplace and chimney at the far end. Jonathan rubbed his hands briskly together; he felt relieved and all of the worry seemed to wash off.

"Put it down there."

Otto lowered the big trunk. He was sweating heavily despite the cold. "Mister Marlowe he slep' heah too. He got sick, went home. . . ." Otto's voice trailed off.

Jonathan turned to him, looking at him coolly now. His face was craggy-featured, with sharp cheekbones and yellow eyes. The Negro shifted. He wants to smile, Jonathan thought, oddly. The sense that the man was a child came to him. Give him something to do.

"You are my orderly, Otto."

"Yassuh—I reckon."

"Are you a private?"

"Yassuh."

"Did you have a job, a duty? . . ."

"Nawsuh . . . nawsuh. Dint have no job, don't reckon."

"You want to be my orderly, Otto?"

"Yessuh, I reckon . . . ain't got no job."

All right, he thought. All right.

"What's your last name, Otto? Private what?"

"Stimson, seh . . . Stimson."

"Well, I am Lieutenant Seabury. Now listen. Go and find me a lantern, Otto. Do you think you can do that, you can find one? Fine. And go down and see Captain Smith and tell him you are my orderly. All right? Fine. . . ."

"Yassuh—getcha lantern, an' go see Cap'n Smith . . . yassuh. . . ." He went out. Jonathan had sat down and felt how tired he was, and scrubbed at his eyes with his fists.

7

THE WINTER HAD PASSED BEHIND THE TRAVERSE, THE WHITE
officers and non-commissioned officers talking in their mess,
laughing and smoking cheap cigars and playing cards into the
nights, slab-faced men with small eyes and scraggly beards, laughing in gulps and heehaws. Jonathan had walked in among them
and introduced himself. They looked up from cleaning weapons or playing cards or eating and nodded back. They had
looked at him, running their eyes over his tailored uniform and
his sash and shining sword. Then the head of the man near him
turned and said something softly to the other men sitting at the
table. They measured the words against him insolently, and
then laughed and turned back to their food or cards. The mess
room seemed greasy and close, and the sweating Negroes brought
out the thick, chunky food, beef and corn and beans. The tin
plates scraped and tinked, the faces bent furiously over the food,
thick lips and stubbled teeth catching it from the spoon end and
chewing and biting into slabs of cornbread, all of the men talking in grunts between bites.

The other officers and white sergeants looked at him not
with contempt or even suspicion, but just with indifference. He
had spoken up once at the second meal he had taken with them.

"What action has the regiment seen to date, Mr. Smith?"
Smith looked at him, holding the spoonful of beans inches from
his mouth, and he looked around the table at the other white
men. Then he bit into the spoonful with a snort and chewed
and screwed up his eyes, looking cagey and wise. "Against
which?"

"Sir?"

"I mean to say, boy, against which have we seen action? You might say we been in action against everything in sight. We been in action against white soljers down in Memphis on provost duty. The white soljers, they don't like to have no niggers come around tellen them what to do. So they take offense. . . ."

Jonathan felt the light, warm and thick and palpable, close in tightly on him. All the other men at the table were smiling to each other and looking at Smith and pursing their lips, sucking at small stringy bits of meat caught between their teeth, and resting, waiting.

". . . So they take offense. Now we had us a big nigger sergeant name of William Bee. Big ol' nigger. He took a patrol of niggers down to Memphis, and caught some drunk Pennsylvany soljers raisen hell. He set in to stop 'em. They jumped William Bee and took his gun away and stabbed him fo' times with the bayonets in a place I won't mention because it's too indelicate . . ." he waited ruminatively while the others laughed ". . . and these Pennsylvanians, they took off all the others' clothes and stripped 'em buck bare, and sent 'em back to us.

"So you might say that's one thing of action we've seen. And another time I recall, a couple of them niggers down to Company J started a fight amongst themselves, with bayonets and knives, and cut up se'm, eight of theirselves pretty bad. So that's another spot of action. But we ain't seen no rebels, if that's what you mean."

All the men at the table had laughed and grinned at Jonathan. Jonathan had opened and closed his mouth trying to interpret, to regain his balance and force a smile.

"Sit down, boy. Yore food'll git cold," Captain Bischoff, fat-jawed and pale, had said, and everyone laughed. "Sit down. Yore safe up here."

A great deal crowded into his mind, a great deal he had to ask.

"But . . . but . . . why . . ."

The faces turned a grey-edged seriousness on him, eyes narrowing and lips together. He looked from eye to eye; all of them were expressionless, pitiless.

"Why are you serving with them, then? . . . Are you joking? . . ."

Smith had grinned around at the others. "Me, I'm servin' here because in Ohio there was a conscript law, and I had to serve one way or another. An' I'd seen how the pore beggars in the infantry live, 'cause I had been one. You caint laugh at officer's pay. You caint laugh at it a bit. An' we're liven a hell of a lot better up here than we lived down in the Forty-third Ohio Volunteer Infantry. A hell of a lot better."

Bischoff had said, "An' it's a hell of a lot better service too, than serven with white men," and for a moment Jonathan felt things slip back into place, a surge of relief, but: "Because these niggers ain't got the sense of a white man. No sir, they ain't. You tell 'em to do somethen and they do it, they fetch and carry. They get in fights with each other and cut each other up, but, what the hell, no adjutant general is going to give a damn about a colored regiment. Just turn it out on a parade looking good, that's all they care 'bout. That and having enough men to dig a ditch when they need. Nobody rides herd on you, here. You do as you please. Let the niggers alone, let 'em cut themselves up. We live up here, they live down in the lines and they can do whatever they damn well want to do. They don't talk back or act up like white men. They caint count so they don't mind their pay. You go down, drill 'em three, four times a week, that's all you have to fool with 'em."

"How . . . how can you tell, sir, what they will do in a fight?"

"How can I tell! Hell, I know! In a fight, they going to turn tail and run like hell. That's what I know they do. Hell, you heard about that time down on First Street they run into those drunk white soldiers. You think you can trust them to stand up to fire like a white man? Boy, you are crazy. Ain't no rebel going to try and take Memphis, otherwise I'd be long gone." He snorted, and the others bent over their plates, and a moment later Jonathan went out into the night, chilled, bewildered. He heard a snicker and someone say, "Don't that about beat all?" and a lot of laughter.

After that second night at the mess, when he had eaten three mouthfuls of stew beef and then gotten up mumbling and walked out into the night with the laughter gathering around his coattails, he had made his irrevocable error. He had known he was making the error at the time but, like the question of finding a Negro orderly for himself when he had passed the lines, he had not been able to force himself to avoid it. He had put on his uniform the next night, smoothing it and putting on the sash, and then he had not been able to go down to the mess. He had stood with his hand on the door and counted to three, and then to five, but he had not been able to. He took off the coat and he called Otto and Otto brought the food to him, cold by the time he put the tray down on the table. Jonathan had not gone to the mess at night for a week. He had slipped in for a cup of coffee at breakfast; he had not taken lunch, going instead to lie on his cot, staring up at the whorls of plaster on the ceiling with one hand dramatically resting, palm upwards, on his brow.

And one day in front of the company after a week of this, all the time knowing that there was a wave of resentment building against him on the other side of his silence, Captain Smith had called him aside and said, "Seabury, I don't give a damn what you do but lissen, you might as well know that we ain't got room for uppity second lieutenants. Not putten on airs the way you do. Now you in my comp'ny and I tolt you. You in the wrong regiment to git uppity ideas. Might do you some good to come to mess once in a while." He had stood there near tears and amazed at the shock and unfairness of it all. And that night he had gone to the mess, holding himself miserably upright and going in, expecting to be ridiculed or greeted or acknowledged in some way, but everyone instead had paid him no attention whatever, not even slowing down their conversations, pausing to perceive him and then going on as before. He saw that Smith had not wanted to get him back in the fold as much as get him where they could punish him. He tried to say, "I've been feeling weak," to a couple of the younger officers and some of them snorted and the rest looked him up and down and then turned away.

They had found out, concurrently with his disappearance

from the mess, that he had received a large crate of schoolbooks sent by a Boston society. The crate of books had been left in the sally port unnoticed since he had not gone to mess and so had not received the message, and it was finally opened and seen by the officers, by Captain Epenter in particular. They did not only despise him for being withdrawn, as if he found himself better than they; but they also accused him, he came to realize, of all but fomenting a rebellion. Epenter even went up to him that first hideous night back at the mess as the men were leaving or settling down to poker, and said, "We have no need for men comen in here and stirren up things. You got those faincy ideas you take 'em back to Boston, boy." And he had stood with one arm in his overcoat and his face puzzled and worried and twitching, saying, "What, what?" A lieutenant from K Company said from near him, "You know damn well what," and when in desperation and even reaching out for the man's arm he had still said no the man had almost hit him. Epenter held the lieutenant's arm, and fear and surprise and tears were visible in Jonathan's face. Epenter said, "This ain't the way, but I know how you feel," and the others looked curiously at them, seeing the fear and surprise and child-like incomprehension in Seabury's face, and turned muttering contemptuously to each other so he could hear: "You hit ol' Bahstan one time he fold up" and "You know it, little chickenshit coward." He had stood still with his arm in the overcoat, the cloth achingly cold, looking around helplessly and with his lower lip trembling; then biting the lip until it stung.

He could remember running back, then, running back to his hut and jerking the drapes shut and closing the door and lying on his belly for two hours, still in his frock coat and brasses, puzzled and shaking his head and his mouth bubbling, his face red and swollen with anger and rage and helplessness at the unfairness and incomprehensibility of it all. The next day he had heard about the books, McGuffey readers with mauve and brown covers, most of them by now thrown into the mud and kicked around near the sally port until he picked them up and threw them away. He walked around his company during drill feeling marked and spotted and hated, and he kept his eyes on the ground sadly and walked with his shoulders slumped. He knew he could not outlive this, ever.

And it was so hideously unfair: every night before going to the mess he rehearsed exactly what he would say in pride and scorn to them all, and every night he sat in silence and said nothing, the bitterness gradually, slightly, assuaged by the talk and the food and the cigar smoke and the fact that he could at least sit there. They could not or would not take that from him. He would sit in the same place and eat and listen and laugh a little at the jokes and then carefully leave, right after the younger officers left to go down to the women's quarters or the fleshpots in Memphis and right before the older ones, the colonels and majors and captains, settled around the poker cards. He measured his leavetaking carefully, so he would not impose on either group. There was no place he could turn.

The older officers were living in their niche of beef and whiskey and cigars and cards, and the younger men, with shifting, quick eyes, were tired of insults and knowing they were true. After a week they were indifferent to Jonathan, with an indifference which turned to hatred, sparkling-eyed, when he pricked at it. And he could not go to the Negroes. That too was a wall, yellow and greasy and musty-smelling, with different faces like things hacked into grotesque masks out of coal or wood. The winter world was a thick sinkhole of greasy smells and slab-sided faces, of beef stew and nigger lines and filthy tents, of cold and the mud-stained rime of snow-ice along the edges of the latrine sheds.

He had thought he could go to the Negroes and find great, dusky-skinned children and he had thought the officers would be dedicated men with fine-boned faces and delicate hands. And there was only a business sense, a sense all over the cantonment of so much flesh on the line twice a day, so many hands to handle shovels and so many bodies to stand watches. The white men were dealing in human flesh, putting it there on the line, watching and tending it and feeding it and ministering it with the indifference and contempt of a zoo-keeper shoving the chunks of meat to the animals, pushing it out and then turning and slamming the cage door in one motion; not even seeing the crouching animal but already going to the next cage, thinking of other things, of pay and beer in brown bottles and food for himself.

Jonathan endured time. The spitting winter sky drove hailstones and snow and rain down onto the earth, and whipped the river into pockmarks and foam. The wind howled around the corners of parapets, and the Negro sentinels buried themselves deeper in their coats and made their meaningless rounds, sure not of their authority or of their duty but only of some inscrutable malice that would fall upon them from the other side of the traverse, where the buckras lived, if they dropped out of the stinging wind to the warmth of a fire. Parade and muster and inspection, and drill, with the white sergeants shouting at the ranks and cursing the niggers, with feet slopping through churned mud and the yellow liquid eyes brimming with water from the chill, hands claw-shaped and bodies hunched. Yellows and clay-reds and brown earth colors stained everything. Jonathan lived, he felt, desperately near the traverse; he could not stomach the white men, and he was repelled by the Negroes. He walked over the paths cutting through the cantonment, and down the steep bluff to the river. He cried to himself in desperation, and found himself saying, "If only I could see the sun, if only I could see the sun."

The white officers had a special kind of ostracism; they would look at him with a half-attentive, vaguely contemptuous glance, a glance a man might give a piece of shoddy leather as he lays it back on the counter to pick up another, not even recognizing him as another human. It seemed they did not look with the eyes: Smith would pick up the duty roster and glance at him, taking a quick, sensate impression of a shadowy form before his desk, and then giving a flap of the fish-belly white hand for dismissal. If he spoke, white men like Smith or lantern-jawed Captain Bischoff looked at him with silent indignity.

A slow and unwilling agreement rose in him; he was worth no more than a quick, vague, eyeless glance not admitting his personality or his appearance but only his flesh presence. It dulled him, and made him feel dead and whipped and weary inside, a sick, hollow pain in his throat. His loneliness and disillusionment felt out for the insensibility of a thing. I will be a thing, then. Until one day he recognized, suddenly, finally, that he was being treated like they treated the Negroes. He was at the duty desk and saw Smith look at a Negro recruit the same way, a hollow, contemptuous half-glance, serving as dismissal of him as man even while he was being sworn in. Why, I am being treated as though I were a Negro, and he suddenly saw the tents, yellowish now from the smoke, and the carved, grotesque faces and the jargon and guttural monosyllables and the grease and sweat smell, enveloping and folding him voluptuously.

So he spent much of the night writing a letter, long and almost desperately cheerful, talking of progress and educating the blacks and of his noble, dusky soldiers, scratching away at the paper while the candle sputtered and rain drummed against the roof. He had sent the letter and then walked back to the fort, empty and hopeless again, lonely and afraid and humiliated. He picked up a book of Tennyson from the little table made out of a barrel, but there was no longer that hollow secret sense of pleasure and warmth and cleanliness he got from immersing himself in the printed words. They have taken even that from me. His eyes stung. He threw the book against the wall.

Later that week he had found Dan Van Horn, Van Horn who had just been driven with curses and blows from cabin number 7, clutching at bedclothes and spitting curses back into the cabin and standing in the mud and snow. Van Horn was thin-voiced and reedy, with wisps of a black moustache and a pale, white face; he had made himself totally unacceptable to the other two in the cabin, with the weeping endlessness of his monologues, and they had kicked him out. Jonathan had helped him with his gear and they moved in together in his cabin; he had started the game, baiting Van Horn for a reply, for the snarling, cursing contempt which at least was not indifference. At least it was not the same look they gave the niggers. "Dan, why don't you please try to keep the floor clean?" "God damn you you sonofabitch you are worse than any damned wife! I be damned if I come up here to the army to be nagged at! Be damned if I will!"

The Third Winter of the War   93

> . . . and now, Mother, I have a roommate, a capital fellow named Dan Van Horn. He is no relation to the Van Horns in Brookline, but he is a good friend all the same. . . .

"God damn you Seabury, will you stop that damn writen while I'm tryen to get some sleep! I be damned if I know why I let you talk me into liven with you. . . ."

So now, Jonathan thought, on the wall at Fort Pillow with the spring night fresh and clear and a few lights on the Arkansas shore, now I have a cushion both ways; there is Otto to deal with and Van Horn to deal with. . . .

One day in Fort Pickering he had folded loneliness and self-pity around him, and it had given him a surprisingly good feeling. He bit into it, his eyes ached, he walked across the parade to his company forming in sodden, weary ranks for drill; he wrapped the loneliness and sorrow around him, and it was so warm and so intense he did not want to break from it. He lived with it as a tear-stung disease, a steady, dull headache and a catching pain in his throat, and only occasionally, when he was exercising the big field pieces with the Negroes, did it leave him.

Once a week, he and Sergeant Gaylord would take a platoon out from the fort and man one of the redoubts along the railroad line. They marched out through the grey city streets, past other details, cavalry looking contemptuously at them and white civilians looking at them with open hatred, and Gaylord spitting tobacco juice and grinning back saying, "They're black sonsofbitches, ain't they?" Jonathan marched near them, holding up his sword in the crook of his elbow, trying to avoid hearing, feeling. The Negroes laughed and joked and capered, and it made him mad and he felt betrayed. They carried the rifles like shovels or picks, they slopped through the mud. He was afraid to give an order, because Billy Gaylord would ruminate on it and grin and turn around without a salute and saunter down to them and begin shouting "All right you black bastards. . . ."

They would file into one of the abrupt little walls of earth, pierced for two twelve-pounder howitzers which frowned straight down the railroad tracks into the hazy distance. Jonathan liked to touch and slap the guns; they were solid and clean and sure, with the cold, thick feel of solid metal. The Negroes would play cards endlessly; he would send out pickets and details, and get some of the Negroes busy deepening the ditch or cleaning the big cannon or digging latrines, and then he would sit in the half-light of his tent, alone. He would listen to Gaylord pace back and forth cursing at the Negroes, and to the tink of shovels and the laughter from the card games. Jonathan would wait out the endless hours, leaving his tent just to slap the breeches of the howitzers and letting Gaylord change the pickets and reliefs. He and Gaylord had worked out a tacit agreement, Jonathan saying: "You can handle everything better than I can, Sergeant, so I'll just leave you in charge and be in my tent or at the guns," and Gaylord would grin through blond stubble.

Looking out the embrasures, down the railroad track to the vague and mystery-clothed point where it came around the spidery grey hillock, he sometimes thought of rebel soldiers, and fancied swarming grey figures between the far trees and in the ravines. All winter, Forrest was a palpable word in Memphis, a word that felt like a lead musket ball when it was spoken.

Forrest had dealt in land and slaves and horses in Memphis and was remembered by the merchants and businessmen and farmers. Even while they were selling beef and corn and leather to the Yankees they were remembering Forrest's cold grey eyes and the tall man looking over an acre of property, not sharing your jokes in the cold winter fields but sizing up the land and feeling it with his hand and walking along the boundary lines and the fences, looking and poker-faced estimating, judging; finally putting a clear, sharp-edged price on the piece if he wanted it, and even after the deal was finished not the sort of man you would invite to the house for some peach brandy or whiskey, and not the sort who would accept even if you offered. Always the last name, "Forrest," never Nathan or Nate; the businessmen of Memphis, watching the loaded packets come in convoys and the cotton leave for the North by the boatload under the bayonets of Yankee sentries, the businessmen stood in the cold streets and worried. Planters and the aristocracy and the West Pointers didn't worry them, but a man who could size up a field or a slave or a horse and cold-eyed give you his first and final price, and turn and walk away if you bantered; a shrewd, smart businessman with a small layer of fat as tangible prosperity on his frame—though that would by now be eaten away to a rock-hardness; a man who knew how much to buy things for, and when the price was too high would not buy, that man scared them deeply. The fear too came not only from the skill of the man but his brute, puritanical, flint-hard inevitability. He would not be invited to your home but he would be on the board of aldermen, cold and unflinching and inexorable. It was not that the price he offered you for the land was what the land was worth; the price he offered was the fair price, the only price, and in the manner of the man was the hint that to ask any more would be to somehow defraud, would be consciously immoral, not because of piety or soft honesty, but because of his hardness and clarity and tight-lipped certainty.

Jonathan felt the fear and the shuddering that ran through the Memphis merchants and Unionists; all the Northern soldiers felt it. The man was legend, and beyond the parapets and the range of the howitzers and seige guns, where the greyness of winter came down and mingled with the earth, the land was populous with Forrest. The unsparing winter earth, shoddy and flint-hard and dirt-scrabble poor, seemed part of the skein of the man. He was always out there, Forrest the raider, and sentries shivering on cold earth walls strained their eyes toward the horizon and awaited the inevitable; the telegraph wires set traps and made dispositions, trains clanked by the outposts loaded with troops, the roads swarmed with nervous angry patrols.

Jonathan had often crouched over the howitzers and looked at the far hills and thought: He is a dragon; this is what confronted the knights and their ladies in their castles. Out there, there was always that animal, ruthless, skilful, cunning, in the long run victorious. It is out there now. He would not write that home: he always wrote quite the opposite, platitudes about how the Negroes knew Forrest and his slave-pen and would fight to the last, teeth-clenching, vicious moment. But all the Memphis garrison—all Hurlbut's Sixteenth Army Corps—

wrote the same meaningless assurances. They were giving themselves confidence and certainty which they achingly needed. And their confidences echoed by telegraph and messenger and routine all over the department. One moment a commander in one of the loopholed outposts would wire his ultimate and complete confidence, and the next moment surrender to a handful of half-armed rebels and a bluff and a name written, forged, on a slip of paper. Hurlbut and his division commanders would set trap after trap, and plan defenses and strengthen outposts, and yet feel as soon as they boarded the train or shut down the telegraph that that outpost would melt to water; that they were trying to strain an ocean with a fork. Helpless and desperately resolute, the Memphis garrison waited, and all they had to judge by were the whipped details flooding into Memphis, symptomatic bursts and dribbles of men from the scattered outposts placed to protect the rails or from the expeditions sent out to capture him. The men were received and treated with kindness, like survivors of a natural disaster, the soldiers themselves dazed and dirt-stained and chattering to out-tell the others about Forrest.

Hurst's Tennessee Cavalry was driven back in, white-eyed with fear and Hurst without his hat. There were small details from the railroad line blockhouses, brow-beaten and bluffed out of their timber forts, leaving their guns in the loopholes and now shamefacedly sitting beside the railroad tracks while Hurlbut himself cursed them.

Finally Sooey Smith's huge cavalry division had set out, all splendidly mounted and singing "Rally 'Round the Flag" while the garrison troops admired and envied and pitied them. They had gone out swinging past the redoubt where Jonathan had had his men stand and cheer them on the walls. Some of the white troopers had made obscene signs to his cheering Negroes, cavalrymen clanking in swords and carbines, braced in columns of fours behind the snapping regimental flags and the striped guidons, passing in a gleaming, endless stream. And of course two weeks later, somewhere out beyond the grey line where the winter sky greasily lay over the bare hills, they had met Forrest and inevitably had been whipped. Not just whipped but routed and driven pell-mell and in dry-mouthed flight all the way into the center of Memphis, some of the men too weary to find their own cantonments and lying in the streets. They came back weaponless and blanketless, mixed in huddling clusters without company or regiment or brigade, a whipped rabble.

They had not met Forrest, Jonathan learned, head on, but the name of the man had haunted them for miles into Mississippi, past the burning fields and houses and barns, and guilty columns of smoke marking their way. And when they had come up to him, up to Forrest who had two weak and scattered and half-armed divisions, they had immediately been formed in a desperate column of retreat, Sooey Smith desperate and nervous and unsure of himself. They had broken and broken and broken again until their officers could not form them in line and gave up and the whole campaign became one agonized, whipped, cowering retreat. Jonathan watched them ride in, shaken and weaving sleepless in their saddles, streaked with mud and stung with cold.

So Forrest is out there, Jonathan had thought, and then thought of a rebel attack pouring out of the far ravines toward his redoubt; his men, the Boston papers would have it, fought to the last. But he knew they would not fight. The whole command knew Negroes would not fight. They would make a fine show marching out, happy and cocky, and shoving white people out of their way, but they would not fight. Jonathan imagined them running in bunches, eyes rolling in fear.

And he then would have his chance. The rebels would be wizened, hot-eyed men in brown and grey, scrambling over the ditch, yelling, and perhaps Forrest would lead them. Jonathan would stand alone and Gaylord would run, and then he would have his chance. Then the only thing he would have to do would be just stand there; not even walk or run, just stand in one place and jerk the lanyard on the howitzer once, and then stand and fire his gun. He practiced unconsciously in the winter nights. He would stand in the middle of the tiny redoubt with the cold moonlight and the chill on the brass gun muzzle in front of him, and take out his big Navy Colt, and practice steeling himself; the back of his legs and his knees and his spine rigid, standing there firing the empty gun and then slowly putting it back in his holster and drawing the saber and looking at the imaginary faces of the rebels coming over the wall. The bayonets would gleam in a circle around him. He would die. Forrest would look down on him, and salute the torn and tangled body, and somehow the Sixth United States Heavy Artillery Colored would enshrine his memory, the officers, Smith and Bischoff and Van Horn coming out to look at his grave, maybe even Hurlbut standing over them (or Forrest, that would be better, marching the captured army corps by his grave) and saying, "There, there is how a man dies for what he believes. There is the way a man conquers death." He would stand and play the game of emptying his revolver and drawing his sword and standing his ground, until a thick lump came to his throat, filling him with the beauty of it. And then the Negro sentry would pace by one of the embrasures and Jonathan would duck into the shadows, waiting until he was past to begin the pattern again.

Jonathan paced along the wall at Fort Pillow. The air was pleasant and clear and clean after it had rained the night before, and he could smell the spring, and was glad to be out in this fort and away from Memphis. The winter had been the worst of his life, he knew. He would sooner die than go through a winter such as that again. I know I must rely on myself. I must wait, for that moment will come, and then I can at last measure myself against this hateful universe and find what I am made of. Even if I must die to do it. Forrest is ultimate enough; he is the inexorable, the inevitable. He is not unlike a force from Nature coming toward me. He will free me, in a moment of destruction. After all, is not the final willed action that of self-destruction, the final moment of selfless action? And Forrest will give me that chance, to die for others, as I have been unable to live for them.

The thought choked him, momentarily, and he wished he could write it to Emily. It was a beautiful thought. Perhaps they will try to take Fort Pillow. He thought a little more about the grey-coated rebels clambering over the walls, the Negroes running, he alone standing to meet them. He was afraid, for a moment, the Tennesseans would fight. But perhaps they would run if the Negroes did. Even if they stood and fought, if the Negroes ran he alone could stand and fight in their section of the abandoned parapet. Then many would see him; the white Tennesseans who had stared at the landing Negroes, and had whispered, "Look at that air nigger officer," when he passed, just loudly enough for him to hear. That would be even better, to show them.

As he stood on the firestep at Fort Pillow, the feeling came to him that his dream, of gallantry and sacrifice, was suddenly possible. He reworked the images of his death again, and pictured them to himself. They seemed much more consistent with this fort than they had with Fort Pickering, or with the howitzer embrasures along the railroad. He shifted with a sense of excitement. He sensed that the place was exposed; more exposed, he told himself, than Memphis, anyhow. It was a heady feeling. He felt himself both free and exposed, along an edge where his heroism would be exercised.

With that feeling, of course, returned others; he began to retrace some of his dreams—of teaching the Negroes, in particular—and they too seemed infinitely more possible, here, he told himself, on the edge of Secessionland. He managed to convince himself, exuberantly, that the patterns of his life at this fort would be much changed from the patterns and cloyed, distasteful conditions of last winter in the Memphis cantonment. Encumbrances seemed to drop away. I have never met Major Booth; but he will certainly be a much finer man than Colonel Brickland. After all, he is facing the enemy here, every day. That seemed to hallow the man. Yes, he would, he decided. He would ask Booth for permission to start the school. New enthusiasms were bursting in him.

He walked along the wall, a handsome young man with a clean-shaven face, clear-eyed. His collar was open and spread, showing his clean-lined neck and throat. He began to feel the spring air and, smiling at the traces of his youthfulness, allowed himself to think a while of Emily.

BOOK TWO

*The Winter and Spring
of 1863-1864
Trials and Preparations*

I

THEY DRILLED DURING THE WINTER FOR THE FIVE WEEKS THAT THE
Federals and their own command gave them, in the meadows
east of Oxford toward Panola, behind the line of the Talla-
hatchie River. Acox, who had held his captaincy in some ephem-
eral Sixtieth Tennessee Mounted Partisan Battalion, found
that he was reduced to the rank of lieutenant. He was placed
with his men in the new regiment of cavalry that Forrest assigned to Colonel Russell and called the Twentieth Tennessee
Cavalry, of Bell's brigade, which was expected, and Buford's
division, which was not. The prairie land was flat and the soil
was black and tawny with the winter; the days were cold and
grey or cold and bright. They did not drill like the numerous
regiments had, that had marched off four years before. Back
then they had been given a bare overlay of military terms, and
had learned a sequence of neatly ordered movements coming
from the chessboard patterns of a drill manual. In those days
they had drilled not so much to form an effective machine but to
satisfy the urge to play bloodlessly at soldiering. This time, in
Mississippi under Forrest, they were not given a meaningless
overlay of military terminology (which almost always proved
worthless in the thick and swirl of battle amid copses and
swamps and honeysuckle anyhow) because in the first place
there were no military manuals left, and in the second place
Forrest did not do things like that.

Forrest had seen how things that were done in that fashion
totaled more often than not an unwillingness on the part of the
officers to descend to detail and to reality: how like at Fort

Donelson two years before, such military terms, such careful delineations on textbook paper and designed not only for victory but with a sure eye toward textbook immortality, had led to a lost victory at Donelson, where the plan though not the men had failed, so an army was lost. And again in Kentucky and at Stone's River and at Chickamauga, where the Yankees were beaten but kept on fighting so everyone at headquarters in a flash of gold braid and heroic posturing assumed that the plan had failed, while the shoeless ranks had charged over and over across the fields and through the thickets. And the South, even a slave trader and a property owner and a street fighter could tell, the South was running out of men in its effort to find a winning plan, and was already out of time, maybe irreparably out of time.

Acox could remember the taste of the early days of drilling and inactivity down at Pensacola, which had given a false sense of confidence that melted in the hideousness of Shiloh; where the parade drill commands, whether executed smartly or stupidly (or not at all), only sent ranks of living flesh and thumping blood straight into massed battery fire. Everything suddenly had been placed on a different plane, a different level, the man to value becoming not the man who knew the book but the man who could get the job done. The man who could go there and stay there and endure in that spot until finally the Yankees couldn't dislodge him; or if they did dislodge him had bought time in such a way as to get out with most of his men alive. Hamilton LeRoy Acox with his sad eyes and his deep chest had been precisely that sort of man.

For that reason he had been placed into the skein of acquaintances across the state that Tyree Bell kept up with, and had been saved and then attended to when Forrest had come back to Western Tennessee; a good man to be folded away and then called up with the same arguments and the same force used to call up all of the good men Bell had kept in touch with for a year and more against the time Forrest, who could get the job done, would come. Forrest had come and, in the six thousand men he had wrenched by force of personality alone, force of personality transmitted over that skein of business and military and property and political acquaintances a man of means builds up in peace and in war, in this six thousand there was a sure leavening of company and staff and field officers, veterans and men of conscience.

So now, because of these men and their experience, the six thousand were shaped into an efficient if untested force, not by drilling and drill manuals but by day after day of working out patterns on company and regimental levels. The men from the same homes and counties and towns were placed under officers they knew; but men culled and selected by Tyree Bell and by Forrest himself, not chosen by the pathetic and naive demo- cratic elections that persisted in the major armies of the Con- federacy even now, while the slaughter and the butchery per- sisted as well.

At Pensacola LeRoy Acox had walked up every day to the headquarters tent of the ——th Tennessee Infantry and had found posted orders for drill and for inspection, signed by the adjutant and countersigned by the colonel, and on the salt flats they had industriously and with sweat dripping on the manual pages puzzled through and carried out the movements, until they had been a well-drilled regiment. But the lessons they had had to learn to survive had only been learned after, again and again, they were butchered and chopped up. Finally they had learned that there were flaws in the manual and that the rifles and the artillery could and would chop you down while you were dressing the line or marking time, at impossible distances according to your textbook. And then the posturings had gone at last. They had learned that as soon as you stopped anywhere you burrowed and dug and you didn't try to keep a straight line but you followed the line of the ground. They learned to study minutely every tree and shrub and stump; they learned when you charged to run for anything that looked like shelter and then to settle down and try to outshoot the Yankees.

Acox had learned those lessons and had put them to good use and become one of the men who could get the job done, but his will had been eroding away inside him all the time. That had been the price of the lesson; that had been the reason he had learned it, in the first place. Forrest knew that, and he knew that Acox and the other veterans who had been conscripted had one more lesson to learn before he could use them.

Because Acox was a man, and human, there had been a time when war seemed not only necessary but good. And this had died hard in him. All of the print-like, song-like enthusiasms and illusions had died; the resplendent uniforms had faded and there were no clear victories, not for Confederate arms in the West; and cleverness and courage did not pay off immediately and indeed often as not went unrecognized or even regarded with suspicion. Rather than the clear and crisp panoply of war there had been the screaming wounded, all of the screaming, dying wounded, the rags for uniforms and the rotten pork and the captured hardtack soaked with human blood (surreptitiously scraped off) and no coffee. These disillusionments had made war unpleasant, repellent, but they had not made war unacceptable. For war had seemed to offer, finally, victory. Victory, surcease, cure.

So when he was wounded at Chickamauga he had found out that victory was a hollow thing, a lure, a bait. His knowledge of war had been completed. He knew how to maneuver a company under intense fire. He knew that war was ignominious and horrible; and he had finally accepted—not learned, but accepted what he had learned, but refused to believe, much earlier—the fact that war was futile. His war; that war; he did not want to fight any others to learn if they, too, were illusory. It had taken him long enough and longer than most, but the proof was forthcoming after Chickamauga, when he dawdled and gladly lied and willingly hid and refused to go back.

So while Acox—and the other veterans—had all of the talents and all of the knowledge, he did not have the will. He would desert. There was nothing, any longer, that would keep him to the colors. So Forrest knew that he—they—had one more lesson yet to learn. Forrest had one more lesson yet to give them before he could give them their victories, which of course would make that last lesson unnecessary. And he knew that he could give them those victories.

Of course, it was not only the veterans; most of the men that Forrest and Bell had wrenched out of Middle and West

Tennessee needed the lesson. They did not accept the fact that if they did not stay they were liable to be executed, and they didn't accept—indeed consciously rejected—intimations that the army had any rights over them and over the conduct of their lives whatsoever. They said in flat, nasal tones that they had 'y God done their share, and let some of the bombproofs step in for a while, or they said that they could not leave their families to the mercy of the Yankees and the niggers and the Tories.

After a fortnight of tentative and small and therefore successful efforts at desertion which tiptoed around the edge of the six thousand men and reduced them silently but steadily, a whole body of nineteen men one day agreed that they might as well die trying to get home as trying to kill Yankees and you couldn't kill all of them anyhow. They took all of their gear including the new rifles Forrest had somehow found for them. They got ten miles up the road, riding now in loose formation and laughing and grateful for slipping away, when some of the tall, big men of Forrest's own personal escort came down upon them and of course the deserters did not fire or break. They just laughed and said, "Come on, boys"; and then they cursed but they went back to camp, still not realizing that anything they had done was in the least wrong. After all, they had pieced out their lives in the hills or in the small scratches of their land in Tennessee and the big planters and the county magistrates had never paid them mind, before. Nothing they had done had ever carried consequences or effects five miles from the location of their homes or their fields or the places they held their prayer meetings or did their Saturday drinking. The veterans among them had even deserted before.

So it took the severest and the sharpest and the simplest cutting-edge that discipline had to make them realize that they were no more their own men, and Forrest had that cutting-edge to hand. He sat them in a tiny, overheated classroom in the school building in Oxford and despite the pleas and recriminations of the townsfolk who still did not know what war was about sentenced them almost out of hand to death.

They were shoved from the courtroom that had been the classroom and still had the picture of Washington on the wall, and they were taken and thrown in the town jail. There they were fed and petted by the people of the town but there, as well, they were kept in cells and guarded by troopers with loaded guns. And then the priest and Bell and their regimental commander came and took them, to the thumping of muffled drums, out to the ravine where they were permitted to dig their own graves, turning with each spade load of winter earth deeper and deeper into the sure knowledge of their own mortality and death. All nineteen of them sweated in the winter cold, their foreheads glistening while they worked at the frozen earth which finally gave, breathing through their clenched teeth and some of them crying. None of them swore. On three sides in rigid precise formation stood Bell's brigade of Forrest's cavalry; men in dun-colored uniforms with greasy, worn leather belts and battered hats and thorns instead of buttons, standing squinting into the bright sunlight and feeling the stinging cold air on their cheeks, no one saying anything and watching the spades bite the earth.

Hamilton LeRoy Acox shifted behind the line of his company and hated Forrest who not only was killing nineteen men but was killing something within himself because up and until this moment he had still not known that there was no escape. He had felt and believed and even known that one day, if things got too bad, he could pull up and desert. But he could not do that any more. It was another edge of reality cutting into his world, painfully, just as the other realities, that war was without glory and that he had to return to it, had bitten into him. It was not a game. He could not quit, or he would be as summarily killed as those men out there.

And he listened to the minister reading the words above them as they stood at the edges of the graves they had cut, and thought of the relentlessness of the man Forrest, of his steely eyes and hair and the tight-lipped mouth and the nasal drone of his voice, and he thought, *he* is a goddamned white trash, and will have us all dead. I had heard but had not believed that he sought only personal glory, but I see that now. This is the most barbaric thing I have ever seen. His stomach hurt and he did not want to watch and he flinched away, and wanted to break across the dry earth and the frozen corn and get to his horse and get away from the war and from this insanity and from Forrest.

The firing squad came up and the minister went away, and the blindfolded men sat on their coffins with tears running down their faces. One of them was sixteen, maybe, with long blond hair and it blew in his face, and another one named Murphy was bent over double holding his belly and his face was twisted. There was complete silence and the officer in command, who was officer only by token of a small red sash around his waist and a collar with three bars sewed on it and was certainly not appointed of God to kill these men, just as Forrest was not appointed by God to judge them, brought the squad to attention. Everyone in the three-sided brigade square came to attention.

And then, of course, as everyone told themselves they had known all along, a man came up, his horse's hooves hammering over the frozen ground and yelling, and everyone turned to look and Acox could see the tear stains on the face of Bowles and Clark next to him with his kepi, and he turned too. The firing-squad captain had just said, "Present arms! Make ready! Take aim . . ." when the man came pounding up on the horse so there was no question, none at all, that this was the dramatic and deliberately plotted last-minute reprieve, but still there was the breathless race against time. The messenger on the horse tumbled off and caught his boot in the stirrup and did an insane and circular little dance around the side of the horse, while the firing-squad captain stood with his hand half raised and his mouth open, and then the man got free of the horse while the brigade shifted and twisted perceptibly in the long regimental ranks. Then pulling his short blouse square, the messenger, who had a blond beard and creaking, high hip boots, ordered the men to stand at ease, and then turned to the culprits who were still blindfolded and sitting stony and rigid on the plank coffins. He turned to them and shouted above the rustling noise of the brigade: "General Forrest has requested me to say to you that it is unpleasant to him to shed blood!" and he gasped for breath and then, "And that, through the petitions of the clergy, the prominent citizens of Oxford and your officers, if you will now promise to make good and faithful soldiers, he will pardon you."

And the patent fact that he had rehearsed and written down and read off the little speech which crowned the deliberateness of the drama, this fact slid away unnoticed when all of the nineteen shouted, "We will!" And the brigade cheered over and over and dissolved. The nineteen of course at any time during all of the proceedings would have gladly and honestly shouted, "We will!" and signed or made their mark on any and all oaths, but they had no more been given the chance than a stalked deer is given the chance. The blond-haired boy with pimples was half insane when they pulled the blindfolds off and was led gibbering to his horse.

As Acox walked with his company back to their mounts he was fully aware of the deliberate drama of it all, that of course it had been the simplest and most rudimentary of object lessons. So simple that he felt ashamed and offended, ashamed for the feeling of fear when all along he should have known it was drama, and offended that Forrest would have such a low opinion of his intellect as to believe that such a trick would work. But work it had, he also had to admit, because all around him the men with winter-reddened faces were gesticulating and laughing and relieved, but they were saying as well, " 'Y God I don't ever plan to be caught by ol' Bedford like that" and "I reckon those men were suren hell lucky" and "I ain't no mother's son to be counten on ol' Bedford changen his min' like that again."

And he knew that it had worked in him too. He was involved in an incredible, miraculous reprieve. But there would be no more such second chances. Were he ever to be caught, no matter how genuinely penitent, they would still push him in a matter of hours up before a firing squad and he would not have merely lost an incident in a game, he would have lost his life.

On the way out to drill the next morning, feeling the motion of the horse between his legs, he began to appreciate what Forrest had done. They say he has no use for the rule book, but you look at that spectacle yesterday. The muffled drums. It was all taken straight out of the drill book. All of that textbook-perfect procedure gave a rigid, an inhuman cast and tone to the thing. All of that made it supremely obvious that disobedience is the cardinal and unforgivable sin, no more to be pardoned by human efforts than by the hand of the Lord Himself. But he did pardon them. . . .

He guided his horse around a solitary, dead blackjack tree on the plain while he thought about it. Of course. He produced it and he dismissed it. And they know it. They understand his power over them; he has the power of life and death over them. It did work, he thought. This was not a farce, or a spectacle; he imagined Forrest's implacable, steel-grey face. It was a warning; a ritual.

"All right, all right. Bowles take a section out on the left, and Clark out on the right. Horseholders to the rear. . . ." The hooves pounded and drummed over the tawny, black earth, the little fir trees slapped as the horses were led past at the gallop.

It was a show of power, the first time that Acox had ever seen the power of life and death that was balanced over him; that had been balanced over him ever since they had marched into camp at Pensacola, beneath the arcades of spanish moss and pine, with the flowers still stuck in their buttonholes. Starting it, starting all of the legal and penal forces into work, that was nothing, though the spectacle of it was awesome and frightening and weird. Bragg had had men hung for desertion. But Bragg, sallow and lean-faced, had not been Forrest. Bragg had not been able to stop it.

Forrest's power was a personal thing. Bragg had not been able to stop all of the cuttings and feuds and desertions and straggling. He had not been the same thing as the power he wielded; but Forrest was. Bragg had been strong only because of his rank.

"Is that ol' Bedford, over there?" Orrison was pointing at a column of rebel soldiers riding down the Panola road, drumming dust out of the winter earth. There was a shudder, a lift; Acox squinted. The wind ran chill fingers across his eyes, and they watered. "Hell naw," Clark said. "You'll know him time you see him." The riders passed, clattering, capes fluting with the wind. Acox still watched, face stiff with the chill.

None of them would try their power with Forrest. He was implacable, inexorable.

Acox drilled the company in getting set properly in line of

battle, in disentangling themselves and running for cover while the horseholders led the horses to the rear. "Orrison, cut to the other side with the horses . . . the other side, damn it. . . ." Clark and Bowles grinned in the cold afternoon while Acox swung his arm in arcs, and Orrison looked vacantly at them from the distant hillside.

You did not want Forrest for an enemy; that was your first reaction. After that might come the adulation. For the recruits in the cold Mississippi winter, eyes smarting, wrapped in their cloaks and lying along the grey-brown earth in line of battle, Forrest was personal, legendary, implacable. If they deserted, he—not the provosts or the bombproofs or the damned planters —he, Forrest, would seek them out. 'Y God, I don't never want to face him alone and he mad. Bowles shivered inside his cape, at the foot of a small pine tree.

He's a mean son of a bitch, Acox thought, and shivered too. "Get into that stand of pine." But he keeps them in line. They know him. And so do I. I will be damned if I will cross him. He stopped it, he stopped the execution. He balances it over me; it has been that way all along, but I never knew it before. I am glad I did not know that, when Bragg took command. He was tired and he simpered at the thought. Ohhh, I am glad I did not fully understand it then. If I had known it before, in Pensacola, I would have been better prepared for Shiloh. But then, I might have deserted and have tried to swim to the Yankee warships in the bay.

Bragg was a little man; his power was caprice. Forrest swings it in his hand.

"Clark, get your men down in that swale, and on their bellies!" He rode over the grass, golden with the tawny colors of winter, and the late sun throwing long shadows, and the far hillsides dark blue. Forrest would not waste horseflesh in a battle and Colonel Russell had told them not to waste time with mounted maneuvers. Acox made a hand signal and the horses were brought up smartly from the grove of pines and the dismounted men ran to the saddles, and the whole thing went off beautifully. Acox told them well done, and it was gathering dark so they went back into camp.

2

A WEEK AFTER THE MOCK EXECUTION ACOX WALKED ACROSS THE chopped and frozen earth to the house. It was dark and the wind whipped his cloak around his legs and bit at his flesh; there was a velvet tinge to the purple sunset. The house was lantern-lit, and he went up to the dogtrot in the center of it. His mouth tasted of brass from the cold and the exhaustion, and his lungs pumped and ached.

He went into the first door to the left, into the room he shared with Captains Tarkenton and Wheelock. Tarkenton, who was the regimental adjutant, was asleep on his bed, and Wheelock was not back yet from exercising his company. The room was rank and stale, with tobacco smoke and the grainy smell of dirt, and the old, rotting odor of the wood in rooms which have stood empty to the rain and the wind. There were the various congenital smells of the juices of men's bodies, baked and impregnated into the cots and the blankets from the flesh and the clothing of the three officers, smells as fully a stamp of soldiering, Acox thought, in their pungency, as ever was breastplate or rifle.

Acox warmed himself at the fireplace, rubbing his nose vigorously and lifting his coattails to warm his backside. He took off his grey hat, and his scarf and his gloves. His cloak was made from a blanket and his pants were standard issue of the federal army. He unbuckled his sword belt, and the sword clanked against the stone of the fireplace. Tarkenton turned and looked up, and then shuddered and sat up and drew up his knees, and pulled the bedclothes to his throat. He looked at

Acox, rumpled and thick-eyed from sleeping, and blinked furiously.

It was cold in the room, and the wind whistled insidiously through cracks in the floor and between the logs and chinks of the wall. It was grey and dark in the corners, and the custard light was pressed and compacted by the shadows back upon the lantern itself, a spotted pool of yellow in the middle of the room. There was the gleam of shiny metal and polished wood from the weapons, and the tangle and disarray of dun-colored clothing. Wheelock, Acox thought, will have to make that Negro boy of his come in some time and clean this place up, instead of polishing those boots all the time.

He sat down and laboriously pulled off the big hip boots, and in so doing felt a stab of pain in his buttock. I feel eighty years old; too old for this anyhow. His crotch and his hips hurt from riding.

Tarkenton was a very dashing young officer from near Pulaski, Tennessee, where his father and his uncles owned all or at least most of some small community. He had been with Earl Van Dorn, who had been, along with Morgan, a sort of personal god to the young man. He had been hideously wounded outside Holly Springs by a lone sentry who had fired more from surprise than from duty when the advance company of cavalry had come pounding down upon him in the fog of his morning ruminations; the minie ball had bounced up from the pommel of his saddle and torn out much of his chest and his throat, exposing part of his lung. He still had the shiny blue scar from his chin to his rib cage. He was dedicated in a fanatic and naive way to all of the romance and the glory of warfare; a certain worldly awareness had never and indeed never would manifest itself upon him. Almost no one, even in Van Dorn's command, used a saber, yet he had personally sabered a man to death in the old style—the Holly Springs sentry——and had then fallen from his horse hugging life to his wound and shouting in the best fashion to his men to press on, a yell most of them had not heard.

He saw himself as a Pelham or a Morgan, but it was a harmless affectation. He did not have personal qualities of leadership to succeed; but he was not blinded so by his fanaticism as to be dangerous. He was never at a loss for enthusiasm, and Tyree Bell had sought him out with the same and even greater diligence than he had sought out men like Acox. Tarkenton was not really handsome enough to push himself over the edge into vanity. He had a huge and bulbous and pocked nose; which somehow made his wound seem not tragic or even noble but just hideous. It was because he came so close to being what he wanted to be and what he pictured himself as being, yet he was so perceptibly and obviously doomed to failure because of his nose that he was well liked and respected.

Tarkenton said "How did your company do today?" Acox, who was struggling with a soaked stocking, almost laughed because he always made it sound, somehow, like an English officer of horse talking to a subaltern in a novel.

"Well now, they are doing all right. They are almost all veterans, and they know what to do as well as I."

"Good. Good." Tarkenton ran a hand through his thick brown hair which hung to his shoulders, and immediately tucked the naked arm back into the warmth of the bedcovers. He rocked a little and looked around the room. Acox went on with the undressing and then poured some water and washed himself as best he could, splashing at his white chest and his armpits. He felt the stubble on his cheeks and neck; on campaign he always let his dark beard grow, for warmth and to save the trouble of shaving. It bristled now, a series of dark, thick individual hairs, prickly and ugly and not really well started. He and Tarkenton said nothing, waiting for Wheelock.

Acox sat down after putting on his other shirt, and adjusted the lamp and sharpened the quill of his pen and rummaged through the clutter of things on the table top for some paper. He wrote every day to Amanda, having reached a place in self-discipline where he was able to devote just a certain amount of time each day to gut-sick worry about her, and was able, therefore, to spend the rest of the day working out the myriad of details about his company. This was an enormous expenditure of will. He was exhausted by nightfall. He lowered his head and held it in one hand and let the pen run across the page, scratching industriously and filling out the spaces with words.

He was halfway through the letter, pleading with her to look into the possibility of finding a room in town, and so deeply buried in concern and worry there were sharp physical pains in his throat and his diaphragm, when Wheelock came in like a furious bear, stamping and blowing from beneath the thicknesses of his clothes and coats and equipment. Acox noted this on the letter and then put the paper in a drawer and turned, still worried and as yet unabsolved and unreleased since he had not yet expiated himself by finishing the letter. He had come to establish a relationship between his period of concern for Amanda and the careful completion of the letter, the working out with hand and pen of the patterns of worry and love in his mind, and when that was interrupted it was like an interrupted church service or story, wherein the emotional context and atmosphere would have to be maintained until he could return.

But Wheelock of course had to say something. He was big and husky and had a thick beard, and whereas he was a younger man than Acox he was somehow more permanent, not just in contrast to Acox but in contrast to anyone. He had thick black hair and a strong thick nose with deep lines beside it, and his cheeks were pocked with a pattern of black holes that you always found yourself looking at. Wheelock came from outside Jackson and was of that peculiar type of man who is a small businessman—in this case in timber, catering particularly to the railroads—but who is really a politician. He spent periodic amounts of time in local public office; by heredity and position and personality he kept abreast of what every segment of the population felt, and was of incalculable worth to the bigger politicians, and had been employed by many. He could and did conduct the affairs of the state and county and city in his lumber office, answering letters or meeting people with the friendly hand placed on the knee. Or—and he was cultured and polished enough as was necessary for this—at a banquet or dinner or dance, rough-hewn and vital and holding a brandy in one thick hand, bulging into his worsted and smiling at the ladies and sweating but unconcerned by the heat, saying, "Yes, of course, but they won't stand a piece for that over in Jackson."

And if Tyree Bell had worked energetically upon Acox because he had established himself as a man who could do the job, and upon Tarkenton—though of course not as hard because he had only been awaiting the healing of his wound—he spent virtually all of his energies in getting Wheelock transferred from ———— brigade and then had ridden all over Tennessee at the right knee of the man, recruiting, re-establishing through Wheelock key parts of that skein of ties and personal relationships which enabled Forrest to bring the six thousand men out of Tennessee in the first place.

Wheelock took off his overcoat and his sword belt and his gauntlets, and went to work on his boots, calling all the time for the boy Franklin, who finally appeared in time to help with one of the big hip boots. Franklin was then told to bring out a pipe and to start putting dinner on the table and to look in the saddle bags and get out a bottle of whiskey and mind you don't touch any of it, and to put the horse away. Franklin was tall and angular and crevice-faced, and had a bony skull and was not a boy by at least twelve or fifteen years. He seemed to fathom the instructions, nodding "yes seh, yes seh," and finally going out to perform them, in such a fashion of carelessness and incomprehension that of course most of them would have to be redone; but then this was accepted as part of the privilege of having a slave boy in camp.

Tarkenton got out of bed naked and white-fleshed, with the spill of his hideous scar running from right under his throat all the way down his chest, an icy blue and shiny thing not looking like flesh or even anything human, but rather some sort of transplanted metal. He pulled on his shirt and his trousers and took a chair at the table beside the fireplace. Acox splashed some water on his hands from the chipped bowl and dried them and went over to the table too, and waited patiently with Tarkenton while Wheelock closed his eyes and ran his big hand over his face, and then looked up enigmatically and pensively at the ceiling. Wheelock came back each day and they all immediately went to the table and Franklin brought in the food. They would eat and listen while Wheelock talked, since he knew as much as anyone about the news out of Tennessee; many of the troopers after reporting to Forrest or Bell or Chalmers would report then to Wheelock, informally.

Franklin came in with the food, a big pot of mustard greens and some cornbread and a little bacon. The food was of course as greasy and thick-larded as only Negro cooks can produce. Tonight they even had some roasting ears of corn, which was a surprise, and some of the real coffee which one of Wheelock's troopers had traded tobacco to a Yankee outpost for; they ate in the thick light with Franklin coming in carefully and impassively.

"Well, word come out that ol' Sherman is planning to move on Meridian," Wheelock said, "and that he has put himself together all the cavalry he can find in Tennessee and they are going to come join him through our part of Mississippi." They all thought about this while eating, pushing the cornbread through the thick, congealing grease on the plate and while swilling the coffee around in their mouths. Acox figured it meant that they would fight then, and soon.

"Not too soon, I do not think. The rivers are up in Tennessee this time of year, and hear tell that the Yankee general is having a time of it getting his men together. And I reckon he knows ol' Bedford is down here, and he will go slow. Man name of Smith."

"Will we be ready for him do you think, Ben?" Tarkenton asked.

Wheelock looked at him under his eyebrows and then refocused his eyes on the lighting of his pipe. "I reckon we will. We worked 'em hard so far, and they will be ready. Barteau's Second Tennessee is with us now, and that will help stiffen us. We ought to be ready."

Acox was thinking, I will have to be careful for a while, since I have no idea how Forrest handles his men, nor how the men will behave, and a good many officers get killed right at first when their men cut. He was ashamed for thinking that way but he thought, well, I have to take care, it don't hurt to take all the care I can.

But then Wheelock was saying, "Let me tell you 'bout what happened to me, this day. Damndest thing. Damndest thing I ever saw. . . ." He was fumbling with his pipe. Acox and Tarkenton sat back and listened; normally Wheelock did not have to make a formal beginning like that. Normally he just began.

"I took my company out the Oxford road. Well, you all know that burned plantation out there 'bout six miles . . . you know the place." Acox did not, but he kept silent. Tarkenton said he did. "Some of my troopers come riding back in about noon, and tell me to come out there quick, there's been some trouble.

"Well, I ast 'em should I bring the company, and they said well maybe, so we get on out there. Come on the place, an' I see two of my men standen in the door of one of the slave cabins, out behind the house. One of 'em—Williamson, you know his brother, has a law office over towards McMinnville?—" Again, Tarkenton said yes, he did. Acox listened, whitely. "—Well, Williamson told me I better take a look inside.

"Well, there was a white woman inside, and on the floor, a dead man. The man had a knife sticken out of his back, and it looked to me like he had been dead three, four hours. . . ."

"Soldier?"

"No, he wasn't. Let me tell you. He had on a broadcloth coat, vest, fancy-dressed. The woman, though, was older than he was, and poorly dressed. She was thin and her hair was all down in her face. . . ." He made a motion in front of his face, with his hands. Acox could tell that he had not yet had time to polish and finish the story; he was relating it for the first time. Wheelock pulled at his pipe. Franklin, in a captured Yankee jacket, was clearing off the table and putting down the bottle of whiskey. Acox sucked at the taste of grease and vegetable behind his teeth, and finished his coffee, and kept his eyes on the black holes in Wheelock's cheek.

"Well, I ast what has happened here, and Williamson says,

'She says a nigger killed her husband, and then vi'lated her.' The woman nods that that's right. How long ago? About three hours. I looked down at that body, and at the woman, and wanted to get out of that cabin; it still had a nigger-smell, know what I mean?" Tarkenton nodded that he did. "But I just wanted to get out, into the air. It was close and dark inside that little ol' cabin, and that dead man was staring up at us all, and his body was sort of humped up, where that knife was sticken out of his back. . . ."

Acox felt a steepling anxiety, a pain, a foreboding. He knew the rest of the story, the next steps of the pattern. He had always known the story, but he had never heard it before. It was the South's oldest story; its first fear.

"I did not know whether to believe her or not." Wheelock kept his eyes on the bowl of his pipe. Acox knew what he meant, precisely. Wheelock had had no choice; he had known the story all of his life too. He had been—was—beyond questioning the story. It was a pattern, a confirmation, not a story of a crime or a murder. "But what the hell . . ." Wheelock looked around at them, for the first time, quickly, and then looked back into the bowl of the pipe. Franklin shuffled around them, a shadow, bat-like, behind them.

"There was somethen about the whole thing . . . somethen about the whole thing. . . ."

"What?" Tarkenton said. His eyes were shining and expectant.

Wheelock frowned. "Somethen sad." Tarkenton seemed to be disappointed. Acox nodded.

"You . . . you found the . . . a . . . a man?" Acox struggled with his voice.

"Of course."

Of course. A man was always found, a nigger. The voiceless, mindless fear always found the single man, a single man; it feared the shadow, but it found an inevitable, single nigger.

Acox listened, horrified; there were two anxieties. The story only had one variant, not conclusion. The conclusion was so much a part of the pattern—so changeless—that there was no volition connected with it. Volition, guilt, was attached to the variant. That was where men had a choice. "What did you do to him?"

Wheelock shook his head. "Let me tell you. We searched about half a mile, in each direction, and came across a nigger hiding in the brush, other side of a rise."

That was the unvarying fact too. The man had been hiding. And the next would be that he had no reason for being there, for hiding or for being there. The nigger never did; perhaps, it came to Acox, perhaps they have their own patterns, and when you look for one of 'em, anyone that will do, perhaps you cut across one of those patterns, and they can no more tell you what they are doing there, at that second, than you can. Perhaps that is just the final and inexorable fate of their race; just to be handy when you need one, like a bullock strapped down for the sacrifice, when you arrive at the altar. It was a quick thought; he glistened in horror and in anticipation.

"Poor ol' nigger, about fifty. He had no idee why he was there. Couldn't give me a reason. Errand? Nawsuh. Run off? Nawsuh, just there." Wheelock looked at them both, now, full in the face.

"Prob'ly run off," Tarkenton said.

Wheelock nodded. "Anyhow, we dint find anybody else, not in a mile of the place."

"What did you do to him?" There were twin anxieties in Acox's mind; the unexpiated, unfulfilled worry and concern in the letter, and the old, renegade, bitter anxiety for the caught nigger. It was unbearable, that they should mingle and fuse.

"Well, let me tell you. We took the nigger back, and the woman, who had recovered somewhat, the woman said that that was the one. The ol' nigger was bug-eyed. Said he had never seen the place before. We just stood around, in that slave cabin. The soldiers had pulled the knife out and the body was under a cavalry cloak. Williamson pulled back the cloak and ast the nigger did he ever see the man before. Nawsuh, nawsuh, never did. . . ."

Wheelock looked into the bowl of the pipe for a minute. "Damndest thing was, the woman looked at the man too. Normally, I'd never have brought 'em face to face, not a woman violated and a man who might have done it. But you knew that with this woman, it made no difference at all. And there she was, looking half crazy, staren at the face of the dead man. . . ."

"Prob'ly was crazy after that," Tarkenton said. Acox wanted to say—found his lips working to form the words—of course, of course, it's always that, isn't it? He said nothing.

"Then she reach out and pull a gold watch out of the nigger's pocket. She said it had been her husband's. Said it had his name on the back: Thaddeus Willingham . . . Thaddeus Willingham. And it did. . . ."

Of course, Acox thought. He—or they, or someone—made you a present of that. Franklin moved behind them, to get the captain's boots. They noticed him and did not notice him.

"Well, I be damned," Tarkenton was saying. "So what did you do?"

"Well, I sent Williamson and three others to take the nigger and the woman back to headquarters. But the woman wouldn't ride with him, in the same group, she said, so Williamson took him off by himself, and came back and said the nigger tried to run off, so he killed him. . . ."

"Of course." Acox said it aloud.

"Naw, Williamson's a good man. The nigger did try to run off, I'm certain of that."

Acox started to say of course, again. But he did not; it made no difference. It had not been as horrible as it might have been; the variant was less guiltful, less willed, than he had known it could have been. He rocked back into the shadow, looking into the clustering greyness in the corners of the room.

"Well, the damndest thing was, that I am certain as I am sitting here, that that is not the whole of it. What was a man in fine broadcloth and shirt doing in a nigger cabin, with a woman of that stripe? Eh? An' why would an old nigger kill a white man and rape a woman and take a watch, and he fifty years old? Now a buck, I could explain. . . ."

"With a nigger, you never can tell though, can you?"

"No, you can not." That was part, too, of the pattern, Acox

thought. "And you can not explain away the fact that he was there, and with that watch, and without reason. . . ."

They were silent. At least, for Acox, the anxiety had resolved itself. It is true. With a nigger, you never can tell. And Amanda, my Lord God, is there alone with them.

Then Tarkenton started telling a story about what some Mississippi soldiers had done to some nigger whores who had been down servicing the Yankees in Memphis. It was a cold, brutal story, but Tarkenton told it without guile or lechery, just talking to fill the space, and it was oddly not inappropriate. The two of them listened and laughed. "Well, he says, he says, it was not of the best, and it was not of the worst. It was just a little too well done, for my taste." The story was mindless; patternless; it rubbed the air clean around them, it seemed.

Then Acox was thinking, if they run off, it serves them right; and again he thought of Amanda out there alone, and whereas he knew Sam and Buck as well as anyone he had ever known black or white the fact remained that with niggers you could not be sure, you just could not be sure since they were not, after all, white men. The pattern, without the horror or anticipation, had entwined him. He listened with half attention. Tarkenton was telling another story, about a cousin of his in Georgia and what he had done one night in the slave quarters. "So he pulls out this hosspistol, and he says, 'Nigger, get yourself out of that bed.' The man starts up at him, and Craig cracks him too, across the side of the head with the barrel of the gun, and then he looks down at this high yaller and he says, 'I be with you, too, in a minute.' So then he goes to the next cabin . . ." Tarkenton had a wealth of stories. He smiled, not lecherously or even convivially but just smiled around his big, pocked nose, when he reached the climax of the story.

Wheelock had measured out three fingers of whiskey into three glasses, and pushed a glass to each of them. He frowned and swished the liquor from side to side in his mouth, and said he had never held with that, of fooling with their women. Tarkenton said quickly, of course not, that he had not either, and that he had made his feelings known to his cousin, but on a fair-sized plantation, if a man had a mind, there was nothing you could say to him, was there?

Acox said that on the small farms, where there were one or two niggers, things went on that would make you ill too. Wheelock nodded judiciously, and reached for the liquor bottle again. Franklin padded back out of the room, with Wheelock's boots and belt over his arm, silently, bat-like with the flapping leather. They had said whatever they wanted in front of him, but they waited, in silence, until he was across the dogrun and in his own room. "Of course," Tarkenton said, "it is not like the abolitionists say."

"No, it is not."

"No." There was agreement; they had nothing to say, for a moment.

Though of course Wheelock himself and Tarkenton had indeed learned eagerly and hotly about flesh and lust and sex from Negro women and girls. At a certain time of their lives on the large plantations with the blood running hot the young men would get together on a night ride, or in one of the rooms and fill it with tobacco smoke—unless indeed the moment came even before they were permitted to smoke or drink—and there would compare notes and grin with shining teeth in the lantern light, and then hollow-thighed and anxious and nervous would run down the lines of the slave quarters. Not viciously or even sinfully; because it was there, the raw female flesh was there and it was owned. Whereas the white women were inaccessible to the point that it was ridiculous to even think of them in terms of amounts of flesh, ridiculous and horrible and unnatural. And the Negro girls themselves would be simpering and complacent and that would further remove any signs of the guilt whatsoever, unless you were of a peculiar sensibility and might therefore set one of the girls up in some sort of independent fashion or at least lessen the work load upon her.

Acox had not done this thing, and therefore did not have any idea that the men in front of him had. He had not done it because in the first place their farm was not large enough to really be a plantation and therefore to have plenty of more or less nameless and faceless Negro girls. He knew and had known every one of the Negro girls and women from the moment of his or of their birth, since they presided over or paraded past his cradle, and all but concurrently he had had to assume the responsibilities of feeding and clothing their daughters. In the second place, after all, he was Hamilton LeRoy Acox and the Acoxes had come from the seaboard and had had years of not prosperity, which might have created that sense of the easy fullness of life in which you might take a Negro girl, but adversity and the Negroes were fully as much of the family, and indeed knew more about the family, than most of the white people. But neither the fact that his family was not a big plantation family or that they were one of the old families had made as much difference as his own personality. It would, before the war, no more have crossed his attention that there was accessible female flesh than it would have struck him to come to the evening meal without washing his hands. He was secure in his innocence because Wheelock was long married and because Tarkenton was engaged and also assumed from Wheelock's manner that such things were either not done or not prated about, so he said nothing either.

Wheelock then changed the subject slightly, not because he was uncomfortable or ashamed, but because there was nothing to pursue in discussion once three grown white men had reached the same conclusion. He was not ashamed of what he had done twelve years ago on his uncle's plantation because it was never borne to him to be ashamed of something like that. Any more than he should be ashamed of testing his first smoke away from his parent's knowledge. It was a part of growing up, and there was simply no need to discuss it; and it might tend to throw some unfavorable light upon his wife and that was unthinkable. So just for discussion he changed the subject and said: "You know, I caint think how the Yankees intend making soldiers out of them. They will not stand, I will bet."

And Acox, because after all Amanda depended upon their faithfulness and, perhaps, their courage, said:

"Oh, I have known some of them to be as brave as any."

"Yes, but not in the main, and not in sufficient numbers."

"Well, they have been slaves so long. . . ."

"They would not have been slaves had they been able to stand up in the first place. They will not fight. I would at no time be hesitant about approaching a whole brigade of them with my company. At no time. . . ."

Acox said nothing, and looked down at his hands. He would be hesitant, yes, but he had to agree. He did not think that Negroes would stand and fight either.

"Give them a gun and a uniform and teach them to drill a little, and you don't make a good soldier," Tarkenton was saying, "but you are certainly ruining a good field hand."

"That is right. Niggers have no sense of proportion, nor of right or wrong in our sense of the word. You cannot tell what they will do if they have the upper hand. They might be as meek as dogs, or as merciless as savages. The Yankees are upsetting the order of things by arming the Negroes, and mark my words we will have to pay the price of their experimentations in changing nature's pattern."

Tarkenton was nodding somberly, and Wheelock emphasized his points with his pipe-stem. "They may well touch off a racial blood bath such as western man has not seen. Given the chance, they will bring into our society and our home their tribal heritage of blood and cannibalism and destruction."

Acox shuddered, and tossed down the last swallow of the whiskey, drawing his mouth back. He thought again and again of Amanda and of the unfinished letter which now seemed not only inadequate and pathetic, but even misleading in the mildness of its tone. He ached with worry, and he rubbed his hand over his nose, and he thought, if any one of them touches her I shall kill him slowly. I shall cut and feed to him parts of his own flesh. His head ached he was so filled with hate.

Tarkenton said, "We got to stop them. We got to stop the Yankees." Wheelock of course agreed. Tarkenton said, "They don't know niggers like we do, and we got to stop them. We got to beat them in the war."

Wheelock said yes, and then got up to get a clean shirt, still talking. "Yes, we have to stop the Yankees, but then they have done a lot of harm already. They do not know these people like we know 'em. They seem to think niggers are just like white folks, only with black skin. But that ain't so. You know and I know, but you take the abolitionist that only saw the educated nigger or something. He don't know about the nigger in the field. He's all so dead set on setting them free he don't much give a damn about who is goen to take care of 'em once they are. We are, damn straight we are, just like we always have. He's all set to put rifles in their hands and turn 'em loose. Hell, I never yet seen a nigger I would trust all the way with a gun. . . ."

He was muffled a moment while he pulled the shirt over his head. "You give a field hand a gun, I say, and he right away gets damn fool ideas. I hear they push the white women off the streets in Memphis."

Tarkenton nodded. "I heard the same thing. I hear a white woman isn't safe alone at night in Memphis. When the Yankees armed the niggers, they suddenly put this ol' war somewhere else. Before then, I had a lot of respect for the Yank. I didn't when it started, but I did after a while. But now! Why hell, man," and he was leaning earnestly forward talking, "why hell, they are trying to get the niggers to rise up. They are trying to get them to revolt. You know ol' Lincoln would give a hell of a lot to get the niggers to revolt. It would tear the hell out of this war, and that's for sure. . . ."

Acox found his voice after he tried to say something once. "Why . . . why, I'm not certain that that is what the Yankees want. They know the niggers will by and large stay loyal to the families. . . ."

Wheelock turned around at him. "No, Lee, no they won't. We might as well quit fooling ourselves about that. We figured that the niggers would stay around the places while we went off because they were used to us taking care of 'em, or that they would be loyal to us the way we been loyal to them. But that ain't so. It hasn't worked out like that. The first time a river boat come along they all run off to the Yankees. Yank cavalry move across this state, you and I both know before they go five mile they got more niggers than you or I can shake a stick at. The Yankees and the abolitionists have stirred the whole thing to a boil." He slapped one glove against the other. "God damn it! God damn it, Lee, why didn't they let us work things out our own way? Why in the name of God did they come down tearing things up?"

"You can't convince me," Tarkenton was saying, "you can't never convince me that God didn't intend for the nigger to be a slave. Everywhere he has come in touch with another race, they've made slaves out of him. He is suited to it. . . . And the minute the Yankees come and start trying to turn that around . . ." he searched for a word ". . . they are messing around with something that is too big for us to handle."

"Well," said Wheelock, "I got to be goen: Tyree Bell is haven his poker game tonight, and I got to get on over there." He pulled on his cloak and walked out, and they heard him yelling to Franklin for his horse.

"Yessir," said Tarkenton, who was still watching the door where Wheelock had just left, "yessir, when the Yankees gave guns to the niggers, they were asking for trouble. I am not planning on holding my boys back next time we have a fight. Nosir. They want to fight like that, all right."

Tarkenton kept staring vacantly at the door, and Acox turned back to the table, and put his hands on it, and looked down. They are right, he thought. They are right. The Yankees want a slave revolt, and they will get it, and the whole South will go up in flames. They will violate the women because they are savages. I can not deny that they are savages; only a savage would take arms against the people that have cared for him, and that is just what they are doing. Amanda nursed some of the young through every disease that came along, and they will kill her and violate and mutilate her. I have heard them singing at night, I have seen their funerals, and they will not and can not fit into our world. We should not have brought them over.

The wind whistled emptily through a crack in the wall, and Tarkenton got up and began to pull on his overcoat. The flames danced in the candles and the lantern.

We didn't bring them over, he thought. The Yankees brought them over, and made their blood money. The blood is on their hands as much as it is ours. But we will have to take the penalty, yes, because the niggers are down here. Oh, you can bury yourself in the war, but in the back of your mind you know where your vital spot is. You know where you haven't got any armor. Your wife and your home. They are behind enemy lines, and oh I would trust them there in safety if all Yankees were like that Illinois captain we took at Murfreesboro. For a time, we thought they were. But now they attempt this. They are callous as they can be, they will let the niggers despoil and loot and violate and murder, and they will give them the guns to do it with. I thought we could fight this war the way it should be fought, between men, but they will not fight it that way. They will make war on women and children, they will not only burn them out but they will also turn loose the most savage and backward race in the world upon them.

He thought, a man tries to build something for himself, a place of refuge and shelter in this world. I had that, before this started. I had the law and I had Amanda, and the goddamned war came along, started by the abolitionists and the hotheads. I had to leave the sheltered place I had built for myself, and while I was gone it began to crumble. Now it is almost gone; so I found out I could not keep a sheltered place in these times. But tonight I realized something else. Wheelock and Tarkenton are right, though Tarkenton is a boy and Wheelock is a politician and nothing more. But they are right. There is no way to read the arming of the Negroes other than that the Yankees are trying to encourage a slave revolt. So in addition to losing that sheltered place, I am to lose Amanda. Right now, right now they could be raping her. Right now they could be busting in, Sam and Buck maybe. Maybe Sam and Buck took up with the Yankees, and run off and got some guns and some brass buttons. Maybe then they got together and slipped off, 'cause they knew where there was a defenseless white woman. Of course they would know. And maybe right now they are raping and violating her, and she will die in the most degraded and hideous way possible. And there is not a damned thing I can do about it, except take revenge. I will catch them and they will suffer, Lord.

On the desk in front of him, his hands began to curl in anger, the joints stiffening and the flesh over the knuckles reddening and then paling again as the bones slid and tightened under them. I do not think I can stand it. God, I do not think I can stand it.

Tarkenton left the room, making a bustle of noise and clat-

tering across the dogrun, calling too for his horse, and Acox
knew he would go and ride out his anger, or maybe just ride for
the exhilaration of it, or maybe he knew where there was another poker game.

He wished he could ride hard but he had to save his horse,
he knew, because he had pushed it all day, and he could not
ride it into the ground. He unclenched his hands, and he put
his face into them, and he prayed. Dear God, dear God, one
thing is all I want. It has finally gotten to the point where there
is only one thing that matters any more. Keep her safe, dear
God. Keep her safe. Maybe it is sinful to pray like this, for one
thing or one person. But if it is sinful, then do not punish her.
Punish me, but leave her alive and inviolate. And then, let us
go back into Tennessee, dear God. Let us go back and clean up
this mess. Let us go back with this man Forrest, and show us the
way to win, and show us how to beat them so bad they will not
think about arming the Negroes. Let us put fear into them, dear
God. Arm us and steel us, and let us hit them hard.

And out back during the hour of conversation Franklin—
out back being of course a euphemism which in this case really
meant the slightly smaller but still intact room across the
dogrun—Franklin was eating his greens and some side meat and
some cornbread, pushing the cornbread through the grease in
the platter and snapping at it in his pinched, dripping fingers
before the bread slipped away. He had gotten the place fairly
warm with a fire and he had wrapped his blanket around his
legs. After he finished eating he began to rock slowly, back and
forth, in a chair he had found in the room half burned through,
with the stuffing coming out, a rocking chair in which the previous owners had doubtless taken incommensurate pride because of the fine rosewood and the leather upholstery, which
they themselves probably found half busted and with the
stuffing coming out in some old deserted mansion or beside the
wagon track to the ferry. He rocked in the chair and hummed to
himself about Jacob's Ladder. He pulled the thick, filthy coat
around his shoulders, the coat that Mist' Ben had thrown to
him one day with a wide grin, saying, "Franklin, I reckon
this'll do your worthless hide more good than it done its last

owner." He stopped humming for a while and thought, Mist' Ben and Mist' Lee, they are right, I reckon. Any fool nigger fiel' han' gets him a gun, he gets uppity. Hell, he grinned half to himself, hell better not let ol' Mist' Ben cotch him. Nawsuh! Mist' Ben he hit him up side the head so hard it tech that nigger somethen. And then he went back to humming and rocking, and waiting for Wheelock's return so he could take the horse back into the old barn and rub it down and blanket it against the cold and then help Mist' Ben off with his boots. Maybe Mist' Tark'ton would come back first, and law but he was a wil' gen'man, yessuh! And he started on Jacob's Ladder again, tunelessly. Deep in his mind was the single thought which had and which would govern his actions until he was killed by a Yankee shell outside Nashville—any nigger run off to the Yankees is a fool, and any nigger take up a Yankee gun is twicet a fool, and any ol' nigger mess aroun' with white women is the biggest fool of all. 'Cause whatcha do is bide your time, nigger, bide your time. It ain't gone hep any, getten caught on the Yankee side lessen they win, and Mist' Ben ain't gone lettum win, and hit won't hurt nothen just sitten still. 'Cause if freedom's comen after all, it'll come and this nigger'll just be sitten here waiten, and if it don't, this nigger ain't goen to have any bad en'mies at all 'mongst the white folks. But he did not really think this in any sense of the word—he knew it and he recognized it and it was born in him and nurtured in him through the long nights when the white man had his way with the slave. He kept on humming and rocking. He had a full belly and he was warm, and there was nothing for him to do until Mist' Ben came back magnanimous and drunken, and then he would help him and then go to bed, and maybe sleep most of the morning after breakfast.

In the officers' room Acox had tried to finish the letter but he could not because of the roil of hatred and anxiety inside him. Everything suddenly sounded puerile and empty and naive and he ached to be killing, or in any case to be doing something. Hamilton LeRoy Acox had never at any time owned more than twelve slaves and now had only about half a dozen; he had been a respected young lawyer with a lovely young wife and had been noted as being unusually liberal on the question of slavery and had even set two of his men free when they were on the verge of senility because they at last were his and he loved them both. He had been popular among the slaves and Negroes and had twice ridden off and left all he loved most in their trust, the first time trusting completely and the second time with only the slightest of doubts. And now he tossed restlessly in bed feeling the guilt released in him and the fear set in him by two other young men who were careless because they had no one to worry about behind the Yank lines, since their people had refugeed to Atlanta. They had the natural human propensity to relish in predicting the worst and suspecting the worst, in the form of all sorts of combinations and depths of intrigue set against them—who indeed because they came from large plantation families and who had fornicated among the Negro women might be expected to have the sense of guilt and fear; but who of course did not because they were not so nakedly exposed, and they still trusted their sword arms to keep the Yankee away from their women.

But Acox had to pay the price for both of them, and he felt the horror they talked almost academically about, and whereas he should have been the one of the three—indeed the one in the whole regiment—who through his education and personality and the respect men had for him as a person, whereas he should have been the last man to sink into the frenzy of doubt and fear and concomitant hatred, he did—because he believed what the others said, and because he had had to leave his wife alone and all but in the hands of two of his slaves too many times.

All of his family history had combined to produce the fact that there was nowhere she could go, and circumstances had put his home behind the enemy lines irrevocably. This made him frustrated and desperate and sick with worry, and yet because he was conscientious these things also made him the best and most competent company commander in the Twentieth Tennessee and perhaps in Bell's brigade. Now he not only had to get back, but the getting back itself was suddenly dependent in his mind upon how he came back—not as a survivor but as a victor and a man who was fighting for his home and the life and sanity and chastity of his wife.

The next day, grey-faced and with blue circles under his eyes, he took his troop out for a company practice in the morning under wintry skies. They did well, moving at his signal and handling the complex patterns involved in getting a company dismounted and into line of battle in three minutes, with the horseholders to the rear and the men realistically hugging the shelter in a loose line and the officers crouching behind them. Bowles, the buck-toothed lieutenant with the big moustache, came up blowing from a leg-aching race to the horses at the end, and said they were going real well, and said also that Acox looked tired, and whyn't he take the company for a while and drill 'em. Acox told him no, and pressed his lips together, and looked across the Mississippi prairie toward a lone tree, wind-blown and silhouetted on the side of a swale.

Everyone in the company was relaxed and laughing, and Sergeant Clark, who had a little grey kepi and was very thin and boyish, was telling them all a story about the first time he had been detailed into Memphis, and what he thought the whore-house was. Clark's cheeks were red and glowing, and they were all laughing and turning in the column to listen to the story. Then Acox suddenly kicked his horse and dug in his spurs and the animal bolted in surprise and pain and the whole company turned and rose in a start, and their horses rolled and whick-ered. Acox stood up in the stirrups and drew out a heavy cavalry saber he had bought from Tarkenton that morning. Acox waved the saber over his head and yelled, and rode down on the hardwood tree. His wrist could not quite hold or wield the sword and it swung dangerously, but he got enough of his shoulder behind it to chop out a huge, shingle-like section of the blackjack when he went whipping by, the snap and blow and check to the blade when it hit the wood almost jerking him out of the saddle, and making his arm ache. The heavy saber bounced out of the wood and as he was reining in the horse it cut down and into the leather of his boot. He felt the sharp pain bite into his calf, and immediately turned the horse back to the

The Winter and Spring of 1863–1864   *133*

column, grinning ruefully at cutting himself with the saber. There was a slit in the leather boot, and he could feel the hot red sting of the wound like a snakebite. He felt like a fool, but the clenched rage had gone from his jaws and his hands. His foot was wet and he knew he was bleeding down his leg, but he didn't care. The men were laughing and whooping, "Ol' Captain, you sure did lay that tree low!" Clark said. "If I had been a ol' Yankee 'stead of that tree I would have dropped down dead from th' fright, I swear!"

"See if you get out of this camp to see that ol' girl of yours tonight, Clarkey," one of the younger privates said and everybody laughed at that.

"All right, Clark," said Acox, grinning despite the pain, "all right, let's see you take that Navy six and hit that tree with it from a gallop."

Clark, grinning, threw back his cloak and pulled out his revolver, and loosed the strap of the cap and pulled it around his chin, the way the Yankees did. He got the big gun out and took off at a gallop, angling toward the tree, and he fired three times before the men saw the wood chip and fly. Each time the horses jerked, and the smoke hung bluish for a moment and then couldn't be seen against the thick grey sky. Clark came back laughing and there was the acrid smell of gunfire as he put the gun away.

"I got him one hell of a lot faster than you did, Corporal."

"Naw, Mr. Acox, I used up that first and second shot to give him a chance to give hisself up. Soon as he saw me, he knew he dint have a chance in hell."

The leg wound made Acox flinch because it was cooling painfully, but he grinned with the rest of them. He was stubborn about it, and he ate lunch and still wouldn't take off the boot and look at it, until he got off into a stand of pine trees on the pretext of defecating. Then he pulled it off and his face turned white with the pain. The skin was pulled back from the cut; he had just slit the flesh with the tip of his saber, and the skin was drawn back until there was about three inches of wound. His whole lower calf was stained and riveted with blood and the hair was matted down. He poured the blood out of his boot—there had been about an inch, and it spilled into the pine needles and the ground sopped it up. He tore off one of his shirt sleeves, shivering without his jacket while the wind came through the pine needles, and the grey sky began to drip and rain. He got the bleeding stopped and made up a story about a pine spur ripping his calf, and hobbled back to the regiment, which was spread out in dismounted skirmish lines below the pine stand.

Russell, a tall man with that kind of rounded, large forehead that makes it look as though he is wearing a helmet of flesh and hair above the back-set eyes, looked over at his regiment through a pair of field glasses. He was wearing a brown civilian overcoat, with a colonel's stars sewn on the old stand-up collar— it was his working jacket, and he saved his regulation grey overcoat for battle. He looked around and immediately frowned at the wound.

"What happened, Lee?"

"Damned pine spur stabbed me, sir."

"Bleeden pretty bad. Well, you better go have a surgeon take a look."

"I bandaged it myself, sir. It will hold until the end of drill."

"No, you better go have him take a look. Your company is doen fine. Run on."

"Yessir."

He hobbled over to his horse and turned it toward Oxford where the surgeons were huddled around sitting-room fires, talking to the ladies of the town and keeping in their hand as doctors and southern gentlemen and keeping up their knowledge of gossip. He started to throw away the heavy saber, figuring it was too much for him to handle. But then he thought of the fierce slash it had made in the blackjack, and he remembered the feel and heft of it when he had gotten up in the saddle and gotten his weight behind it. This, he thought, is a thing which I reckon can break some heads. And that is exactly what I want. It can cut me when its through but at that moment it hits I can handle it all right. And that is what I want.

The Winter and Spring of 1863–1864   135

3

BY THE RIVER, IT WAS COLD AND CHILL AND GREEN-DANK; THE early sun was a white pool behind the white-grey sky. Mists like smoke drifted along the banks between the winter-grey trees. The sounds of skirmishing rattled across the river.

General James Ronald Chalmers sat his horse beside his two aides, in the road space between the shriveled grey-brown winter woods. His hair, thick and curling over his collar, was sodden and cold and padded. A general did not, would not, put himself into the midst of a developing battle until he knew the limits and circumstances of his command; Chalmers had just arrived to take his promised division of Forrest's new corps.

The firing along the opposite bank would cluster and they would strain towards the spot; it would dissipate, surge, cluster again. Their horses shuddered and stomped. The green water slapped against the causeway at their feet and rustled into the reeds and brush. They could see the figures move and scurry, and the rebel horseholders near the bank. Chalmers' fine grey uniform was a shade darker with the dampness, and the buttons and leathers shone. Wind caught the edge of his cape, trailed a corner, the cape belled out blood-red against the grey and green. He was a slight man, dressed splendidly and flamboyantly, but his eyes were petulant, lidded, deep-set; lawyer's eyes, in a general's uniform and coiffure. He sat with studied indifference.

Chalmers turned his pale face over his 'shoulder at the sound of hoofs on the winter road behind them. Fingers of wind spread over his face. Forrest came up, with one aide, suddenly, furiously, surging down the causeway and standing up in the stirrups, his face agleam like beaten brass. His hair was tousled and his plain grey cloak was dirty and flapping. Chalmers, posed, confident, sat at the sort of ease a professional man can muster when he is determined not to be committed too early.

Forrest was not Chalmers' general; he had known him in Holly Springs before the war, but they had had no more than a business acquaintance. Chalmers sat his horse amid all of his codes and lidded his eyes. Forrest was already shouting at them but his horse's hoofs drummed away the words; his face was brazen, gold and grey, and the eyes were hard. He was wraith-like. The codes, Chalmers knew, were on his side.

Forrest reined in beside him, face a foot away; Chalmers stiffened. Forrest's voice was shrill and edged. "How are things up there?"

Chalmers reserved himself. "The firing, sir, indicates a skirmish, but I do not think it is a serious affair."

Before he had finished speaking Forrest said, "Is that all ye know?" more incredulous than contemptuous, and while Chalmers' jaw dropped a fraction at that, spurring his horse again: "Then I'll go up and find out fo' myself."

And with that spurring his horse on across the causeway and toward the timbers of the bridge. His aide was a tall man in a tattered jacket and had five revolvers in his blouse and belt and saddle and large cross belts slung over his shoulders. They whipped their horses out from behind the angled protection of some willows in a race across the bridge, and Chalmers still framing a reply in his mind turned and watched them, pale-faced and silent. Forrest and his aide were out in the open and some of the Yankees had worked their way down to the side of the river, and began shooting at the figures on the bridge at two hundred yards' distance. Chalmers glanced at them—tiny blue and pallid white forms scrambling among the tangled trees and logs and branches at the water's edge, and smoke from their rifles hanging in the timber. The bullets whizzed like small angry insects over the causeway. The fire flicked a dead brown leaf from a tree over Chalmers' head, and kicked up splashes of water in the stagnant green backwash along the causeway.

Chalmers could see the bullets spitting against the logs of the bridge where Forrest pounded across, and he immediately turned and ignored the glances of his aides and spurred for the bridge too.

He and his aides were on the bridge and then clattering across it, the aides hanging onto their hats and Chalmers' cloak flowing open and beckoning behind him. The Yankees pumped their carbines at the new targets but were annoyed considerably by the wetness and the tangle of limbs at river edge. Chalmers heard a ball skitter and ricochet along the wood and his horse's hoofs drum hollowly on the planks. Then he was across and up the slope, right behind Forrest, whose horse was lagging. Forrest, though of course Chalmers had no way of knowing this, in his encyclopedic, ground-covering way of fighting had been up all night with part of his escort tracking through the freezing bottom lands and the pitch-darkness a column of Yankee riders off across the Sakatonchee on a raiding expedition; tracking them down and cutting them off by a chilling and head-first mounted plunge through a half-mile of swamp, and capturing them, thirty disgusted and surprised regulars of the Fourth U.S. Cavalry Regiment.

But Forrest was not exhausted so much as furious; his will surged and coursed around him, beside him, in the grey morning. The blood was up and pumping with his will and he stood up in the saddle and his face flared and shone. It was an animal reaction, the sort of reaction that the codes proscribed and curbed; at Shiloh they say Albert Sidney Johnson directed the battle with a silver coffee mug, and he bled to death out of courtesy, because he sent his personal surgeon to look after the captured wounded. Chalmers had admired Johnson while he still thought of Forrest as a slave-trader. Forrest whipped his horse up the slope and like a surging animal in full stride he reached out with his instinct and will and soul, to feel of the land and to judge and evaluate the Yankees. Behind him Chalmers could sense like steam or mist the relentless, brutal, inevitable will.

Forrest went right up the slope, and suddenly, towards him and looking backwards, stumbled a rebel cavalryman, hatless and without his gun, his short coat flapping about his hips and his eyes wild. By the time Chalmers got to the man Forrest had in one continuous motion stepped, literally stepped, off his laboring horse and taken two giant strides straight for the man. Chalmers could see that the Confederate was a boy, narrow-faced and pimply and with stringy blond hair. His mouth was open, his nose dribbling and splattered and rubbed red. Forrest pitched right into him and knocked him down with his shoulder, and stood over him with his face hideously frozen. The boy shuddered and squirmed to look up at him, and Forrest plucked a thick switch from the brush by the road. He dragged the recruit to his knees and began to whip at him, the stick raising welts on the flesh and beating dust out of the jacket. The soldier writhed and twisted and Forrest dug his hand into his collar and held him, thrashing at him. Chalmers stared wide-eyed and listened to the skirmish fire and the whine of bullets going overhead and through the leaves and bare branches. The stick fell and fell and the boy was slobbering and waving his hands over his head and face, and Forrest kept thrashing him. Then he stopped, suddenly, with the boy terrified and in pain and quivering like a cornered rabbit at his feet.

Forrest threw the stick away and hauled the boy up, the muscles in the side of his face twitching and his mouth still shut tight. "Now then, now then God damn ye, go back to that front," and he panted, "go back and fight; you might as well be killed there as here, for if ye ever run away again ye will not get off so easy." The boy scrambled backwards and stumbled and nearly fell, and then broke into a trot for the lines, loose-limbed and shaking and rubbing at his sides.

Forrest threw himself back on the horse, settling into the saddle even as he put the spurs to it, and, kicking, rode past the horseholders who were crouching and squinting between the trees toward the fight. They saw him and cheered and Jeffry Forrest came over from a tree he had been leaning against. Forrest leaned down from the saddle, his wide-brimmed hat almost touching his brother's forehead, and listened and nodded and looked around while his brother talked to him. Jeffry would be dead before the day was over. Chalmers sat his horse and stared, his eyes wide open and bewildered and disgusted. But Forrest was now oblivious to him, restlessly stirring and straining in his stirrups for a look at the Federals, riding down the line a little and watching while the men saluted and yelled up at him and waved their caps, and bent back to their firing.

The trees were sparse, and wounded men were clustered in little knots on the ground, and the horseholders were passing their ammunition to the front. Chalmers watched a boy limping away with half of one cheek gone, and waving and yelling hoarsely at Forrest, blood all the while splashing down on his homespun checked shirt and leather crossbelt. Forrest looked down at him and nodded and almost smiled, and the boy slapped his helper on the back and said over and over, "Ol' Bedford done smiled at me. You saw it. You saw it, Chucky." When he talked the wound bled more, and Chalmers could see a tooth through the hole.

Forrest was gathering the feel of the thing to him, sucking at it, listening to the reports and thinking about the lay of the ground immediately ahead, peering through the trees at the Yankees. Forrest came to his conclusion; the desultory skirmishing was a bluff and Smith, burdened by his own fears, was pulling back. It felt that way. He suddenly turned and began to yell, high-pitched and unnaturally: "Cap'n Tyler, fetch up Cap'n Tyler!" Chalmers turned away and began to talk to a wounded lieutenant about the fighting, still dismayed and puzzled and concerned. The firing began to end almost when Forrest shouted for Tyler, and Chalmers shook his head at that, and wondered how Forrest had known the Yankees were breaking off the battle at that moment.

Forrest got hold of Captain Tyler, a Kentuckian with an oblong-plain face and a walrus moustache, and sent him forward with his company. The men were shifting and yelling back and forth, and the horseholders came up at a gallop with clods of earth pitching up from the horses' hoofs. Chalmers, still with his two caped and mounted aides, came nearer. Forrest signaled toward his escort, and two men, one with a thick, long beard from his eyes to his belt and another in a blanket poncho, came up. He scribbled away at an old telegraph pad in his palm.

"Tell Ginral Richardson—you find him over to the west about twelve mile—tell him to git across Line Creek bridge before the Yankees burn it. Tell him to get toward Okolona with ever'thing he got." The big man with the beard and the man with the poncho spurred off along the river. Two more men came up and Forrest bit at the stub pencil for a moment, almost unconsciously controlling the motion of the horse which was jerking with the bustle of the mounting troopers. Forrest wrote again on the pad. "You men git over towards Bell's brigade an' fin' Colonel Barteau. Tell him to git to Okolona by midday tomorra." He looked up at Chalmers and Chalmers noticed that the edges of his mouth dropped for a minute. His face was still flushed and brazen and the flesh around his eyes was bone-white. He looks like a man in the fever, Chalmers thought. Forrest pressed his lips together in a hard blue line. "Git Gholson," he said, and for a minute Chalmers thought he was talking to him. "Git Gholson," he said to a blond boy who came up with a lieutenant's bars on a faded yellow collar, "and tell him if he's got anything that kin stay on a hoss to git it over towards Houston. Tell him we got the Yanks on the run, and if he can keep up the scare we can git 'em all."

He twisted and watched Tyler lead out the Kentuckians. The Mississippians were yelling something and Chalmers leaned to hear what they were saying, and then Forrest shouted, "Go with 'em one time, 'y God, go with 'em one time and see if they will whip!" The Kentucky company, most of them wearing caps with leather visors and with braces of pistols stuck in their cavalry jackets, whooped when Forrest yelled at them and cheered, and Chalmers could see their teeth shine in their beards. The mounted Mississippi soldiers across the road, re-settling cartridge pouches and sliding their rifles into place, yelled back at Forrest and he turned and showed his teeth in a smile to them, and they let out a whoop. Forrest turned to him then, and Chalmers lidded his eyes carefully while behind the man like a living wall the grey- and brown-coated soldiers began to wheel into the dust left by the Kentucky troopers. "Foller me, Ginral Chalmers. Foller along, and let's go." A trooper with the square battle flag of Forrest's escort fell in beside him, and

Jeffry Forrest with the star on his collar showing just under his hair took up at his right hand, and Chalmers waved to his aides. The soldiers filled the road and Forrest talked a little to Jeffry and nodded and smiled, and then there was firing ahead and he spurred on to the lead and his escort—all big men with beards and revolvers and clattering rifles—came close behind him.

4

LIEUTENANT SEABURY, HANDSOME WITH THAT THIN-BONED DELI-
cacy of bone and flesh that makes the eyes look feverish and the
nose ivory-white, sat on the bunk in his room alone because Van
Horn was off with the Negro women down in the town. In the
rain-stung darkness outside two Negro women, wet to the bone
and their dresses clinging to their flesh, walked clumsily by and
saw him through the window by lantern light, and one said,
"Law but that white off'cer one han'some chile!" And the other
laughed, her feet making wet, flat sounds on the parade.

   Lieutenant Seabury had not written home in three weeks,
since his letter the first night at Fort Pillow. Instead he had
spent his time watching the shadows come and go in his room or
across the small earth fort, and trying to recall how the thin
purple and blue veins crossed Emily's temple just beneath the
transparent, luminous skin: and waiting for Forrest to come. He
was surrounded and encircled and pressed upon, by Tennesseans with sharp, bony faces and porcine yellow teeth, and by the
Negroes with black, thick flesh and wooly hair beneath their
kepis and splay-footed indolence; he washed himself with soap
every day in his room, pressing the strong, scented soap over his
white body and working up the lather and shuddering when the
icy water splashed against the quivering skin. Van Horn was
growing a beard which was a shadow of stubble on his chin and
a knot of longer hairs on the moles; Van Horn laughed at him
every morning, lying in his thick, dirty bedclothes as Jonathan
pushed the soap over his body, and said, man you are goen
crazy. What you need is a nigger woman.

Every day Van Horn stayed cuddled in the twisted blankets with his long, bony white legs protruding unless he had drill or the guard detail, snoring fitfully, and if Seabury stayed he could smell his musty, thick breath, since Van Horn was perpetually snuffling and ill. Occasionally Jonathan would call out his platoon and they would drill. They had been assigned the section of the fort near the fifth sally port, facing northeast toward rolling, breast-like hills and the brush-choked bed of Coal Creek. He had a howitzer and about twelve paces of firestep, so he drilled a crew on the gun and the others stood wide-eyed and giggling or, as time wore on, sprawling along the wooden platform, still watching but now making crow-voiced comments. The days were full of spring—of rain and the moving, thick earth and sudden warm gusts of wind in the midst of cold mornings—but the river was flaccid and pale and unchangingly muddy. Seabury would remember the crispness of New England springs which did not drowse into prurient lushness but gently budded the tree limbs and came in an aura of gold and green with the melting snow.

He sat now in his room by lantern light, staring at the sheet of paper on which he had written "Fort Pillow" and the date, which was probably not right by a day or so. The shadows clustered thick around him, twisted shadows by Van Horn's bed things and clean, sharp-edged shadows from the military purity of his own. He stared endlessly at the paper. He did not want to do anything but stare, and thoughts came and crowded at him like animals, furry and warm and reeking and black: thoughts of the thick, jiggling flesh of the Negro women and of the sunken-chested easiness of the white women.

To Jonathan, it seemed that the availability of women was fantastic; legion. He felt squeezed, with the whole command, into the tight confines of the fort and the town down the bluff. There had been no new beginning, of course; rather the opposite, a compression, an impact. The fort had grown in his mind to resemble a cyst. He was steadily amazed at the cruelties and duplicities and tangled infection of the daily life at the small, puckered fort. Leaving the mess, the white officers—Carson, Mc-Clure, Van Horn and the others—would laugh and slap each other on the back, and talk about which of the whores they would visit, and whether 'twould be dark meat or light. The niggers' sexual capacities were fantastic, it was agreed; both the nigger women and the nigger men. Carson and Bischoff held a ten-minute discussion in front of the whole mess concerning the performance a nigger man had put on for them. Booth scowled his disapproval, and they straightened and finished their coffee, and then stepped outside with most of the officers to finish the description. Jonathan was alone with Booth, feeling humiliated, not knowing whether to slip out (will he think that I—I?—am going out to listen?) or sit helplessly in front of Booth while he swilled the last of his coffee.

And it seemed to him that the Negroes' capacity for punishment, for endurance, was fantastic as well. More and more stories crowded up the bluff about beatings and whippings. They said one of the men in his company had been flogged by some of the gunboat sailors. The man was missing for two days from muster, and then he was back, silent, undemonstrative. Jonathan did not ask him about it. Two men in Bischoff's company cut each other up in a knife-fight, and Bischoff was laughing about it at the noon meal the next morning. "Got a slice cut out of his forearm this long, I swear." There seemed to be no such things as pity or compassion. Jonathan was assured by Delos Carson that they thrived on the pain. "By God, boy, they are built to take th' punishment! Anytime you give one of 'em an order, you better kick him if you want it done. Ain't that right, Ep? Eh?" But Jonathan could see it for himself. The Negroes seemed to caper, as always, and he could hear the loud Negro laughter in his tent, as it drifted from their lines. The lights in their tents sparkled and danced in the nights, and Jonathan could see the shifting dark forms moving in and through the yellow-white circles of lamplight. When he tried to pity them, he was repelled; the Negro women sauntered through the sally ports, smiling lasciviously at the sentinels, and late at night he could hear the Negroes slipping back into the fort from the shanties and whorehouses and card games in the town.

He pitied himself. He was staggered by the licentiousness

and then attracted by it, by the shifting flesh of the Negro women beneath the cheap cotton dresses, by the hoots and soft, swirling laughter from the Negro lines late at night. But the fort was not deliberately or uniquely depraved; common military brutality and the uncaring attitude of the white officers and the similarities and dissimilarities—both irreconcilable—between the Negroes and the white Tennesseans; there was simply no measure of human contact. It was not unique, save to Jonathan, who was not a practical man. He was squeezed by the impacted smallness of the post and by his own duties into a stifling and unfamiliar presence.

He tried to recollect the look and the caste of the thin purple and blue veins across Emily's temple. Thinking, I have not even got any longer the right to pretend that I am superior to the demands of the body. Or that I would not take one of the Negro women—and he thought blindly of the fierce thrust of the bodies and the wonderful and ecstatic release—because I would, Lord knows, if I could, if I could. If I could walk down to the Negro huts or the places for the women in the town, and seize one of them, putting my hands on the flesh and the thick pelt. But of course I cannot, no more than I can lift this cabin by the strength of my arm. The room was stuffy and he was sweating but he did not open the door. The rain beat against the wooden roof and since the hut was poorly chinked gusts of rain splattered through, some of it he noticed staining the paper and blurring the word "Pillow" into an ashy, layered mark.

This is not the crime but the penalty. I wanted to exalt myself by service and sacrifice and oh I made the great show, even, yes, the show to Emily with whom among all the people I should have been most honest. Then after collecting the credit and the profit I was not strong enough to take the first step. Not of course that I knew the first step, or even the correct one. But in all my delusions I did not realize how deep the selfishness and cupidity of these white men go, or how the Negroes smell and react and think. Or rather do not think but surge like animals by raw instinct. I flee from contact with them during the day, and would I search them out at night? Not the sweat-lubricated motions of the drill but the musty—I assume they are musty, since Von Horn is frequently explicit—hair-entangling, fierce body thrusts?

I would transfer, but to where and away from what? How after all can I go back, having failed? How can I talk to the frock-coated men amid the glitter and the violin music, to tell them that I have been totally unable to effect anything? Or the women with the kind hand placed on my knee, or Emily? Or of course my mother? Or Mr. Higginson? There is no place in the creeds I have been taught for the utter failure of the human will. They do not write treatises on the shrinking away from physical and spiritual contact that a man instinctively makes. They talk with praise of the generality of men but they do not mention the yellow teeth or the beard stubble or the smell of sweat or excrement or the glandular-quick demands of the flesh.

The second day at Fort Pillow, he had gone to see about setting up a school for the Negro soldiers and their families. He had been partly under the new enthusiams of the departure from Memphis; and he was partly trying to seek out, recollect, his old sense of purpose and duty. He was trying to return to a starting point, an initial dream and desire and self-impression that had been real for so long and was dying so hard. He had been aware of a place, a land, that he must try to reach, and his actual gust of enthusiasm and purpose had little to do with the Negroes, or with the school. He had known, of course, that he would fail and be humiliated. It was not unlike the involuntary, spasmodic way in which he called Van Horn's reedy contempt down upon him.

He had walked resplendently across the parade in his third new uniform, as yet unworn, with the red sash and the shoulder bars and pipings and the saber glittering and swinging at his side. Lieutenant Lippet, who never wore a uniform at all, had said, "Come out of them fancy clothes I see you in there," and the Negroes of his detail laughed, crinkling their eyes, and white Tennessee soldiers dusty from a patrol sneered.

He passed the sentry and the desk. Major Booth, sitting in a nest-like, filthy cubicle with a rolltop desk and a thick lantern burning at midday and the shutters pulled, invited him in without looking up. Seabury stood rigid and handsome, holding the kepi under his elbow and looking covertly about the room, at the framed picture of Lincoln and the yellow wood of the furniture and the scattered stationery all printed officiously and lined and dated, waiting for the clerks to fill in a few numbers and a line or two of writing.

Then Booth had looked at him, a bleary-eyed man with a mouthful of grey teeth and grey-brown beard. He had served out his limbo in the regular army as a lieutenant, passing into middle age in the dim monotony of dusty barracks and endless drill, with a wife as cold and plain as ice water but almost prescribed, in the old army. When the war came he had expected immediate promotion, but due to his age and his continuing lack of connections he had not even reached captaincy by the time his cavalry regiment reached Stevenson, Alabama. And then at the promptings and scoldings of his wife, he entered a newly raised Negro regiment where promotion was certain anyhow, the First Alabama Seige Artillery. And had then done long and combatless tours of garrison duty at Corinth and in blockhouses on the rail lines and in Memphis. He was finally promoted to captain and then to major and then almost coincidentally with the death of his wife was given the post at Fort Pillow, a perfect post with an independent command. But a man commands a battalion of nigger laborers for so long and the old instincts and prides and enthusiasms die out; and he knew better than to trust the white officers either. So the Fort Pillow command was just a bitter summation instead of an accomplishment. All of this endless long experience, of faulted trusts and disappointments, was in his eyes; Booth was beaten flat, he was of a piece with the odor of stale cigar smoke and ink, and the pale, sooty lantern light.

Jonathan shivered inside his uniform and his unmarked, uninitiated newness. Standing there even now mouthing a request he did not really want, since he no more wanted to teach the Negroes than to live with them or train them or fight beside them. But he was doggedly making the request, his mouth shaping words. He had the odd sensation that he was trapped inside the body of someone else; he knew the consequences.

"Sir, it has come to my attention that the Negroes at least

in my company are woefully ignorant and unlettered, and if indeed Mr. Lincoln's"—this with a motion toward the framed picture which he did not know was as standard issue as the ranged guidons in any commanding officer's quarters—"proclamation is to be effected, this condition must be alleviated. So I respectfully request permission to set up a classroom in one of the unused storehouses in the town and to purchase some primers and to teach them. . . ."

Booth began to laugh flatly. Jonathan stopped talking and realized sweat was rolling cold down his side; he thought, suddenly, desperately, of a little pointed fir that grew outside their summer cottage on the Cape, a little tree perfect and careful against a green, warm background and salty fresh wind.

Booth said, "Why, you don't really believe they would come to your schoolhouse, do ye?" Jonathan had expected this; he did not know; he stood speechless but with his lower lip trembling slightly. "Hell, you would have to order them to attend." Booth laughed flatly again, and bent back over the forms on the desk.

Jonathan said, "But sir . . ."

And then Booth said, shortly, "Do any damned fool thing ye like. Only do not do it on battalion time." He dipped his pen in the inkwell, paused, readjusted himself to one of the rectangled and printed slips before him.

Jonathan had not expected to be given permission; he thought of his corporals, Gator and Lexington and North, slab-faced, black, no longer even stooping to mimicry when he was trying to exercise the platoon. Just snickering occasionally, along the walls; he knew better than to order them to work the howitzer too. Booth still paused, waiting for him to leave. His eyes were no longer on the pad in front of him, but looking at Jonathan's waist, through his eyebrows. Jonathan was trying desperately to recollect one name, one face, from his platoon, which he could fit into one of the classroom scenes with himself and his primers. De landis; the one with the yellow face; Otto; Jessup . . . he could remember no other names, no other faces. Just the crossbelts and the wide, wide black hands and the dark circles of sweat coming through the wool frock coats.

Booth said, "Well?" Time hummed in Jonathan's ears.

"I . . . I need permission to use one of the government storehouses. . . ." This, he knew, was his last chance; he would have no other gambits.

Booth frowned. "No. I do not think so. You will have to . . ."

"But Major, you are willing to lead them. Are you not willing to make the effort to see that they are taught?"

Major Booth looked coldly, steadily, at Jonathan; his eyes were flat and hard. It was not the principle, but the challenge, Jonathan knew. He was slipping back into his old role, his old posture. There were relief and humiliation, both old friends, both equally welcome.

"I lead 'em; I will put 'em on the line behind me. That is the extent of my duty to 'em. I ain't being paid to teach 'em a god-damn thing outside of the drill and the regulations; the gov'ment ain't paying a damn thing to teach 'em. Mister Lincoln freed 'em, Mr. Lincoln can do that. When he tells me, I will turn over government property to you, so you can teach 'em; not a damn second before."

Almost without thinking, without thought, the body that Seabury was in made another baiting lunge. "But Major, you do not think that your responsibility to these men ends . . ."

Booth sat back in the chair. The tip of his pen touched the pad, made a wide, spreading, blue-black circle on the buff paper. His eyes were full of hate. "Time I need you, boy . . ." his voice was stiff, waxy ". . . time I need you to tell me my duty, I will call on you. Time you show me that you know your own duty and have th' stomach to do it, you can talk to me about it."

"Major . . ." It, he, had gone too far. He needed to explain.

Booth tore the top sheet of paper from the pad, dipped the pen into the inkwell again. He seemed to forget Jonathan's presence. "Damn young pup. Time I need a young pup with damfool ideas and a cute face and a new uniform to tell me my duties . . ."

"But . . ."

"Get the hell out of here." Booth looked up. "I do not care for you, boy, because I have seen too many of your type in this war. I said get out of here and do not bother me farther about this."

Jonathan had turned to go. To his horror, he found that he was about to cry. I cry so easily; it is so absurd. His eyes were brimming and about to run and he thought, oh no, not that too. Oh God, let me get out of here before I start crying.

But Booth had called him. There was a tone of dutiful magnanimity in his voice. Jonathan stopped and stood with his back to the desk, his face stretching tight with the effort not to crumple spasmodically into tears.

"Boy, listen. Listen one time." Booth had a lesson for him; it was the pattern of his magnanimity. "I have been with these niggers for a lot longer than you have. And I know more about them. Now . . . turn around here. Turn around here when I am talking to you."

He had turned, but Booth was looking down at the pad, holding the pen poised and putting his thoughts together, so he did not see Seabury's mouth and jaw trembling, or his eyes running.

"Maybe they could learn to read, I do not know. They been slaves so long, I do not know. But that ain't the matter. To the army, men are so much beef on the hoof, and it does not matter what color the beef is. That is why they raised the nigger regiments, to get more beef on the hoof. . . ." He seemed to think that Jonathan was about to protest; his hands made a temporizing motion and his head bobbed; but he still had not looked up. "Oh I know, I know. About Shaw and Higginson; but they did not prove anything 'cept that niggers might stand fire, and could be drilled. They gave the army an excuse. Maybe they taught their niggers; maybe their niggers were better. That did not mean a damn to the army. They needed men, they raised the niggers. They do not give a god-damn whether they are taught to read or not; so I don't. I do not see that it is my concern.

"But I know this too. I don't trust my men a damn sight farther than I can throw them. I know this from serven with 'em. They are straight off the plantations, and maybe this is the reason: but they are lazy and shiftless and I don't believe they will stand fire as well as a white man. I don't know, but I 'spect they won't. None of the other officers do either. Right now, I tell you this, these niggers are as worthless a bunch as I have ever seen, and I'm glad we got these dirt walls and these artillery pieces to keep the rebels at a distance, 'cause if they ever get close God help us. The rebels will be rough on the white Tennessee soljers, ain't no love lost there, but they will be murder on these niggers. And on us too. . . ."

Jonathan was not really listening so much as absorbing this. He was choking back the tears and keeping his jaw stiff and tight and praying that Booth would not look up and thinking step by step about the walk back to his hut; he was feeling the trickle of sweat and wishing he were not wearing his fine uniform. But he had dimly perceived that Booth was about finished. He took a shuddering silent gulp, and said, as was expected, "But is not this war . . . is not this war being fought for the freedom of the Negro?"

Booth did not look up; Jonathan had another moment. He fought the twitch in his jaw, straightened himself.

"You and your abolitionist friends, all you people in New England, do not know how things are." Booth sounded like a man who was repeating a familiar argument which he had had to use a wearying number of times. "You think this war is about these niggers because you have talked so long about 'em. But it ain't. We are in this war because the South tried to split up the Union. Now you caint argue with me about that. I saw it coming, and I know what Lincoln said when it was about to happen." Booth was ticking off his points. "I know why the boys from the West—Ioway, Ohio, Michigan—I know why they are in it. They do not like the niggers much better than the rebels themselves; I served long enough in this regiment to know that for a fact. . . ."

He looked up; Jonathan was pale and his face was wet. Booth thought he was about to argue, because his lips trembled.

"I know. 'Th' Battle Hymn,' 'let us die to make men free.' I know. But they—we—were not singing that, when we came down river in '61, '62. We were singing 'Rally 'Round the Flag,' 'the Union forever.' The rebels are traitors. That is all that they matter to me; a Union man, and he owns slaves, is no enemy of mine. Nor of Mr. Lincoln's.

"Oh, it helps. It helps a damned lot." Booth was looking distantly, vacantly, into the corner of the room. "It is like the nigger regiments that Shaw and your friends raised on th' coast. It makes things look a great deal better. It is another fine, noble reason. But that is the way this army, and this country, that is the way they are; you do the job to hand, the reasons, the fine reasons, they will come. And th' arguments. Lord God, the arguments . . . but the first man to put his money down, to do the job . . ." Trailed off.

He looked back up at Jonathan. "I tell you something else you probably did not know. You people up there do not know the nigger, nor the southerner, nor a hell of a lot about this country.

"You think once the blood and the killing is over everything will be all right. The nigger will walk the earth like a white, and everything will be all right. But it will not. If this war goes our way—and as a professional soldier I do not see how but it can—then you are just starting to clean up the mess. My war—keeping this country together—is goen to be over. But your war will be just starting, and you and all your fine, self-righteous . . ." he searched for a word ". . . tea-drinking friends had better hie themselves down here to take care of these people they set free.

"'Cause these are the sorriest people I have ever seen, worse than the Indians. They will starve or freeze unless you take care of 'em hand to mouth. Why that is, I do not know. Maybe it is because of slavery, maybe because of race. You will find the reason, but I misdoubt you will find the answer. This is none of my worry. I am keeping a certain amount of beef on the hoof. But you and your people who got blood and lightning called down and destroyed slavery, you better figger what is coming next. I am going to stay away from that end of the stick, because whoever gets involved in it is going to be a sorry man; and after this war there are goen to be a damn sight more rich men than sorry men. So get out, run along and take a good long look at 'em, and do not come to me tellen me my responsibility." Some of the bitterness returned to his voice; Booth had enjoyed his lecture. He bent back over the desk and the buff pads. "T' tell th' truth, you have got a hell of a lot more responsibility than I have."

Booth's ink-stained fingers had flicked out for the inkwell; Jonathan had pivoted and left. There was an aching irony to Booth's talk. It contained a warning of sorts—the crate of books?—but that was not important. Jonathan had fought his way across the cold parade ground, still struggling to master his face. He had been chastened, scourged. The picture, the image, the land, was unobtainable; there was no dream left. Blood and lightning? Very well; on my head, as well. Even the lies which he had attempted to hoard had been taken from him. Since that day Jonathan had been waiting only for Forrest.

He sat now in the lantern light with the storm pounding outside, thinking absently, that was quite a wind, and looking at the paper with the "Fort Pillow" blurred and nothing else written. He relived the moment of humiliation with the curious fascination of a man probing for a sore tooth and finding it and continuing to play at it with his tongue. And what else did he say, and what then did I say? Was I that much of a fool? Yes. That was the last time he had tried to write home, writing to his mother, "I had not been previously aware, I suppose, of the depths to which our natural instincts frequently lead us, for though I blush to say it I would willingly have struck the man, though he is my superior officer and I owe him a token obedience." He had torn up the letter.

He folded his hands behind his head and looked around the room. Then he leaned forward and picked up the pen, toying with it. Booth was right. They were different.

Jonathan got up and began to pace around the room. Garrison and Higginson and Colonel Shaw can stand up in front of the crowds, and even the snag-toothed, furry mobs, and hold the hand of one of their pet runaway slaves, hold it aloft in theirs, coupling the white and the black flesh. They can form regiments and lead them against the rebels. But they are starting and not ending the process. They have the easiest part; all they need is courage. Some of them are even dead.

Could it have been done any other way? Would the rebels ever have done it? Who can trust them? But we did not purify the land, the way we thought we would, with fire and sword.

It will take more than the exorcism of slavery to free the Negro. I do not know anyone, not anyone, that has the forebearance and patience and sufferance and courage—that has all of these things that will be needed. And it will take more than one man; it will take a whole nation of men.

And I know this. He went to look into the pane of glass, where he could see his face. Droplets of rain pelted against the glass and it faintly buckled with each gust of wind. I know that I am not of the stamp of man that will be needed. He thought of his platoon, their coats stained with sweat and grease, shuffling through their drill, capering, dull, insolent. Child-like, but what does that say? His own white, stiff anger had beaten against them ineffectually and he could not make them pay attention, much less understand. He had no appeal to make to them. I never thought that I would simply not be strong enough, and that for three months in a Negro regiment I would pass each and every night, with the exception of the steamboat here, in a whitewashed cabin, alone. I had thought I would be down there listening to them sing spirituals and recording the words to compare with Mr. Higginson's notes. But here I am. I do not think, in this battalion, they even sing spirituals.

But looking into his mirrored, dark face, he began, once more, to feel dramatic and noble, and tragic rather than ineffectual. I am not of the sort that will be needed to lead them to the promised land; so I will be like Colonel Shaw. I will prove myself in death the way I could not in life. He was back in a familiar place.

He got out his overcoat and buttoned it, feeling the need to walk through the evening. The rain brushed across his face and he had to blink. He had thought in the tiny, stinking cabin that it would be dramatic to walk outside, with the swirling cape and the hood of his coat raised and the wind on his flesh, dramatic and perhaps expiatory. But it was only difficult and unpleasant, since the three walls of the horseshoe earthwork caught the wind up off the river and sent it swerving. The rain came at him each way he turned. He could not bear the thought of going back to the room with the single sheet of datelined paper and the twisted pile of bedclothes and the crouching shadows. He went to the south sally port and stood for a moment in the wall, hoping for the rain to turn away from his face. It annoyed him, and he bit his teeth in frustration. He swept the rain away from his face, over and over, and pulled his collar up.

Down in the town, he could see, there was a haze of thick light, refracted in the rain, and he went out of the fort and down the slippery path toward it. He passed three troopers in greatcoats coming up, swearing under their breath in flat, nasal drawls, 'y God this rain don't never stop, and what does that ol' fool want this night when were I free I could be samplen some of the nigger ware down yonder at the ol' shack. They gave a sketchy salute as he slipped off the path into the ankle-high weeds to let them pass. He heard them when the wind brought their voices back to him. Who he? I never seen him before, and he is one of them white nigger officers. I wouldn't have saluted him then. Time I salute nigger rank and know it that ol' river will be dried and blowed away.

He kept on down the path, feeling the shaft of pain in his chest from self pity and fury. The Tennesseans scared him, stubble-cheeked boys with yellow teeth and stringy hair, always walking in tight knots of three or four, hands inside their breeches pockets and spitting tobacco juice and laughing raucously. They were slope-shouldered and sunken-chested, with sallow skin. He had expected young men with ideals and clean muscles who by virtue of their personal heroism had not been taken into the trap of plantation-run secessionism. And instead there were small groups of slouched, ugly, arrogant boys, picking their teeth with loud, smacking sounds.

He got down to the town despite the slipperiness of the two hundred yards of path. It was in one of the shallow depressions of earth near the river, a clustered group of boarded government warehouses with official stencils and numbers on the sides, and rows of chinked huts with barrel chimneys. Weak and watery lantern light flashed in circles over the pocked, dirty earth, where they threw out the garbage. The white soldiers were quartered there, since evidently Bradford, and certainly Booth who relieved him, expected immediate conflict between the Negro soldiers and the whites.

But this had not come immediately, principally because the white Tennesseans were for the most part so incredibly poor and so incredibly filled with choking, searing hatred for the planters that they regarded it cacklingly as the greatest joke of all. The slaves—or rather their owners—had kept their families crouched in arrogant pride and inbreeding on the hilltops, and in the small and sprawling cities among the cotton sheds and po' white districts, instead of working the rich fields. Slaves gave anyone with money an insurmountable edge. The slaves were both the instruments and the symbols of the planters' ascendency. And now here the slaves were too, fighting those same planters. The things they had brought over to work for them, now, in delicious irony, leaguing with the very men they had kept from the richer fields.

So for a while the white Tennesseans had forgotten that the nigger was worse off even than they were and they had clustered down at the landing when the boats came in and walked by and looked at them working the big guns or drilling. During this time, which lasted about four days during which Seabury was vastly relieved and his brother officers were nervously waiting, the Negro women began to slip down to the fort from the plantations to see the men. To see confirmation that maybe their husbands were still alive somewhere, or to see confirmation that niggers were indeed and truly armed and paid by the white men. And to merely see the new black flesh that had come in after their own young men had run off. They had slipped down in the same way the white women in the neighborhood had slipped down months ago to see the quality and texture of the white men that had come down in the gunboats to the fort; and certainly in the same fashion that before the war the girls came over to the military academies in carriages chaperoned and beribboned but nonetheless for the same reason—to see the texture of the white cadets and the young gentlemen, fascinated not only by the uniforms but also curious and with the most delicate stirring inside them to see an aggregate of finely toned young man-flesh, attractive and as yet unbreached by the world of women. So the Negro women too had come and had walked through the sally ports in joyful, splay-footed profusion, talking to the Negroes, hey nigger you in de stripes an' all, and then breaking into gales of laughter. Eventually they were picked over in a spate of marriages, many of them to men already married. All of the marriages were performed by the uniformed chaplain and ceremoniously attended by the white company officers, most of them making loud, lewd remarks and smoking thick seegars but Jonathan impressed and holding himself erect and spotless in his second new uniform. Until the tasteless and tactless nature of the whole thing came to him: the laughing officers and the wide-eyed Negroes and the sleazy, cheap, almost pathetic women's clothes stolen or given from plantation drawers and already work-stained; and the complete, faithful seriousness of the Negro soldiers, impressed into silence and awe by the ritual and the glitter.

But during this time the Negro women who married and those who did not were picked over by the white men too. There were even some marriages down in the town, some of them drunken farces and others presided over by the disdain and open-eyed hostility of the officers. There were fights they heard about the next day, over or because of the Negro women who had been married out of love or drunkenness or probably defiance. Then with the cooling of the mood and the slackening of the great sense of the huge joke, the women were regarded as more or less communal property by the unmarried white men, since didn't the planters treat them that way and 'y God ain't we as good as any damnfool planter? Fights at first broke out between the white men and their wives or between the white men themselves. Then came, naturally, the fights between the white men and the Negro soldiers, really vicious, belt-swinging knots of white men catching and flailing lone Negroes and spitting curses. The white troopers then wandering back down to where the Negro women in the scattered outlying cabins, still laughing, waited in their shebangs, and in the stinking, smoke-stained, yellowish wood huts and gave their bodies thickly and pungently for bits of ribbon or material or coins or even for slaps and belt blows and welts.

Once the spell of curiosity was over the whites for the first time in their lives realized that they had some men trapped here in close proximity who were more despised than they. They brutally beat them in wet-smelling evenings by the river, and they went to their women repeatedly and openly. If they had lived close to the plantations the whites had already known that while the plantation man rode you said nothing to his face, but if you caught his nigger that was a different thing; since it was the nigger's fault you weren't on that horse in the first place and he was bound to feel better than you in the second place. So you whipped him or wanted to, depending on the strength and personality of the man that owned him. Their mindless hate centered on the women; they were the principal occasions.

In that spate of four days when the Sixth first arrived the Negroes too, suddenly out of Memphis and the garrison cities and with all of the women coming down and into the fort and even treated by the po' white men better than ever, the Negroes too not so much out of rebellion but out of opportunity had begun to change. There were shallow-chested white women with hot eyes who in the reversed pattern of things came up from the town where the white men beat them. They looked at the man flesh regardless of the color, so there were even some marriages between strapping, handsome Negroes, well-set-up men with good straight teeth and square-shaped heads, and the white women. Again the white officers presided at the ceremonies, not with so much levity and cigar smoke but with a sense of foreboding which passed immediately into non-caring. Jonathan had stood, again immaculate, when the man named Arnold had married a sutler's widow with greying hair and yellow eyes, and thought at first in a sheer burst of emotion that this was the way men were meant to live. Until he had passed the bride and noticed the hot, lascivious way she looked at the Negro and the way she held his arm and ran her fingernails over and over across the back of his neck. There were other marriages between the sallow and welted white women from the Thirteenth Tennessee, who now in the sheer sex-urge looked on the men of the Negro regiment as on prize bulls, machines which would fill them and yet not demand the long hours of working, since how could they, ain't they niggers?

This too worked itself out in hate with Jonathan watching and horrified and beginning to formulate the idea that here was sin and retribution for sheer, Godless lust. The white soldiers caught one of the Negroes on the fifth day, near the latrine above the river, and even while a ship was blowing for a landing at the slip they dragged him to one of the empty federal warehouses and there they castrated him with his own bayonet. Of course the white officers could have demanded and might have received the guilty troopers. But Booth, grey-faced and weary, did nothing, since that might spread to Memphis and he was not sure whether Hurlbut would sanction the marriage in the first place. Seabury was the only officer in the Sixth who would have asked for some sort of justice, the others all deciding it was right and proper or just not caring, and Seabury had by this time tried to get his schoolroom and had failed, and was not going to face Booth again. He merely told Arnold, perspiring from working the big guns despite the stiff spring wind, to quit living with the woman or to stay out of the town and don't leave the walls of the fort. Arnold of course nodded yes seh, yes seh, and the very next day was caught near the outer lines by a group of mounted Tennesseans coming in from a patrol, and run down like a fox. They beat him with the flats of sabers until blood was all over the dark skin and his nose was severely broken. The Negroes in his company rustled in the lines the next morning when Arnold came to drill, but they did nothing more. Seabury assumed they did not complain because of their whipped and conditioned fear, but really it was out of the identical reason that the white officers did nothing—they had expected it and they had told Arnold that he was getting into trouble and they knew it was bad business to fool with white women.

Now, in the night, Seabury stood at the edge of town, watching the light sparkle and bounce in the rain near the corners of the huts. There was no noise from the huts, except occasional strains of a mouth organ, lonely and wailing, and sometimes a pattern of mindless and disembodied laughter from the maze of shacks. Everything was cold and wet and rustling in the wind and rain. After a time of standing empty and aching all over physically with the sorrow for himself and with the intense loneliness, Seabury turned and walked back up the path from the town, the two hundred yards to the fort.

5

THE NEXT MORNING JONATHAN AWOKE TO THE BUGLE CALLS, STAR-
ing upright at the whitewashed ceiling of the hut. He washed
himself in the chilling water and put on his shirt and blouse,
sniffing at the armpits of the shirt and deciding it was clean
enough, and then his sash and pants and equipment. He shaved
in the corner of the room, having long ago dispensed with the
pleasure of Otto's stumbling search for hot water because of the
embarrassment of hearing the man grumble and curse while he
stood guiltily in soiled bedclothes with his razor dangling in one
hand. His flesh smarted and stung from the cold water and dull
blade. Then, on the verge of leaving, he prodded and shoved at
Van Horn. Van Horn's mouth was open and his yellowed teeth
chewed at the air; and then the mouth closed and he rocked his
head upright. Jonathan left the room pulling on his gloves.

The river mist crowded into the fort. The air was cold and
chill and snapped into his mouth. Sunrise was purple and red in
the upper half of the sky, and everything else was bathed in cottony mist. The ranks of Negro soldiers were dark, regulated
stains, changing, as he walked toward them, into familiarity. A
private, encasing bubble of open air seemed to walk with him,
finally including the nearer ranks of men. They had turned out
in frock coats with red pipings and chevrons, lighter-blue pants
and dark, embrassed kepis, holding rifles rigidly in their hands,
breathing steam into the air.

He was told as he walked over the spongy ground that Captain Smith was indisposed this morning and would Lieutenant
Seabury be so good as to take charge of the company. This ritual

was accomplished by the yellow-faced, boyish orderly who always buckled Captain W. T. Smith into his sword belt for the officer's poker and drinking. And who unbuckled him in the early dawn and then awaited the bugle to give the message to Lieutenant Seabury crossing toward the company. He got to the company front, hearing the white sergeants call the role, crisply, with a nasal twang at the enns. Gaylord was their company sergeant. Seabury looked up at his sharp face while he finished the role. Gaylord then called them to attention with a blurred monosyllable and then turned and saluted him rigidly with his blue eyes looking vacantly into the fog. Seabury went to his place in the rear of the company, past the four thick, shortened ranks of dark faces and shining rifles. First Sergeant Weaver, a big white man with a long brown beard, called for the report. The sergeants answered and Gaylord said, "Presenanaccountedfaw!" and then the command, "Post!" was given and Seabury walked out to the front of the company.

Then Major Booth stood in front, today no more than a thick figure in an old-fashioned Hardee hat blurred by the mist. He gave them the orders of the day himself, letting his voice ring out through the hollow of the fort. In the middle of the colored ranks the men yawned and leaned on their rifles and drowsed, knowing their white officers could not recognize them and would not dare call them down, just as they had known back in the plantation fields they would not be sought out and called down. The white man, ol' buckra, he doan know one nigra from the other, Gator knew, and stood to his place while ol' Booth shouted. He doan know but he pretend he do.

Seabury listened vaguely to the orders of the day, broken and parsed into syllabic military patterns making them even more meaningless. Company A on duty and Company B send out a work detail to the slip, and C and D exercise the guns and drill. All of this echoed metallically around the parade while the officers rocked on their heels in anticipation of coffee and bacon and the Negroes slept or nodded or looked around at the fog. There were bugles over the parapet, down in the white camp. Some of the Negroes leaned together and whispered, ol' white man he up early today, must be feelen mean early.

The Winter and Spring of 1863–1864   *163*

Then Booth stepped back. There were more vacant military commands and the officers pivoted or turned lazily and called the sergeants to dismiss the company, most of the men falling away to the breakfast lines even before the sergeants got to the front of the ranks. The officers streamed off to their mess table on the other side of the partition in the headquarters cabin. Seabury went in, toying with the button on his glove silently, while Van Horn came in scrubbing the sleep out of his eyes. Delos Carson and John Hill came in, having missed the parade too, talking together and rubbing themselves from the chill. He sat down after Major Booth took his seat, going to the place he had sat in since he first came to the regiment, at the foot of the table and on the left side. Captain Epenter sat next to him, smelling of sweat and hair grease, and Hill, who was post adjutant, on the other side.

The Negro waiters brought in the food after Booth, with sleep marks still on his face, gave the solemn, lengthy blessing asking health for the President and even for General Hurlbut, and for God's strength in doing His will this day. Seabury drank some of the coffee, passing the food on to Epenter, who took eggs from the big plates, and grits and bread. Epenter shoved egg-crusted bread into his bearded mouth and chewed almost without breathing. Hill leaned over to Seabury and whispered "Ol' Ep is sure a ball of fire with that food, eh?" Jonathan smiled and nodded and sipped at his coffee. Epenter was from some place in Indiana where he had been a school teacher, a small, round man who had grown a scattered beard, and who wore rectangular spectacles. Johnny Hill was a clean-shaven, lean boy with eyes that sloped upward above his nose and a lower lip that made a half-circle when he talked. He was sleepy-eyed and earnest and always ready to smile.

Smith and Bischoff and Tom McClure and the other officers were unshaven and thick-eyed from the poker game which the regular army had made into an institution in Booth's mind, played in the absence of much money or light or air until early dawn. Red-eyed from that, or from a night of plunging wild lechery down in the town where they all went to a certain shed which the officers of the Thirteenth had told them about in a spate of brotherly kindness. The officers of the two regiments got along very well, the Tennesseans for the most part, Seabury surmised, being small politicians and lawyers who had opposed secession. They were practical men, who appreciated power. They had as little as possible to do with their men and welcomed the officers of the Sixth as brothers in arms.

After breakfast Seabury left the table in silence. There was a conversation still in session, about the course of the war, Booth holding the lead and the captains flicking big cigar ashes on the floor and drinking endless cups of coffee and picking the residue off their tongues critically, while Booth said, "This man Sherman now, I knew him in the regular army, and we called him Cump. . . ." Hill walked beside him in silence for a moment, Seabury thinking, well, at least he is still on speaking terms with me. Then Hill said, "I reckon this would be good farmen land. You ever been out yonder?" He indicated vaguely the other side of the earth wall, pierced by the howitzers and sally ports.

"Just down to the town."

"Well, there's some good fields around, some good farmen land. I know of some I think I can get not far down the road toward Memphis. I would like to have a little land, for after the war."

"Down here?"

"I reckon it to be as good as anything I can get back in Ohio, and a good bit cheaper too."

"Hunh . . . I never knew anyone that wanted to stay in the South after the war."

"Well, I haven't got anything to go back to up there."

They had a while before they had to get to work. Indeed before anyone got to work since most of the officers were still crowded around Major Booth's reminiscences or still in bed or out taking the air around the walls of the fort, staying, of course, well away from the Negro quarters and the river face. Jonathan and Hill sat down on the firestep.

"How . . . Why, uhh . . ." Seabury had trouble starting. "How did you get with this regiment? I mean if you care to say."

Hill pushed up the wrinkles in his forehead with sincerity. "I was in an infantry regiment out of Ohio." He pronounced it Ohiah. "We come down to Shiloh and get cut up, and then over to Kentucky and get cut up, and then Stone's River and get cut up. Finally we were mustered out, and I did not have enough money to do anything except go back in. So I figgered I would rather be an officer than a private if we got to get cut up again, and they put me here." And he smiled and the wrinkles went out of his forehead. For the first time it did not sound so horrible to Seabury, enlisting as an officer in a Negro regiment for the added pay.

"I came here, myself, really wanting to do something good for the Negro, you know? I really thought this was the best way to fight the war."

Hill nodded. "I heard them talken about that," and they both laughed, Seabury with a burning in his heart. "Not many of you from the east come down to this part of the war, I reckon," Hill said seriously. His sloping eyes and slow smile made him look very sincere.

"They fight over on the coast; I knew Colonel Shaw of the Fifty-fourth, and Mr. Higginson who raised a Negro regiment out of South Carolina, I think. They talked to me a great deal about it."

"How come you went west?"

"Oh, Mr. Higginson was disbanding his regiment and Mr. Shaw was killed, and besides they said I was more needed out here. . . ." He said this before he thought and he looked sideways at Hill. "And I had never been west, so I came."

"Yeh . . . my ol' pap heard about me doen this from the boys that went back home, and he was really madder than a wet ol' hornet." He smiled again, slowly. "He tol' me to come home if I wanted to work like a nigger. Said he had a place for me in the shop." They both laughed.

"But you stayed?"

"I was tired of the ol' man I reckon, and I like it down here well enough except for the rebels. I want a piece of land somewhere, maybe here or in the West. . . . I been talken to some of the officers and they say that you can get out to the West and get some nice land."

"That's what I've heard. . . ."

"But I might want to stay down here."

Jonathan was sitting with his knees pulled up to him, boyishly, his hands locked in front of his shins. Hill was sitting sideways on the firestep, his hair tousled, looking at the sun burning away the mist. For a moment neither of them said anything and then Hill was about to move, so Seabury said hastily, "Do . . . do you have a girl back in Ohio?" pronouncing it Ohiyo.

"Naw . . ." Hill was smiling and then serious again, "No, I had one, but time I got mustered out and joined this regiment she married a messmate who got back home."

"Oh."

"It tore me up for a while, but my ol' man said she had been runnen around for a time anyhow." Then of course Hill had to ask him the same question. Jonathan said, "Yes," and it became all important to him to convince Hill that she was lovely and a lady. They sat together, Hill squinting and listening earnestly and looking up at him with his eyes slanting upward, while Seabury leaned and talked and smiled.

Later in the day Jonathan worked with his men at the howitzer along their section of the wall. There was a new warmth in the air and he felt sweat stain his shirt. For a while he took off his jacket, but the chill was still in the air and he put it back on. The Negroes stood at the chest-high, gleaming tube of metal, glistening too with sweat. They worked in relays, learning again through endless, cadenced repetition the patterns of loading the cannon. They handled the rammer pole and the sponge, looking vacant or trapped, and moving with clearly no comprehension from one part of the gun to the other. Jonathan shouted at them or called out the orders, having long ago learned that any attempt to explain the function of one action in relation to another was wasted. They came out of the fields where presumably they had known nothing more complex than the great wooden screw of the cotton press, which doubtless they had worked under the scrutiny of a white overseer, Jonathan thought, and they cannot now learn, in a month or so, the precise functions of manning the guns.

The ones who stepped up to the cannon held the pieces loosely, and the others stood back in line, grinning and slapping the men at the gun on the back, saying, Hey man, doan you know how to hannel that ol' stick? When ol' massa come ovuh that wall you got to get thet thing in quick if you wan' to blow him to kingdom come like you say. Gator was grinning too, at Lexington going to the breech and sighting down it, and saying, "Hey niggers, I see ol' massa comen up with a whole passel of secesh," and then bending over dramatically and squinting down the thick, round length of the barrel and pressing his lips together more and more firmly, and finally jerking at the imaginary lanyard and saying, "Woo man, he blown all over Tennessee I reckon." The others, who were perspiring and weary, laughed too. Jonathan grabbed the linstock out of Lexington's hand and knew instantly he had made a mistake but pressed on, saying, "Why damn it, Lexington, this is no time for sport. Your life may depend one day on doing this right." Lexington's face changed and a flicker of anger came into it as Jonathan took away the pole, and then his expression froze in place. When Jonathan turned away, rubbing his blond hair out of his forehead, Lexington of course made some sign so that all of the Negroes laughed. And Jonathan completed the ritual then by turning and looking at them, and they froze too, their eyes tightened or white and the corners of their mouths twitching.

"All right now then. All right now then, the second crew come up and take over the implements. All right." He took deep breaths. "By my command—Numbers one and two, handle sponge—" beginning it over again, the manual-ordained motions with the frock coats swinging and the black arms reaching down into the ammunition boxes for the imaginary cartridges and passing them to the men at the muzzle, they in turn handling spaces of air exaggeratedly and ludicrously. The small, yellow-skinned Negro who was Smith's orderly pretended to drop the make-believe shell, and danced away in horror holding his hands up and his eyes wide. The others laughed mindlessly; half of them did not know why they laughed at all. Jonathan looked around and tried to laugh too.

"Load cartridge—ram cartridge." He tried to bear down in his voice. While his back was turned, one of the Negroes thrust the spongestaff through the legs of the tall Negro who was standing by one of the handspikes, eyes half lidded and blank, mouth slack. The man with the spongestaff twisted it and the tall Negro fell over the trail of the cannon. The others laughed and jeered, and slapped their knees. The tall Negro picked up the heavy handspike and jabbed it hard at the chest of the man who had tripped him. The ornate sequences of training fell away, leaving Jonathan alone, exposed, while the two men circled each other warily, with fear, animal hatred, in their faces. Those around them moved backwards, giving them room. Hev at him, Tawm! Hit him up side the haid. Scrush his skull, nigger! Jonathan could not move to separate them: he was helpless and uninitiated, transfixed by the savagery, viciousness, brutal humor which had surged up, it seemed to him, from nowhere, without warning. Gator and North watched him while the two men sparred and circled; then they stepped forward and separated them, and Gator knocked the tall one off of the firestep with his open palm. But they were both laughing too.

Jonathan pulled the handspike and staff away from the two corporals. "I have to take these things away from you as though you were children." He was talking to fill in the depthless, suspended sense of his own helplessness. The Negroes were still laughing in their dark ring around the cannon; who knew what they thought? Jonathan looked around quickly. Some of them were stamping their feet against the wooden matting.

"The third crew, then. Step up here. Handle the implements."

"I handled mine, Cap'n seh. I handled mine already." The yellow-skinned boy made a cupping motion toward his genitals, squeezed his hand, cupped it again. He winked broadly, and they all burst into laughter again, standing in a circle around the gun. Jonathan looked hotly at him. The third crew came up after Gator said, "Step up theah, nigger, and quit yo' foolen and lissen to the cap'n." But he too stood smiling in Jonathan's face, and Jonathan would not meet his eyes.

They worked some more with the gun and then racked the sponge and worm and rammer and the chests, again without having actually fired the piece. Seabury was still burning with anger and shame. He told himself that if just once they could fire the gun they would be more appreciative. Of course they cannot learn by this rote and pretense, and it makes them mad. If they could just once fire this gun! But he still rankled and while the Negro soldiers walked away loosely toward the cabins, their opened coats swinging, he watched the yellow-skinned boy's back and thought, I should so like to strike him. God damn him.

He turned and looked down the slope toward the Tennesseans' camp, and watched a patrol ride out into the spring land. The trees were deep with new color, with green leaves and purple shadows, before the sun burned the colors flat into the land. The patches of torn earth around the camp were black or reddish and moist, and the grass and sedge were green. He could see, away working the distant fields, some of the men who came down to the shelter of the camp. There were white men from mustered-out regiments or returned from refugeeing, and freed Negroes working for the bombproofs and cotton factors in the North. The men were sullen but they were grateful for the chance to work the land in the shelter of the guns at the fort, coming in at night to one of the camps, depending of course on their race.

Out on the river a gunboat, its metal shield gleaming in the sunlight and the ports open and folded back to let in the spring winds, passed with a flutter of signals, the sailors' tiny blue figures standing on top of the shield and around the pilot house. The Negroes of course scattered to watch the boat pass, some of them yelling and waving their garrison kepis and the women in bright-colored dresses amid the profusion of wash putting their fists against their foreheads and staring too. They are, Jonathan thought, like children in a way, but children rendered insolent and obscene and unlettered. He was still furious at the yellow-skinned boy. His anger had centered upon that one. He walked back to change clothes, sweat thick and cool around his armpits and down his back, from handling the long spongestaff after North and a short Negro had persisted in dropping it in trying to fit it to the muzzle. He did not like the greasy feel against his flesh, and he wondered if he had a fresh shirt left. Or if he would have to go down the scattered tents and shanties behind the fort, to the Negro woman who did his washing, amid the chicken dung and charcoal chips and stumps and scattering children with cloth in their pigtails. He hoped not, sincerely enough. He washed with the water in the chipped basin in his room, and made his bunk, looking in distaste at the crumpled blankets of Van Horn's bed. He thought that he might request permission to fire the cannon.

Jonathan found the clean shirt and put it on under a fresh blouse, and went out into the spring morning. He saw Hill (no, John, he thought) standing with Dr. Chapman Underwood by the sally port. Of course, he thought, of course I will talk to John about it. As he approached he was already framing the words in his mind and thinking, this is a good idea and he will see it is, the fact that Hill would see it as a good idea being very important. He timed his step as Dr. Underwood drew away so that he came up and Hill turned to him immediately and smiled.

"I was having trouble today with my company," he started and Hill grinned and said, "Yeh, I saw they was given you some."

"The trouble is, you see, they are not mechanical-minded . . ." and Hill laughed again. "They are not mechanical enough to grasp the purpose of it all, of these movements; when we practice with no powder or shot, they think it is a game. Now, I think," and he began consciously to make his voice as colloquial as he could, always watching Hill's face desperately and covertly, "now I think 'twould be best to really give them some powder. To set off a cannon in practice every so often, and show them the—relationship between the motions we teach them and the gun. . . ."

"If they don't kill themselves. But you caint get any powder out of ol' Booth, you know it," Hill said, earnestly. "He will not give you no powder, ner shot to practice with."

"Umm. I know. 'Twas just an idea." And then the thought came, no this is not what I wanted. Hill said again, "You caint get powder though." Jonathan stiffened and was silent, and then asked him about the gunboat that passed and did he know which one it was. Hill treated that with equal studied and earnest seriousness, saying the *Peosta* he reckoned but maybe the *Comet,* he did not get too good a look but they could ask Bischoff.

In the afternoon B Company worked under the bluff, hacking away at the scrub and pine and tangled branches and refuse nearer the river. Jonathan, like all of the white officers, stood posed on the slope without working, his feet dug into the soil and balancing with his sword, his blond hair and sash blowing in the river wind. He watched while the Negroes in fatigue jerseys sweated and tore at the earth and made rasping jokes or sprawled worked-out along the bank above the slip, watching a riverboat maneuvering for a landing. He stood unmoving and silent and tight-lipped, watching the bending backs of the soldiers. There was a fitness to the work; a release from the tight ritualistic humiliation of the practice, in the hard labor along the river bank. With some of the off-duty Tennesseans sharp-faced and sucking at straws, laughing as the Negroes cut at the thistle and the ferns.

Down at the landing the forty men from the Second Light were unloading the landed boat, standing in long lines, laughing and passing the bales and crates down from the deck of the boat across the stages onto the dock. The sailors stood on the decks watching and guiding them to the new piles while the boat, hollow-mouthed and ornate, blew steam and dark smoke spasmodically into the clear sky. The captain came up the path with his frock coat swinging about his legs, looking for Booth, with the artillery officer from the howitzer stationed on the boat. The crew sat atop the bales and swung their legs and watched the Negroes work. Jonathan's men were stripped to the waist by now in the heat of the work, their spines rigid lumps along the black silk-like flesh of their backs. He looked down at the boat deck where the sailors sat spitting tobacco juice over the side and watching the Negro gunners of the Second at work.

The Negroes there were small, light-skinned, agile men in shell jackets and bright buttons and commanded by Captain Lamberg who was a Jew from New York City and who spent most of his time in Memphis, and Lieutenant Hunter who was

Irish, from up the river. The two of them did not pass much time at the officers' mess and stayed with their men. Lamberg was dark and long-nosed, and Hunter, who was working over them, had an open face with thick sideburns and a tall body. The Negroes in that single section sent to Fort Pillow were better niggers, it had been decided a week ago in all solemnity at the mess of the Sixth. They are better niggers and more intelligent than the average nigger an' they do their work better, Captain Carson had pronounced, and the others had sagely nodded yes. They were themselves of course victims of some vast and unconscious conspiracy that gave them the poor niggers from Alabama that were blue-black and didn't have enough white blood in them. Jonathan had agreed, comparing the light-skinned boys that were always laughing and crossing the parade with their buttons gleaming, to his own men with bulky, greasy frock coats, more like caricatures of men with thick flesh and jutting skulls and black skin. Even if I had just been sent down to the Second Light things at least might have been different; I might have been in Hunter's place.

Hunter, tall and Irish and black-haired, spent his time in the main with the artillerymen while Lamberg was gone to Memphis doing some sort of work in the judge advocate's or maybe the quartermaster's staff, again on behalf of the Negroes. Rumor had it that he was thereby limiting all chance he might ever, despite his Jewishness, have had for advancement, since this brought him into direct political and military conflict with Hurlbut and with Johnson the governor. It was generally common knowledge among the mess of the Sixth that Hunter shared a hut with Lamberg and with a Negro sergeant from his company. They were trying to get a commission for the nigger, and this of course prompted some obscene comments from Bischoff. The others had laughed, but Booth himself, reaching for the mustard pot at the time, had told Bischoff to shut up and said that the Second was a better regiment than the Sixth and perhaps it would help the officers of the Sixth to get to know their men. Everyone exchanged momentary panicked glances, thinking, is he going to send us out to bunk with niggers? But they all knew the only reason Booth particularly cared about the

Negro soldiers or even got incensed when they were ill-treated was because always in the back of his mind was that army career, and he meant to hang on by doing a sound job. After the war, if they mustered out the Negro regiments he might well be dropped from the regular army, and then he would have to enlist into the ranks. So Booth made his protests or his suggestions within military channels and without rocking the boat, so they in turn went generally unheeded by men like Captain Turner on the transport, and even by the company commanders in the Tennessee regiment after the castration. The officers in the mess recovered their poise. They knew he would go no further in his suggestion, and when Booth reached the mustard and put it on his beef, he chewed in silence, a bit of yellow clinging to his beard. The stir of conversation had grown again, though Bischoff saved ramifications on his obscene thoughts concerning the officers of the Second until he was alone with Carson and Smith and Epenter.

Now in the afternoon above the river Jonathan stood posed and handsome above his working men while they raised to rub at their backs and then bent down again to cut at the growth. He thought about everything they said about the Second. He looked down at the deck of the riverboat and watched the Negroes unloading it quickly and with despatch, and he saw Hunter among them at the head of the line. He was stripped to his waist, bending over a box and lifting it and passing it to a Negro sergeant. It rocked along the line with a seeming motion of its own and then was placed in the yellow-brown stack at the edge of the slip. The sailors stood immobile and did nothing to help. They were watching Hunter with suspicion, snickering among themselves and pointing out the next box with a toe. Hunter finally straightened up and said, though Jonathan only heard the words later and second-hand, "Why don't you give us a hand with these paint crates?" The three sailors, tall and high-cheekboned, looked one to another quickly and then reputedly one said, "We ain't niggers." And another in a second moment of inspiration, perhaps hearing the intake of breath and the rustling halt to the work, added, "We ain't even in the service. They your color meat. You do it." Then Hunter, bare-chested and towering over the man, said, "Now you don't mean that, do you?" and the first man replied, "I said we ain't niggers." Then Jonathan and most of the men on the bluff saw Hunter backhand the man suddenly and with sufficient force to send him sprawling open-mouthed back against a bulkhead. The other two sailors stepped forward and with a tiny motion that was somehow visible on the hill, Hunter stopped his sergeant from coming in, and with another quick flick poleaxed one sailor in the belly. While he broke in half Hunter stepped to the other and clapped him, close-fisted, across the side of his head and spun him around. Then the other sailors were beginning to move from their seats down toward Hunter. He picked up a belaying pin, and made a move toward them which halted them frozen at the top of the companionways.

Then the Second Officer came forward and ordered the white men to give a hand. Hunter smiled affably again and threw the iron slug he had somehow fisted and used into the river. Jonathan and most of his Negroes on the hillside saw the incident and one of them whistled and said, "That ol' buckra I tol' you could fight." Jonathan made stirring motions with his hand to get them back, bent over and scraping at the weeds and small bushes. He watched Hunter, though, choked with envy and thinking, I know I am separated from that man by a century of street-fighting, but I wish I were like that. I wish I could enforce my will like that. Christ, why can I not? Why is there nothing I can do? Jonathan felt the old choke of frustration. That is the sort of man I need to be, and would have to be, to serve here. All of this is rank, rank pretense. I should not even be here at all. To be effective here I must be another person, and since I can not be effective I just have to sit behind this pretense. The breeze through his hair annoyed him and he brushed his fingers through it.

6

BISCHOFF BROUGHT UP THE SUBJECT IN THE MESS. HE HAD HEARD
tell that ol' Hunter had stooped to nigger fighting and had
busted up some sailors when they wouldn't stoop to nigger work,
making a rhythmical sort of statement out of it so that everyone
looked up.

"Yeh . . . I heard that too."

"I was there," Jonathan said. Epenter looked attentive but
Booth just bent over the spareribs with lines forming stiffly
around his eyes, and the others turned their mouths down. "I
was there and saw it. They called his men niggers," and
Jonathan realized, why so does Bischoff, and everyone here.
He kept talking desperately, "And he got mad, I understand.
He hit three of them with a slug of iron he got in his hand, and
after that they straightened up and helped him unload the
boat." He looked from eye to eye hoping that it was colloquial
enough. "And I swear it is the first time since I have been here
that I have seen river sailors set to and work with a will."

They relaxed with that and Carson said, "That's God's
truth, they are the laziest sonsofbitches on this earth."

"I heard it too," Bischoff said, running his tongue over his
shiny, thin lips, "that they said they were not niggers and after
Hunter laid them out he said do not say, 'We ain't niggers,' say,
'We are not Negroes.' That's the way I heard it. But that
Hunter he is a big bastard and a mean un, but if he gets work
out of them sailors he is a better man than I, I reckon," and they
all laughed at that.

"That ain't much of a compliment, like in Cairo they always say the least ugly daughter is the family beauty" and "You better shet up with thet face of yours, Carson." Jonathan sat still and relieved. He chewed at some of his spareribs in the thick sauce the Negro cooks put over them. The meat, sliding off the ribs, tasted greasy, thick, warm.

After the meal, amid the coffee pots and the mugs and the silent, padding Negro waiters, the thick cigar smoke and the glow of brass and braid, the officers of the Sixth United States Colored Heavy Artillery sat and mused and speculated and bragged and talked. Van Horn rocked restlessly back and forth and finally left early, in a flush and his black hair tousled, to the obscene comments of Ellis and Carson. Epenter pontificated and looked judiciously at his cigar the whole while, watching it burn. Booth sat back smiling and drumming his squarecut nails on the baize table cloth, waiting for the time to begin the poker game; Lippet leaned forward hatchet-faced into the flood of cigar smoke, talking about the coming election, and John Hill listened differentially. Smith was talking about his coming trip to Memphis and getting licentious advice from McClure, who had thin, shiny eyes, about the whorehouses. Everyone knew McClure knew less than Smith about the whores in Memphis. Cleary was going with him and left to get to work on the reports for the quartermaster in Memphis, officious and gangling.

The others talked about sex or politics and wondered vaguely what Forrest would do, after ol' Hicks had knocked him one at Paducah just the other day. They all began to talk about Forrest then: he had broken into Tennessee, or rather followed through the hole left by the broken cavalry of Sooey Smith. That was the reason they were at this place and that was the reason that the Thirteenth Tennessee hadn't left yet to report to Memphis where its Fifth Company was to be mustered in.

Booth said, "Forrest has tried his hand at the river fort at Paducah, and I do not think he will be back at us for a while."

"Yes sir, but I heard 'twas only the gunboats that kept him out. I heard that the nigra troops broke and ran and Hicks and the Fortieth of Illinois and the gunboats kept him out."

Booth looked at McClure. "I do not know." He always got mad when they openly questioned the fighting capacity of the

Negro troops in the mess. Nobody knew how they would behave but no one really thought they would do too well. Jonathan sat at the end of the table, having heard about Paducah where Forrest had been whipped. How the Negro troops had run under the levee and the *Peosta* and some other gunboats had shelled the rebels thin. The Fortieth Illinois had stopped their charge on the earthwork. Everybody in Fort Pillow was interested in it since, of course, it proved that here was a combination that Forrest could not break, earthworks and the river gunboats and a strong defense. The gunboats could keep the rebels from massing, the theory went, and then the rifles and cannon could stop their rush. If the Negroes would fight. He looked over at John Hill; he was slouched back smoking a cigar, and watching the smoke rise to the ceiling, unconcerned.

"Yes, but Forrest took Union City."

"An' ol' Poyles—you know Poyles, Del, you know, yeh— well, Poyles of the Thirteenth Tennessee was tellen me that Forrest whipped Hurst out of Bolivar pretty bad. Whipped him and cleaned him out."

"Naw, I don't think Forrest is through with this state by any means."

Lippet said, "Well, there ain't any reason he ought to be here at all. They had the bastard trapped back in December, was it, had him cut off when he was raisen his command, and damned if he didn't run over 'em without firen a shot."

"Cav'ry leaders ain't worth a damn in this army. Grierson was supposed to be, but Forrest took him once in Tennessee and then again down at Okolona."

"Wasn't Grierson he took at Okolona," Epenter said, " 'twas Sooey Smith."

"Yeah, I know. But Grierson was with him and I heard tell," Delos Carson said, beard jerking, "I heard tell he treated him pretty rough."

"Well, that is the truth. This army ain't got a cav'ry commander worth his salt. The rebels have got 'em all. Ever' one."

Jonathan wanted to say, well, of course this is cavalry country, the rebels don't have one good artilleryman, nor one good riverboat commander, do they? They do not. It is not a question of which produces the better fighters; it is just a question of which, North or South, produces the geographical opportunity. Of course the rebels have the best cavalry commanders. But he said nothing.

"Well sir, I say this: I say till Sherman wakes up and gets rid of Hurlbut this department won't be worth a fiddler's damn."

"Umm. That's the truth, Del. That is the truth."

"Hell, he had two—no, no, three—three chances to catch Forrest back in the winter. He had a chance to hit him and keep him out of Tennessee. But he won't move out of Memphis. He got enough men to bag ol' Forrest any damn time, and he won't move 'em out of Memphis or the garrisons."

" 'Y God, that is the truth. That is the truth. We out here can holler our heads off for help but we won't get any from Memphis," McClure said.

"I hope, I swear I hope that Forrest cleans him out of there. Goes in an' takes Memphis right out from under him. Before God, I hope it. Maybe then we can get somebody out here that is worth a damn."

They talked, pulling at their cigars or drinking coffee. Their uniforms were loosened at the throat and the room smelled of woolen uniforms and lantern oil and cigar smoke and just faintly of man sweat. The Negro waiters padded in and around and out, probably, Jonathan mused, seeing no more than which coffee urn needed to be refilled, and removing the china still smudged with red grease and ribs and flecked now with cigar ash.

Outside, the sun had gone down in a pink and red blaze under the blue curtain of the sky, a lovely, warm sunset that had the Negroes in the rows outside singing and taking the air and talking as their faces blurred indistinguishably into the darkness and the dust. They were listening to the birds and the bats wheel and squeak and the hum of the insects and the frogs down by the water, talking and slouching loose-shouldered against the wooden cabins or along the parapet. The clouds caught at the sunlight, clouds coming over fast and thick now, and there was the smell of rain all of a sudden. The Negroes in the darkness saw the first lightning bugs that night, and slowly began to drift back for the lights of the cabins, hearing the noise from the officers' mess.

Inside the mess the table was cleared of plates, though dirtied in spots by coffee and grease stains. The officers listened mainly to Bischoff and Epenter and Major Booth, or talked in groups by themselves. They were oblivious to the coming rain, feeling their full bellies and smelling the thick smoke and the now prominent man smell, in the close warmth and comfort of the mess and the military talk. There were two wine bottles on the table, red port wine, sweetish and tawny and throwing purple shadows on the table. The officers poured the port into their glasses, compliments of Captain Smith who had left in the minute for the packet to Memphis. In the closing of the red wine with the clear glasses and crystal they felt rich and full and masculine, and their talk or perception of the talk became more affected and rhythmical.

Major Booth, his grey teeth hidden now in his reddish-brown beard, sat steady and old and constant amid the chatter and pretense of the junior officers and the opportunists of his command, listening half amused to them ridiculing Hurlbut. Their ridicule was gradually turning to pomposity. "Now if I had been in Memphis instead of that ass, I would have sent my infantry out along the rails and stationed them, brigade by brigade, at each major crossing point." Lippet was illustrating this on the tablecloth with a fork. "That way, with an engine for each one brigade, I could have concentrated three brigades at any point where Forrest came through, you see."

"Yeah—well, it is a damn sure thing that Hurlbut could not concentrate one soldier at any major point."

"Yes, but look what I mean. Look here . . ."

"That is good, Ep. Could not concentrate one soldier! He could not concentrate one set of hindquarters underneath him, though he has enough of em!" Everyone laughed except Jonathan, and Booth and the lieutenant, still trying to explain his trap for Forrest. "Now look. Now look here. This is what I would do now. We have Fort Pillow here on a parallel with, say, Nashville. Well, I would assign one division to each. . . ."

The others were still laughing at the concentration joke

and saying, "Tell 'em, Lip. Tell 'em, Lippet. Walk into Hurl-but's office and lay out the plans for the man. Give him his pro-motion," and they all laughed. "If he don't trust Lippet he got more sense than a woman I know up in Kankakee. You tol' her yet about your little southern belle, boy?"

"Well hell, if you boys want to kid, all right, but I thought a long time about this. Now divide the district into four regions along the roads. . . ."

Then Epenter broke in, still looking at his cigar ash through his square spectacles. "Well, if Forrest was to hit this fort, gentlemen, what would happen? What would happen then?" Everyone turned to look at him, Epenter with the skill of a schoolteacher putting out the question everyone was think-ing anyhow, underneath the talk. He leaned forward into the si-lence. "I hope we have the assistance of the Navy. I do not trust the rebels when they go after these nigras here, nor when they go after these white Tennesseans we got. Fear is a strong thing. The rebels will be mean. They might not take any prisoners."

"They will not get into the fort. Paducah stopped them cold. They will not get up to the fort."

"At Paducah there was Colonel Hicks and the Fortieth Illinois. I knew Hicks before the war; knew him well. A stout, fine man of principle, and the Fortieth a good regiment of white men. Now what do we have here? We have two untested battalions, one of white Tennesseans and one of Negroes, both likely to raise the devil hisself in the rebels."

Yes, but look here, Epenter. We can keep the Negroes loaden the cannon and we can hit them with six artillery pieces. We are behind this wall, and they caint come over the wall to get at us, can they? We can pack the fort and the white Ten-nesseans ought to fight well enough. We got a gunboat on sta-tion out there to hit them with shells. I say we are as safe here as in downtown Memphis."

"That ain't too safe with Hurlbut in command." Everyone laughed but they kept looking at Epenter who was pursing his lips and looking at his cigar, and at Carson who was arguing with him. "Can we keep the Negroes at the guns? Can we? I doubt it. . . ."

And then Booth came in harshly, saying in a hoarse, steady

voice, with his hand thumping the table, "You cannot doubt it, Epenter. You cannot." Epenter raised his eyebrows and looked up with watery black eyes. "Neither you nor any of your men. I am sick of hearing this sort of talk, which will decay the heart out of this regiment. They are your soldiers despite their race and if they do not stay at the guns it is your fault. This is the strongest earthwork, I am convinced, north of Memphis. We have infantry, six cannon, a mounted battalion of veterans who know the region and a gunboat on station! Any officer who doubts his men and doubts them to the extent that he believes this fort will fall is a stupid and incompetent fool who should be relieved of duty!" His voice was parade-ground hoarse, Jonathan thought. He was snapped up by it. He doubted too. His final expectancy was predicated on doubting his men and that was wrong; and he was a fool. All of the men held their cigars without moving and watched Booth who was still looking straight at Epenter. Epenter lowered his eyes and seemed frozen. "You men all forget this fact. You are not officers over nigger troops. You are officers over soldiers of the United States Army, paid and armed by the government. Think of them as soldiers and treat them as such, and we can hold off a dozen Forrests. You are not paid to look at the color of the skin of your rank and file, but to look at their muskets."

He stopped for a moment. Jonathan remembered what Booth had said to him in the office when he asked for the schoolroom. He thought, oh, a hypocrite, as in college when he found that his Latin professor was having an affair with an actress. But he suspected more; the distillation of the purely practical into solid advice, into comfort, into idealism. Booth, he thought, knows the Negro, perhaps he can tell me how I ought to approach them as their officer, or at least how I ought to look upon them. He was expectant. The whole room was; Booth was attempting to inspire them and they needed it badly.

But then Booth went on, a moment after the tension and the expectancy lessened. "Oh I have no brief for the abolitionists who got us into this," and he looked straight at Seabury. Jonathan had been following him and in his mind saying, yes sir, yes sir, go on, and when Booth looked dark-eyed at him he felt like a school child being punished unfairly; he felt an end to his gust of hope. Jonathan dropped his eyes from the hollows of Booth's face.

". . . for the abolitionists. Or for the Negroes. But despite the mess they have gotten us into, the Negroes and the rebels and the abolitionists, we have got to persevere, until we win. We cannot let our Union be dissolved. We cannot, and as soldiers—and since I am a professional it is doubly true for me—as soldiers we have the duty and the opportunity to keep it together. By licking the rebels. You men think of them as another army, but they are not. They are the ragged populace of a countryside in open and envious rebellion. And we must whip them and teach them a lesson.

"Now then, I have no illusions concerning the nigger soldiers in this command. Unlike some, I have no illusions," and again Jonathan felt the bite like a sinking of teeth into his flesh. but unnecessary, a cheap appeal to the others at his expense. "I do not know whether they will fight effectively. I know they are not as good as white soldiers. But I also know I'm going to stand behind them with my revolver out and shoot them if they break, and I expect you to do the same. Shoot them if they break. You would shoot a white man for the same reason, and out of hand, so you can shoot them I reckon. Our duty is clear; that is to give our services and if need be our lives to the army and to the government. This is government soil and government property, and they are rebels. We will give our services and if need be our lives. Now for the sake of Christ have no more of this damn worrysome talk. Resolve to stand and do your duty, and you have nothing to debate." That last line came from a speech given impromptu by the captain of his company when they were barricaded in an adobe hut listening to the Indians outside and waiting for the next rush, and of course it had been more effective then. But the officers looked at their burning cigars and sat in silence, each encased in silence and unwilling to break the spell. Until Booth again said, "Pass the wine this way, boys, and we'll have some more and then a hand or two," and the room stirred. Jonathan got up in the shadows almost unnoticed and slipped out.

He got back to the room thinking, well, now I am still young and in good health, so I must not let this sort of abuse take that away from me too. Van Horn had left the lights burning and his clothes in a twisted disarray of sweat-stained shirts and dirtied jackets, in his wild and hollow-loined effort to prove his manhood upon the Negro women. The effort had grown so that it evidently required a perpetual, night by night, surging rush upon them down in the town, and it was becoming the joke of the regiment. Jonathan took off his sword and laid it on the table, where it gleamed in the lantern light, silver and brass and leather. He sat down with his back to Van Horn's armoire, but the pile of clothing grew in his mind like some weird, live crab and his neck twitched.

He picked up the sheet of paper with the now completely blurred "Fort Pillow." Jonathan looked absently at the haphazard spread of the ink stain across it, a watery wash with a black border and faint purple and green tracings. He crumpled up the paper and tossed it over his shoulder onto the floor next to Van Horn's clothing, and he pulled the pen and the ink and ream of paper to him again. He got out the fresh sheet and dipped the pen and wrote "Fort Pillow" again and "April 5th" and then he started to write, "Dear Mother, Forgive my long absence," but even as the words formed in his mind he felt the worthlessness of it all. To tell her the truth would kill her. No. It would kill something of me, in her, that I value. Just as to tell Emily would kill the same thing, and of course if I tell Mother I might as well tell Emily. I shall write to them soon. As soon as something happens. I will certainly write nothing out of all of this cycle of drill and work and humiliation at the hand of Negro and white alike and the constant seedy efforts to find something or someone worth attaching myself to. And only ending up in the cigar smoke and the parryings and thrustings of all of those men.

Even when you think Booth is the man he turns on you. He has no right to be correct about the Negroes, but he is. He was in a soundless frenzy of bitterness; it would have all been so different had the Negroes not so disappointed me. Since I left my world and came down here, he thought, the people that have offended and disappointed me the most have not been Booth and Bischoff and the others. I have been the most disappointed in the Negroes. I had expected to be reviled by the whites. Perhaps I expected too much, he thought: but he was feeling particularly betrayed. As if, somewhere, there was that world of light-hearted and full self-sacrifice, where the Negroes were not only downtrodden and mute, but were clean, noble, innocent, sufficient witnesses.

The complexities, personalities, odors, tastes of this world clustered around him. That world was being withheld from him; rather than the purity of witnessed self-sacrifice, he had found a grey nether world of flat, brutal, mindless, sensual practicality. He was restless, encrusted, trapped; nothing he had discovered, none of the warnings he had received, seemed relevant.

He got up and walked out of the room. He buttoned his coat against the pelting rain. I did not notice the rain was coming. He walked across the parade between the earth walls pierced for artillery pieces. These walls and the sally port path down to town (and that only for forays at night) encompassed his world. He felt choked to death. I cannot pretend. I need the fellowship of people, the sort of fellowship we had at college with the rooms and pipe smoke and the talks, with the balancing of ideas or rather of personal experiences, always enlarged just a little by the lateness of the hour into things that never happened. I am not made of steel. At least when I wrote home I could talk to someone. But that turned out to be too much of a lie.

He climbed up the firestep, alone except for the hooded sentinels walking in the darkness and the lantern arcs. When they walked beneath a lantern their bayonets glistened. He rubbed the rain out of his face and looked out north from the fort, into the woods. There were two points of light, one reddish and the other more yellow, in the distance, the yellow one twinkling because of the rain and mist. He could hear the rain falling into the trees. The rain was drumming off the wood and coming down harder and harder. His cap sluiced it down his back and across his temples. He was cold and chill, but he looked out into the distance. There is a tall, white sycamore out there that looks dead. I can not remember exactly where it is.

He paced up and down. Something must happen. This routine has to stop. Perhaps Forrest will come. Yes. Forrest will come. Then I can have that death I used to dream about and half believe. Wherein to prove myself all I have to do is stand still, just stand still, and hold my sword up while Booth looks on and the Negroes and the whites all turn and run, standing there and smiling. He half crouched in the crouch he would use and he worked on the smile. The rebels will cross the wall and pause for a second and then they will call out from—let's see—there at that ripped board, for me to surrender. And of course I will not, I will say "No . . ." and then what? I must work this out.

But that is not important. It will come to me. All I will have to do is stand still and not flinch and hold out my sword, perhaps spreading my arms to shield the backs of the retreating Negroes, cowering like children. All right, I will say, "Shoot me but not them" . . . or, "Take my life for theirs." And then the gunboat will drive them back—no, it must be a victory for them. The gunboat will pick up Booth and the others and they will remember how alone I stood off the rebels and sacrificed myself.

He paced along the firestep oblivious to the sentry who came by smelling of sweat and rain-soaked wool, working out his scene on the boards of the firestep. He tried to imagine the bite of the rebel steel into his flesh, but he could not. He could readily enough, though, picture the despairing, penitent men on board the gunboats watching the fort where the rebels would ceremoniously stand with uncapped heads paying more honor to him in death than ever his companions had in life. This is the beautiful thing: all that I have to do is just to stand still when they come into the fort. Just stand and face them, and all of this complexity will be reduced to simply holding the body rigid and firm and in place. I can concentrate all of my physical energies upon that one moment and that one action. He tried to imagine again how he would brace himself for their rush.

The sentry shuffling by again awoke him; he sobered and thought of course this may not happen. But, oh please God, let this much happen, that Forrest comes. Let him come. Give me the action, God, let it come to me. Dear God, break this inactivity and motionlessness. Let there be an action which will oblit-

erate this world and cleanse it. Let it be Forrest. Forrest, the
rebel who, you have to convince yourself, is indeed only a man.
He paced up and down in the night, down the long, creaking
length of the firestep and back, passing the changing sentries,
praying for the action to come. The rain did not let up; it beat
the river into a wild pattern of splashes and pocks. Lantern
light sparkled off of the heel-marked drill ground and parade,
and the cannon dazzled in the light with the rain splashing off
of the brass. Jonathan finally went back, soaked and happily
drained, and fell to sleep almost immediately. His clothes made
puddles on the floor, and the dye from his uniform coat had
blued and ruined his shirt.

7

BOB PERRY HAD BEEN HOME TO WALLS, JUST ACROSS THE MISSIS-sippi line from Memphis. Perry was in Major Perry's Fifth Mississippi Cavalry with Forrest's command, near Jackson, and he had heard one day at morning muster that ol' Bedford wanted the Memphis and Charleston railway scouted, from around where it hit the Alabama line all the way over to the river. He had stood in the rain, with his hands in his pockets, thinking, and then without even heading for breakfast he had gone over to the headquarters tent, and knocked respectfully at the tent-pole, and then walked in and saluted Major Perry. Major Perry was some relative of his, he wasn't sure where; he thought maybe a cousin. Philip Perry, though, was a good man, with a care-worn, lined face with a lot of wrinkles around his neck and chin, and small, lidded, friendly eyes. He had big hands, and he liked to put one of his hands on a young private's neck and walk a few paces with him, telling him about different things to help him along or cheer him up. He was buttoning on his frock coat in front of a mirror, and he turned around and smiled his weary, friendly, sincere smile. His eyes closed for a moment and then opened, emphasizing the smile.

"Oh yes, Robert."

"Major Perry, sir, I hear tell Forrest wants somebody to scout the railroad south of Memphis."

"Yes." Major Perry was still smiling, so Bob had gone on.

"Now Major, you know I'm a good scout, and I know that section like the back of my hand. I was raised there, and I hunted and tracked down niggers all around there, for some of

188

the plantations outside Memphis. I sure would like to scout over that way. Maybe take a day or so, look in on the homefolk, carry some mail back . . . you know."

Major Perry's thin lips closed tight. He frowned and then, moving his large hands expressively, said, "Well now, you be sure and come back, you hear?"

So he had gotten out of camp and headed for home, dodging Yankee patrols once he got up around Memphis. Which wasn't too hard. He had a real good horse, and he knew the land about as well as he reckoned anyone could. He liked the feel of being in the night air, of ducking through the shadows with the cool breath of the moon on his cheek, or into the solid blackness, finding his way half by instinct and half by the horse's sense, knowing that here he was on his own, and there wasn't another damned soul out here but what were crouched around fires or lanterns. It wasn't too different from fetching back niggers; only he didn't move in the daylight as much.

When the planters had come up to his place, the little dog-run house set back off the road a ways, with a dusty, huge oak in the front yard and him sitting on the porch with his feet up, a tickle of excitement always went through him, and he went and got his tracking stuff wordlessly, beginning to smile just a little. He was a good nigger hunter, about the best. He never hurt one of them, not the first one. He carried a double-barreled shotgun, one barrel loaded light with birdshot to chase off any plantation hounds and sting the nigger, and the other loaded with a ball and three buckshot, but he had never yet had to use the second barrel, nor the old horse pistol either. He always moved like a big cat, trying to surprise the runaways before they had a chance to bolt, and he liked to rest one foot on a stump or log, and just set and wait for them to wake up, and then flick the barrel of the shotgun down on them, and watch their eyes widen and go white and blank with fear. He hardly ever used bloodhounds. Hounds might tear up a nigger. He liked just to outthink and outhunt them, by himself.

He had grown up south of Memphis, two miles from where his little shack was before the war. He had been one of maybe fourteen children, being cuffed out of the way and working in the fields and listening to his father alternately drink and cuss. He had spent his time wandering through the hills, sometimes spending two or three days out in the autumn woods just letting the shadows and the breezes play across him, hunting his own food and staring up at the sky and feeling himself blend down into the ground. He had splashed through every creek twelve, fifteen miles away a hundred times, and wandered over all the hills, skirting the big plantations ripped out of the land because he did not like planted ground. He liked the swamps and bottoms and the leaves and the little natural meadows.

Until he moved in with his brother Simms, who cut out a little raggedy hillside farm for himself. One day word came a nigger had escaped from the Murphee place down south, and was probably headed up toward Memphis. And he had said, hell, he could track any nigger down without no dogs. Simms had laughed and said, "Le's see you it's about time you started payen for some of the food you eat around here." So he had got off his haunches and spent two days out in the countryside, patient as an ol' house cat hunting down jaybirds, not fuming and wanting to move and get it over with, but enjoying and relishing being patient because that was part of the hunting, just as much a part of it as drawing a bead. And he had fetched the nigger back to the Murphee front door, joshing the man, "Well, here we are back again. You been here before, you say," and laughing and getting paid a whopping big sum of money.

After that, and once or twice more including a time he caught a nigger before even the bills were posted, the planters came up to him, and he always smiled and obliged. He never did push at the niggers or kick 'em around. He just hauled 'em up by the scruff of the neck and kidded with 'em, fed 'em a little side meat and pone he carried with him, and started back, letting them ride every now and then while he led the horse. He had never had to shoot a one, and he had only had to knock one up side the head once, and that one was there with his wife and maybe four kids and Perry figured he was showing off. He had hit him once with the stock of the shotgun and the nigger was never the worse for it save a lump side the head. You couldn't hurt a hard-headed nigger that way. He liked niggers; they were funny, and you could fun around with them, and while a white man would try to hide something he felt, a nigger just splashed it right out, all over his face, like surprise or fear or pleasure. And, besides, they paid pretty good, and he didn't have to come too close to 'em.

When he got his leave from Major Perry, he had no trouble at all crossing the railroad three or four times, back and forth. He kept mind of which crossings were well guarded and where long stretches had nobody over 'em at all, and he tried to keep track of the trains he saw as well. He made it home in four days, and could have done it in half the time wasn't he scouting for ol' Bedford.

Bob Perry was a big, broad-shouldered man, maybe twenty-one years old. He had sandy hair and freckles and a big blond moustache, and his face didn't have any lines at all, except crow's-feet when he laughed. He liked to laugh. Perry had hunted niggers from the time he was fourteen, which only gave him about four good years at it, since the war came and he had jumped right in. He had been in an infantry regiment for a couple of years and shot two Yankees for sure, and strangled a third, all at the battles up in Kentucky. When he got the chance, he joined the cavalry.

He reached home in a driving spring rain. The place was deserted and weed-choked. He kicked his way inside after stabling the horse and tending it, and got a fire going. The place was musty and dank and it leaked. Simms had pulled up and left a long time ago, he figured. He had gone to sleep with the rain driving down outside, smelling dust and rotting wood. The next day was clear, so he spent the morning delivering the letters from his company around to the families. A lot of people weren't there any more, he found out, and at one place there were some niggers and a Yankee overseer working the fields, and some bluecoats with rifles out back of the house. He had put Jaycee at the gallop and cleared out, shocked and rather bothered at the thought he might have just ridden up and smiled and gotten shot right down, hadn't he seen the Yankees out back. Things shore do change.

He had lunch at the Tige place, and kissed old, withered

Miz Tige on the cheek and told her Tommy was doing just fine, and lent a hand clearing stumps for about an hour with Mr. Tige, who was too old to do much good by himself.

Then he went up to the Blackford place, and when he had seen Suellen out behind the house in the pale spring sunlight, red-headed and round and short, he had instantly gotten excited. He rode up and she looked up from a washtub and shaded her eyes and then came running over, shiny-faced and sort of jiggling all over. He climbed off the horse grinning like a fool, knowing damn good and well this was why he had even asked for the job in the first place. He hugged her up to him, feeling her breasts and thighs through the dirty print dress and his own grey jacket and jean pants. He ran his hands along the arches of her back, and then looked at her face, and kissed her, and then held her at a distance, and looked some more, and kissed her again. She came about to his neck, and she had a tiny little waist and a good figure. She had big brown eyes and a slightly twisted small nose, and a full, tiny mouth. She was even better than he remembered. He kissed her some more and then she jerked away, embarrassed, and said maybe her parents were looking, and besides give her a chance to get cleaned up. He gave her the letters from Jamie and then she asked him over for supper that night. He squeezed her again and said sure and went on back home after they had talked a few more minutes.

He found a piece of mirror in the storm-scattered rubble on the floor of Simm's old place, and spent five minutes or so straightening himself. Whew, if she got so excited looken at this pore ol' face, wait till I get slicked up a whit. He shaved himself with the old razor from his kit and a little piece of soap Mrs. Tige had given him. He brushed off his jean pants as best he could, and sewed three buttons back onto his single-breasted grey jacket. When he strapped on the crossbelt he figured he didn't look too bad—at least he looked military. He took the faded pine sprig off his battered grey hat, and found a blue-jay feather, pearly-white shading into brilliant sky-blue, with purplish markings. He tucked up the side of his hat and pushed the feather through the slits to hold the brim in place. He was whistling, and he got excited again thinking about her, and hoped it would wear off with the ride.

Mr. Blackford, yellow-faced and splotched with liver spots, talked about the war and how things were going, and how if they had Lee out here instead of Johnston and Bragg and that ruck, he reckoned it would be a different story. Supper, side meat again and greens and some onions for flavor, which Suellen and Bob Perry studiously avoided, was served on cracked chinaware plates in the kitchen of the Blackford place. Mrs. Blackford, lean and sag-hipped and almost toothless, cackled and beamed with pride when he told her what a fine trooper ol' Jamie was making. The fire in the hearth was stifling; he desperately wanted to get Suellen out in the backyard or at least in the front room. He poked at his food, laughing and carrying on about some Blackford relatives over in Holly Springs he'd never heard of. "Yes'm, I bet you was surprised at that." He sure did want to get alone with Suellen. The thought made him excited all over, and he had to shift in his seat. He had brought some canned meats for the Blackfords that they had taken from the Yankees back at Okolona; they raved over that, and Mr. Blackford kept on about what a fool Jeffy Davis was, how he'd known Davis back before the war and 'y God, back then he was no planter and that was God's truth. The hearth fire bubbled in the ashes. Perry kept on thinking, well now, I must have gotten the hard part of it over with, they must be about through. He kept looking at Suellen, and her eyes flashed at him, and he shifted. I'm sweaten like an ol' stuck pig, he thought nervously, and then wondered what a stuck pig sweated like. He fidgeted around the edges of his plate. There was a cold draft down his neck; bad crack in the wall, mud must've gotten loose from the heat of th' fireplace. God, God, whyn't they go ahead and leave me an ol' Suellen by ourselves?

Mrs. Blackford said, "Well, le's leave the young folks to theirselves," but Mr. Blackford kept on. "Well now, when I heard tell that Johnston was in command over at Dalton I said to myself I said now there's a change for the better. . . ."

"Yessir, of course, anything after Bragg would be bound to be for the better I reckon. . . ."

"Just what I tol' myself. Just what I said, I said . . ."

God, God, will he never shut up? Suellen was moving around clearing off the table, but he couldn't trust himself to glance at her, since he would get excited again and it would show, and he had to get up when ol' man Blackford left. If he ever leaves, which is about as likely as snow in July. He wished suddenly he was out in the cold, clear nighttime. That was his place, outside in the night. He was choking.

Then they were gone upstairs to the attic bedroom all the family had taken to sleeping in ever since Memphis had fallen and the Yankees had started using nigger troops. Blackford kept a big shotgun loaded at hand, up in the attic room.

Suellen smiled at him across the table, and she looked so round and her breasts were so soft-looking he nearly died. She smiled at him from under her eyebrows teasingly. He nearly made a lunge for her right across the table.

"Let's go outside for a little air, hunh, Suellen?"

She balked. 'Twas cold outside. 'Sides, she mightn't be safe.

"Hell, take a coat. I'll protect you."

"Whose goen to protect me from you?" Giggle. " 'Sides, you shouldn't talk to a young lady like that."

He slid around the edge of the table. 'Y God, I got to grab hold of her in another minute. She was smiling and her lips were gleaming and soft. Her waist was so tiny. . . .

"I'se sorry, Suellen. Listen, le's go outside for a while. Just for a while."

"All right." She turned her back and pulled on a shawl and then smiled over her shoulder. "You be good now, you hear?" He nearly died. Sweat was drooling down all inside his uniform blouse and checked shirt.

Outside they sat on the porch. It was sheltered by the roof from the attic window, he noted. He reached immediately for her, and tried to kiss her.

"Hold on." She smiled at him. "You oughn't go grabben for a young lady that way. You promised to be good. Let's sit here and talk like white folks."

He thought, I ain't never promised to be good. But he was outside at least. The night was clear and moon-washed, and he knew the rains were over for a time. He felt he could blend into the shadows out here, and it was cool and he was part of the sweet spring night. He could wait. They talked aimlessly about things, about Jamie and the war and he listened while she told him how hard things was getten since they couldn't travel safe even in the daytime because of the freed niggers, and the Yankees had nigger troops and a decent white girl wasn't safe in Memphis anyway.

"Aw now, Suellen . . ." he said doubtingly.

She flared up. "Why Bob Perry! I sweah you don't know what you are talken about. You caint trust 'em one step, sure enough you caint. Why, they'd as soon as . . . as soon as . . . as look at you!" Her voice broke. She was looking away and her chin was tilted up.

So would I, he thought. As soon as look at you. He started talking about his plans after the war. He wanted to move out west. To Texas, maybe. Wanted to farm some land of his own, or maybe something . . . he wasn't sure what. He was tired of Mississippi, and he didn't think whichever way the war went there would be much left to hold on to around here. She flustered for a moment about of course the South will whip, but she was interested in his plans, so she shut up after a sentence. He almost said, "Anyway, there won't be much use for a nigger hunter," but he didn't because you just didn't go around sayen that you were a nigger hunter. So he said "trapper" instead, since it sounded good and she knew what he meant, even if he didn't say nigger hunter. Hell, he didn't even know what a trap was. "But I reckon I got a good pair of shoulders and hands, and I can do a good job at whatever I take a mind to. . . ."

She nodded assent. They both sat and looked for a while longer at the moon. It was a clear, washed silver coin, and the sky was purple around it.

He pulled her over to him, much more gently this time. The hot urgency had drifted away, and he felt sweet and warm inside. He kissed her on the lips. Her lips were soft and after sort of nibbling experimentally at them he put his arms around her and hugged her and kissed her over and over. She leaned over to put her arms around his shoulder, and her breasts were suddenly right in front of his hands. Well, now, I be damned. They were pushed out, the way she was leaning. He carefully fitted his right hand around her breast. She made a snuffling noise of protest, but he pushed his lips against her mouth again, and never let off squeezing her bosom, softly.

She drew back and put a hand to her hair and said something, trying to look calm again and cool, and he nearly busted out laughing because all the time he had a hand on her tit, and kept on squeezing it. They kissed some more, and he slid around until both his hands were on her dress front, and started handling the buttons. She had her arms around his neck, and kept on kissing, their lips making tiny wet sounds. She would gasp every now and then. The buttons were the most maddening things he had ever come across in his life, he decided. And she wasn't much help, not by a damn sight, saying, "No, no, no," over and over in a whisper, between kisses, and fumbling around with his hands. Finally he had the thing open, and he was so excited he was about to explode, a white pleasurable pain all through his genitals. But he didn't quite know what to do, he couldn't just throw her down or push her back and get to her. He fumbled around some more with her breasts. There was some coarse old thing in front of them, and he tried to push his fingers over it and it sounded like she gasped with pain, and then finally he was just about to say to hell with it. But then she said, "Hit buttons too," or something, and she made some moves with her hand and there he was. Her breasts were hanging there all of a sudden, soft and round with small brown nipples, and he squeezed them and worked them in his hands. They were so smooth, he had never felt anything that smooth before.

"Hit's the war. I'd never ever let anyone do this . . . if hit wasn't the war."

"Hunh? Oh yes. Oh yes."

He bent and kissed the exposed breasts, thinking, Now that was one hell of a funny thing to say.

"Do you love me, Bob? Do you love me?"

"Yes. 'Y God, you know I do. You know I do." He kissed her warm, wet mouth, pulling her against him. He did, he really did love her to pieces. He was just about to make some other move, do something else since he was still about to bust all over, when there was a noise behind them. Instantly he felt hollow and afraid and his heart caught in his throat. Her hands flew in the moonlight, soft white birds flickering over the dress and buttoning it, and he was left with a sickish, empty feeling, and still as damned excited as ever. It was quiet again in the house, and they breathed easier.

Suellen said, "Bob, oh Bob, I never let anyone do that, I never did."

"I know, I know." She did look beautiful though in the clear light from the silver moon, and her eyes were big and moist and there was spring everywhere, and oh Christ he wished he was this minute laid up in a big old feather bed with her.

"Did you, did you ever make love to a girl . . . before, Bob? Hunh?"

"No, I never did. I never." That was a lie. He had loved old Betty Crawford over in Natchez, long time back. But she was skinny as a pole and twice as ugly. No tits. Chewed snuff too. There just wasn't any comparison.

"You musta tolt girls you loved 'em before, Bob. You musta. . . ."

"Well yes, I did, but I never meant it before this minute, I never did. I swear to God I never did. . . ."

"Did you ever . . . did you ever go to bed with a girl, Bob?"

"No." No dammit, that was the damn truth. He had never.

"Oh Bob," and suddenly they were kissing again, and he held her in his arms and felt all full of love, like the darkness and the long hours in the moonwash hunting for runaway niggers could just be washed out of him by his love. Then her mother was calling and he was saying, "Yes'm, yes'm, I got to be going back tomorra. Yes'm, I'll tell him, I surely will. . . ."

He kissed her once more, and promised to think of her every day just at dusk. He stood in the moonlight holding her to him, arrow-straight and rigid and her pulled tight to him and everything was round and lovely in the white light. He set old Jaycee at the gallop, and they fairly flew along the muddy roads, a wide, dark shadow thrown out in front of him, and he wished he had him a whole passel of Yankees right now right in front of him, so he could ride right over 'em.

The Winter and Spring of 1863–1864   **197**

The very next day he sure did get the chance to. It was one of those early spring days, cold enough the night before to frost, but warm and glowing in the sunlight, with the earth just beginning to move and stir. In the fields on each side of the road winter-browned stubble lay matted over the red earth, and gave, slipping, when his horse pushed down. He had just taken off his overcoat and thrown it across the blanket roll behind him. The sun was warm, and he moved his shoulders inside the blouse, and thought some more about ol' Suellen. He was figuring how he could slip off and spend some more time with her, and whistling aimlessly. He got excited thinking about her and shifted in the saddle and just let the horse have his way.

The road dropped down beside a small stream, which was rocky and choked with green ice and red mud. Now he knew exactly where he was, and where the road was going: he knew it would dip once more, down beside the stream, and then it would cross the railroad tracks beside a trestle and a blockhouse. The blockhouse was garrisoned by maybe two platoons, and he figured he would have to cut back into the woods and he even knew just the knoll above the railroad cut where he could lie in a stand of pine and take a long look at the blockhouse. But he got his ground mixed up: for the first time in twenty-one years his sure instinct let him down, not severely but by a distance of perhaps thirty yards. Because in the first place he got the dips mixed up in his aimless prurient driftings beneath the hot winter sun already thinking about asking Major Perry for another bit of leave, thinking about the next time he would see Suellen and maybe how it would be late spring and would be nice outside and how the tall, soft grass in the fields would feel beneath their weight, thinking about how nice and soft the air was. In all of this he had miscounted the stretches of the road, and he had already passed the first dip down beside the stream. And in the second place he ordinarily would have sensed the presence of Yankee troops but somehow in the smell of the fields and in the delicious feel of the warm air and the crisp, cool breeze, he missed that too. So naturally, in a moment out of context and unlike any other moment in all of his life, he had abandoned himself to the purely sensual animal enjoyment of everything with absolutely none of the accompanying instinctive caution, and of course he rode right into the back of a group of Yankees.

They were out washing clothes, about ten Yankee nigger soldiers. Their rifles were slung and they were taking halting, short steps with the great baskets of laundry held in front of them, and they were leaning backwards and talking. And he could not have been more than ten paces from them; he saw in one moment of self-accusative clarity and horror and humor the blue uniforms with the sunlight warm off the cloth, and the black shining flesh and the brass button on one of the kepis winking in the sun, and the kinky hair of the nearest one and the musty smell of them and the thick smell of the soap, and their bootprints in the mud. They were going back to the blockhouse which was right in front of them.

Fear and the hot need for action rose through him and his hair bristled, but he was grinning too, grinning at his own stupidity and thinking somehow, what a story this will be to tell, what a story. He got the horse turned around on the muddy road at the moment the nigger sergeant heard the slopping of the hoofs and turned and saw him. His back felt curiously exposed, cold now that the sun was off it and in his face and he was not wearing the overcoat. He twitched, and while the horse gathered its weight on the hind legs for the thrusting first stride, he shoved his fingers past the trigger guard of the rifle across his thighs. And he was laughing. At the sheer humor of the thing; at the irony of having for years done precisely the opposite to runaway niggers, slipping up on them, and how he had to go and ride right into a mess of them. But he was laughing at the horror of it too; much more horrible than having stumbled into an ambush, because he had come across them out of a clear blue sky. Out of warmth and lasciviousness and the innocent pleasure of the flesh, he had ridden right into them and they were there in a close, heart-stopping proximity.

He got the horse turned around and there was a field on his right and the creek on his left, so he spurred it to the right straight for a stand of little pine trees about fifty yards down the road at the edge of the field. He turned around in the saddle and swung the rifle, still in his lap, in the direction of the Yankees. He saw the sergeant with his blouse open and the buttons winking, and there were spilled white baskets of laundry.

He squeezed the trigger of the rifle; it hurt his wrist when it went off. There was the clear sharp odor of the rifle smoke, and then he bent low over the horse's neck and concentrated on making it to the stand of pine. The horse was having trouble in the mud and its hoofs tore up clods of it and made a pathetic, hollow sound. There were rifle shots and he quivered all over; things went past him. Twenty yards. Still the clatter and suck of the horse's hoofs, and the beat of the warm sun, and shouts behind him. 'Y God I never felt so damn helpless in all my life. I ain't goen to make it. Then it was ten yards and, yes I am, I done made it and oh my Lord but won't this make one hell of a story. He was pressing the side of his face against the horse's neck and really flogging it; and he was looking suddenly at a little pillar of ice that had come out of the mud bank on the right side of the road, in the shadow of a clump of sedge, pale-white and stained with traces of mud. Thinking, five yards beyond that and here we go into the woods. And then something went right past his ear and he heard it hit the horse's skull right behind the ears. He heard it hit and he could hear the reverberation inside the skull, and he thought, just like a bullet in a watermelon, and then the horse died right under him, in lurching midstride. The ground came up and hit him, all the world spinning up against the left side of him.

He was dazed and he shook his head and it hurt; his face was a few inches from the tiny, fragile columns of hoarfrost in the road, and the ground was cold and there was blue pain all over his left side. Ol' horse was dead fore it ever hit the ground, he thought. He fished out his revolver and looked over toward the stand of pine trees and thought, I'm close enough to make it easy. Then the great weight on his left leg came to him, and he looked down and realized that the horse was pinning him to the ground. Well, I be damned.

He turned his head painfully toward the niggers, his neck stretching. One of them fired at him, a fragile burst of blue powder smoke, and all of him jumped into his throat, and then the bullet thudded into the horse. He hefted the revolver, and it felt good and powerful. Hell, there's a dozen of 'em. I'm in one pretty ol' mess, I am. "All right, all right." He pitched the revolver away from him. The sky was bright and fresh-washed, and the sun was dazzling, and he could hear the voices of the Negroes and the drip from the ice-coated pine needles in the woods.

The Negroes were standing in the muddy road, their wash spread in bundles and strands and soaking up red stain from the mud. They were loading their rifles and some of them kept on banging away at him. He flinched and yelled, "All right, goddamnit, all right, I done give up! Come ahead!" The sergeant was yelling at the others. They all stood and stared at Perry. "Come and get this ol' dead hoss off me." The sergeant pulled out his bayonet and put it on his gun barrel. They all started toward him, walking as if on fragile ice. He watched their steam breath rise in spurts as they walked. They holding their breath, 'y God. They're more scared of me than I am of them.

They stopped and stood in a cautious semicircle, ten yards away, holding their rifles still on him. He shifted restlessly. The horse was hurting him, his leg was all afire it seemed and at the same time it was going all numb. "Come on, come on! Get this hoss off me!" He sucked in air through his teeth in pain and frustration. Goddamn stupid niggers. Glad to be shet of 'em, yessir. The sergeant was a big ol' nigger, with welts across his face and his jacket unbuttoned, the bright buttons hanging loose. Ugliest nigger I ever did see, Perry thought. His leg was really hurting him, cold and numb and yet prickling, and he felt like he couldn't breathe, pressed down against the road, and that was making him angry.

"Well goddamnit, get over here an' get this hoss off me I said!"

They started walking down on him again, still holding their rifles pointed at him and stepping heel-toe, heel-toe. He made frustrated pulling motions at his leg. Tears were trickling down his face, but he knew that was the shock more than anything else. Damn it, damn it. Good ol' joke on me though. Yessir, ride right into the back of a roadful of niggers, could've smelled 'em a mile off. Yessir, tracken for a liven and then ride right up to 'em. They had stopped a few feet away and were looking down at him now. He squinted and started to curse and then thought, hell, that ain't goen to get anything done. "Come on, boys. Come on. Lend a hand." The Negro sergeant put the tip of his bayonet into the trigger guard of Perry's pistol, and then tossed it into the grass. Then he stepped forward. Perry was struggling with both hands at his knee, trying to get the leg free, with his tongue between his teeth.

The Negro sergeant with the pale-yellow face and the pink welts across it rested one foot on the horse, and Perry looked up suddenly and querulously and then the sergeant touched the bayonet of his rifle against the flesh of Bob Perry's neck. Perry was about to say, "How about lenden a hand down here?" and then he didn't say anything, he just looked up that shining-bright steel blade and the long rifle barrel, up at the Negro's face. And at the mottled hands holding the rifle, and then he saw that the Negro was smiling. Not the others standing around open-mouthed, but this one was smiling.

"I know you, white boy. I seen you, ain't I?"

His teeth were small and black and his lips were pink, the same color as the welts. "I remember one time you fetched Lonnie Boy back to the ol' Isbell place, I remember that time."

Bob Perry started to grin and nod and say, yes he remembered that too, but then the bayonet shoved harder against his throat and he felt he was going to choke on it. He put his left hand up on the blade and frowned, and tried to twist away from it. But the sergeant just pushed harder. Another Negro came over, with a wide, large nose and a thin moustache across his upper lip. "Yeah, I remember him too. Name Bob Perry. Ol' Isbell he used to say, he said, you han's take a notion to run away an' ol' Bob Perry he track you down."

All of the Negroes had crowded around now, a circle of brown and yellow and black faces, anonymous under blue caps with brass buttons and letters on them. Perry looked down at his leg, still under the horse, cold now and hurting. "Unhh— well now, how about given me a han' with this horse, hunh?" He stopped struggling after a minute, and then looked up and blinked, handsome and blond and white-faced. He ran his tongue over his lips.

But he was only scared for a minute, the minute it took all of his natural reactions to take hold of him again, the minute it took him to forget about his leg and how it hurt, and how heavy the horse was and how the bayonet seemed to be choking him. Hell, these are niggers. Don't know any more than any ol' fiel' han' about killen. Won't kill no white man. No sir. Too smart for that. Nigger ain't gonna kill any white man.

He put his hand on the hard, cold steel of the bayonet, and he didn't smile any more. He looked straight up at the sergeant with the flesh-colored welts on his yellow face, and he pushed the bayonet away, or tried to. "Get that thing out of my throat, nigger. And get this hoss off of my laig."

The Negroes were all closed around him, on the road, their shadows blocking out the sunlight, and the sergeant shoved the bayonet right back in his throat and brought a sting of blood. "It ain't that way no mo', white man. It ain't never gonna be that way no mo'. You ain't never gonna run ol' nigger down in the swamps with yo dogs an' yo shotgun. Ever. I'm goen to kill you, right here."

"Naw you ain't, you know it. . . ." He pushed again at the bayonet at his throat, and was about to tell them to quit and to get the horse off and get him to a white man. It no more occurred to him that they would kill him than that his dog might tear out his throat. He was thinking about how bad his leg was hurting, and how they could get the horse off and maybe look him up a doctor. He was also mad because they were clustered around him in the road, and he felt like they were like to smother him to death. If you ain't goen to get this thing off my laig, at least get somebody that will, he was about to say.

The Negro sergeant raised the rifle, and it wasn't in his throat any more, as he was forming the words. But out of the corner of his eye he saw it; it was against his ear lobe, and the long length of the rifle barrel was shining in the sunlight. And suddenly he knew he was about to die, and that tickled him. It sure did. In another second the whole goddamn thing was so stupid he would have laughed, he knew.

The sergeant with the yellow face pulled the trigger, and in the split second of time, amazement and amusement and the continual sensual perception of life—the cold, prickling feeling of his leg, the blue feel of pain, and shadows making him cold across the shoulders after the blaze of sunlight—all of this came to him. So he really died just like he had lived, with the uncaring and unselfconscious feel of the world, and he didn't have any sense of loss or sorrow or even fear, just a series of physical perceptions suddenly cut short by a blow against the side of his head, the last thing coming to his eyes being the hair of his horse's mane where mud had caught in it, and him thinking, got to wash that off Jaycee.

His head was blown off, for the most part. The ball-and-buck army issue splattered his brains and his bone fragments and blood and blond hair all over the ground and across the legs and shoes of the Negro soldiers standing around him. A couple of the Negroes jumped back, and the others showed shock in their faces for a second, but the sergeant raised his rifle and slung it on his shoulder without hesitating and turned away and said, "Buck and Whitemeat, y'all fetch that ol' nigger hunter's body over this way fo' me."

"Ol' nigger hunter, he sho was one fooled man," Buck said. "Sho was."

They all got the horse off the body of the nigger hunter, shoving at the carcass and then pulling the body free and laughing and talking again, like they had been when they were washing their clothing and blankets in the creek. "Ol' white man he sho was su-prized I mean to say."

"Seed he once over at McCollum."

"He was sho not thinken he was goen to die way he come riden up like that."

"Nawsuh he wadn't."

When they got him free, covered with mud and blood and his leg at a funny angle, they carried the body about a mile down the road, in the early morning with the fields tawny and the sky blue. Their breath came in steam, and the yellow-faced sergeant found a tree by the side of the road, a stunted old blackjack oak. Buck and Whitemeat were shiny with sweat from the carrying. They had worked on the Isbell plantation, where the yellow-faced sergeant had been the chief field hand, so they did what he said. Sometimes the others would not. Give a nigger a gun, the yellow-faced sergeant thought, an' he don't have no more sense than a ol' mule. Gits ideas. But he could make Buck and Whitemeat do the work that had to be done at the blockhouse, even if the others were worse than any passel of house niggers.

They put Bob Perry's body up against the stunted grey tree, and spread out the arms, and strapped him down with his own belt and cartridge crossbelt. The body sagged down, and the flesh was white and green. The whole back of the skull had been torn away, and while they were carrying the body blood had splattered out over them and over the ground. "Man this white man sho do bleed heavy." When the body was in place against the tree, one eyelid closed and the other blue eye staring emptily at the sky, the yellow-faced sergeant opened the blouse and the trousers, and went to work with his bayonet, carving and hacking just like he had carved and hacked up the meat after the hog-killen back on the plantation. The other Negroes stood around loosely, talking and laughing some. Most of them had known of Bob Perry, the nigger hunter, best in the State of Mississippi.

After the yellow-faced sergeant had finished and had stepped back, so there was more blood on the white, white body and on the ground and on the dried mud, they all looked and one of them, Bentman from up the river a ways, whistled and said, "He sho is dead. Sergeant, I reckon he sho is dead!" and they all laughed. The sergeant looked up at the body. "Come heah, nigger. Get this hoss off me, nigger. I fetch you back, nigger." He started laughing, his whole chest and shoulders shaking, and saying, "heeheeheee." Then he said, "I'm gone fix me a sign fo you, white man. I be back in a while."

They all turned and walked back down the road, loose and swinging their arms and wrists, and talking. The yellow-faced sergeant walked behind them a ways, moving cat-like and wiping the bayonet off on a leaf.

They put the laundry back in the wicker baskets, and went

back to the blockhouse. The little blockhouse stood on a cleared spot near a long trestle of fresh-cut wood stretched out in fantastic rectangles and beams and sap-drooling pilings over the stony little creek. The place smelled of the wood, and shavings from the lumber were scattered over the raw dirt, amid the tree stumps. The little blockhouse was so small that they could not live in it, so there were two tents, built up and boarded and furnished with mud and log chimneys next to it. The place was isolated and lonely, and mist still hung in the trees near the creek, and the snow and ice from around Christmastime was white and black below the crests of the hills above it.

Lieutenant Schumacher was waiting for them in the door of the little blockhouse. He had put the rest of the detail on duty with their rifles balanced in the loopholes. The laundry detail came straggling up the road, carrying the baskets of laundry.

He put the revolver back in the holster. "We heard the shooting, sergeant. What was it?" He was tall and pinch-faced with big muscles in his jaws and cheeks, and a wide brown moustache. His eyes were pressed, and there were ridges between his eyebrows. He was nervous and mad.

"Jest shooten at some ol' jackrabbit, sah."

Schumacher played with his sword hilt. "Well goddamn it all, man, we were all ready for a rebel attack after that volley."

"Yes sah."

"Well man, you should have told us!"

"Yes, sah." The sergeant was impassive, ugly, his face thick.

The lieutenant prodded with his gloved hands into the basket of laundry. There were red mud stains on a white shirt. Oh Lord, he thought, oh Lord, are these niggers stupid and dumb as the beasts of the field. And he thought, three more days, three more days out here before they come with the relief. He paced up and down the track next to the blockhouse, listening to the Negroes laughing over at one of the cooking fires, hearing the rattle of rifles. God, are they worthless creatures, he thought. They will surely kill us all! Waste powder on a rabbit. Drop washing in the mud. 'Y God, are they worthless. The

206   *The Falling Hills*

smell of the Negro tent, musty and thick, came to him. And they smell to high heaven; don't smell like any white man.

The hills closed down on him, and he was nervous and mad because they had scared him to death, with half his men out washing clothes and him hearing all the shooting. He quit pacing after a while, and thought, well, hell, nothing came of it, did it?

He smiled, and walked back into his separate tent, feeling with a keen sensual pleasure the clean, scrubbed board floor and the precision-folded blankets, and the play of the clean winter sunlight across the canvas. He sat at his desk to continue to fill out his reports, and he thought he might write a letter this morning to his wife in Indianapolis.

By the fire the Negroes were squatting and staring at the coffee pot, and laughing occasionally. "Ol' white man, he sho was fooled when ol' sergeant pull thet trigger." And they all laughed, not from vengeance or satisfaction but from just the innocent humor of seeing a man that surprised by what had happened. No one felt sorry for Bob Perry. Or even very glad that he was dead. He had been a thing from the times of their slavery, and it was interesting to have seen him up close. In open-mouthed innocence they had watched the sergeant kill him, but then the sergeant would do things like that 'cause he was the overseer, the top nigger, over at the Isbell place. "Ol' sergeant, he one mean nigger."

"Yeah, white boy he found that out I reckon." And they all laughed.

The yellow-faced sergeant squatted in the winter-thinned trees above the creek, near a patch of unmelted, rotten snow. He had a thin shingle, and he wrote on it with a thick piece of charcoal. He finished the sign and knotted some rope to it, and stared with yellow eyes down at the water. Ol' nigger hunter, he thought, ol' nigger hunter brought back my people with dogs and with handcuffs, and with a shotgun. I had to stand there while they came back and got tol' off, or got cut with the whip. I didn't have to stand there this mawnin, I reckon. He sho was su-prised when I blew his head clean off.

8

WHEN FORREST FIRST MADE HIS PRESENCE KNOWN IN WEST TENNES-
see, the skein of Union garrisons, blockhouses, river forts and
railroad stockades reacted all along its length with a spasmodic
quiver and jerk. They threw into Memphis report after report
along the toy-like military telegraph systems, all of the reports
claiming Forrest in their immediate neighborhoods and all of
them calling for reinforcements. The federal garrison commanders, colonels for the most part commanding hometown
boys riveted and locked into narrow stinking blockhouses or
stockades, looked into the distance at dust clouds and listened
to distant plosive sounds coming out of the prairie distance
or the breast-like hills, and were desperately afraid. They paced
up and down past the holstered revolvers and racked guidons
and pictures of Lincoln and stroked their beards. The federal
colonels would think about the young men they commanded
and what would Mrs. Schumacher think with Davy dead. They
would watch Davy standing at mindless ease at his picket post,
and they would think, this is a stinking war. It is a damned waste
to ask fine young men to die for this forsaken corner of Tennessee. What will happen after all to the course of this war if one
more post falls? A career is not worth the spattered blood and
brains of Davy Schumacher and Lloyd Elliot and the other boys.
They would take more pacing steps and stop and look at the wall
and think, of course this place is not strong enough to hold out
Forrest. They would have a quick image of Forrest, wrathful
and animal-like, his bare hands tearing through the doorway to
get at the young men inside. With that lack of perspective that

comes to men closely connected for a long time with a military operation or a political campaign, they were absolutely confident that their post, constructed though it might be by the finest military engineers of the department, could not be held; indeed, that it was not worth the holding. One by one, and often not to Forrest himself but to the name Forrest, sent in by one of his grinning brigadiers who would refuse to present himself "because Forrest is not in the habit of conferring with officers of lesser rank," the forts and blockhouses fell. Everything ended anticlimactically with the boys marching out without rifles and squinting in the light, tousle-haired and drained of emotion, while the tough young rebel troopers loafed and grinned at them. Duckworth took six-hundred Federals out of Union City that way, from a Yankee Colonel Hawkins who had the incredible bad luck to surrender twice to Forrest's commands. He did this while General Brayman with a trainload of infantry was coming down the rails an hour away, to detrain in a flurry of oaths and curses and the settling dust of the rebel cavalry.

Forrest kept companies and battalions of his men in to the roads miles on either side of his main column. They hit anything in sight, busting into the hated Colonel Hurst at Bolivar and sending him hatless into Memphis. By the end of March, after being in Tennessee for a two-week period, Forrest was sending out a column of six-hundred federal prisoners and feeding and mounting his men all over West Tennessee and Kentucky. Forrest himself, the day after Duckworth captured Union City for him, took his men into Paducah after horses and saddles. Some of the Negro soldiers ran away from their posts when the rebels came into the town, but a federal Colonel Hicks packed six-hundred Illinois troops shoulder to shoulder in an earthwork. Hicks had been waiting for Forrest for two weeks and saying, "There is an awful shaking among the timid but the righteous are as bold as a lion," this sort of thing in the middle of a telegraphic dispatch to Hurlbut. It must have been received sardonically to say the least, because Hurlbut had thirteen thousand men with him in Memphis and was still afraid for the town.

In Paducah, Forrest pushed his men through alleys. They

kept up a steady fire on the fort, kicking up flashes of earth and splintering the timber palisades, and the Federals in turn kept their heads down. The *Peosta* came into the dock area and opened her ports right on top of the cobblestones and shelled the rebels hard. The sailors and their officers, packed and stifling inside their iron shell, peered around the fat black guns trying to see the effects of their firing. Bullets whined and ricocheted off the sides and occasionally came into the ports and hit the sailors. They would drop to the sanded deck bleeding and whimpering, and the din was hideous and it was very hot. But of course, with the professional certainty of their own effectiveness, the Union sailors were very sure they were keeping the rebels scattered. Their officers enjoyed the work and the sense of being able to flick away a whole wall of a house.

The rebels hid in the muddy ditches or the alleys or under the houses and kept up a steady rifle fire and there was finally a truce for an hour and they came out and stretched for a while. Forrest sent in the standard surrender command that, despite his shortcomings in the language, he had evolved on his own and which was undeniably effective: "If you surrender you shall be treated as prisoners of war, but if I have to storm your works you may expect no quarter." Hicks of course laughed and said, come and take it. Meanwhile Forrest was very happily burning bales of cotton, a steamboat and a drydock at the river, and even finding some splendid horses and new saddles for his command. They settled back to the exchange of gunfire and the *Peosta* kept up the thundering salvoes which were ripping great holes in the houses and tearing up strips of earth.

Then Colonel Thompson, a southern cavalryman in the grand style and wearing a lined cape, came up the street with his brigade of four-hundred Kentuckians. Captain Tyler, who was trying out his revolver on some Federals scampering for the fort, asked him where he was going. "To take that fort." Tyler assumed it was under orders so he asked if he could ride beside him. They kept formation down the length of the street, behind a row of houses which kept the federal shellfire off of them. Then, again in the grand manner, Thompson whipped off his hat and let out his long hair, creased by now with sweat, and pulled out his saber. His gold-braided sleeve flashed in the spring sunlight, and his uniform was dark and brushed and handsome since this was his homecoming. The bugler with a tasseled trumpet gave the charge and they hit the open space going full out for the fort. It was senseless, since there was nothing they could do if they got there except mill about outside, because of the ditch and the abatis. But Thompson had brought his men home, and this was the way things were done.

Forrest had not ordered and did not even know about the charge until they told him Thompson was dead while he was counting out the saddles and inspecting the horses on the other side of town. But the Kentuckians charged straight for the fort whooping and with the banners flowing and flapping, the blue St. Andrew's cross on the red field brave in the sunlight and the horses' manes tossing and the men waving their hats and giving the yell, a mass of beautiful horseflesh and young and handsome men with the edged brilliance of swords and uniforms and rifles. Hicks, leonine, watched them coming and walked down the firing line telling his men to keep low and he'd give the word, magnificently oblivious to the rebel rifle fire which was spitting all around him. They got to within twenty-five yards of the earthwork and then the six-hundred Illinois boys rose up on the firestep and sighted just for an instant into the hurtling mass of men in front of them and then squeezed the triggers and immediately reached for cartridges. But when the smoke cleared there was no need for any further volleying, and Colonel Hicks rejoiced in the Lord's strength that had littered the ground in front of him with shattered men and horses. Thompson had been chopped out of his saddle and went down still unhatted and still sad-eyed, almost at his own back door. The live men scrambled back for the rebel lines around the houses, feeling burned from the rifle fire around them, with spit still hanging out of their mouths. The wounded struggled to crawl away.

They then settled down to some more desultory firing and small wounds from flying splinters or glass. Forrest cursed Thompson for a damned fool and for costing him twenty-five dead men and a hundred wounded, but Thompson of course was stone dead in a splayed clump, his sword outthrust and his face in the ground, and his clothes jerked up around his chest and over his neck. The cape and blouse and white shirt had pulled up and over his tangled, muddy hair, and the fat white flesh of his back was showing in the chill March wind. Forrest pulled out after staying ten hours and doing everything he had set out to do, including finding the horses and leather. The Federals in the fort stood up and cheered and patted each other on the back and then set out souvenir-hunting among the dead rebels until their officers told them to stop and Hicks said a prayer. On the riverboat they stopped shelling the houses and the captain sent around grog for all hands, the men putting their porkpie caps back on and the officers congratulating each other on their gunnery which had stopped Forrest. They counted it a big victory. The news spread along the skein of the river and railroad forts and suddenly everyone assumed Forrest was just bluffing. Hold on, do not surrender to a handful of rebels, and you can drive them away even if Forrest is with them, because did not old Hicks do that at Paducah?

Every day Bradford with Leaming at his side made his way up the tangled, weed-choked path from the town to the fort. His men said, why hell, don't he live there anyhow? Bradford always followed the same ritual, walking across the wooden footbridge and through the sally port pierced into the wall, where the Negro sentinel came to a crashing salute with his leather and brass and gleaming rifle. Then Bradford would return the salute and smile and fish elaborately in his pocket and find a coin and put it into the man's blouse. This bewildered the Negroes at first, but later with huge smiles themselves they would say, "Thanky suh." Leaming always grinned sardonically and returned the salute viciously behind Bradford's back and they would go into the fort. Bradford carried out the ritual partly of course because it was in precise imitation, even to the elaborate fishing in the pocket, of the bigwigs in Memphis and Chattanooga and Nashville, going into the Gayoso and the Reed House past the liveried Negro doorman and giving him the coin. And partly too out of a desperate and earnest desire to ingratiate himself with the Negroes; smiling at them and talking to them and calling the sentry on cold nights into the office for coffee. In his mind he was playing out the nightmare of when the rebels finally crossed the wall or came into the town to get him. Hoping then that there might be a Negro soldier who would thrust himself in front of the raised saber (it was always a raised saber) in return for the numerous pennies handed out on coming into the fort or perhaps the cup of coffee or the cast-off frock coat. Or that the Negroes might, while he walked down behind the company lines, stiffen when they saw him and perform better and thus keep the rebels out.

Bradford in any case had not found any sort of protection at all in the Thirteenth or any sense of security, coming more and more to detest the fact that these were not the fine, eager boys but the second and third and fourth culling of the state for men. They had served and run away from every Tennessee regiment in perhaps both armies, and they sat and nursed cold, hard hatred, like a scruffy, snot-nosed baby with one tormented rag doll holding immovably onto that filthy doll. They did things to the countryside that he did not want to hear about and would not hear about, thinking desperately, well perhaps this will free me of complicity in them. Most of these things were senselessly cruel, like burning barns or stealing cattle or burning fields, and sometimes murder as well, though no rape because they did not think in those terms. They left the woman holding the starving children at her skirts and they rode off laughing, faces silhouetted in the glare of flames and breathing steam into the coldness of the night and still laughing. Bradford drew up duty rosters in conscienceful parody of the rosters he had seen the Yankee regiments issue in Memphis. He heard the patrols clank out according to his orders, but he knew conclusively that they went where they wanted once they were past the picket post.

They pushed their horses down the roads in mindless laughter, with their stringy long hair flopping in the wind. They kicked viciously at their horses, which was the finest horse flesh the Yankees could buy for them and therefore to be doubly abused, because they themselves in their scattered poor dirt farms amid the dusty firs and blackjack could not ever have afforded anything so fine. The secesh, they pushed their fine ol' hosses didn't they before the war. And we are as good as they 'y God you better believe it. Their horses were rolling-eyed and foam-mouthed with bloody flanks from the roweling. They would yell and kick down the roads toward the lonely houses; unless they had an officer like Leaming who kept them in line in which case they rode muted and grinning at each other and whispering in the ranks behind the stiffened back of the officer.

Sometimes from the evening patrols they would return with clocks or china or silver held in gunny sacks over their thighs or clutched under their arms. They would come back with beaver hats or claw-hammer coats, clapping and laughing and the thin flesh sliding over their high cheekbones and long jaws. Bradford would sit upright in bed sweating and listening to their talk of victory, Ol' Sim got hisself a coat I warrant, or, That is one fine ol' clock, buddy boy. When they had passed his hut he would listen to the wails and laughter and noise from down where they kept the nigger women as community property. He would shudder deeply and feel the long shadows reaching for him. This is ridiculous, I am a major of federal cavalry. But he would shake anyway and finally bury himself under the dirty quilts and blankets in their warmth and anonymity. They won't fight, I know they won't fight, and they do hate me. Like I hate them. I had thought they would be the best of the country, but they ain't. They are the very worst. The rebels wouldn't take 'em. And God, they would slit my throat for a dollar I do believe. What will the rebels do then to me? I turned 'em loose out yonder and what will Forrest and those Tennessee boys do to me? Those Tennessee boys with Forrest are somethen. God, what would they do?

In the white Tennesseans he could see, because of the way the flesh went and the porcine teeth and the chin stubble, the long stringy hair and the sallowness under the eyes and the almost feverish, thin way they laughed, he could see where they came from and what they would do any time they could. But the Negroes were dark and they were always uniformed and sharp-looking. They are my boys, he would think. I will take care of 'em and they will take care of me. Why hell, these niggers have got no choice about fighting. The rebels won't take 'em alive anyhow and they know it. They will fight. I will win 'em over and they will fight for me.

And every day having passed by the sentry and given him the warm, dark penny, he would then go to the headquarters office, where once with Booth and behind the walls and the cannon and the nigger soldiers, amid the military clutter and the lounging messengers and sentries and secretaries and orderlies, he would feel safe and relax. Outside he was always taciturn and nervous and tight-faced, but inside the headquarters he would feel relaxed and the fear would come rising to his eyes as he let himself out slowly. His eyes would blink and squint and jump around in the long, bony face and he would laugh too loudly and grin and slap people on the back. He talked incessantly and always did favors, Here lemme give ya a hand getten over that desk son, and, Well if I was you when I get to Memphis I would go straight to the Gayoso first. The first thing he would do in the room was look over at the orderly and say, "Put my coffee on please, Joe boy."

He would then go first to Booth. Booth, sitting still sleepy and normally with the corduroy marks of his bedspread on the side of his face, would inevitably look up, questioning. That always bothered Bradford, the "What do you want?" look. Did he always have to want somethen just to talk a while to a friend? Bradford would come in smiling and blinking, and sit down on the edge of Booth's desk, sliding his right buttock and thigh onto the desk and swinging his booted calf. He always played absent-mindedly with the little silver inkstand. "Well, sir. Well what is in the air today? Any messages about our frien' Forrest?" Without saying anything Booth would wearily gesture to an orderly who came back with the sheaf of reports that had come over the wire or on the steamboats, written in precise penmanship and on the lines in official military slips. Bradford would put a hand in his beard and read them aloud judiciously, Booth hearing them for the second and perhaps third time. Bradford would comment, "Well, it looks like he is going to have a try at Columbus next, eh?" and he would smile wearily at Booth, who wanted Bradford to get his damn rump off his desk and shut up and leave him to command the fort. Then Bradford would always go over to the wall map of the region next to Lincoln's picture. He would rock on the balls of his feet, one hand folded behind his back and the other holding the sheaf of dispatches and reading them again carefully and then looking up at the map and back at the dispatches, occasionally saying um or yes and squinting at the map. Then he would settle into the chair in front of Booth's desk with his steaming cup of coffee and sip it loudly and talk about the whole course of the war, saying, "Well now, Sherman has got his hands full don't he?" or, "I figger Lee has two more months to go before Grant whips him into the ground." Booth listened uncomfortably and concentrated earnestly on his dispatches and his reports and rosters. Both of them were uncomfortable but that only made Bradford more anxious than ever. At the end of the conversation—or really, monologue—he would always say, "Well, how is your battalion doing?" and then, "Well, do you think Forrest is going to come at us here any time soon? I just want to know your opinion." This last comment got more and more earnest when Forrest went at Paducah. Then, in obvious relief when they found Paducah had held out, Bradford was almost radiant, grinning all over the fort and whistling to himself. But Forrest slipped away again and they heard about Hurst getting routed and again the grey tension came into his face. "He whipped ol' Hurst pretty bad. I tell you them Tennessee boys don't like us much, men like us who went with Lincoln and the Union. Nosuh they don't. But I sure thought Hurst could hold his own. I thought he had a good regiment. Humm."

In the next week they heard hundreds of reports from the scattered post commanders, each immersed in fear and saying, everything is quiet on my front, but I hear rumors that Forrest is coming. In this week Bradford's nerves almost made Booth strike him. He kept up a steady monologue about Hurst getting routed: "Ol' Hurst goen into Memphis without his hat. And I thought he had the best of the Tories. He did. Boy, Forrest would chop up the ol' Thirteenth in no time." In the spell of quiet it was absolutely natural to assume that Forrest was coming at them, just as a man in the dark, when he knows there is something there, figures it is stalking him. Bradford repeated, almost as a litany, "Those Tennessee boys are somethen else." He spent all day, each day, in Booth's office talking aimlessly and rereading the dispatches and looking at the map. "Now if I was Forrest I would come down on us here along the Brownsville road, I reckon. What do you think, Li'nel?" He was the first man in Booth's service life who ever called him "Lionel" or even tried to.

Booth would watch him and feel the rise of almost nauseating contempt for the man. Booth had been schooled in the scattered and leaky army posts from Florida to the western desert, watching on innumerable nights the dust swirling in miniature tornadoes across parade grounds. Until whatever imagination he had had was worn out of him, but along with it whatever fear. What will be, will be, and he would turn in all loneliness on his bunk, under the pegged, gleaming tunic and cap and swordbelt. If they come, they will come and there ain't nothing to do but wait and then do your duty. Booth was unique among the post commanders in the Sixteenth district, grey-toothed and beaten or worn into a single train of thought, knowing the army schemata and nothing else and caring about nothing else. He was not unlike Thomas, or even Grant; everyone else with his dogged determination and his single-minded attention to duty and grey-souled methodicity had gone places in the war. They had needed them. But they had not needed an aging lieutenant of infantry and when he had gone at his dying wife's urging into the Negro service they had doubly not needed him.

The other post commanders, political colonels or drunkards or timid, clean-shaven Midwesterners, were all afraid and bedeviled and against them Forrest had no trouble at all. But Booth was regular army. He no longer even cared about promotion. He just wanted to be back in the army, the regular army, at the end of the war. He was not sure whether he would make it, but maybe he would. And for right now, he had learned enough in all his years to support him; do your duty and nobody can get at you. There ain't nothing to be afraid of except your own army's system of justice. Certainly not the rebels and if you die you will not know it anyhow. They had made him over the years into the perfect soldier except he still was slow-minded and not particularly imaginative or smart. He had gotten that way during endless, long nights and blistering days all over the country, feeling the same trickle of sweat during all the years beneath the thick, woolen, blue uniforms. The only embarrassment he had ever known and the only fear was once when he had lost some cartridge boxes and had had to turn in a remiss account. Then he had waited in supreme and soul-tearing and nerve-killing fear while the morning hours passed and the spanish-tiled roof gleamed under the heat, watching nothing but the shadows dwindling on the parade ground while his commanding officer eventually came to and read his report. He had been called for and had walked steeled across the parade ground at a brace, and gone into the office seeing nothing, his eyes white-ringed blanks. And his commanding officer had asked him about it and he had said, "No excuse sah!" knowing full well the cartridge boxes were out in the desert amid the brush and dust. He had been almost able, in his intense concentration, to feel the heat on the black leather and brass plates. Booth had been rebuked for a mindless, careless fool and it went on his report and his pay was docked the amount of thirty-seven dollars and eight cents necessary to replace them. Then he had pivoted, not even minding the personal insults and that afternoon parade, still in front of his platoon, was sweetness to him. It was like the taste of sweet water, the fact that he was still an officer and still in command of a platoon and still on the parade in his hot, high-collared frock coat in all the heat. That had been the moment of fear in Booth's life, and then he had known the worst and since then nothing else could bother him. Except that through circumstance or the vicious plottings of the people up there (meaning anywhere from Memphis to Washington) he might be tripped up in his duty, and therefore have to submit again to the merciless military judicial process.

He had sent in his dispatch to Memphis on April third, an honest and completely fearless report which was in direct contrast to the reports sent in by almost any other post in the Sixteenth army district. He wrote to General Hurlbut, "Everything is quiet within a radius of thirty or forty miles around, and I do not think any apprehensions need be felt to this place being attacked or even threatened; I think it perfectly safe." This was received and shown to General Hurlbut at his desk. Hurlbut did not mark down Booth's obvious competence or courage or even the fact that his report was so markedly different from that of the other commanders who saw Forrest every day in the drifting shadows under the spring clouds. He only thought, well, that is good, and he looked at the map and it convinced him that Forrest was concentrating after all for an assault on his own position in Memphis. He dictated half a dozen encouraging answers to his secretary with half a mind, while he was looking through the drawers of his desk for the plans of the defenses of Memphis and then thinking, I shall have to get in touch with the Navy; Forrest is probably going to make his move on me, and I cannot lose Memphis.

But at Fort Pillow, Booth, in the certainty that he had done his duty and utterly unmindful of fear because he had not the imagination to particularly catalyze that fear, sat back one morning and showed a copy of his confident dispatch to Bradford. Bradford said almost immediately, "Are you sure we . . ." and then, white as a sheet, turned again to the map of the district.

"Well now, Major, you told me what your men found. Either you trust that or you do not. In any case we have a full battery of artillery, a battalion of fully armed infantry and one of cavalry, and a gunboat on station at the fort. Now either you trust them or you do not, too."

Bradford looked around the room desperately. He smiled weakly with his gums showing and said, "Well, had not we better see Commander Marshall? Had not we . . . just to be sure had not we better see him about organizing our defenses?"

Booth then thought, well now, if Forrest does come I could be considered remiss in my duties if we had not worked out some sort of a plan with Marshall. And of course this will encourage Bradford. Maybe he will stop coming in here every morning to be encouraged. Booth sent out one of the Negro messengers and then sat back and listened to Bradford who was worrying about Forrest. "Well, he might be—my men have not been as thorough you know—he might be out there. Those

Tennessee boys with him anyhow can be down upon us in no time. Those boys are somethen; they can ride forty miles in a night. They could be down here on us. . . ." Booth looked away to the wall of his office while Bradford talked and finally he stopped talking and his voice trailed away.

That afternoon Captain Marshall of the gunboat *New Era* came ashore from the ship, which was being coaled. He was a tall, dark-haired man, clean-shaven and with a large, rounded head. He walked up the path to the fort in a black frock coat and a stiff round cap with bars of gold braid around it and he saluted and then shook hands with both of the officers in the corner of the south wall. He was very affable and smiled, with crow's-feet coming into the flesh beside his eyes.

Booth sat on the firestep and they talked for a few minutes about coaling and how things were in Memphis, and then Booth said, "Captain Marshall, I desired to speak to you concerning the defenses of this fort. Forrest may come at us as he did at Paducah. . . ." and Marshall nodded vigorously and it made Booth stop for a minute. Then he went on. "Well, if he does I want to work out some sort of system of fire control—I mean of spotting your fire, you see."

Marshall nodded again, somehow like a big dog. "That is a good idea, Major, and I would have mentioned it myself. You see the bluff is high and we cannot see over it. Now . . ."

"Yes. Yes, well. Look." Marshall stopped talking and they stood up on the firestep. Booth pointed out over the direction of the town, and they went over the positions one by one the rebels might invest, starting at the outer parapet which they both agreed was too far to shell, and then coming down toward the fort. "Now I will put a signalman up here with two flags. One signal on the white flag will mean to the south of the fort, and the red to the north."

Captain Marshall pulled out a small leather notebook and licked the tip of a pencil and began to write it down, breathing loudly through his nose and quoting the words. "Red north, all right."

"Now if they are massing over in the center . . ." and he pointed out the small elevation with the orange mud scar of the abandoned trenches along it, ". . . if he comes there the man will wave both flags one time." Again the snorting and nodding and "One time all right, sir."

"Now I figure the range from the river to the hills to be about five-hundred yards. Can you get canister or something onto them at that range?"

"Well now, humm. Well, it ain't that far. I would say about three hundred from the bank to this end. Over there may be four. Yep, maybe four."

"Well, can you get shells there all right without 'em hitten in the fort?"

Marshall squinted with his crow's-feet showing. "Oh yes. Oh yes. Only how about this? How about giving me a set of signals so I know whether my shells are effective or not?" He pronounced it *eefective*.

"All right then. Once you fire a volley . . ."

"Nawsuh. A broadside." He smiled.

"Broadside. Then the signalman will give two pulls on the white flag for way low. Then one pull for low but closer. Then the red flag, one for over it and two for way over."

Marshall wrote, again licking his pencil first and quoting under his breath while a group of officers wandered around them and talked and nodded solemnly. The pencil made large grey marks on the thin lined paper.

"Those hills over yonder, Cap'n Marshall. Now there." He pointed to the rising hills choked with shrubbery and weeds and small trees, humped and green and brown. "Now they may get down in there. You can put some effective fire on them there. I make it five-hundred yards, or maybe more. . . . Those hills . . ."

"No sir. No sir, I make it less than that again. Maybe seventy-five yards left. But n' mind."

"Well those hills have a slight elevation on the fort. Can you promise to keep a good fire down to keep the rebels off?"

Marshall stood on tiptoe and looked from the river over to the hills, studying it. Booth almost said, well man, why not test the damned wind too? Marshall looked back twice. "Well Major Booth, we could come upstream another hundred yards and hit 'em pretty hard I think. Yes sir. We'd have to come upstream a bit but we could get 'em there as well as anyplace."

"All right, all right. We will use the same range finden signals. . . . Now . . ."

But Marshall was slowly licking the pencil and turning the page and writing down, "Shift position" and then some figures, and snorting and licking the pencil again and "same . . . signals . . . for range . . . for fire . . . yes, sir."

"All right, now over toward the crick . . ." but Bradford who was rocking on his heels and had his hand pressed into the small of his back and was squinting endlessly at the hills said, "Major Booth. Major Booth. Whyn't we work out some pattern of signals for firen to the left or to the right? Then we could put the fire right down on the rebels."

"All right, we will. We will do the same thing . . . two for way far, one for a bit like a hundred yards. . . ."

"Make it fifty yards, Major Booth. I can promise you to work pretty well with fifty yard corrections. . . ."

"All right. Fifty yards and a hundred or more for one flag or two. Now if you are shooten to the left, we will use a yellow flag. To the right we will use a blue one, all right?" And he thought, why hell, this man is a damn fool. No man I ever seen can promise fifty-yard corrections with gunfire at half a mile or more. But aw hell. Bradford was smiling and still rocking up and down and now with both hands behind his back, smiling and contented-looking. Aw hell, why bring it up? Marshall bent his heavy, rounded head over the pad again and wrote laboriously, "Yellow for left . . . blue for right," and he looked up and smiled and Booth started to go on to the next position, but again Bradford cut in. His face suddenly seemed to shatter with worry. "Now Cap'n Marshall, you know that means to correct your fire to the left for a blue flag. I mean you will not get that backwards, you see don't you?"

Marshall said, "I will not get it backwards," and his face clouded too, but then he wrote another notation in the pad and looked up and smiled. "That is just to be certain. I wrote 'shooting to left of target,' see? That will make sure."

Christ, thought Booth. I am surrounded by imbeciles. He snorted and put his hand into his reddish stubble and frowned at both of them, but Bradford was craning over to look into the book with his face radiant again, and Marshall turned his mouth down a little in deprecation and showed him the notes. They went on to the Coal Creek side, getting the ranges down for the fire and Marshall hesitating and then saying, yes, we can chew them up good if they get into either ravine, the town or the other one. He got the notes in his pad, a Negro orderly taking down the instructions too for the use in the fort.

"All right, then. And thank you, Captain Marshall." They stepped down off the firestep and walked toward the bluff, Captain Marshall stepping slowly and with his hands behind his back and turning his feet out, and Booth walking with hands in his pockets and scowling. Just as they turned and commented on the nice soft air and would not Marshall do them the honor of taking supper and, well you see, Major, then Bradford said, "Captain Marshall. Captain Marshall, listen." He caught up with them by running across the muddy ground, his black hair flopping. "Listen." He looked quickly at Major Booth, white-faced and breathing heavily, but not long enough to catch Booth's eye and then, "Listen, Captain Marshall. If the rebels push us out of the fort, le's do this. Le's do this. We will fall back down the bluff side. We can put some ammunition there. We fall down the bluff and you can watch us and sweep the fort with grape from the river. All right? We stop down at the water's edge and you can shoot right over us into the fort. If the rebels push us out. All right?"

Both Booth and Marshall were launched already into the rigidly courteous deportment between officers of two different services. Except for that, Booth would have dressed Bradford down, since even without considering it the idea was a stupid one. And in the second place it implied that he would not be able, even with the strongest of naval support, to hold the fort. But since Marshall was there he could not curse his second-in-command for a fool. He shook his head slightly in refusal and rejection and anger, but then Marshall was saying to his surprise, "Yes. It seems logical to me. All right, drop down below the fort and we will put shell fire right into it for you. We can drive the rebels out and you can retake it."

Bradford said, "Thank you, thank you," and he fumblingly shook hands with Marshall while Booth thought, again, oh what the hell. What the hell, while I am here and in command I don't reckon it will come to anything as stupid as that. If we fall down the slope we are dead men as any damn fool can see. We will not be in any shape to have naval fire goen over our heads into the rebels with them shooten down on us and the niggers prob'ly runnen like chickens with their heads cut off and Bradford's men not a damned sight better. But what the hell. I can keep the rebels out of the fort I reckon. An' it will make Bradford maybe sit up if he figures he has this to hang on to. He got this decided on the way back to headquarters, Bradford at his side and talking while he was paying no attention at all and thinking about what a fool Bradford was. They got to the headquarters and Booth began to consider the afternoon retreat, worrying at the details of his uniform as Bradford took his leave. Booth was already forgetting the plan to fight on from down the bluff, and indeed forgetting the plan to control naval gunfire which he thought was rubbish anyhow. You could not do anything like that.

But Bradford thought, well now. Well now, even if the rebels cross the ditch and the wall we still got a place to go. There is still a way out. We won't get caught like rats in a trap, and the niggers I know will fight to the last man anyhow 'cause they will not have any choice, thinking this as he passed and tipped ritualistically the Negro sentinel. We got a last resort, and a way out, even if the fort don't hold.

9

THE SAME DAY THAT BOOTH WAS SENDING HIS UTTERLY HONEST AND
frank and unimaginative report to Hurlbut in Memphis, Forrest in a communication likewise to S. D. Lee, nominally his
commanding officer, was mentioning plans for a move against
Fort Pillow. There were reports concerning two weeks of action
in Tennessee and Kentucky to the effect that his loss was fifteen
killed and forty-two wounded; on the disposition of his soldiers
—most of them, the Kentucky soldiers especially, allowed to go
home on honor to refit and re-establish themselves, emaciated
wraiths in tattered uniforms grinning wolfishy and embarrass-
sedly at their women and leaning out of the saddles to receive
the first embraces—and a request for a brigade of infantry
which of course would never be available to him; and notices
concerning the federal concentrations against Richmond and
Chattanooga. Sandwiched between these lines, recopied in precise language for him by a young and educated lieutenant, was
the Fort Pillow notice. "There is a force of five or six hundred
at Fort Pillow, which I shall attend to in a day or two, as they
have horses and supplies which we need." But Forrest and no
one else put it as "attend to." He did not even reflect any more
upon his choice of words than that, because when the time came
he would indeed attend to it. So far nothing in his life except
the Confederate high command itself (and that because he ac-
ceded to it from choice) had ever been removed from his ability
to attend to it. He was certain he could capture Fort Pillow
because he had heard precise details concerning the fort and he
knew it could be taken and taken rapidly, and without a prohi-

225

bitive cost in men. Some of the back-country families had told their men the details about the position; old men, perhaps veterans of the Mexican War, and still agile and concerned and arrogant enough to send down the information to their sons. And a few of Bradford's men had redeserted and re-enlisted, and others had been captured outright. So Forrest never doubted his ability to take the place.

After a quiet two weeks following the Paducah fight, and while the Kentucky soldiers were reassembling to a man at Trenton, and Crews outmaneuvered Grierson at Raleigh, Forrest called a conference with his two division commanders at Jackson. The force he had entered Tennessee with was scattered in encampments and on furlough all over Tennessee and Kentucky, some of the troopers getting home but most of them, including Bell's brigade and of course the Mississippians and Missourians in McCulloh's brigade spending their time in idle encampments in misty creek bottoms and small towns and muddy fields. They rose each morning to the bugle call and sent out their foragers with wagons and then the recruiting officers with frock-coated local magistrates, impressing the horses and the men and the grain and corn. They lived and sufficed and ate, and cleaned their guns in the scattered and roundabout encampments. They sent out patrols into the spring rains and the flat, new, green fields to look for and fight the federal patrols. The whole body of two divisions of cavalry was spread out loosely across Western Tennessee and Kentucky so that Sherman would receive simultaneous reports that Forrest was crossing the Tennessee in Alabama and moving at the same time of morning against Cincinnati.

If a federal column came against the scattered sections the division would recoil into compactness for action. But the Federals did not have the cavalry yet to supply Sherman and Grant at the same time for their big offensives, and simultaneously keep up the numbers of good cavalry for garrison duty. The federal government was finally learning that the sheer occupation of space was meaningless and that you had to strike not even at the enemy armies but at his cities. Take Atlanta and Richmond, after which their armies could not gather and be supplied in numbers enough to threaten you seriously, and you could mop them up. The key cities were the things that the Confederates had to fight for and therefore when you went straight for them you had the initiative and if you outnumbered them it was a question of time. So they stripped away the cavalry from Western Tennessee and Kentucky and even from the far west, from Missouri across the river and from the Dakotas where the Indians profited, and they sent them by convoyed boats or overland in long winding columns to Sherman at Chattanooga and to Grant in front of Richmond.

Forrest had been separated from the dual center of the stage, Atlanta and Richmond, by one night in the tent of Braxton Bragg following the empty victory at Chickamauga. Bragg had stood in his nightshirt after a hard and punishing day, blinking in the raw lantern light, and Forrest refused his hand, standing soiled and weary too but furious. Forrest's face had been a bronze mask and he was still in leather and metal equipments. He called Bragg a coward and a dog and said, "If you were any part a man I would slap yo' jaws an' force you to resent hit," and turned on his heel, out into the night. And then he was sent across Alabama with a handful of men to Mississippi. He knew the theater better, but it was nowhere as essential to the Confederacy as North Georgia or Virginia. He earned a reputation on his own, but a reputation for being a "guerilla fighter" or a "raider" which of course carried the implication that he was not really fit to work in conjunction with anyone else on a complex plan for a major battle. It was damning by faint praise.

So Forrest stood in the silhouetting light of the doorway of his headquarters at Jackson and welcomed first Chalmers and then Buford, having heard them come up the road. They arrived like local bandits, their escorts armed with braces of pistols and impressive beards and crossed leather belts, dusty and weary after the ride. Chalmers came in, still sad-eyed and aristocratic, not having given up the lined cloak, but the cloak was a bit more shaggy and worn than it had been a month earlier on the cold approach to Ellis' bridge. He smiled and gave Forrest his hand and noticed how weary Forrest looked, and then went to the proffered brandy decanter in the sideboard in the thin-lit room. He took off the cloak and stood in his frock coat, with the yellow-facing buttoned back at the second button down each side and the collar rising into the mass of hair behind his ears. He sniffed at the brandy and paced a little to work out some of the soreness of the ride and looked at the things in the room. It was the parlor of a one-story house, with a fireplace and an ancient flintlock over it and brass kettles beside it, tables pulled together in the center of the floor to make a desk and the carpets rolled up in one corner. The room smelled of cigar smoke and sweat and there were burned marks on the floor near the desk from where the officers had let their cigars fall. Uniform jackets and cloaks were hanging like slain birds along the wall; and there were cots near the fireplace with the blankets in confusion on them and on the floor, and spare boots and a sword and some pistols laid out for cleaning on the sideboard next to the liquor.

Buford came in and said, "Hello Ginral," and then, "Hello Frank," large-faced with dollar-round circles of flesh under his heavy-lidded eyes, and a straggly moustache. He was short and rotund and belted into a frock coat with brass buttons and yellow facings like Chalmers, but the thick massed braid along his sleeves was tarnished and black.

He helped himself judiciously to the brandy, looking for all the world like a small-town politician settling himself into his office in the city hall or county courthouse for a long night at the files or books. He found a cigar somewhere in his pocket and sat at the table on the other side of Forrest. Chalmers sat down and crossed his leather-encased legs and admired them for a moment, and the warmth of the brandy. Forrest got out a map, and they both leaned closer, Buford pulling absent-mindedly at his cigar. Forrest neither smoked nor drank, giving up both as a savage affirmation of his will when he courted a woman who did not like either habit.

He sat thin-lipped and grey-faced. Before the war he had been what was called well set up; the flesh was thick all over his big frame and it was full on his face, but the war had tightened it all over him like drying leather, the cheekbones and jaw bones strong and marked now and the eyes framed by hard bone and the nose straight and long. The moustache and small spade beard were tinged with grey and his hair was shot with it. His eyes were always hard and full, now even when he laughed. He reminded Chalmers of some of the patriarchs of the hill families he had heard of as almost legendary during his youth, seeing Forrest as one of them, grey and tough as a wolf and with a long rifle avenging some implacable hatred, saying almost nothing and possessing even in repose none of the small, snuffling, humanizing sounds a man makes; sitting in self-contained rigidity and silence and speaking crisply and with a strong accent, and the anger rising quick to his eyes. But before he got started Buford interrupted through his cigar smoke. Buford understood Forrest from dealing with men just like him in Kentucky before the war; in any case he had achieved an insensibility of his own from having two brothers fighting for the Union. Buford flicked his growing ash and said, "Ginral, after we hit Paducah I found some newspaper," and pausing, Forrest who had as yet not said a word looking at him straight. "It said the Federals put all their stock in an ol' mill I know about across the river. The horses we got were local animals gathered up by the Yankees. If you want, I kin get the others for you, suh."

Forrest considered. "All right. Take your division then and move on 'em. Send out some men to make a scare at Columbus too."

"Yes suh."

"Now look at this," and they leaned over to look at the spread-out map. "I told Neely to take his brigade down this way on Memphis, and to put out the word we are moven on the city. An' I sent out a messenger to Dan McGuirk down in Mississippi. He is goen to come on Memphis from the south. That way we ought to keep ol' Hurlbut shut up tight."

"Yessir, Ginral."

"Now then, Ginral Cha'mmers. I want you to take Fort Pillow for me. Take what you figger you will need from yo' division."

"Yes sir." Chalmers leaned over the map, and put two fingers on it at the bivouacs of his brigades, and then put a thumb on Fort Pillow, represented by a U with a flat base on the map. "Yes sir. Le's see. . . ." While he thought he could hear Buford breathing and sucking at his brandy glass. He thought, well I ought to take two brigades. That will be enough. He has sent Neely's brigade and mine on Memphis, so I cannot take it. Now then, my other brigade, McCulloh, will be at Forked Deer Creek, around Sharon's Ferry. That is, le's see, that is forty mile or more. Start at nighttime, be there by the next day if we keep moving. He thought about his brigades, and was sorry he wouldn't have Neely. He had McCulloh's brigade and Lord knew McCulloh was a good man, but he would need another brigade too. McCulloh's men were all from out of the state, Mississippians and lanky Texans and some Missourians, the Second Missouri being the biggest regiment and the rest of the men scattered in small battalions. The brigade was tough; the men were yellow-faced and wizened and hairy.

"I will need another brigade." He looked up at Forrest. Forrest looked straight at Buford. "How many men will you take to Paducah, you figger, Ginral? . . ."

"Ohhh . . ."

"Cain't you hold it to one brigade?"

"Yes . . . yes suh, I can. Only I got to cut down on the demonstration toward Columbus. But I reckon one is enough. I got some good enough men to put up a show."

"Well then, sir, I shall take your Tennessee brigade, Bell's, if 'tis all right. I guess you would want the Kentuckians for your raid."

"Uh-hunh. I will take Thompson's brigade; you can take Bell's then."

Forrest looked rapidly at them both. His eyes were slate-grey. "All right. All right, you reckon you can do the job at Fort Pillow with two brigades, Ginral Cha'mmers?"

Chalmers wanted to ask for another brigade, but he saw Buford looking somnolent, his eyes barely open and his fingers locked, and thought, he wants those horses at Paducah. I figured I could do it with two brigades because I hear the Federals have six-hundred men, Tennessee whites and niggers. "Six-hundred Yankees at the place, General Forrest?"

"Five or six hundred."

"I hear the fort is small and there is good cover around it on all sides. . . ."

"That is what I am told; it ain't too strong. Brush enough

to keep a good fahr on the fort and keep 'em down, and the boats caint get a good shot at you. All they got is some nigger soldiers and some Tennesseans. Nothen too strong."

Chalmers thought, all right Buford can get those horses at Paducah. He sat back. "Why, yessuh, I can bust the place with Bell's brigade and McCulloh's I think." Forrest looked at the two of them again, first at Chalmers and then at Buford and at Chalmers again, quickly. He is measuring us, Chalmers thought, but it was a quick thought and he was not certain.

"When can you git yo' command on the road for Paducah, Ginral?"

Buford stirred, his eyes still almost shut, and Chalmers smiled, thinking, look at him, you would think ol' Buford would say next winter sometime, but I bet he says tomorrow.

"T'morra."

"And you, Ginral Cha'mmers?"

He thought he would say tomorrow too, but then he thought while Forrest raised his eyebrow in his direction, no, no I better give myself till the eleventh, and then move 'em in one night. "I will get them on the road at dusk on the eleventh, Monday, sir. Move 'em into Lauderdale County and the fort in one ride, and be on the Yankees by midmorning."

Forrest looked at him steadily without moving his eyes. Chalmers felt his cheek muscle twitch. Forrest said, "I will bring up my comp'ny and come with you then. I can get some wagons of ammunition, I think I know a place, and bring 'em along to the fort right after you git there. You will need the ammunition."

"Yessuh."

"All right. Why not start yo' men earlier, and hit the place at dawn . . . which way you think to go?"

Chalmers was thinking, why dammit he planned to command all along but then, yes, we will need the ammunition, and where will he get it in two days in this part of Tennessee? "Umm . . . what, sir?"

"Which way will you take to the fort?" Chalmers traced out a route along the map between Sharon's Ford and the fort. Forrest watched him carefully, and then said, "I see if I caint find you a guide too. I ain't sure about some of that this time of the year. . . ."

"Umm. Good idea, General." He was still a little angry but beginning to get wrapped up in the idea, already plotting his orders and rations and counting on the ammunition and thinking about the horses in Perry's battalion. He hunched forward a little more over the map, his eyes open and intense. Good. This can be a good move. We can go in and bust them fast and come out in two days. Buford was making his goodbyes at the door. He nodded quickly at him slipping out into the night. Forrest came back to the map and sat down.

"Frank, how about doen it this way? How about goen in at dawn? Leave in the afternoon or so, and give yo'self the time, and hit 'em at dawn?"

"Yessir. Yessir, we can make it pushing hard in one night. McCulloh can take the road marked here, down like this. If they got a picket in front of the fort, 'twill be here. I can take Bell's brigade into 'em myself and we can pitch into 'em and keep 'em in the fort until you come up, sir."

"Yeh. All right, keep 'em in the fo't and penned up."

"From what I hear, the fort is open"—he checked himself from saying vulnerable—"especially along a creek on this side that goes into the river, eh?"

"That's what I hear."

"All right then. Take one regiment of Bell's brigade an' move 'em into the creek. . . ."

"Umm. Yeh, and bring along another regiment on the straight road from Brownsville to the fo't, that'll put 'em in along the lef' of the creek and between where McCulloh's men ought to end up."

"Yessir. Yessir, that would do it, eh?"

"Ought to. Reckon hit ought to."

They both looked soberly at the map, silently. Then Forrest said, "I will be along with part of Wisdom's regiment and my own comp'ny about eleven. Keep up the push and keep yo' men moven as close as you can to the fo't."

"Yessir. Yessir, I will."

They looked at each other for a moment in the hanging

smoke of Buford's cigar, Forrest in thick army pants and shirt-sleeves and Chalmers in his braided grey coat. "Well, General. What do you know about who is at Fort Pillow?"

"I am told that a man name of Booth is in command. Know nothen about him. He came with the nigger battalion. Bradford . . ."

"Yessir, I heard of him."

"Bradford is still there with his battalion too. The Tennessee boys will be wanten a chaince at Bradford, I reckon. They want this one pretty bad."

"Yessir. I can see why."

"We ought to have some fahr in the boys for this one, Ginral. Some fahr in the boys."

Chalmers, the traditional inbred stubbornness in him quiet and forgotten, got up and made his goodbyes, thinking in terms of work to do getting his brigades ready, and parenthetically about rousing out his Negro boy to make some coffee once he got back to Sharon's Ferry. He thought of the late hours to be spent with the papers and the figuring and the maps, and the men on his staff tousle-haired and grinning and rubbing sleep out of their eyes. It would be a good night, and he felt the rising blood in him. 'Twill be a good attack.

Forrest stood in the doorway feeling the nighttime air and watching the clouds, black-bottomed and swift, moving overhead in the sky, showing under the thin film of the spring moonlight. It was a good night, with the smell coming from the creeks and the fields, the smell of water and plants and the sounds of the frogs and croakers grating into the cool air.

He turned back to the office, his face still set, and thinking. They were going to hit Fort Pillow and everyone had known they were going to, from the minute he had brung them across the line of the ol' railroad into Tennessee. That Fort was a cankering, infested boil on the men's minds and it stood for everything they hated and he was going to take them in swift and hard and they were going to lance it. It would be a relief and a purgation, and he figured Chalmers could do the job and the two brigades would be more than enough. They want this'un. He needed the horses and the rifles and maybe the artillery pieces and the strap leather and the clothing, but the men needed this'un themselves. Some of them had come to him, coming back in from their furloughs all filled with love and pity and new worry for their womenfolk and their land and families with a place like Fort Pillow, and they asked to be allowed to stay. Pathetically they asked, just to be allowed to stay and swearing, Ginral we will fight 'em we sweah we will, only we caint leave our womenfolk like this with Bradford and his niggers over yonder tearen up the place. They were loyal to him and came back choking and desperate on their worry. Or just on their hate, like the Mississippians hated.

Some of the Tennesseans hated Bradford's men because of the fear but also because of the fact that if these people were right then they were wrong 'cause they had been brought up the same way in the same state hadn't they, and these people were turning against their own kind and had to be hit. And the niggers of course, you can't trust the niggers with a rifle, you got to teach them their place. It was a constant raw feeling, worry and fear and concern about the unprotected women, and the hatred of the goddamned traitors, men they had known and who were now fighten with the damned Yankees and the niggers and all, and Fort Pillow stood for the whole thing, Forrest knew. Fort Pillow was where, not the Yankee boys from the Midwest, but the Tennesseans, their own renegade flesh and blood, huddled behind the animal-like niggers and the steel of the gunboats, and it was where the Yankees brought in the armed niggers with fancy uniforms to rouse up the countryside. You couldn't hate the boys that much from Ohio and Iowa after you had seen how they did, all of them at Chickamauga and Shiloh, and even little bunches of them at Okolona. You found grinning boys who when you captured them showed you tintypes of their girl friends and agreed, hell yes, let us go home and let the damned politicians settle this, get the bombproofs up here instead of us. You could like boys like that, but bring in the homemade Yankees and the niggers and that was something else. And that damn Bradford standing for all of the Tennesseans who were not fighting the Yankees but helping them, sitting now in ease and comfort. It was so easy to assume since your own political views were so incoherent (and irrelevant) that theirs were the same, only they wanted to sit in ease and with women and liquor, growen fat off your cotton and your land. You had to go and suffer and they stayed and 'y God grew fatter each year off your suffering, and when you caught 'em you would make them pay for all the damned nights worrien about your wife or girl friend and about your land. (What if they won? Would Bradford get the farm? Why wouldn't he? He picked a winner, 'gainst his own people.) And the niggers. Bringen in the niggers was too damned much. A man asks for some decency in the middle of all this and a nigger with a rifle don't know right from wrong. Let the niggers get away with carrying a rifle and a uniform and you wake up the others like animals with the bloody beef put in front of 'em. You reverse the process of things, and turn all the niggers loose on your helpless people. Git 'em excited and they ain't like white people; they are savages.

Forrest, who had traded them and therefore lived with them, knew of course that this was vague and groundless fear, that the Negroes lived up to your expectations if you put the expectation into them. But he knew his men felt that way, and it would make them fight harder, and by God he had to get as much out of them as he could. War meant fighten and fighten meant killen no matter how you looked at it. He had to take that fort for the stuff he needed from it, and to boost up the spirits of the region's people, and because were he to have any command left during the next summer of campaigning back in Mississippi he would have to let his men hit Fort Pillow and get rid of all their frustration and anger and fear by carrying the place. By capture or by storm, they would take Fort Pillow which stood for the formal and embodied establishment upon their land of everything which they detested with an iron-hard detestation and hatred.

He began to clean his revolvers and work out his plans for the step beyond Fort Pillow, since he had to keep on the budge and keep tearing at the Federals while he was in Tennessee. Maybe one day they would be driven away, but till then he had to come at 'em like a bobcat in a pack of dogs, moven and hitten every which way at the same time.

10

WHEN RUSSELL'S REGIMENT ASSEMBLED ON THE MORNING OF THE eleventh of April, coming in from the scattered fields and homes surrounding the farmhouse which served as Russell's headquarters, tousle-haired and swearing thickly and looking for their coffee, Russell himself stood in front of their lines. The regiment was spread along a narrow creek bed, grey with stones and the spring mists, and Russell paused and then said, "This afternoon at three-thirty the regiment will lead out on the Brownsville road," and then he paused again and rocked on his heels. "And from thence to Fort Pillow, to arrive there on the morning of the twelfth April." They all, predictably and dramatically, turned and looked at each other with their mouths open. Then everyone cheered wildly, "Yaay, Yaay," which was almost the fighting yell. Russell read the rest of the orders when they finished the cheer and then went back to his house. The company officers gathered their companies around them, small groups of men in dark, wet-looking, grey-brown uniforms standing in the new green grass and surrounded and silhouetted by the mists. They could hear cheering from the other regiments of the brigade, from the Second which was separated by a small round hill, and from the Sixteenth Tennessee about a mile away toward Jackson.

Acox's company was thirty-nine strong, including seven new recruits they had picked up along the Kentucky line, during the Paducah campaign. They knotted around Acox; the thirty-two veterans of the Okolona fight squatted or stood or clustered as if each man had his own familiar position and place around their captain. The seven recruits stood at the edge of the circle, awkwardly; they could not yet imitate the judicious ease of the veterans. Acox reminded them about their horses, and asked if any men were ill or felt they should report to the surgeons before making the march. None of them did this time, though Orrison and Van Nest had both gone on sick call before the Paducah march. They want this one, Acox thought. "Now, about your ammunition . . . ."

"What's ol' Tell goen to do with that ol' Yankee peashooter of his?" All of the veterans laughed. Acox pretended to be angry.

"What's that? Are you still carryen that breechloader, Tell?" Johnny Tell, sitting on the grass at his feet, blushed while the men laughed. He was a slim, red-haired boy with freckles and wide brown eyes; he was the company pet.

"Yesseh, Cap'n. . . ."

"Hell, Cap'n, he ain't big enough to tote uh Enfield. . . ."

Acox raised his eyes, despairingly, to the skies: it was a ritual of sorts, pretending to be angry, frustrated, with Tell. This morning it gave him a chance to mask his surging anxiety. They cannot call this one off. Not this time. But I will wager they will. . . .

The seven new recruits grinned and shuffled. They were not fully aware of the jest, and they did not feel that they could laugh openly with the others quite yet. Three of them had fought under Breckinridge, deserting after Stone's River—but they were not yet veterans of Forrest's command. They smiled and looked down at their crossed arms, and then listened again as Acox resumed his instructions. "Now, when the ammunition wagon comes, the sergeants'll pass it out. . . ."

The thirty-two men who had gone through the Okolona fight with him and had followed him back into Tennessee filled the space around him with affection, respect, silence. They were extensions of his own will, they would do what he told them instinctively and well; they were as close as brothers, even the ones such as Orrison and Van Nest, who Acox knew would hardly have held his affection or trust in peacetime. They were bound together by victory, confidence, arrogant self-respect for themselves and their company and Forrest's command. Forrest had given them the one big victory, where they could see and sense the effectiveness of their courage and initiative and training.

It had not been a brutal fight, such as Shiloh or Chickamauga; or a soul-wearying one. They had fought all morning and into the afternoon, and the Yankees had run and rallied and run and finally broken completely. It had been particularly exhausting. They had driven in the Yankee rearguard at Okolona in the morning; had driven them again with a mounted charge at Ivey's Hill, where Forrest's brother had been killed; and had finally broken a charge by the Yankee rearguard in the late afternoon. They had fought and chased all day, through a chill, bright winter landscape with the fields tawny and dotted with fir trees.

Acox could remember terrible weariness, exhilaration, doubt. He had been desperately afraid that Forrest would not keep up the pursuit each time they had broken the Yankees (that would have been like Chickamauga). Then when Forrest's brother was killed, he had been afraid that Forrest would throw away the whole thing. He had been close to them, Forrest kneeling over the body of his brother while twigs and dry brown leaves were showering down as the Yankee fire went over their heads. Acox had been thrown from his horse in the charge, and his shoulder blue with pain; but when he had seen Forrest hurl himself back on his horse and, alone, whip down the road after the Yankees, he had mounted a dead man's horse and followed. Forrest had plunged into a platoon of Yankees in the yellow road, a tangle of men in kepis and powder-blue capes, and Forrest hurtling into them; all around Acox the rebels had checked their horses out of concern and fear and impulse, and then McCulloh had been among them, his bandaged hand mauve and crimson with the fresh and drying blood, yelling, "Will ye see 'em cut him down!" and they had all whipped down on the Yankees. Only when they got there they saw Forrest in the midst of them, his face still in that hardened, molded bronze masque, his long sword hacking and spraying blood and slicing away the powder-blue capes, and the knot of Yankees pushing their horses in terror away and back, and six, seven of them lying dead already in the rutted back-country road, their bodies flecked with blood and sprayed spittle and foam.

Acox could remember that—the terrible helplessness of the Yankees, Forrest's wild, long saber, and suck and intake of breath as the men reached him and the Yankees plunged away into the woods on all sides or fell sobbing and pleading in the roadway, trying to avoid the saber. After that, he had kept up all day, even to the end when he found himself hurling back the final Yankee thrusts with some Missourians of McCulloh's brigade. Tarkenton and Tom Morse, another company commander in the Twentieth, had found him and helped him back up the slope and back to the regiment, and he had slept feverishly in Russell's own headquarters.

But he had had his victory. He had finally seen the Yankees broken and beaten and run to earth, littering the roadside with their fine new carbines and pistols and dazedly surrendering in the blue-grey evening, with the air in the nostrils like brass. They had done what Forrest had told them and they had not only beaten but destroyed a much more powerful force; they had seen it whipped, their hunger for a real, consummated victory, with the prizes and sights and sounds of such a victory, had been satiated. They had implicit confidence in each other and in Forrest: part of the legend of the man had been enacted before them. "Did ye see him hit those bluebellies in that air road, after they killed Jeffry? Did you see that?" Now the only thing left, they told themselves, was to get back up into Tennessee, and attend to the Yankees up there. And Forrest had taken them back, and tomorrow he had said he was going to let them have Fort Pillow.

Acox dismissed his company and felt a rising surge in his throat, standing in the mist watching them walk off toward the breakfast fires. They passed Morse's company; Morse, tall, heavy, shy, was reading the Bible to his men. Acox remembered how he had done that in the field right outside of Okolona, on the morning of the fight. It was a sharp-etched detail of his recollection, like the moment they had gotten to Forrest's side and seen how he had decimated the Yankee detachment—Morse with the sunlight falling coldly over his shoulders, reading the Bible to his men as they had hunkered behind a snake-and-rider fence and whistled at the size of the Yankee column down the slope and spreading through Okolona toward the northeast.

Acox's throat, chest ached with the fierce hope and expectancy. *I hope Morse is not reading to them of charity. Now we can hit those people. Because up to now we have done nothing really. They have not even let me go home, but now we can go and hit those people where we ought.* He kept pushing his fist into his other hand, over and over. His beard was full and dark. The sun above him was a gleaming, creamy pool over his head, and the place smelled of water and the sharp smell of mist. He was almost afraid to keep on thinking about it, he wanted to go at Fort Pillow so badly. *If I keep on thinking they will send down a messenger and call it off. Even if it is Forrest, he is still a military man, and he might call it off, just like they have stopped us every time we have done something worth doing in this war.*

They spent all day getting ready for the ride. In the early morning, which turned out to be fine and rich, they worked with the horses, currying them and examining the hoofs and coats. They cleaned their own equipment, dragging patches through the rifles, spinning the chambers on the pistols over and over and sighting down them. Acox went down the company line taking especial note of the seven new recruits they had taken out of Western Tennessee and Kentucky, keeping his mind on the things like the leather and the rifles and not even letting himself think about the campaign. Wagons came down the road and stopped by the regiments, and a large corporal with two Negro helpers handed out the rations, captured federal hardtack and bacon wrapped loosely in paper, and a little beef. Company by company the mess cooks went up and put the rations in large haversacks, swearing at the corporal and the Negroes, the Negroes grinning and the corporal sweating and swearing back. Acox listened to the talk and the noises the horses made, and caught himself staring at the showers of sparks from where the regimental blacksmiths were shoeing the horses.

Inside himself he was in a pet of nervousness. *They can not* stop us this time. They can not. He got his cavalry saber which he had practiced with but which was still not very handy for him, and he went out to the rear of the house where there was a grindstone. He had to wait in line, during the time it took three big Tennesseans from Wilson's regiment to sharpen their bowie knives. Acox thought irritably, normally they don't look like that, normally their eyes don't flash that way and they don't let their faces smile that much. One of them finished and straightened up and spit on the knife once more and then ran his thumb along it experimentally.

"Wowee, that will take care of airy nigger I ever see, just flash hit his way oncet!"

"Ol' Dexter, he feel strong about niggers." They all laughed.

The second man stepped up to the grindstone. "An' them goddamn Tories too, don't you forgit it. Don't you forgit it. I know me of some that I aim to look up in that ol' fo't."

Then Acox couldn't hear them any more since he was pacing past the garden which was chopped and battered by heel and hoofmarks into a mass of turf and weeds. But there was a stand of jonquils above the black earth, in a corner, shielded by some brickwork where the movement of people and animals hadn't beaten them down. He felt irritable at the Tennessee troopers. What is wrong with me? They should not feel that way. No. They have to follow their officers and do what we say. We can not take that fort if the men lose their heads and forget to follow orders. The third man finished, and then Acox brushed past them regardless of the exaggerated stare one of them gave him and stepped up to the grindstone. He laid the long sword on it, from the honed tip where the sharpness stopped, and he set to work. The day was cold and yet warm; it was spring and the air was full of moist smells, and it was cold in the shadows but warm in the patches of sunlight. Acox did not know much about sharpening metal and it took him two hours, working hard, to get the sword sharpened all the way down its length. They say ol' Bedford has his this way. It does make sense. You hit a man with this sword and it don't kill him unless you get him with the four inches at the tip that are sharpened.

He was sweating by the time he finished, and he reached down and put on his frock coat. He looked at his watch.

Messengers still ran in and out of the house and Russell nodded to him from the porch and then bent over the stack of papers in front of him, still writing. His personal equipment was already packed. Acox looked at the russet leather pile of equipment at the foot of his chair, pistol and sword and glasses-case and map-case and knapsack and belts, on the floor in a warm stack like some patient dog. Like some of the retrievers my friends at college used to have with them. I have never seen dogs like that since. He realized that he was staring at the equipment and he shook his head and went back down to the company. Most of the men were eating their food down quickly, but he was not hungry.

He paced and fidgeted and played with the bits of his own equipment, and walked endlessly around his new horse, looking at it from every angle and saying, "Caesar, Caesar, you had better hold up. Yes you had. You don't hold up this time and old fellow I swear I will shoot you. I have to be there this time, old fellow." Tom Morse came down the line, his face bent and worried and clean-shaven now. He looked soberly at Acox walking around his horse. "Hamilton, my men are really excited about this one."

"Umm. So is my company."

"They ain't skitterish. They are quiet and they smile and talk low and polish their things. I mean to say, they are really ready."

" 'Twon't do to talk about it, Tom. Not at all. They may call it off. We got an hour to go, and they might call it off."

Morse laughed softly. "Naw. Naw they won't. Forrest, he knows he got to give us this one crack at that place. He knows."

"I hope you are right." He straightened up and looked at Morse. "You know, Tom, ever since I have been in this army I have never had the feeling that anything I . . . anything I was doing was for Amanda. And this time it is. You know?"

"I know. How is she, by the way?"

"Oh, Bowles went home and I got a letter from her. She says not to worry and she is all right. . . ." His voice trailed off and he looked out across the glistening wet fields. Morse got up and went back to his own company.

The regiment mounted by the bugle call. They assembled in the old creek bed, nervous and waiting, and Russell waited with them on the slope above, talking to Davidson who left his company to sit his horse beside him. They waited and waited and Acox got down off his horse out of nervousness and picked at the grass and pitched away the small pebbles.

He stood up and buttoned back the yellow facings of his jacket. He was sweating. Oh God, let us have this one, let us get on the road. Oh for godsake, get on with this thing. This waiting is sickening. Caesar, you better hold up underneath this ol' carcass of mine or you will be dead soon. I mean to have this one. We weren't there when Neely whipped ol' Hurst. All we have done is go to Paducah and what the hell, that is not even in this damned state. Oh come on, come on, let us get on with this. He looked up and hated Russell. Sit up there then. Whyn't the hell you send somebody like that Davidson over yonder and find out what the shit is the matter. He saw Bowles was looking up at Russell too, hollow-eyed too and slapping his hands with his reins. Clark was whispering and grinning but he kept on shifting himself in the saddle, throwing one leg over the leather and sitting easy and then back again and putting his feet into the stirrups. Orrison and his cousin were talking softly to each other, and then Orrison threw back his head and laughed. A bluejay flew down the length of the column, and one of the new recruits made a motion to shoot it, trailing it and squeezing his fingers and pretending to jerk from the recoil. The one beside him pointed up and told him something like, you missed hit boy. You don't lead right. Here lemme show ya, and then both of them were somehow joining hands and scuffling and bending their fingers when their hands met, trying to pull each other off their horses. Whyn't the hell they sit there and lick their lips and swallow all the time like the other damned recruits? He stood up and glared at them. One of them looked at him in surprise, and tried to disengage his hands but the blond one kept on pulling at him and laughing, and then he too saw Acox, only Acox looked stiffly away as soon as their eyes met. Oh come on, come on. He looked at all of the details in the creek bed. Lichen pale-pink and green on blue-grey rock. Why does not this creek flow? I wonder.

Then there was the clattering and the messenger came down, with a bugle glinting and slapping across his back. Oh, here it is. Shit, here it is. He was so anxious that he was certain the man would tell them that the orders had been canceled. The messenger was stopping and saluting at impossibly long range toward Colonel Russell and Russell raised his eyebrows and the bugler nodded and kicked his horse around, and Russell lowered his eyebrows in understanding and said, "All right, Company A will lead out then. By column of fours, to your right." He gave a circling motion with his hand and all of the horses and men pivoted and everyone cheered. Acox climbed into the saddle and cheered too, screaming into the stillness of the valley. "Yaaaaa Yaaaa."

They rode out through the old campsite where the blackened circles of fires, the cuts for tents and the latrines were scattered through the new grass and the black, moist soil. Acox thought, we are like an animal, sloughing off an old skin. His back quivered and he wanted to spur the horse ahead. Let us just get out of sight of this house and then no one can call us back. They trotted past the headquarters house where the regimental flag had been taken down. The square red flag flapped at the head of the column. They caught up with the Second and Barteau came back, wizened and yellowish, and nodded to Russell and the two rode along together. The Sixteenth was farther ahead and could only be seen when the column of cavalry rounded one of the hills and on the fields below it in the distance they could see the head of the Second and the end of the Sixteenth just curling out of sight, pale, tiny grey figures with bobbing guidons like the lances of knights.

So we are. We are like the knights, Acox thought. And anyhow we feel like it, we feel like a crusade. We are not jittery like we were before Okolona, and they don't ride in one tight clump. The men spread out and gather into messes while they ride. He looked back at his company behind him, talking in small, strung-out groups, all of the men bearded except Clark and Bowles and one or two of the recruits, and all of them with large hats with the brims turned up on the side or in front except for Johnny Tell and Clark who were wearing grey kepis with yellow trim. Orrison was riding beside him, whistling, leaning his cheek against the long pole of the guidon. Up ahead they could hear the Sixteenth singing something that sounded like "The Yellow Rose of Texas," and some of the companies of the Second singing it too.

They were out of sight now and Acox's back trembled once more from the tension and then he thought, well, I can think about it now. The afternoon was slanting away with blue shadows coming out in the green grass and the grey woods, the blue-purple brought out by the sinking light and all the moisture in the earth. Everything seemed a blue haze and blue screen, and above them there were large, puffy, thick clouds in a deep, deep, blue sky, the clouds with grey bottoms making them look substantial and full, and above the moving clouds a thin, gossamer-like white scarf of cloud. The land was broken with gullies and rising, rounded hills on each side, furred with evergreens. Dogwood was out; the pink and white looked water-soaked and rich, and glowed through the masking, grey-blue woods. Acox looked far up on a ridge to his left, and he could see the other face of the ridge at one break in its crest. The sunlight was painting it orange and gold, and the side to the column was grey and still. Between the two colors on the high ridge he could see one tree, a redbud or a dogwood, standing in a raw, bare spot, the tree having no color but the base of it dark and above it chinks and flecks of pure gold where the sunlight caught in the petals. He could see the golden chinks flick and glow and disappear like dying embers of a fire as the sun went down, and he could see the golden light spread, shift and slip away down the ridge.

They had been out an hour. That was impossible, it seemed, but a rest was called, and the column stopped and turned to the side in the roadway. The men dismounted and sucked at their canteens and rested and stretched. Acox dismounted and tossed the reins to Tell and paced. We oughtn't be stopping, we could go on I know for another hour. While they were sprawled around talking in low voices the shadows began to sink upon them, the blueness turning all of the men to dusky, dark forms, and along the fringes of the forest early fireflies began to twitch and flicker and weave. Acox sat in the dimness on a log next to Morse and Davidson, and watched a match flare at Davidson's beardless young face and glow and sink twice while he pulled a cigar alight, his eyes shining against the flame and his face ruddy-looking and rounded at the cheeks. Orrison was talking to Van Nest who was urinating loudly behind them, wet sounds splashing against the leaves and trees. Then Russell blew his whistle like some weird, insistent insect and they mounted again.

He rode on in the darkness. Up ahead he could see one rider drop out and wait, and he knew that it was Morse, waiting for him. On the way into Kentucky they had together endured a sleet storm in the last spiteful blast of winter, and ridden hooded and in silent company together, and since that time Morse always waited for him after the first halt.

"Lee?" Morse sounded hoarse and embarrassed.

"Umm. Won't be too much in the way of company tonight, Tom."

Morse made some kind of strangled apology and fell in beside him, and Orrison reined back to let the two into the road together. Acox watched the moon through the trees on the right after the ridges and the hills broke. It was large and scimitar-shaped, probing through the trees. There was complete darkness in the road, and the talking had already died away. Far up he could hear someone playing a jew's harp and someone else singing "Lorena." The men made rustling noises up and down the column as they began to pull out coats that they had taken off to exercise their flesh in the cool air during the afternoon. Acox's jacket was soaked with sweat, he suddenly noticed, and the cold, tight press of the cloth under his armpits annoyed him. He shivered and began to tug and pull at his cloak behind him. He could not get it free and Morse wordlessly settled his horse back a pace and unhooked it for him, and he said "Thanks" and folded himself into it and unbuttoned the cold wet jacket.

We will see the moon circle us tonight, he thought. 'Twill

circle us and then we will be at Fort Pillow. I have waited a long time for this, a very long time. He was still very excited about it and he smiled and shivered. When the moon is on the right—no, no, it will be right ahead of us for we turn west sometime during the night (I heard Forrest found a man that was in Fort Pillow and who is guiding him—I hope he knows his way) and then we will be going due west. They passed a creek running through a press of trees. There were dark fences and a cabin with no lights, and all of the men shivered from the darkness and huddled into themselves. They could see the shack and the fence by looking out of the corner of their eyes at them; the creek smelled moist and then the whole sky smelled like rain, and there were toads and frogs rasping and clacking in the tangle at the creek. The jingle and clatter and squeaking of the leather frightened them into silence but on the other side they kept on methodically, pushing a freckled sound at the men. Morse said something and he grunted and gave a kind of chuckle.

Well now, this last month has been an agony. Because he was so close to home. Now that they were back in Tennessee he could have gotten to see his wife if he had deserted. When they were in Mississippi there was the thought and the fact that, well, even if I did slip away I could not get there. But he could have gotten there from Sharon's Ferry because after Hurst was so thoroughly shattered, there was simply no federal cavalry in the area. Every morning in the dawn he had gotten up slightly ahead of the bugles, when the more conscientious cooks were the only figures stirring except for the cloaked and sleepy sentries. He had taken his horse out with a wave past the company sentry for a ride through the fields, saying he was exercising the horse but really almost slipping away, just over one more ridge and one more creek and then south, establishing a pattern (so they will not miss me tomorrow) which he somehow never completed. It became consistently harder not to ride off and find her because of what they themselves were doing to Tennessee.

When in Mississippi and along the Alabama line they had requisitioned grain and horses and cattle and especially men, down there it was a terrible necessity of course and it hurt the men, but it was happening in a foreign state to people from another area and with other thoughts and land and history. Here it was a local disaster and you sensed no longer only the inequity of it but also now the disaster. What it meant to the families to lose food and cattle and men, especially still the men. You rode into a farm that was exactly like your own farm and the woman protested she had three sons or maybe a husband and a brother in the Confederate army and here were their pictures, see? "Here," she would shout, "look here!" even as they were dragging the animal off through the dirt or holding a gun on the sullen-faced man, "Here, look at this!" And it would be a paper signed and made pathetically formal-looking, saying: I am a privut (or privit or privat) fighten (or fiten) with Lee in Virginny and our Colonel says do not take our property and food from our family's mouths or we will not fite or you will answer to me. Evidently they had started doing this in some one Tennessee infantry regiment because it was prevalent in the region. The officer always answered, "Yes ma'am, yes ma'am, but we got to have the stuff. Now here is the payment." "I don't want that money which ain't worth a cent, a damn cent, an' you know hit, and I got to feed these chilrun, these three chilrun." Sometimes the women would say, "Why yore Tennesseans too, ain'tcha? Ain'tcha? What more we got to give? We give every thing including our menfolk and do you now mean to take our food? Do you now mean to take the only boy I got left? Whut would you say if 'twere yo' wife?" To that they devoloped a standard answer: "Why ma'am, a loyal Tennessean would be happy to make the sacrifice."

This scene would be re-enacted in a hundred scattered homes by one officer, standing under the winter-dulled oak in the front yard or maybe the cedar, and looking at the stragglyhaired, desperate, praying, cursing, begging woman. Listening to his men breathing through their mouths as they dragged the calf off or kept a watch on the boy in their midst with bound hands. While the woman kept on saying, "Please now then, I beg please don't," and "Even the Yankees, even Hurst or Bradford wudn't take off our boy. What will we do? Tell me that, officer. What will we do?" The slouch-chested woman holding a baby athwart her hips or the young woman with the potted plants on the porch crying or trying to act noble or pleading too, parading always the children and begging. Until Orrison said one day in all seriousness as they wound back down with a horse in tow, "I swear I have seen more chilrun in West Tennessee than all the goddamned schoolteachers and midwives put together. I am an expert on the women and the chilrun of West Tennessee." Everybody laughed, even LeRoy Acox, laughing and laughing until the tears came because Orrison was so deadly sincere and it was true. But he thought as the brigade wound into a ridge and then over it, the reason is not that they will take our food though that of course is partially it. No. I am not worried about that. Amanda will not starve. And we have no children. He did not think anything for a moment after that. Any more.

But that is not the thing. The thing is what is happening to me. I feel nothing any more. It is an annoyance and just once you wish you could find the wife who needs—Christ on the cross, they all need—but who will let you take the things. Even in your own state. You know the disaster and you even feel it but you think what you are doing is not only necessary but even moral. That is the thing, the change that happens to you. So like the Schafer boy, we trap him on his wedding day, or we sent the family hounds after the other boy, what's his name. Acheron. That is the thing. That we sit in our saddles scruffy and hairy with the vaguest pretense of uniforms among us and say our lies and become so completely callous about it. Yes. The callousness at first, and then inevitably we feel the rage. The rage that comes so that Fire would have split open that old woman's skull when we took her sixteen year old and she would not turn him loose. Fire took his rifle and calmly lifted it to bring down on her head, and of course he was stopped but not until there was a moment in which we stood and nodded, yes goddammit, get it over with. And only then did our moral and virtuous thoughts come in and only then did we stop him.

Even in your own state, among the limestone and cedar trees you feel only coldness and contempt and fury and rage when you are thwarted. You callously take and behind the taking is not patriotism or self-sacrifice but the fact that you can as a last resort get twenty rifles to bear on the woman and manifest your will to shoot her if need be. Make it clear that you will shoot. And you will kill the husband or son or brother if he will not serve. You will shoot him dead. You have to make them see that because they are past all appeals; they have been through this so long and so often. You cannot appeal to them but you will shoot them readily enough, and only when they see that can you requisition enough to keep this war for independence and the home and hearth going. That is what it takes. This brutal callousness, some part of you squeezed and wrung dry of emotion and buried and never showing. Until you still hear the wail as you are going down the next ridge and then you flinch, but even that flinch is going too. Because sometimes in the last week we were only laughing or saying, "Good job," calculatingly. "Only move in faster next time from the barn side." All right and, "Yassuh, that was sticky, but we will hit 'em faster next time." At first, like in Mississippi, you thought, this is horrible but it is necessary, and you always had to convince yourself of that, but I have seen what follows then. Then the convincing becomes so much a pure, single thought that you don't go through the process again, you just accept. And then past that you only feel the tiny twinge of pain. And then and soon there is not even a twinge, just a dull indifference. But that is followed, and here is what I mean, that is followed by a final step wherein you exult. Wherein you are so used to the whole thing that you go the last step. You become angry when they argue and think, don't they see? Then the selfish fools are deserting the cause and they ought to be killed. And all the time you are fighting for the hearthside and the home and the family. You are not even fighting for a change.

But they work it out; that is why they never send you to your own family to get the youngest brother and the only cow left. Of course not.

Acox knew that these things were happening inside himself, and inside all of the men in Forrest's command. When you were in the infantry with Lee or with Johnston, you were never faced with this. But here, and especially during this last month foraging in West Tennessee, assurance wore thin, and then wore out; they were always justifying themselves. To most of the men, Wheelock and Tarkenton and Morse and even Davidson, it was not too difficult, since certainty settled easily over them, and they had no time or interest or even capability to imagine that there were other sides and other conditions. This did not mean that they did not suffer nor did it mean that they had not changed. But change had come to Acox only with pain and misgiving and doubt.

What we should do is just every man stay at home and fight from his front stoop. Every man of us until the Yankees get glutted with the slaughter and leave us alone. Yes. Increasingly, he had come to depend upon that answer; that the Yankees just leave us alone. It was the only answer that he could envisage.

The Yankees do not have to do this. The war is not up in their land. It is here and the losing of it will not affect them if they lose, but it will affect us if we lose. It is an expedition to them, but it is a hideous nightmare visited upon us.

Why did they come? Why didn't they leave us alone? They have always hated us because of our slaves: did they not realize that we would have taken care of the slaves and slavery in our own fashion, if they had just left us alone? Acox had come to depend upon this too, as he depended upon the thought or hope that the Yankees might someday leave them alone. We would have taken care of our slaves and slavery, in our own way, in our own time. He had come to say it to himself by rote; he could not envision what he meant by it. It was so much easier to recollect the hypocrisy of the abolitionists, their professed love, their blood lust; they had to have their pound of flesh, we had no choice. There was no question in his mind concerning himself and slavery: it was caught up, spun, flamed, by his sense of antithetical forces, threats, dangers. It was not only slavery; it was our culture, our religion, slavery only gave them an excuse, a patina of reason. We would have taken care of slavery in our own fashion, in our own time. Anyhow, is slavery such a sin, if you treat them well? I know of many people that have freed their slaves upon their death.

Look at what they are doing now, look at what Sherman

did to Mississippi—they had better keep him out of Georgia—
and Hurst, and nigra troops shouldering white women off the
sidewalks in Memphis. Look at Fort Pillow. He shifted restlessly, straightening his back. Anger and determination settled
upon his shoulders; Acox had the strong certainty of a man who
sees himself move with purpose against his enemies. His home
was threatened; his way of life—and by this he imagined patterns of faith and culture and gentility—was menaced. They
mean to bring us to our knees. They had better beware.

Imagination still plagued him, but with the awareness of
the price that they were paying. There is the spiral of destroying our homes to save our homes and shedding our gentility and
even moral sense to preserve culture and gentility and morality.
The price we have to pay is not just measured in cattle or even
in human souls. I always see this scene. Amanda is around the
house planting or sewing or making soap or cooking. Then she
hears the patrol and she rushes through the back of the house,
past the little table in the entryway where she keeps a basin of
soap and water and some scent and perhaps by now even a
morning coat and she freshens up there. Out of that sweet,
tender conceit that is half-conceit and is half a desire to appeal
in order to somehow make a spot of color in the world for the
man that beholds her. She hears the troop and sees the grey
coats for a change and she runs and changes, desperately shouting at the cook (if we still have one) to put on some tea. Then
she runs to the door and out to meet them, radiant and smiling,
warm and full. And there of course she meets a Confederate
troop, dull-faced and weary and hairy, smelling bad and coated
in lice and dirt and thick captured blankets, and an officer with
enough tarnished lace showing to identify him trying to make
the social response while the men simply sit slack-jawed and not
even interested. And she in an excess of pity for these things
and, thinking of me, she invites them in and they come in tracking red and black mud and crushed grass and odor. She asks of
me and asks about them and their families and they remain not
guarded but just calculating. Then the officer asks and not even
toning down the demand (I know I would not at someone else's
home; indeed I have not) makes the requisitions. And she

would pale and by some sort of indication he would impress upon her the fact that he would shoot her if necessary and if it came to that. A cheek twitch or something or a gesture and there would be a clank of a rifle being lowered even while the man holding it is balancing the teacup. And she of course would give what they requisitioned, which she would have done in the first place, since she has lived at such remove from reality that nobility and courage and self-sacrifice are not parodies. But she would die inside. The awareness of the price steeled him further.

The rest-stop came, this time in the middle of a field freshly plowed to the side of the road. There was a light and some of the men from Morse's company went over toward it in the expressed hope of finding liquor. Morse had to track across the field on stiff legs to reprimand them, leaving Acox dismounted and sitting on his side, fisting his hands in bitterness in the complete darkness. The moon was out but clouds were covering most of the sky, clouds and mist, and there was the definite and never-ending, hollow smell of water and moisture. Some of the men smoked but most lay still in the grass, cradling their heads or working the soreness out of their thighs. More of them urinated this time, in a scattered line across the field, making weary jokes about, Reckon this is the las' and first time you ever been on a skirmish line, hunh? Russell came by. "How is it goen with you, Lee?"

"Fine, sir, just fine." He stood above him for a moment, and then turned away on down the line, his boots crunching through roadside weeds.

There was a sudden, far rumbling of thunder then, and the whistle blew to get the men mounted in case lightning frightened the horses and they got loose. They climbed stiffly into the saddles which felt warm and comfortable and yet stiffly painful, as the muscles readjusted after the stretch. The men got their ponchos out and put them on, pulling on cloaks too with hoods so they looked more than ever like knights with huge helmets. The moon was gone completely the next time LeRoy Acox looked for it, and Morse was practically indistinguishable in the depth of his hood. Orrison said, "God I wisht I was in bed, this would be a good ol' night to be in a bed." Somebody said, "Yes, with a woman I reckon," and everybody gave a tired kind of laugh. The whistles sounded and gradually they moved forward again, with a drizzling, cold rain beginning to come down on them and a chill, cold fog coming up out of the earth, squeezing at them.

They rode on in the wet and complete darkness, huddling together now because of the driving spurts of rain that seemed to come out of the trees and the constant drizzle that worked underneath their clothes, and the close-edged blankness of the road. Everyone bared his teeth in discomfort, and swore. The guidons flapped wetly against the poles for a time and then plastered to them. Officers stood to one side peering at their companies and saying, "Move up, move up," and three times in the next hour they had to wait and sit their horses while straying regiments and companies and individuals were brought back, by flatted bugle calls and squinting shouts into the darkness. Acox felt the water soak into his shirt and he fumbled with his wet gloves to button his blouse at the throat, and cursed and had to take off a glove and almost dropped it. A crack of lightning came down through the clouds, freezing everyone in weird, bulky, hooded cloaks and slick ponchos, against the eye. The second bolt followed the first and they could see bare-limbed trees and ridges to their left in the sudden white-blue glare. The horses jerked and skittered, and the men who were tired and nervous kicked at them and swore.

So, Acox thought as he settled down into the shell of his overcoat but tightened his hold on the reins, so there is no mercy at all in West Tennessee, not for anybody. Nosuh. Not for my wife, I reckon, not now. Not with the niggers out back planning to do God knows what, or maybe already run off to that fort and planning to come back and do God knows what, which since they are niggers and have always wanted the white flesh of a woman they of course will doubtless be planning. And there are those damned white Tennesseans fighting for the Yankees and, ah God, there ain't pity with them I know. We passed too many houses where they been, where the woman said they took every cent she had and showed us the ripped-up pictures and clothing—not of course that it made any discernable difference to our foraging—those white Tennesseans coming out of the darkness; and everybody heard what they did to those officers of Forrest's old regiment they caught. How they cut off the nose and punched the eyes out of one, and shot the others out of hand and then mutilated the bodies. I didn't see that but I did see what they did to the houses we went to where there was just a woman and her family and a few slaves. How they choose only the bigger houses and then put the sword to the furniture and rip out the books and steal the picture frames, all half driving the woman out of her mind.

And they know how to hit you where you are the weakest. "They" had come to stand in his mind for many things beside the white Tennesseans: for the Negroes and the Yankees, all of them faintly imaged as a great, faceless, eyeless, Godless host, in grey and dim-blue, bent on his own destruction. They were part of a vast conspiracy; certainly the pattern of war so far had shown him that. That there was a great arcing conspiracy and that his own leaders were culpable at worst, foolish at best, incapable of dealing with it. It was a curiously intellectual fear; visceral realization of it was never plain to him, or to any of them.

And I know that they know how to get you where you are weakest, and oh my God I am weak at that point, at my wife's soul and delicacy and yes even body and beauty, that is where I am weak, because I love her so. Maybe it is not right to love like that and there is always a guilty edge to it, I know, and sometimes God help me that guilty edge only adds a kind of relish to the lovemaking. Oh I love her so and she God knows is the only world I got left to put any trust in and any faith in and the only world left to fight for. She is the only thing after four years worth fighting for in West Tennessee anyhow, and dear God dear God I mean this like I never meant anything I ever said or asked for before, dear God if the two of us have to be punished for what we did, for lovemaking and for loving each other so much, if we have to be punished for this (and I always somehow thought we would be; that you can't love that much without it being somehow wrong), then let me take it all. Put it all on me and strike me dead this instant but oh God don't let it be her that has to suffer, oh God in all Your might let it be me that is struck down. Do anything to me (oh no, there is one thing you know you don't want Him to do to you), yes anything (but if He takes that what have you got left then?), well don't make her suffer Lord, don't make her suffer. I will put it that way then. Don't let her suffer and of course You realize God that to have to live with me if I were . . . were disfigured or mutilated, that would double her suffering. No, no, I won't say it like that. I won't put myself into this because I do love her enough. Strike me down Lord, do Your punitive will against me, in anything. In anything or any way do it against me. I will have nothing left if it is against her that You move, and dear Lord I have always tried to live properly and correctly have I not? Maybe not in constant awareness and perception of You (no, no, Thee), in perception of Thee, but always in honesty and righteousness with my fellow man. Maybe I haven't. Maybe I haven't or if I have it has been because it has been comfortable for me. Well then, I shall. Well I shall (saying this despite, and into, the constant image of a round window in the county courthouse with the sunlight coming through in the late afternoon and him standing having just won a case listening to the stir of the people behind him and their rustling departure and the knot forming around his table clapping his client on the back and then clapping him, and the huge surge of pride that was always his reward. Black and sinful pride). Oh God, deliver her from this war and I shall burn in hell for an eternity and with gladness because of our dual sins. Only she hasn't really sinned, Lord. You know she hasn't. I have led her to it, awakening her body in a way that was immoral and taking delight in the pleasures thereof and oh I knew 'twas sin and she kept saying it was sin but I persuaded her (and now the image of her naked beside him under the white, white sheets in the dawn, sighing and putting both of her palms against his chest and putting her head down on him, in the circle of his arms in the coming day dawn. And going gently to sleep and him so filled with love he felt he could die) and so it is my fault. And do not take it on her. Indeed Lord, indeed I must go one step further. I can not protect her Lord (say you never could), I never could protect her really, but now I doubly can not. Now there is no mercy left here on earth, not from the niggers where there never was any, and not from the white men tangled up in this war. The only people I would trust her with are the Yankees now, the Yankees whom I can't hate really and who have not been pressed to the point of desperation. And who have still the distance from the fact of starvation so that they can uphold honor. Even that fact, Lord, almost kills me because of the hideous irony of it all. So dear Lord protect her and look down on her as she moves and love her and if there is punishment then inflict it upon me (no, no, not any conditions now, for godsake), just inflict it upon me.

He looked up into the sky and everything was completely dark and black and rain made him blink and squint and suddenly he almost laughed. Well now, I was really going for a while, I was. His horse lurched and he thought, oh now Caesar, as he steadied it, oh now Caesar you can't give up now. We got to ride all this night. Well, I was really wrapped up for a while. And then as an afterthought he said, "But of course it was sincere, dear Lord, of course it was sincere." He felt weary and drained and exhausted. The wool was gathering in his crotch uncomfortably and he moved around in the saddle. He got a sudden cramp in one thigh muscle and pumped furiously at it in the blind, biting agony of the thing until it subsided. I better watch how I move. I am cold and wet and stiff and tired and I could get more cramps. The wool of his pants gathered and was soaked and it scratched. Well, I will have to wait until we come to a halt. They kept on riding. Aren't we ever going to come to another halt? How long has it been? He tried to see his watch, but there was no light at all and he did not have any matches and there was no hint of any more lightning. Now that the passion of the moment had worn off he was acutely uncomfortable. He squinted and began shifting and turning in the saddle regardless of any damned cramps, trying to get his pants pulled taut again and cursing under his breath waiting for a halt.

His flesh was chafed and stung by the wet wool. He wrenched himself about irritably. The flecked pain catalyzed his fear and his anger and anxiety. The sense of some potent, antithetical conspiracy grew upon him and peopled the air around him. Faces and forms avoided his mind, but he told himself that he knew who they were. He wondered if he would find Sam and Buck at that fort, and if he did find them there, what that would mean. He was afraid that he would find them, and then he was afraid that he would not. Like the story of the Negro accused of raping the white woman, the details of his fear were too familiar, too sharply etched to warrant specific recollection. It was mainly an intellectual fear, with only the darkest surges of imagery thrown arras-like over it. The final fear was that he would be frustrated, thwarted, rendered helpless when he would have to act and to strike the most urgently.

He knew he could enforce his will and his opinion upon most men, at most times; he knew it because that was his experience and the experience of his land. Especially he knew that he could enforce his will upon Negroes. But his hands might be tied, somehow, by that conspiracy. Either he would be disarmed, disentongued, or the final thing to which he might appeal in the Negroes might have been exorcised. They are not as thoroughly civilized as we, that is obvious; that is part of their nature. But if you arm 'em, if you put trappings of power upon 'em and give 'em the power of life and death, you release their savagery. You can not reason with a nigger with a gun in his hand.

The fear carried its own antidote. There was a heady, winy, corded sense of power about him, upon his shoulders, a mantle of power and skill which was at last being applied where it ought to be applied. There was no nipping this in the bud, he thought, because the Yankees sprung all of it upon us. But now then, now I aim to do something about this, time we reach that fort. He thought of Amanda, pouting with sadness and exhaustion, her eyes dark and luminous and big, her thin shoulders. This will be for her, and for all of us. By God it will. The burn in his crotch was an irritant, another part of the price that they had to pay. He sank into his sense of potency, power, ability. Well, they brought me back to the colors because I had certain talents. I did not want to learn those talents, but I had to; and now I am going to put them to use at the right place. I learned those lessons hard, but I learned them well; and now, 'y God, I am going to put them into use for myself and for my own.

Suppose they won't fight. Imagine 'em marching out with their arms raised. He itched with the dread of impotency, of stifled, choked, repressed action. That would be part of the conspiracy. Forrest won't let 'em. But Forrest, he knew, would take the place without bloodshed if he could. Well, hell. His throat and chest ached with this new anxiety. But he had learned enough of men at war and of himself to know that pain and exhaustion conjure up false thoughts. We'll see how I feel when we halt. Christ, we ought to halt soon.

I I

THE WHISTLES BLEW AND THEY HALTED FOR A WHILE, BUT SINCE the ground was soaking and wet and slippery they huddled in misery or walked out the pain in their legs and the cramps in their muscles. No one said anything. Acox tugged and pulled at his pants and then suddenly had to urinate badly. He stumbled off into the dark, thudding against a blackjack and tripping over a root and catching himself and ripping the palm of his hand in so doing. He finally urinated, the flooding sense of relief the best feeling he had had all night, he thought wryly, and then, 'twouldn't do to tell Amanda that. His hand stung. He got back and found that the glove had been ripped open. Well, I will find me a new pair at Fort Pillow. An officer from someone's staff came bouncing along the road asking for Bell and some of the men started yelling, "Mistuh, heah's yo' mule" and "Come outa them high ol' boots I kin see yo' haid sticken out," but there was no heart in it. The night was too bitter and dark.

Then whistles sounded, and the word was passed that for twenty minutes they would lead their horses. They stumbled out stiffly in a long, clanking line. Well, thought Acox, they won't run away. God, that feels better in my crotch. Well, they won't run way because we got held off at Paducah and they will figure they can do it again. His mind, exhausted from two hours of hating and praying, now clinically formulated the details of what they could expect tomorrow at Fort Pillow in the way of a fight. At Paducah he and his company had spent most of the day from midmorning in several old warehouses, all of them painted brown with whitewashed sidings, abandoned and stinking of

260

water and the river and the ground-earth floor, with shattered and boarded windows that the light came greyly through. He had sat on top of a half-bale of cotton, watching his company along the windows and chinks facing the fort and the gunboats, loading and firing and loading, the smoke curling back over their shoulders and the sun slanting through it faintly as it hung thick and curtain-like in the cavernous room. They had kept up a good fire on the fort and got a couple of Yankees, Clark said, and then the gunboat had opened on their warehouse. Suddenly Tell was yelling, "Watch out for yourselves, boys!" Everybody dodged behind the scattered bales of cotton they had pulled near the windows, and then the whole room was filled with a loud, stinging, hot noise and everyone's ears were bleeding and plaster and wood dust and earth sifted down their necks and backs and mixed itchily with the sweat and moisture, and there was fine white and black smoke everywhere. His men went back to their rifles and Acox had crawled over to a window looking out at the two gunboats.

They had closed their ports; he had never seen them so close, so close he could reach out and touch them and certainly close enough to count the twin rows of rivets along the sides, and the wooden pilot house and superstructure and the large number 28 on the side of the one. The cobblestones in the street glistened with wetness. Then the ports came rattling down again and he yelled and everyone ducked. Again the room was filled and this time a whole section of wooden wall at the corner toppled backwards to a piled-up bank of earth. There were hanging splinters and pieces of glass and the room stank like a hundred men had been urinating in it, but no one was hurt.

He yelled at Fire and Whiteside and Clark and they came scrambling over, dragging their rifles at the trail. "We will hit him when he opens those ports. When they go down, cut down on that first one on the right. See it? All right, everybody put a minie or some buck through that port. That will slow him down. Hey, hey y'all up there, keep up the fire on that fort!" He had looked cagily back at the gunboat which was now thudding and scraping alongside the dock under a pelting rain of gunfire from the rebels. Thin walls of their rifle smoke rose like lace embroidery along the house walls. The gunports all came rattling down again and he forced himself to look right at them. Then the muzzles, black and with a shiny circle where the metal ended, came shunting out at them and everyone around him fired and they all ducked and cradled their heads and put fingers in their ears. The wall was torn apart right above them in a series of holes and gaps and ripped boards and splinters. His eyes stung from the smoke and the back of his neck stung from the powder and he got up and thought, we got to get out of here.

An officer had opened the door at the other end and yelled at them to get into the next house over because this one was on fire. They all tumbled away, Acox steadying himself and standing still as they all ran out of the house, some of them laughing. No one was hurt. He closed the door behind him and they ran holding one hand onto their hats up the street in crouching, scuttling postures. They had scrambled in under the next warehouse which already had one company in it, down among the grey-timber underpinnings. They kept up the fire on the fort until after nightfall and when they had run out of ammunition for the most part and completely out of water, another staff officer with a long, bony face came by to tell them to pull out, that ol' Bedford had all he wanted. They had seen Thompson's rush since it had gone right by them, but they heard later as they shifted into their fourth warehouse that Forrest had not ordered it. They had not seen much of the Yankees in the fort, except for some blue figures running toward it from the town in a trickle all day, only two of whom had been hit. They had seen the silhouetted dark heads of men popping up to fire at them, clusters of them every now and again around the gun chambers, but that was all and there was really nothing to shoot at since the Yankees had kept down well and let the gunboats do the fighting for them. Which, Acox reflected, was wise enough since they knocked three warehouses down around our ears and were working on the fourth and tore up a dozen houses chasing Morse and Davidson around.

That was the only fighting we have done on this raid. The

rest of the time we requisitioned and recruited and patrolled. But now. The column jogged past a trickling stream, and he noticed they seemed to have turned west. He could not figure out what time it was; well, we have had four rest-stops. No, five. He tried to remember the halts but could not. Some of the men were nauseated. Someone said it was around two in the morning, but he didn't think it was that late. I hope though that it is. He nodded and almost went to sleep, but his legs ached too much from holding the horse and his back hurt, and the constant drizzle soaked him and brushed annoyingly into his face. They still rode in complete darkness. Morse had gone to sleep, he saw. They rode on and then halted jerkingly and Morse came awake saying, "Oh why not?" querulously. Then he looked around embarrassed and put his hand up to wipe the water out of his face. They waited in the roadway, and after a moment they could make out trees on each side and the pale blur of the road, not so much seen as felt, beneath their horses. What time is it, Tom?"

He fumbled with his watch. "Caint see the face."

"If you have a match, strike it and I will hold the watch." He searched and probed under the rustling wet poncho. "There. Now hold the thing." Morse had to strike at four before one lit. It flared orangely and everyone around them jerked in surprise. Acox held the watch up, letting the image push against his surprised eyes which had not adjusted to the sudden light. He remembered the roman numerals and the hands and the seam of his right glove. "Some time after one, eh?"

"Um. Mebbe one-thirty." The horses fretted and the men peered ahead. Someone said a man had fallen off and they were getting him back on, but it seemed to have taken too long for that. When they started again, his legs twitched with pain. Morse whispered, "I reckon us to be halfway there."

"Halfway. This has been a long ride already."

"We got a ways to go." He leaned over for a minute more but Acox had nothing more to say so finally he straightened and went back to sleep. Well, here we go to the left, the creek down there is running hard, Acox thought (they will fight; I am sure of it). We are rising now, I can feel us. Whups, Tom, don't you slip out of that saddle ol' boy. Here, I will hold the bridle for a time until we cross this ridge. I can see a tree over there and it looks like Russell is under it, yes. Russell pulled into the road next to him. "Well boy, how are the two of you doen?"

Lord, Russell is tired. I never heard him this tired.

"We are doing all right, sir. Clark told me we haven't had anyone to drop out now. I mean yet, sir."

"Yes, the whole column is keepen up for this one."

"Yes, sir, we all want this one I reckon."

"Mmm. Heard something. Word get to you boys about— watch that branch, wuff! We are getten off the road. Push back over that way."

"Yes, sir." He kneed his horse and led Tom Morse's back to the left. He could tell by the vaguely perceived, moving, hooded and gigantic forms on all sides and the smell of sweat and horse-flesh and leather and cloth that they were in the column again, and every now and then they would hear crashes and thuds of men stumbling off the road in their sleep and officers were yelling back down the column. Acox yelled, "Keep in column of fours. Column of fours. Lieutenant Bowles." He did not quite believe that there were really other men in the procession and that he could reach out and get one of them. Then Bowles came up behind him. "Suh?"

"Lissen. Lissen, fall out and check each man and be sure he is in column of fours, and have 'em keep in touch so nobody rides off. All right?"

"Yessir."

All he could see of Bowles in the pitch dark was the hooded, sack-like cloak, a form a bit darker than the rest of the night and close to him. "Lissen, too. You get with Clark and get in at the end of the company and don't let 'em get too strung out. I'll check with you at the next halt."

"Yessir."

He turned back to Russell. "Yes, sir? What were you going to tell me?" His voice sounded tight and querulous.

Russell cleared his throat. "I thought you might of heard what Forrest told one of the Mississippi battalions this morning when they left."

"No, sir."

"Well, pass this along then. They found one of the boys from this battalion where some nigra troops had caught him and had killed him and then multilated the body. And Forrest tol' 'em, he said, 'Now boys, go easy on the niggers, but don't y'all forgit what they did to ol' Bob Perry.' So that is the word, I reckon."

"Yes, sir."

"Lissen. Let ol' Tom sleep awhile, I'll see after his comp'ny. We got about twenty minutes to the next stop. We are going to stop early and then hit it hard till dawn. I heard we are making good time, so tell 'em that."

"Yes, sir." And Russell rode off into the darkness or rather blended more completely with it in a series of tangible and rustling and wet noises, his horse scraping and brushing through the roadside bushes. Acox thought about a sequence of things that were somehow pleasant. So we are closer, hunh? and making good time. And especially ol' Forrest wants us to go in there hard and clean 'em out. That is what he said. Don't forget that ol' Mississippi boy tomorrow. We will go in there hard. Good, that is good. Then the ground seemed to slide up at him and the world spun around. But he was still in the saddle when the spinning stopped, only incredibly tired, and his left hand was weary from holding onto Morse's saddle. He could hear Morse snoring. His hand was stiff and it hurt between the thumb and the palm from stretching over the bridle.

Then Amanda was right in front of him coming at him all round and soft and sweet dressed in pure gossamer, cloud-like white cloth and she was in his arms it seemed and there was wetness and sounds, sounds like men were in the yard of their house and he ought to see who they were, maybe there were niggers around and was that a fire he saw (only the fire had a voice saying "Hits about two by my watch only hits fast")? and he was thinking very rationally, good, good, another half-hour is gone and maybe an hour and a half till dawn only don't let go of the dream and yes there were niggers and we are excited already and stimulated and his flesh was nervous and hollow-feeling with the excitement but there were niggers in the yard, he didn't know how he knew, but there were. And he was yelling at them but they would not go away and behind him still soft and pure and exposed through the white gossamer dress was Amanda, right behind him, and he was still excited and he wanted to hold her and press her up against him and make love to her but there were niggers in the yard with rifles and he could hear them coming toward the house and he was naked and Amanda in the gossamer, transparent gown and he was looking by lantern light only he could not find his rifle. He was going into the chest the family had brought from Virginia but the rifle would not fit into the chest so it could not be there, and all of the time the niggers were getting closer and closer and he could hear them grinning and he could feel their flesh coming toward the house and he could not find the sword. He kept looking for the rifle or the sword and there were so many clothes and coats in the chest and it smelled of cedar and he looked and looked, naked and exposed and his flesh still anxious and revealed for Amanda and him looking and looking and throwing out the clothes in a white pile on the floor. All the time the niggers getting closer and closer and his flesh hot-pinched and tight and him still looking and Amanda could not understand though he kept shouting to her. He kept shouting and shouting but she kept on smiling that smile that he always saw across the pillow from him in the morning and she was reaching for him, her hands and flesh so soft but she would not understand and he could not find the gun. And then he had to run upstairs to find it only she would not run with him upstairs, she would not, she was holding him back so soft and fragrant and he had to make love to her but he had to find the rifle and get upstairs but she would not go upstairs and the nigras were coming in only they were part of the night, just dark and teeth glistening and then she was screaming and he heard her scream whistle-like and then he snapped his head up, and there was the whistle and they were stopping for a rest.

He pulled up and Tom was coming awake. He snapped his head and squeezed at his eyes, and felt hollow and cold and afraid, more afraid than ever in his life, and he had to urinate. He got off Caesar and relieved himself, and then smelled the sweat, the coolness of it running all over his body. Lord, I am sweating like it is the summer in a hot courthouse at noon and I am in a black suit. Oh my God what a dream. He found a log by feel and sat on it, thinking over and over, oh my God what a dream. Suppose it is real. Suppose it is a prophecy. Oh dear God, do not let it be a prophecy. I can still remember how helpless, how exposed; I can remember the thing that came in the door. It was dark and green and a cloud-like thing, and Sam and Buck were smiling. I can remember not finding the rifle and, yes, it was our old chest because I can recall the flesh-colored whorl in the cedar right beside my eye. He shuddered.

Bodies were sprawled around on all sides of him, in thick overcoats and rubber ponchos, no one talking but just sprawled on the ground. A pair of men, Tell he recognized by his pliant voice, were hobbling past. Tell was helping Bob Donald, the new recruit, to walk out a cramp, both of them having pulled back their hoods. They seemed to be huge-bodied and drifting haltingly across the ground, animals with tiny heads and massive trunks. He tried to focus on them but could see only the darkness if he looked straight at them. The log felt oozy and wet. He ran his hand along it, still trembling, actually trembling like a tiny trapped rabbit he'd had in a cage when he had reached down for it, surrounded by the pungency of its defecation but atremble and perfectly frozen. He ran his hand down the log and then took off his glove. This log feels like silk, just like silk. It is an old fallen tree, and it feels like wet silk. He ran his palm over and over down the length of it, as far as he could reach. Oh Lord, perhaps that is a prophecy. It was so real, so very real! Oh for God's sake, don't let it be a prophecy. Don't let that come to pass. Perhaps 'tis a warning. Oh God, I shall go to church every Sunday of my life if only nothing happens to that girl. Oh please God, if there is a God, then let it be only a dream.

Acox hunched forward and felt the play of sore muscles across his back. He put one hand in the other, the gloved hand holding clammily onto the flesh of the other. He lowered his head and pulled off his hood, and let the drizzle fall into his hair. Outside of the casque-like smell of the wool, the wind and coolness probed through his sweat- and rain-drenched hair. He rubbed his ungloved hand through it, and the feel of his flesh was good and refreshing too, scratching at his scalp through the hair and stirring the hair around. Ohhh. 'Twas just a dream. Only a dream. But still God, still I shall live all my life in Your service if you just keep her free from harm. I swear. Well now, I must see about the company. He felt a lot better with the hood down. The rain must be letting up. He stood and stretched, cautiously so as not to cramp the back muscles. Then someone was pressing forward in a smell of wet cotton and rubber and asking his name, and it was Bowles.

"Here, Lieutenant."

"Yessir. . . ."

"Watch the log. Here. Sit down."

"Well sir, we are doen all right." He cleared his throat and spit. "No one has dropped out that I can tell, and the hosses are in good shape too. One of the recruits name of Bob Donald was haven a little trouble so I got Tell to watch him."

"Good." He sat in the darkness beside Bowles and thought, I ought to go back down there with him. I ought to at least take over from him for a while. "Umm . . . you want me to come back for a while? . . ."

Of course Bowles said, "Nawsuh, naw, I b'lieve Clarkey and I can work things out all right."

"Good boy. Well, lissen then. You boys are doen a good job and tell Clark to keep his mind on his work and not on that little ol' Mississippi girl he writes to. Tell him I'm onto him. . . ."

"Yessir." Bowles laughed softly. "He won't like that. He was goen to ask for leave on account of a sick aunt when we git back to Mississippi. . . ."

"Ha! Well sir, I'm onto him. That sounds like Clark . . . all right, lissen. Russell came back . . . what time is it, by the way? We got a minute or two left?" Bowles got out a match and struck it, and looked on Acox's watch. "I make it two-twenty or so."

"All right." He squeezed at his eyes with thumb and fore-finger to try to work away the pale-orange image of the sudden flame. "Russell told me to tell you all this, and spread the word down the line when we mount. Did you ever hear of Bob Perry or something in one of the Mississippi battalions?"

"Oh, yeah! Ol' Bob and I spent one night in Jackson together one time. I knew that ol' boy."

"Well . . ." he squeezed at his eyes again. "Well, some nigger troops caught up with him, I'm not sure when. They killed him and cut him up. So tell 'em Forrest spread the word to the Mississippi boys to be easy on the niggers but don't forget Bob Perry."

"Oh Jesus. I knew the boy. That ol' boy, hunh? Must of been a spell ago. I knew that boy. . . ." He sat and said nothing, and Acox could see his head was hanging down on his chest. He was musing. "Ol' Bob Perry, yeah. Yeah. Clark knew of him too. So did . . . le's see, so did Fire. Believe he was an uncle. . . ." Then the whistle blew and they all began to grope for their horses, stumbling through the briars and the weeds and brush. "Ol' Perry. Well sir, I will tell them, I will surely tell them that. Yessir." Acox got to his horse and managed to mount, his legs stiff and unbending.

For a time everything was the rocking motion of the horse between his legs and the rubbing of the saddle leather against him, and the sharp white pain in his back and the stiff and biting cramps in his legs. But then he began to drift again into a sleep, never really escaping the sense of motion and the noises and the smells of the driving march through the deep night, just no longer feeling the pump of his thoughts. Again he was feverishly searching for something but he wasn't sure what it was, but he knew there was a pressing dark thing right behind him and Amanda was tied up in it; he was blindfolded and muted and seeing and shouting but with his clothes pulled away from his belly and feeling the approaching whisper of horror and of pain and Amanda whom he could not touch or make listen to him standing there and the constant approach of the dark cloud. But then he was in a room on a bare wooden floor with an arched window and the sunlight was pouring through the window in a bright, dazzling flood and the floor was bare and somehow it hurt him terribly between the legs, just being on the floor and he wasn't sure why it hurt him so much, the grey, dazzling flood of sunlight and the hard, bare floor and him naked again and unable to get up and still the hard sharp and steady pain between his legs and in his calves and thighs and the small of his back.

Then he awoke and the horse was still moving forward but there was no one anywhere, on any side of him, and he knew immediately that he was alone in the wet, dark coldness. Spears rose against him and hands plucked at his hood and there was a stinging pain in his leg. He reached down and ripped away the trailing vine of thorns and rubbed at his leg. He was alert and tense, and he listened for sounds of the column. For a horrible suspended moment there were not any, and when he glimpsed some motion out of one eye and turned immediately with a flaring desperation to look at it, it vanished into the pitch darkness. For some reason he knew he had fought the battle at Fort Pillow and now was he dead? Was that it, since of course the battle was over? He tried to turn the horse when he realized that he was mounted, but there was a wall or something coarse and stiff and hard pressing against his side, and again he thought there were hands reaching up and he immediately felt for his saber, feeling the brush of the hands across his leg. Was he dead? Because the saber would not come into his hands and there was still the wall and he had fought the battle at Fort Pillow, he knew, only what had happened then? Had he been killed? But then there was a crashing and a voice calling, "Cap'n, Cap'n Acox!" and he thought, Sam of course, did I kill Sam? I must have. His mouth was thick and cloyed, and he needed water. The voice was still calling and then it was not Sam, it was Bowles pulling up next to him, he could tell by the rubbery sound of the poncho. Then he knew that he had gone to sleep on the march and they still were not there yet. Only what was the wall? He put his hand against it and it wasn't a wall, it was only a tree, and the passing column was still right behind him. The horse had only stumbled off to the side of the road until it had come to the thorns and trees. Bowles got to him and asked, "Are you all right, suh?"

"Yeh . . . yes." He got his horse around and clear of the

woods and headed back toward the column. He managed to reach and uncork his canteen and he sucked at the water. This water tastes as it used to when I would get drunk at college; it tastes sweet. He was back in the column and then he noticed that the drizzle had stopped. He dropped again to sleep; this time the jolting march was somehow the nightmare and the moments of sleep the reality. He drifted off four times and then when he opened his eyes he realized there was a lightness all around him. He could see the column as purple and dark black figures against a blue world. They had another rest-halt, and he went to sleep right away and had to be prodded awake; while he mounted he could hear a man vomiting in the woods and Sergeant Clark saying over and over, "Come on. I be here till yo finish, only come on."

In a little while everything lightened more, into shades of grey-blue and then grey, and he watched it dully and achingly. He looked up at the sky and there were still stars but they were fading; there was then a white sky over him and everything, the brush and trees and the long, mounted column, was grey and light, powdery blue, and they were riding between fields. He jerked his head twice to wake up, thinking, I have made it. This is the morning and we have made the march to Fort Pillow. It is an April morning and there is a fresh, clean taste everywhere and it will be a fine day.

He could see Bowles's square, open face and buck teeth. His lips felt too thick to talk through somehow but he managed to say, " 'Twill be a fine day, won't it?" Bowles looked around and brought up his chin to cover his buck teeth reflectively and said, "Yessuh, it ought to be a good 'un."

There was a smell of water, and the earth smelled fresh and clean. Everything was gradually coming into color, the mauves and greens and browns of the fields and ditches beside the road and wine colors in the leather and red in the company guidons. He rode awake and wrapped up comfortably in his warm, thick clothes, feeling himself inside a tight, small world and looking out of it, warm and content and with a growing excitement inside him. The motion of the horse pleased him and the colors and the fresh morning, and the sounds of the men waking up and shifting in their saddles. Yes; yes, this is fine. He felt again the sense of being wrapped up in a tight, private ball of sensation and animal feeling, and breathing and touching and tasting the rising morning.

But then he remembered, oh yes, this is the day we hit Fort Pillow. He straightened and thought, today we are going to tear them apart. It was as if he had found, or recollected, some precious possession, some precious promise that would be fulfilled for him. A clean, white, thrusting excitement welled up in him. Oh Amanda, take care of yourself today. Just for one more day. I shall be home, I promise. I am going to come home and we will set things aright, but I will need this day. After today when we hit this fort things shall be very different. They will be different all over West Tennessee. All over the South.

He realized he had been smiling idiotically. He froze his face into seriousness and lifted off the hood and the air of the morning was like a balm to his flesh, clean coursing through his tangled, matted hair and across his hot skin. He felt as if his head were being bathed. It is still too cold to take off the cloak; or rather too chill. I had better get my hat. He found the wide-brimmed hat with the flat crown and the pinned-up left side, and he put it on. Bowles was doing the same thing, a hat with a small enwreathed CSA pin. He sat up straighter in the saddle and thought, this is like some animal coming from hibernation. Perhaps this is how the crusaders felt coming from their helms. The air felt good and there was a quick odor he tried to catch with his nose but which escaped him. A smell of something that reminded him of being a very small boy, or of rolling green lawns at college wet with dew and blued in the early morning, and the complete quiet.

But then he thought, ah yes, the fight. He had not thought about the fight itself, only about the fact that they were going to make one at Fort Pillow. I don't know how 'twill be. We will probably just force the place into surrender. Most places surrender. But perhaps after Paducah they will fight; I hope they do fight. If they surrender they will march out and nothing will have been proven. I hope they will fight. For the first time. Why, if they do not, this has been for nothing. He frowned.

Dear God, let them fight. Let them put up a fight and refuse to surrender so we can do our work which this day must surely be Your work as well. They at that fort stand for corrupted and twisted humanity, for men rebelling against the order of things; slaves without gratitude and without mercy and the white man's pity, brutal and threatening to destroy that which is good in the world, and white Tennesseans who are surely the most contemptible of men. Let us do Your will this day, dear God. Let them fight so we can teach them by killing and wounding and chopping them down. Surely, dear God, Your will is not done by renegade, blood-lustful slaves or by scruffy, wizened Tennessee Tories. Let us do this. . . . He began to see what he was saying and he stopped. That is not good. I must not confuse these prayers with those I offer in more and greater sincerity to You about keeping my wife safe. Those are my real prayers, and if I had any to make . . . no, if I had only one prayer that would be answered 'twould be that. But this. We can do this, dear God, in the strength of our own flesh. Just make them fight us like men.

"Bowles . . . what if they don't fight? What if they surrender?"

Bowles looked at him and then pulled up his lower lip reflectively again. "This is the one time I would rather they would fight. Yessir. The one time and I hope 'tis the only time, but I hope they fight."

"Well, after Paducah . . . don't you think after Paducah they will fight to whip us?" He was trying to convince himself.

"Yes suh, yes suh I do. After that and after Duckworth took Union City with no more than Forrest's name, I do think they will figger to whip."

Clark on the other side of him laughed, his face handsome and his hood thrown back and the leather-visored cap tilted. "Well suh, well that is the only time I ever seen ol' Bowles here spoilen for a fight."

"Don't you think they will try to fight us, though?"

"Not if they got good sense, nosuh. Least I hope not. I don't want to fight one more time than I have to."

"Not even against niggers and Tories?"

"Well Bowley, I reckon not. I reckon not. I done enough shooten and being shot at both. Neither one is too much in the way of fun."

"Don't you think we stand a chance to teach 'em a lesson up at that fort?"

"Naw. Nothen we do will make 'em quit usen niggers. That is here to stay. And the Tennessee Tories won't stop joinen the Yankees neither. All we might do is take a few hosses and stuff to keep on fighten with and that is, I reckon, good. And we might tie up with one of them riverboats and lose a sight of men, you know. No, they won't learn anything from taken a whippen today and we might lose some good men."

Acox looked steadily at him for four breaths, and then sat back and thought, well, well maybe the string has been pulled on Clark. Maybe he should stay back with the hossholders. No, no, he is the best man in the company. I can't keep him to the rear. He will fight and I know it. I should not have even thought that. But there is a rankling feeling about what he said all the same. That is why the three of us are so quiet now. He is Bowles's best friend, but Bowles has pulled up his lip and is looking straight ahead and is hurt and disappointed, and showing it by the way he is holding himself. Nobody else thinks the way Clark does in this company. They will not have to be convinced, and they will carry Clark with them and he will do a good job.

He looked over his shoulder, and there was a streak of yellow light right over the road behind them, and white and pink and purple clouds. And while he was looking they heard the gunfire, scattered and then spreading, a series of poppings that you sensed as imprints on the ear tissue, as small tiny fingers not of sound but of pressure. It sounded as if the firing were about three miles away, and it still kept up, catching on and spreading, dropping and then coming even louder. The pace of the column picked up, and Russell came back saying, "All right, pick it up, pick it up. Chalmers has hit 'em. Let's go, let's go." The horses stirred and began to trot, and the men were pulling off their cloaks and ponchos and settling their leather equipment about them and looking to their rifles and revolvers. Acox wanted to kick his horse to a gallop, he was so tense and excited. Oh, keep 'em pinned there, keep 'em pinned there. Orrison shook out the guidon. He looked up at the sky and it was ice-white, with the clouds blue and steep and pacing them running north and south, blue and cold and distant in the ice-white sky.

BOOK THREE

The Battle of Fort Pillow
12 April 1864

I

JOHN SUTTELL WAS DOWN AT THE SINKS—THE WET AND TRAM-
pled latrines near the river at the end of the town ravine—when
he heard the firing. The Tennesseans were up for muster before
dawn, as early as the nigger troops in the fort because Akerstrom
was lieutenant of the day and he liked to get them out early.
Suttell was about to use the latrines but he heard the gunfire
up at the picket on the Brownsville road, and he turned around,
icily handsome with his tousled blond hair and sharply cut features, and stared, and then went running back to his tent. The
other Tennesseans in the battalion were spread hesistantly
about in knots of blue, ranks dissolved after the muster. When
Suttell got there they were all frozen in place, looking at the
dark frieze of trees up toward the picket.

Akerstrom, tall and red-haired and gangling, was squinting
and standing on his tiptoes looking over toward the road and
the sound of the firing. Bradford, wearing his huge, creaking
hip boots, was already halfway up to the fort but he and Leaming were stopped too. All of the tents in the ravine, mud-
spattered and grey with smoke, were surrounded with open-
mouthed, pale-faced, unshaven men.

Suttell ran past them even before Bradford started scrambling back to the camp, or Akerstrom started to shout at the
battalion. He dived into the stink of his tent where Pennell was
spreadeagled in sleep, having apportioned just enough energy
to get him through roll call. Suttell kicked viciously at his foot
to get it off the chest. He opened it and pulled out his hoss pistol and checked its load. He put the pistol into his blouse and

buttoned it closed, and then he took his other oiled and polished and loaded pistol down from the peg and strapped it around his waist. He left the sword hanging. The thing was a damn waste of time. Pennell was making gurgling noises of re-awakening and the sunlight was coming feebly through the river mist. He felt the sunlight on his cheek. Suttell got the short and brassbound carbine and went out of the tent. Akerstrom had gone to his company because the other officers were gathering with their men. Smith was saying, "Comp'ny D over heah! Comp'ny D heah," and waving his arms, and Bradford was running from each of the officers, looking into their faces wordlessly. That ol' Bradford is a damn fool. Get him up to thet fo't and leave us alone. Francis Smith, Suttell's company commander, was short and fat with a thick brown moustache; he was trying to get his sword onto his belt, and kept turning around and around to catch the clasps together. Suttell ran up to him, lithe and feeling good. No one else was around except Lieutenant Barr, a young, heavy-lidded man who was pulling on his gloves and smoking a cigar, and Sergeant Isaiah Jones who had gotten the stripes that Suttell knew he was supposed to get except for Cleary's protest. I get Cleary in front of me this mornen I mean to kill him.

Everyone was in the tents and the huts, and most were searching for their guns. The firing kept up at the picket and the officers were swearing and turning to squint at the direction of the firing, and then trying to catch Bradford by the arm to get some orders. Smith got his sword on and looked up hot and flushed and said, "All right, Suttell, go and put on yo' cap." Suttell swore and turned and saw Pennell coming out of the tent. "Hey Pennell, fetch me that ol' cap!"

"Naw. Do hit yourself."

He cursed and ran back to the tent. He ducked inside and grabbed the hat and started to run back. Why? Now why should I be in such an all-fired hurry? The rebels will keep and ol' Smith'll send me on a thousand damn errands cause he has got a thing against me too. Hell no. He walked easily out of the tent, putting the kepi on at an angle and whistling and judiciously examining the breech of the carbine. Panting men ran by him in squads, all of them bright-eyed and nervous and their hair tangled and matted. Jackson, who had the big star of the quartermaster sergeant on his chevrons, grinned at him, stubble-chinned. He was walking too, taking his time. "Good mornen, John Arness."

"Good mornen. Watcha reckon?"

"Hit's Forrest. I heard tell from a man in heah yestiddy that Bedford was goen to come this way. Hit's Forrest all right."

"We see about that now."

Everyone clustered around Smith, who had already unbuttoned his frock coat at the top where normally it cut into his jowl. The men were all nervous and jerking quick looks up at the area of the firing and then up at the fort, and at each other. They ran their tongues across their lips. Look at 'em. Scared shitless. Suttell felt a cold, stiff joy. The rebels won't run away this time. They will be all the rebels I can shake a stick at this time. We see if we caint hit a few of 'em. Isaiah Jones was swearing at Talley and Kendall, the other sergeants, "Naw, naw. I said bring me Paukey. I said bring me Paukey." Bradford was talking to the officers, his freshly shined boots already daubed with red mud. He was talking in a piping voice, and throwing his hands around. Nicholson grinned through his beard at Suttell, nervously. "Le's lissen."

"Naw. We will be tol' directly." Suttell squatted against the rise of earth at the side of the ravine, and began to throw small pebbles aimlessly with one hand, picking them up and jerking his wrists so they clattered to his fingertips and then throwing. Everyone was booted and armed; they stood in tight knots in their companies and swearing at their officers. Bradford kept jerking his arms and his eyes were wild and red, and his face pale. Poston whose E Company had not even been mustered into the service was saying, "No, no," and the veins in his neck were straining. Ol' Poston he is mad. An' Bradford is scared silly. This mornen is nice. 'Twill be a nice day. He moved a little to find more pebbles. I am in the right spirit for a fight today. Feels good. I know a place up yonder I'm goen to hunker down and pick off the rebs fast as they come up. By a ol' log. Just sit and shoot all day. Soon as they give me some carchidges.

"Get up, Suttell." Isaiah Jones, lean-waisted and broad, with bushy hair and a turned-up nose, was saying at him, "Get up and come over heah."

"Hell you say." Ol' goddamn Jones got the stripes I oughta have had. I'm the best trooper in this heah company, I killed the most rebels of any 'em. But ol' Cleary he took care of me. I didn't even keep the two stripes I had. Ol' suck-aig dawg Jones.

"Get up, goddammit!" He is as nervous as a scared cat in heat. He is a big shit though, and he is a bit too big for me to take. Anyhow I couldn't win a fight with him for losen since Smith would love to git rid of me. I know he would. I better git up. "All right . . . all right."

He noticed that all of the officers were solemn and nodding now. Bradford was running his fingers through his hair and pointing at the different positions they could take. Poston was standing with his arms folded across his chest and his lips compressed in anger, and looking at Bradford under his eyebrows. Smith was nodding and trying to get away, nodding yes and then starting to move and Bradford would say something else to him earnestly. Nicholas Logan looked over at his company and rolled his eyes exaggeratedly behind Bradford's back. Akerstrom was standing with his mouth open, pale-faced and trying to catch every word. They stood in a muddy, tight knot, listening to Bradford who kept giving them instructions and pointing his finger. Small flecks of spittle were flying from his mouth. They had their frock coats buttoned close against the chill, and they were wearing hip boots and sword belts and checking their pistols and sliding their swords part way out of the scabbard and then slamming them back in.

Suttell stood near the group, slouched, and looking vaguely over at the gunfire. A hatless man came running down the slippery bluff at the end of the ravine, and he stumbled panting and wide-eyed, with the sleep plaster still below his eye. His uniform was ripped open at the shoulder, and he had lost his equipment. He ran for the group of officers, slipped and fell in the mud, got up and ran again. Suttell laughed. This is one scared ol' boy. "Shut up, Suttell, or I give you somethen to laugh at." Suttell spit casually and grinned at Isaiah Jones. I know how you got them ol' stripes, boy, and I know why you got it in for me. Yessir I do.

The man from the picket gulped to catch his breath and saluted sketchily in front of Bradford, his chest panting and his mouth open and gasping from the run. He pointed toward the picket and started to say something. Captain Logan yelled, "Act like a soldier, Pulley! Act . . ." but Bradford put his hand abstractly against Logan's chest and pushed him back imperceptibly and said, "Yes . . . yes, what is it?"

"Well seh, well . . ." Pulley took a huge gasp so that his eyes flickered. "Well, we got hit this mornen by a hull division maybe. . . ." Gasp. "They come on us out uv the woods and Sergeant Leonidas he pull what was left uv us back . . ." gasp ". . . back into the woods. We dint leave anybody at the . . . the outeh line. We musta lost ten, twelve men I reckon. . . ."

"Where are the rebels, and how many . . ."

"Shut up, Logan. Shut up. Now then . . . now then. . . ." Bradford looked around at the officers and then at the companies of the battalion, blue-coated and their weapons glittering, standing in clusters among the tents and the horse lines. He must have looked for thirty seconds, during which time the firing got closer and closer to them, coming steadily and seemingly in sight just over the ridge. Prob'ly, Suttell thought, prob'ly they are pushen us in right now. We ought never have lef' that outer trench line. Naw. We can put enough men out there to keep 'em pinned down all day even now, if he will only move us. Damn fool. . . .

"All right then, do what I told you. Do what I said. I'm goen into the fort and confer with Major Booth, so get your men out there." Yessir. They all saluted. Bradford walked quickly, almost breaking into a run. He wants to git up to his niggers and his big cannon so fast he caint stand it. He wants to run like a bunny right now. Look at him holden hisself back. Bradford jerked along the trail toward the fort, Leaming not even keeping in step with him but walking easily behind. The fort, above the thin mist, was in the sunlight now, and he could see the Negroes and their officers standing on the wall and scrambling around the gunports, getting the artillery pieces ready.

Smith came back, perspiring, with Barr beside him looking over in the direction of the firing. "Now then, we got to git out on the skirmish line with Comp'ny E. Bradford says to feel out the rebels and try and keep 'em pinned down. . . ."

'Y God that is the biggest ol' piece of shit I ever heard. "With only two ol' comp'nies an one of 'em not even swore in yet. . . ."

"Shut up, Suttell." Barr had raised his thick eyelids in anger. "Shut up." Hell, I been tol' that once this mornen. He grinned at Barr too. Barr looked away, swinging his eyes around and scowling. Suttell thought, why hell, this is damned fool nonsense. You kin git killed with this kind of hoss shit.

"The other comp'nies are going into the rifle pits the niggers have been building. Now let's go. Get me Paukey up here next to me." Two men came lugging a large cartridge box between them, taking short, awkward steps. The company clustered around them, pushing Isaiah Jones in close against the chest while the two men were trying to open it with bayonets. "God damn it, git back. Git back, the corp'rals'll pass it out to ye." He was sweating.

They stood in nervous, fidgeting lines behind their corporals. Poyles came up with two fistfuls of cartridges for each man. He would turn and reach down and bump into the man next to him. They were all crowding around trying to get their hands into the box, and Smith kept swearing and saying, "Let's go, let's git on with it." They got another box opened and passed out the cartridges faster. Suttell shouldered his way between Pennell and another boy. Poyles handed him the cartridges, pouring the grey cylinders into his hand. Most of the men dumped them into their pouches, but Suttell stepped to one side and counted his out, dropping them into the leather box one at a time. Twenty-nine. Twenty-nine ain't many, and I am plannen to shoot a sight more times than that. I will have to watch and first man I see hit I take his carchidges.

The men of the two companies started out in a group, scrambling over the lip of the ravine and slipping and plastering mud on their knees. They were sweating and licking their lips and their eyes were blank and flicking. Suttell went up the slope easily and kept away to the left, thinking, hell this is damn fool business. I planned to be up yonder in that ol' pit myself. He looked back where the other three companies were spreading over the new-green earth through the scrub and brush, going into the rifle pits scattered like red slits along the slope around the fort. One company went straight east into the zigzag line of trenches along the crest of the hill in front of the fort. They ought to keep that ol' trench. Time the rebels git into that thing they can put fire right down into the fort. Bradford put one ol' company in at least a two-acre earthwork. He shifted his carbine across his chest and thought, this Bradford is a poor scared bastard. Hit don't even look like I can get a shot in at Cleary, does it? Maybe later.

They went southward, Smith taking the right side and Barr the left, spreading the men out three paces apart and then six. Corporal Poyles, a big boy with a scattering of freckles across his washed-out face, was on Suttell's left, and Steward, his bullet head turtle-like out of the high yellow-piped collar, was on the right. Steward was breathing loudly through his nose. Barr, sucking at his moustache, was walking along right in front of them. Suttell was grinning like a fool, feeling the surge of the blood and the excitement through him; he walked springing on the balls of his feet, gliding cat-like past the shrubs and small saplings. There is goen to be some shooten today, I reckon.

They crossed a slight ridge, covered with grass and sedge and small trees with delicate buds, growing up in the midst of a crisscross of fallen brown-grey logs spilling golden chips across the ground. The ridge dipped down on the other side, and they could hear the firing much more loudly. They were out of sight of the fort now, with Company E on their right side, some of the men there new recruited and armed with rifles and still in homespun and jeans, all stepping cautiously with their guns held up through the weeds and timber, as though they were hunting quail. The ground was muddy and slick under their feet, and when they came to the bottom of the ravine between the slopes it moved almost lasciviously, black now instead of red, and covered with reedy new growth. Their boots made splashing noises through the water and crunched the reeds under, and no one spoke. Suttell looked over his shoulder. Now up yonder on that ridge we just crossed there is a white stump —that un—and behind it there is a hole I mind. I just better slide over towards the left a little, and when we pull on back I am goen to aim for that ol' stump. We ain't goen to be out here fifteen minutes. Not with everyone so scared piss-green.

They climbed up the ridge, still silent and nervous, their hands shifting the weight of the carbines, and their mouths dry. Steward kept breathing loudly through his nose, and down the line Scott fell clatteringly over a log. His cartridges spilled out on the ground, and he crawled almost in panic gathering them up, and Sergeant Tate over him saying, "Come on, come on, for godsake." Behind the ridge were second-growth woods and some firs and a thicket on the left. They went up the ridge in a loose skirmish line, some of them slipping and falling and already panting.

"Suttell, goddamn it, close up theah on the lef'." He looked back. Sergeant Kendall was right behind him, bearded and hard-eyed.

"I will do my fighten this mornen, Sergeant Kendall. Now you leave me be."

"Move back over yonder."

"Go to hell, Sergeant Kendall. I got more important things to do than listen to you this day." Kendall licked his lips and looked around, but no one had heard; they were all bent forward coming to the top of the ridge. Kendall slipped suddenly and pushed his carbine down to catch his weight. Sweat was glistening under the edge of his cap. "Do yore fighten then." He moved off clumsily to the left, slipping in another muddy patch. I ain't letten Kendall scare me away from my hole. I need that thing directly. He spit. The carbine felt good in his hands. The firing was loud and pressed in against their ears, and they could hear voices now and sounds and cracks in the air over their heads, swift, fleeting cracks. A recruit looked up wonderingly.

"They are rebel bullets, boy." Barr looked back, nervously. "Keep up. You will hear that some more directly."

Everyone in this damn comp'ny is scared to death. Suttell looked around him, at the men shrinking under the sound of the bullets going over them, and the smell coming to them now of smoke and burned powder. Scared already. They will be a hell of a lot of help, I know. Well, I will have to do as much of this as I can mysef.

They crossed the ridge and saw the line of trees. The trees seemed to move and wiggle and jump when they went over because they were so nervous. Smoke puffed and jetted from the line of trees, and rose in curtains upward into the limbs. There were sucking and small bursting noises at their feet from the fall of the bullets; Smith yelled, "Come on, come on down here!" They began to hop and wriggle down behind the fallen logs and the stumps. The rebels were down in the trees and very close and shooting at them, and they huddled wild-eyed and desperate behind the trees and wood and rock and in the holes, looking up.

Suttell went to his left as soon as he crossed the ridge, heading for a hole he saw behind a stump. He looked quickly down at the trees where the rebels were firing, and thought he saw some vague movements behind the smoke, and thought, I can do a good job at this range, for a time. He looked around, once he was settled. There were men from the broken picket post lying in the ditches and behind tree stumps. They were keeping up a loose fire on the woods, mostly shooting and ducking and loading slowly, and then popping up to shoot again, until the rebels saw them and rifle balls kicked dirt and wood splinters all over them and they got up terrified and broke back for another place. That ol' Winn down there in the black hat? It is. He done a good job keepen this bunch down here at all, way they want to cut and run. Now le's see. He looked around him. The stump was a good-enough shelter and the log ran along near it so he could get other positions to shoot from. The sun was warming and his bottom and legs were cold enough from squatting on the muddy slope so that felt good. He took off his cap and put it in front of him on the ground. He could see Barr crouching and looking around about thirty paces away. Caint see Isaiah Jones at all. Smith is down yonder I think, and ol' Poyles is somewhere around those logs. I can see Steward in that grass. That won't help him. He better git to a hole before he shoots too many more times. All of the men in Company D were shooting and ducking and scrambling around to shoot again. Smoke hung low over the second growth and the saplings.

Suttell put his face over the stump, capless, and looked down at the trees without blinking. He could see the rebels coming out of the trees, keeping down but moving in all the time and shooting. They had tan-colored hats turned up on the sides or in front, and they carried long rifles. I want me an officer. He saw five men, about a hundred yards away, sprint for the cover of a ditch. There. An officer was standing in the open, hatless, in a grey coat with a high collar and some braid down his sleeves. He was pointing up the hill to the men behind him, and making waving motions with his other hand to get them to move up. He was light-haired and young-looking, framed for Suttell by the thick, high grass and the twigs and branches and saplings. Jest wait theah a second more. He looked down and fished out his cartridge and opened the breech of the gun, and slid in the cartridge through the metal rectangles and loops, and closed it. Awright now. He got the sight right down on the officer thinking, I am glad I got me this new breechloaden gun now then hold it there, and he squeezed the trigger and the gun kicked his shoulder and he knew he had missed, that the carbine had carried just a bit down to the right. The smoke went away and he looked judiciously. Now then, I tore that hole in the ground near his left boot. That's right, Reb. Look at hit. Stand there while I load this thing one more time only this time I know it carries to the right and you are dead. His lips moved in his litany, urging the man. Look down at that big ol' hole because the next one is goen to be in you. Don't move but you won't nosuh because you are a shit officer and a rebel and you caint move you got to stand there in all that damned braid don't you? He got the carbine back up and centered it and laid his cheek along it but then the man moved to the right, going behind a clump of saplings and brush about halfway down the slope. Oh God damn it. Well find somebody else.

Suttell moved a little to his right and saw a man with a beard standing looking up the slope, his hat pulled back and a strap across his chest. But then while Suttell got the gun set again somebody came close to the man and he went down. Would rather have some damn ol' officer anyways. He bent around and looked out, but a slug tore right past his head and kicked some wood in front of him, and he jumped back with his heart in his mouth. Well now. Slow down. Well now I got to find that man I reckon. Or move out of here. He has got the angle on me. Let me try the other side of this stump. He crawled to the left, avoiding the edge of the black, striated stump. He saw down into a tiny gully and there were three rebels not more than eighty yards, flat on their bellies and rolling on their backs to load. Well now. He watched them, careful to keep his head down and behind the stump, and he got the carbine set on the center one. Wait till he rolls over on his back, belly up. There he comes now the man with the brown jacket, aim fo' that ol' plate on his chest now jest below it some, like so, and the gun fired, and he didn't feel the recoil. Squinting around the smoke immediately, he saw the man suddenly arch his back off the ground and open his mouth and then flip convulsively against the other side of the depression. The other two men jumped and rolled away and then one crawled over and looked at him and they both, down the far and delicate green channel formed by the grass and buds and leaves, looked up and pointed in Suttell's direction, and immediately dropped onto his side of their ditch.

All around him he could hear scuttling sounds and men slipping and scattering and running back, and he thought, well we got to go back over the ridge. One more shot. He looked to his left and saw Kendall stumble and fall, scramble up and claw onto the other side of a felled log, and Steward roll over it too, rebel bullets chasing them with a shower of mud and scraps of wood. Well I sweah. Suttell grinned at them, Kendall with one cheek covered with rubbed green and spattered mud from crouching in the spring foliage. Kendall licked nervously at the back of his wrist and shook his hands like a man drying them, and then looked back for the next place to run to. Steward was bent flat against the log with his eyes shut, holding on to his carbine so tightly that his knuckles showed ivory-white. Hell, a old man got no right to be scared. Somebody dint tell Steward. I reckon he dint get the word.

He was grinning and looking around for his last shot before moving, and then suddenly he almost forgot the right edge of the stump and the edge of it flew off right in front of his head. That rebel has a good eye with a gun. I better get to the other side. The stump wasn't big and it was thin and hollow, and a bullet came through it almost going into him and tearing a big piece of it away near the base. He could see right through it. He jerked away from the hole and then another shot ripped down more of the stump, tearing away the black wood and showing the grey. I better get out of this place. He crawled backward, cradling his carbine and looking around. I better git onto the top of that ridge.

He slapped the equipment he was wearing so as not to forget anything, and shoved the cap down on his head. Well now here goes. He crouched and then got up running, his feet twisting past the logs and vines along the ground and dodging the small trees. Once he was up it was no longer a world of grass and foliage and men seen through a blue-green haze, it was a flat, warm, muddy slope covered with dead logs and stumps and green ferns and vines and men in blue jackets standing up and firing down the slope. And curling smoke and more men crawling behind shelter and some men in blue staring up wide-eyed at the sky with spatters of red all over them and around in the grass. He ran hard, keeping the carbine held out for balance and watching the ground, jumping over the logs. A rebel bullet spit right into a log when he went over it so he cut to the left, his heart pumping and his mouth open, thinking, git to that ridge crest git up there. The air felt good on his face and his lungs were already panting and slaving but he was laughing, making shuddering noises trying to laugh. They caint hit me now. Nosir they caint. Like an ol' rabbit. Flushed and smiling he reached the top of the ridge and there was a log and he toppled over it to the ground. It was grey and soggy and there were rectangular holes in it, but he was thinking, this heah ain't so bad. Time I catch my breath the rebels'll be ready fo' the picken again. Law, I sho' did git that ol' rebel on the ground back yonder.

He stretched out on his belly after undoing the buttons of his blouse, and he took his cap off again. He opened the carbine and checked the load and snapped it closed, and breathed hard, still laughing. I reckon those two rebs down in that ol' ditch thought they had ol' Suttell. They were waiten I reckon and they started putten ball and buck through that ol' stump, jest waiten. Damn fools. He looked down both sides of him. In fits and starts he could see men in blue coming back over the ridge, running and jumping over it and crawling along the web of logs and stumps and depressions. Steward crawled right up to the log, his eyes blinking and his bullet head ducking into the jacket and then out again. He scuttled over the log and landed on his back, his jacket filthy and his eyes shut tight and his mouth panting, the stubble teeth showing. There was some blood in his mouth; his face was pale, and red and blue thread-like veins stood out.

"Hey ol' man, I thought ol' men ain't never scaired. Hey what about that?"

"Shut . . . shut the hell up. . . ." He was gulping and he began to cough, deep, thick coughs that shook him into a knot, holding his hand to his mouth.

"Hey now Steward, you ain't doen too well, are ye?"

"Shut up."

"Mean ol' bastard, ain'tchee? I thought ol' men ain't supposed to be scaired atall. Whatchee got to live fo', old man, keep on coughen like that you can bring up a lung, hunh?"

Steward rolled over and looked at him. His eyes were red-rimmed, and he was still panting. His head ducked into the collar and then out again. "Suttell, you are the meanest son of a bitch . . . the meanest son of a bitch I ever did see."

Suttell grinned at him, smiling with his handsome, lithe face, tough and bronze and yellow-haired. Steward spit once to the side and turned to look over the log. "Well now Steward, I tell ye, you better take off that ol' cap before you poke yo' head over thet log."

Steward looked at him, his thick trunk still trembling and panting, and finally nodded and scraped his cap off. "All right now, le's see if we caint git us a reb or two from this ol' log, hunh Steward?"

He nodded yes. "Then you git down to thet end . . . go on down thair. Now when I nod you pop up and fire one off, don't matter where. I be watchen and try to see a rebel."

"Don't need to do that, they be comen right up on us in a minit."

"No ol' man, they won't. Not if they got to keep their haids down. Now git on down there. Git!" Steward looked at him for a moment longer and then tried to shrug, but he was too achingly tired already. He crawled snuffling and raising and tucking in his head. Suttell lay belly up on the good patch of grass, resting his head on his locked hands behind him on the log. Ol' Steward won't make it to the next ridge before he dies, one way or t'other. Well now, I better git ready. He rolled over himself and inched right up to the top of the log, and ran his fingers over the smoothness of it. Then he nodded down to Steward. The old man inched up gradually to the top of the log with his tongue running over his thin, blue lips and then threw his head up and shoved his carbine out and fired with it pushed away out from him, crash, and then ducked down again, his eyes rolling back and forth. Suttell was watching and thought, he dint hit nothen 'cept maybe the woods over yonder, but surely enough a rebel cut loose at the log, a reddish-bearded man Suttell could just see standing upright for a second on the slope, not more than thirty yards away with his cap-brim turned up. He jumped up to shoot at the log and his bullet chopped along the top of it while the smoke from his shot was still in his face, so the rebel dodged to the left, standing for a second before he ducked to see if he hit anything, and Suttell hit him in the hip in that second, spinning the man around with his face a mask of pain and surprise and then toppling him into the ground. Suttell grinned. Ol' rebel he was the damndest fool I ever seen.

I wisht this ol' carbine would shoot straight. Hit carries ever which way. I busted that feller in the hip. But he could be daid. Speck he knows it.

Steward was looking up at him with his tiny red eyes and his open mouth. Suttell grinned. "Sure got him. Right in the hip. Slapped that one down. Now you wanna git up oncet more and try that again?" Steward shook his head and blew out his cheeks flabbily.

"No. No, caint."

"Well man, jest sit up oncet mo' and shoot, that's all. . . ."

"Naw."

"Shit yo are the deadest ol' bastard I ever seen. Stay here then, rebels'll be along by an' by." Steward made shaking noises with his head, but Suttell spit and turned his back. He loaded the carbine thinking, well, I don't think they saw me las' time, when I potted that ol' reb. I will try two more shots and then move on. All around him in the brush the Tennesseans were crouching and firing. Some of them were already moving back down the slope behind them, Smith yelling at them and Barr standing open-mouthed and fiddling with his sword and white-eyed. There was drifting, hanging smoke on the weeds and along the ferns and felled timber, and the blue-coated men were dodging back through it, and toppling over. The rebels had sharpshooters down in the woods and were moving them closer, in the ditches and ravines and logs, and pressing the Tennesseans by keeping up the rush all down the line. When the Tennesseans got up to run the sharpshooters had a clear shot at them. Somebody was screaming over and over, "Oww oww oww" down to the left, where he had been wounded.

Suttell put his eyes and forehead over the log, and looked down at the rebels on the slope. He couldn't see from a lot of places behind the log because of the foliage and undergrowth, the green patches blurring as he tried to focus through them, but he found one spot where he could look right down between the brush, and even into the woods. He saw the rebels were coming out in a steady stream, men in light-colored grey and brown and butternut, strapped and crossbelted and carrying rifles, clustering around flags and officers while the skirmishers were pressing on up the bluff. He tried four shots down at them but the distance was too great to tell, or for the carbine to be accurate. Once he thought he might have hit one of the officers but he wasn't sure, and after the fourth shot they had him spotted and he huddled under the log while bullets thudded into it or spattered along the top, kicking off chips and wet flakes of sawdust.

"Well ol' man, I got to be goen." Steward made some kind of whimpering noise, and Suttell ignored him and looked up and down to the left. There was a knot of men in blue over far to the right, in a little hollow, but he thought he detected movement beyond them and that they were outflanked. While he was watching they got up and began to run and slide back down the slope. Hell, I stayed here too long. He gathered himself to go, Steward making snuffling noises and holding out one hand. Oh yeh, Steward'll like this. He stopped and crawled over to him. Steward was breathing thickly and making coughing noises in his throat, and he caught onto Suttell's hand and folded it against his chest, and tried to say something by pulling him down to his mouth. This ol' man is dead already.

He put his hands down gently and said, "All right, all right, ol' man, jest you take it easy." Steward gulped and closed his eyes. He unbuttoned Steward's jacket and worked at getting his other hand into the man's ammunition box at the same time. He grabbed all of the cartridges he could hold in one fist, and slipped his hand out, and then rolled away from the old man. Steward's eyes widened and then he tried to say something, and he shook his head in a panic, gulping with flecks of foam and blood on his lips. "Man, you are dead. You know you are. Thank ye for the carchidges. Now don' look at me like that. Nobody on this green earth kin help you, and I got to be goen, ol' man. I got some rebels to kill this day." He grinned again, put the cartridges into his box, snapped it shut and then gathered himself looking for the place to run to.

Hell, ain't no place (lissen to that ol' man wheezen and coughen, and he is crawlen this way but he will be too late), ain't no place. All right, all right this child is goen all the way over to that hole on the other ridge. You stay down there you caint do anything but keep yo haid down, 'cause the rebels can lay in the fire from this ridge. All right, le's go.

He got up in a motion just as Steward's patting, reaching hand almost touched his legs, and went down the slope hard, again balancing and running and dodging the logs, keeping his eyes on the ground and looking a pace ahead all the time. He almost slipped once on a slick place, but then was down in the flat before the rebels crossed over the ridge and began to open fire on the Tennesseans in the shallow ravine. He slowed down there and looked back up at the ridge. There was some fire coming down on them from away over at the right, and he saw that E Company had already gone back to the inner ridge anyhow. But then Barr came up, sweating and streaked and mud-splattered, and said, "Where the hell do you think you goen, man?"

"Lieutenant, I am goen back up. . . ."

"You ain't wounded that I can see. You set down heah. We are goen to make a line along here." All along the bottom of the ravine the blue-coated soldiers were settling down behind rocks and logs and in the thickets, and looking up nervously at the ridge and jumping every time a bullet came down from the rebel sharpshooters on the right.

"Fo' Christ's sake, Lieutenant! All we done is one stupid damn fool thing after another this mornen an' . . ."

Barr stepped forward one quick step, never taking his eyes off Suttell's face, and put his gloved hand into Suttell's jacket front and jerked hard, twisting the cloth. Suttell shifted his eyes and felt the pistol move inside his blouse. Ol' Barr is mad and I better shet the hell up. "All right. All right Suttell, you dumb chickenshit, you never were worth a goddamn. Now I had enough of you this day. Now you shut up and you git in that hole or I personally will shoot you down. Now I had enough!" He smelled of corn whiskey and tobacco, and his eyes were gathering quickly together and focusing on Suttell. He is not only mad, he is scared too. Suttell boy you better shut up.

"Yessuh, only . . ."

"God damn it!" and Barr twisted the jacket tighter. "God damn it, I don't want another word from you! Git in that hole!"

The Battle of Fort Pillow 295

"Whu . . ." Suttell had no clear idea what he wanted to say, only that he thought they had best get back up the hill but if the lieutenant wanted he would stay there, but Barr didn't wait. His heavy-lidded eyes went blank and Suttell realized he was going to be slapped. He did not have time to get out of the way until, with his other hand, Barr had stingingly slapped him on the jaw.

"Don't you come grinnen at me, Suttell, and you shet your mouth!"

". . ." Suttell opened his mouth and still shocked from the stinging pain tried to say something but Barr was yelling again.

"Now how many times have I got to say it! How many damn times! Git away from me and shut the hell up!"

And Suttell turned and dodged away, blind with the injustice, going blankly over near the closest blue soldier, who was Corporal Poyles, hunched over in a watery spot behind a small thicket of thin, thorny reeds. He sat down next to Poyles with his hand on his mouth. God damn it, he ain't got the right. Nosuh I am as good as he is. He wants to stay down here and git killed that is one thing, only I went to fight this war because I was tired of being told what to do by son of a bitchen bastards like that. That is why I am here. Yessuh. And he better not think he can git away with it. Let him git in front of me one time, one time and I show him. I had enough of thet truck. I tuck that shit off'n the deLaceys before the war but that is over, and I ain't took nothen since then that I could help. I got that nigger bent over outside the fo't two weeks ago and I taught him a thing er two with my ol' belt. He is lucky he still got his balls. That ol' belt messed him up a good piece. He said he wadden one of the deLacey niggers but I know better. But now I done took shit off two of these here officers, off this'n and Cleary 'cause Cleary is arrogant and this'n is scaired, and it is goen to end now. If the rebels don't kill Barr I will. He squinted at Barr, his mouth hanging open. Ol' Lieutenant Barr with his ol' puffy moustache and those goddamn frawg eyes. Frawg eye, yore day is here. You hear that? Yessuh.

They waited in the blue early-morning shadows. Some of the mist was still around in the shallow ravine; the sun had not gotten to it, and the colors were blue and green and stained, misty white, while they waited for the rebels to climb down at them. They were huddling and afraid and looking up at the slopes. Barr paced up and down in front of them, talking to John Jackson whose old man's belly was hanging over his belt, and his big stripes and star filling up the space on his sleeve above his elbow. Barr was fiddling still with his sword and squinting up at the hill, and then trying to hear what Smith was yelling at him. Suttell could just see Captain Smith off to the right, down the creek bed that ran through this ravine. His red face was purple in the blueness of the valley and the early morning. There were some scattered shots from left and right, but the rebels were on the ridge. They heard a bugle from the other side of the hill and everyone jumped and one of the men down the line fired, his carbine flashing and a thin jet of smoke going up into the mist, but the rebels were not coming yet.

Poyles was nervous and smelled like urine next to him. He was lying in the mud, but Suttell was sitting in his cold, hard fury on a log, with the carbine across his lap and his eyes flat, staring at Barr's back. They waited for the rebels. "Wonder where the rebels are, Suttell?"

"Hunh?"

"I said, wonder where the rebels is at?"

"Hell, they are on both sides of us, crossed the ravine that chickenshit fool has got us into."

"What?"

He looked down at Poyles, cold-faced and angry. This old durned fool Poyles has my stripes, I hope he knows it. Poyles's eyes darted over his face, and then back up the slope, and then he cautiously looked up and down the ravine both ways, where it petered out on the left and turned toward the river far down in the mist on the right. He was holding himself up cautiously on his elbows and wrists, not getting above the nest of thorns in front of him.

"I don't see 'em. . . ."

" 'Course not, down in the mud like that, you goddamn fool."

"Well hell, I don't wanna get shot." A bullet came over, cracking, from the rebels on the left. "See there."

"Poyles, you got my cawpral's stripes, you know that?"

Poyles was looking up and down the ravine. "Hunh?"

"I ought to have those stripes you got, you know that."

"You had 'em, but you was too damn dumb and loud-mouth to keep 'em."

"I just wouldn't take any shit off'n Cleary."

"That wadn't it, you know it . . . you really think the rebs are comen on the flank?"

"Poyles, you are the dumbest I ever seen."

"Mebbe so, but I got these here stripes."

"You got to pay that price, I don't want 'em. I got my pride. I took my licks from the goddamned gentlemen, I ain't taken it now."

"Yeh, well . . . lissen, you really think the rebels are comen around us?"

"You think they ain't?"

"Why don't they . . ." he made a gesture toward the hill, still not raising himself above the small clump ". . . why don't they come ahead?"

"They ain't in any hurry."

"Naw?"

"Naw . . . you know what they are doen? They are holden us here, that's all. They are keepen us pinned up in that ol' fort up yonder with ol' crazy Booth and his niggers. They got all day, just so long as we don't slip past 'em."

"Why? Why don't they let us git out, er drive us off?"

"Poyles, you beat all . . . they don't want that fort, they want us. We been tearen hell out of the country, and now they are comen after us."

Barr had gotten out his glasses, and was studying the hillside in front of them, waiting for the rebels. Isaiah Jones, his legs apart, was beside him peering up at the blue ridge. They could hear rustling and shouting, and from over on the right files of rebels were moving down the slope, gingerly taking care not to slip in the mud and the brush tangle. Some of the company began to fire at them, and they could hear Smith shouting to stop the damn rebels. Barr put his field glasses on them, watching the carbine bullets splash and wink in the fern leaves around the Confederates, and them slip and slide and fire back. The men around Barr and Jones were fidgeting and nervous now, some of them counting out their cartridges and others scooping at the black mud and tangled roots trying to get into better holes.

"Them damn fools."

"Hunh?"

"We ain't goen be here long enough to shake a stick at. We are goen to be pullen out of heah in a minute."

Ol' Barr, he got hisself a new toy, thet pair of glasses. Unh hunh, twist them ol' straps, frawg eye. Twist 'em and wait. You ain't goen to come through this day whole, ol' boy. I promise you thet. Well now, I got to git out of here too. He turned and looked back toward the white stump and the hole he had seen going out. He counted it forty yards. There was a path right behind him, a flat place with thin grass and the black earth showing, through the green, blue-shadowed weeds and brush. He could move fast up that, ducking along the way. As soon as the rebels opened fire on them he was going, he figured.

"Whatchee looken at, ol' boy. You ain't goen anywhar."

"Naw? You jest keep waiten for them rebels. I take care of myself."

"You cut and run, I shoot you."

Poyles's face was whitish and the freckles seemed almost blue in the light. The sun was coming down into the ravine, cutting through the mist. In the other ravine it had been warm and moist but here it was still chill. Poyles's hair was reddish and hung in thick, pointed clumps from the water and sweat. He was still on his belly, with a clasp knife by his hand to clean his gun and with the mud soaking through the front of his clothes. Suttell leaned forward, still cradling his carbine.

"You goen to shoot me? Well now, Poyles, that will take some doen 'cause I kin shoot you fore you can think about it. If I run, I might put a bullet right into you."

"Jest . . . jest stay right there. Lieutenant Barr, he tell you when to go."

2

LIEUTENANT BARR WAS STILL PACING UP AND DOWN, TWISTING AND untwisting the cords to his field glasses and talking to Jackson and Isaiah Jones. A lot of the men were moving around nervously and looking over their shoulders.

Then the sunlight came full into the ravine, a golden rich wash coming down on the leaves and the shoulders and capcrowns of the men. They squinted, and the smell of moisture seemed to hang for a moment and then rise and everything felt warm. And then the rebels began to fire from the right and they heard the cannon firing from the left, big, hollow booms echoing over the ridges and short hills. They are past us on the left, Suttell thought. I knew it. Well, I got to be goen. The fire came down from the right, smoke jetting in cottony balls all along the ridge, spreading along the crest in front of them. The bullets went over with cracking noises or thudded into the muddy ground.

Suttell, gathering himself up to run, saw a flat, watery place erupt into a little fountain of white and muddy-brown where a rebel ball hit. He dropped off the log to his knees, hearing more minie balls suck into the brush and the bank along near him. One hit flat between him and Poyles, Poyles jerking his gun and firing up at the bluff and then rolling on his side, exposing the great muddy stain from his chin to his boots, he began to try to work at his carbine, cracking it open and feeling for the next cartridge. He had managed to roll onto the cartridge box and he had to fumble and claw wildly, trying to push his body off the ground enough to free his hand holding the next charge, and making grunting sounds. His eyes were wild and he kept looking up the slope. Suttell was crawling to the left from instinct, thinking, I got to get out of this place. He lifted his palm off the ground and it stung instantly and there was a flattened shiny mark in the earth where the ball had skidded just under his hand. Back on the right Pennell got to his feet from behind his log, trying to get a cartridge into his carbine and running backward with his tongue between his lips, and then he was hit hard and knocked spinning against the bank. He opened his hands once and the cartridge fell out onto the ground and then he was dead with his neck torn open. Somebody else was screaming, "Oh my Gawd, oh my Gawd!" The rebels were all around them and there were splashes and whistling noises and men were being knocked down. Sergeant Tate was on his knees to the left, holding a broken wrist and crying and rocking back and forth.

Suttell rolled back over the log he had been sitting on and ran for the path and threw himself flat on it, behind a fringe of weeds. He hugged the ground, smelling it, rich and thick and musty. He looked away up the long length of the path, at the rising bumps and the roots running just under it. There was sunlight washing across it at the top and blueish morning shadows, and the dew was glistening at the edge of the shadows. It was something out of a dream, like the far-distant, close-cropped lawns of a big plantation with the morning sun on them, and them so inaccessible and dream-like. Well I got to get up there.

Something hot burned his neck, and he saw a quick brown lip of earth flare up from the center of the path a few feet ahead of him. He looked back and saw Poyles trying to load again. Barr had his sword out with the glasses around his neck swinging and glinting, facing his men and shouting something incomprehensible. All up and down the line of the Tennesseans men were being shot and were ducking and squirming out of the ravine and running for the hill. Another bullet hit near Suttell and he jumped up and ran along the path, his left hand swinging in a fist and holding the carbine in his right, and driving hard along the path clenching his teeth. His feet dug into the spongy ground and he dodged around the slight bend and

The Battle of Fort Pillow   301

dropped there, breathing hard and looking back into the ravine. The Tennesseans were breaking now, most of them right at the edge of the ridge and starting to scramble up it, and some, still surrounded by their smoke and scattered cartridge papers, were gathering up their things to run. Bullets were coming in from the right and left and there was no cover at all left in the ravine; Barr was making wide, arm-swinging motions and yelling to the men to get out of the place and back up the slope. Well now, I could put a ball into Barr here and now. He settled on his side and started to raise the gun but he thought, naw. Naw, I got to think about this some more and I better git on up this path 'cause the rebels will be comen up this ridge too. But I will git him.

He looked back into the blue ravine with the sunlight bringing gold into it, sliding perceptibly down the slope. There were a dozen sprawled bodies along the bottom of the creek bed, men dead or moving through the mud and getting more of it on them and leaving red smears which faded right into it. Some men hatless and open-mouthed were coming up the trail in a tight knot right behind him. He could see Poyles holding both hands over his face and blood, purple in the blueness and then bright, fresh red when he ran into the sunlight, covering his hands and his jacket, and then he was hit again and fell face down at the bottom of the slope. Suttell got up and ran hard for the white stump, twisting off the trail near the top of the ridge and hearing the cannon in the fort go off and jumping right into the ditch behind the stump. He lay with his back to the stump facing the fort, breathing hard. It must be about seven-thutty.

The fort was reddish in the light atop the green hillside, horseshoe-shaped amid the scattered, blue-filled rifle pits. The cannon on the south and southeast faces were firing, spewing out thick, white clouds from the red mud walls. He could hear the grape clattering down in the ravines to his left and right. Well shit, if the rebels are down here this hole ain't wuth a damn. I got to git back on that hill with the fo't. He looked over the rim of his hole. All around him the Tennesseans were running up the ridge, stumbling over the logs and through the brush. Their eyes were wide and white and their faces pale with spittle hanging out of their mouths, and their clothes were ripped and muddy from running through the thorns and brush. He leaned against the log and looked down at the ravine.

The rebels were cautiously filing down into it, columns of them in skirmish lines or single file. Their officers were in jackets with yellow facings; the rebel troopers were bending swiftly over the scattered blue bodies and taking the pistols and the ammunition and pulling out the pants pockets like weird, sudden white tumors, all while kneeling quickly and then jumping back into place in their lines. Some of them were standing, firing up at the running Tennesseans, and some of them in jean cloth and grey-brown jackets were herding the wounded and the breathless Tories, prodding them out of the holes and sometimes shooting them, but mostly shoving them together against the bank and laughing to each other. He saw one of the Unionist recruits pitch out of the bushes and run hard toward the path which was now empty. Then a rebel took a pistol and shot at him once and missed, and while the boy scrambled wildly with his hair in his face shot again and knocked him over.

Well now. Well now then. All along the ridge next to him Barr and Smith and the sergeants were trying to get the men into line. They were firing back at the rebels, and hitting some of them. Suttell saw one man with high cheekbones and columns of muscle in his jaw topple and fall squirming onto the ground. The Tennesseans were staying down along the ridge and shooting blindly for the most part, but the rebels were keeping down too, running in crouches across the ravine and getting to the bank on this side, and the ones coming down the opposite ridge were dodging and spreading into the brush.

Suttell forgot instantly about getting back to the fort and thought, well I got me somethen here. It looks like ol' Barr and Smith got this bunch to quit runnen, and as long as they stay 'long here I got some things to do. He checked the load in his carbine. We should of been up here all along. We could of knocked 'em sideways comen down that ol' slope. Lessee, I want me a rebel officer—I hadn't had one all day.

Many of the rebels in the ravine were still standing in

defiant, careless groups. Suttell settled his body behind the stump and balanced the carbine on one of the roots, and moved his eyes over the rebels, who were about fifty yards away. He saw one man with light-colored suspenders and blue pants, who looked like he might be an officer and he put the gun down on the man, and thought, Christ amighty I hate these rebel officers, and squeezed the trigger. The gun jumped into his shoulder and he leaned to the other side of the stump. The rebel was lying on his back, with his legs spread and bent at the knees. There was a spatter of bright blood all over his blouse. Well now I got me that 'un. Caint tell if he's an officer. Might as well be. He sure is dead.

He bent over behind the stump and snapped open the carbine, putting a new, fat, grey cartridge into the sliding bright metal. He looked up again and closed the carbine, moving to another angle in the ditch. Thorns and cut branches dug into his shoulder and back, but he kept his head down and concentrated on aiming. Those damn fools around me, they keep on poppen up and shooten off and doen nothen but wasten good guvment carchidges. Damn fools. He saw a bearded rebel standing loading a pistol, in the cover of a sapling, more hidden than protected. All right. Now you jest hold it a minit rebel. He put the sights down on the man thinking, now this ol' gun which ain't wuth a damn 'cepten hit's easy to load hit carries a bit to the right that ol' rebel is close enough to spit on I do say I knew a boy oncet who could spit that fer all right, and squeezed. When he ducked under the smoke from the discharge he looked with a tingle in his genitals straight down at the man but he was not sprawled out and he knew he had missed him. Git that ol' head down, but he made himself look one minute more, the tingle still in his genitals. I don't see that rebel—there he is. To the other side of the tree in the leaves poken that ol' rifle up heah, down boy, wuff!! He slumped to the bottom of the ditch, already cracking open the carbine and grinning. That ol' reb can sho as hell shoot. He would a taken my haid clean off. All right that is the boy this mother's son is goen to git. He loaded thinking, he caint load this fast not by a damn sight. He rolled to the other side holding the carbine in his left hand. This'll git him.

He won't reckon I can shoot left-hand, maybe I caint. We see. The rebel was looking for him and was kneeling under the partial shelter of the bank and the little tree with its cloud of new, bright yellow-green leaves. His face was slanted just a little to the right of Suttell and he did not see him. He was loading the rifle held sharply out from him, thrusting in the ramrod and looking intently for Suttell. Suttell stretched out his leg in a muscular spasm of delight. That ol' reb he don't see me but he jest a looken all right hold still now hold still a minit with them ol' yaller cuffs and that brown beard and this is goen right through the brim of yo' ol' blue hat all right, and he squeezed the trigger and he knew the man was dead because even before the quick smoke blew across his face he saw him pitch.

Suttell stood up to look, regardless of the rebel fire, standing halfway up against the sky, seeing the rebel spreadeagled with his hat blown three feet from him and his head a tangled mass of red and brown hair. Oh boy you are dead and I killed you. You got up this mornen never thinken you'd die but boy you are dead. You was a good ol' shot but you are dead now. Something plucked at his sleeve and with all of the simple animal instincts pounding in him to jump down, he waved his rifle over his head and whooped and then while all down the line the rebels aimed their rifles at him he ducked down behind the stump. Oh Gawd I did it to that un. I did it to that un. The sun felt warm and good and he was grinning and rolling in joy, shaking the gun and holding it and shaking it again, the silent joy breaking through his lips and a thin spit coming out. Whoo that reb was one surprised ol' boy. Whoo but he is dead; somebody's darlen is sho nuff dead and he no more thought it. He no more thought it. He didn't think I could shoot from the other side. He no more saw hit comen. But then his face clouded into tanned, sharp anger. He wadn't no officer. Yeh. That is what this ol' boy is hunten, and this time I am goen to stay up till I find one. Yessuh. Somebody's darlen, hee hee. Somebody's ol' darlen with no face. Yessuh.

But around him the other pale-faced Tennesseans were still blindly jumping up to shoot; when some rifle-fire began to come at them from away to the right and rear where E had been whipped all the way back almost to the town, they huddled in panic. The sweat ran down their necks past the wet line of their hair, and under their wool jackets. They crawled down the slope, looking to the side at each other. Smith cursed at them hoarsely and waved his sword at them. Barr was standing balanced at a steep part of the ridge behind his part of the company, rubbing at the sweat, his face brown and gleaming along the cheekbones. He had a sword in one hand and a pistol in the other, and his frock coat was completely open and showing the white shirt and black tie underneath and the rows of buttons.

Jones was walking back and forth, slipping and tripping in the timber and brush because of his heavy boots and spurs. The flesh under his eyes was grey and he was visibly trying to ignore the buzz and snap of bullets going into the reverse side of the bluff around him from the rebels who had gotten around the left side of their small ridge as well. When Suttell turned once he could see some of the Confederates in the tangled ground and ravines in front of the fort. The artillery threw a shell at them but it did not explode, and the rebels were standing in the open and shooting up at the Tennesseans along the hillside from about two-hundred yards.

Suttell did not even think about those rebels, since he knew they were too far away and did not have a good shot at him. He was warm and excited inside and it felt like there were too many thoughts for his brain to hold, and this was perfect. The rebels were down there and he had killed two in five minutes and drawn down a storm of useless fire which chopped at the stump and knocked roots and twigs off the lip of the ditch, in an innate fury that was harmless and a waste, and that thrilled him more than killing the two men. Lissen at that. Lissen at that. They are pouren it in and it ain't doen me a bit of harm. They caint tech ol' Suttell down in this place. Nawsuh they caint. Now then I got to git another shot an' this time an officer. He crawled, sharply cutting his hand on a twig but paying no attention, to the northern side of his hole. The bullets still clipped along the top of it and he thought, maybe they are comen up on this hole under all that fire. He got the gun loaded again and carefully slipped the leather thong on his revolver. I might need that ol' boy.

He got to the lip underneath a dark-green clump of a baby pine tree, and looked around the ball of needles carefully. Coming up the trail was a rebel officer and he nearly cried for joy, seeing the man through the blur of the green needles coming up, with a sword in one hand and a revolver in the other, bent at the knees and hips and wearing a uniform jacket with braid and buttons and the top buttons open so Suttell could even see the shirt underneath where the black short beard grew down the neck. Right there, jest keep on not seein' me and looken right there on the stump and I will put this minie ball through that ol' shirt. Yessuh. Jest wait. He closed the carbine again and pressed near the lip of the hole, oh Lawdy this is it oh thank you Gawd oh this is it jest keep on comen man all right. The carbine was right under the ball of needles, its metal against the scaly brown, and Suttell aiming it from an angle, but so close hit don't matter shet up shet up. He was vaguely aware Barr and Jones were yelling something at him and waving from incongruously close; don't they heah that rebel officer don't they see him comen shet up all right, but the second he pulled the trigger the officer saw the glint and dodged. He heard him yell but through the smoke and pine needles knew he wasn't dead or even hurt badly, and then another ball kicked dirt in his face from the rebel soldier right behind the officer. Suttell opened his gun in a frenzy, coming to his knees. I can load quicker than that man and kill him with this carbeen and finish that officer with my ol' pistol, hammering the cartridge down into the carbine and rising on his knees and then jumping right into the path with the carbine ready, expecting to find the rebel trooper reloading his Enfield; so he was amazed and horrified and amused to find that the man had simply pulled his revolver and was kneeling looking at him and bringing the revolver down. Now that was the damndest stupidest thing. The rebel officer was lying on his back, pulling up his shoulder bloodied and helpless but Suttell didn't have time. He squeezed the carbine trigger and it went off and the rebel in the trail with the revolver ducked away instinctively for a second and Suttell was down the slope and running in long, leaping strides with his straps and equipment flying up about his chest. The carbine sling caught on a stump so he let it go, pivoting off the trail and into and skilfully and instinctively through the brush, moving over the logs and never missing a step, while he heard the snap and whistle of the pistol shots coming past him until he was down the slope and out of range.

He dropped into a hole next to some Tennessean but he was laughing too hard to tell who it was. "That . . . they . . . that ol' rebel missen me whoohooo . . . that . . . that officer down on the ground and ol' Suttell whoo . . . ol' Suttell him not even thinken about that ol' handgun . . . nawsuh, a pullen at that ol' carbeen." He was choking with his own stupidity and then the reflex action which had saved his life, the details of it all coming back to him; the rebel trooper in the pale beard with the grey pants and brown blouse, holding up the big pistol and lowering it on him and on the ground the officer with the seams of his sleeve showing pulling himself in the hot sunlight off the ground desperately with strained lines around his mouth and his eyes closed; and Suttell so anxious to kill the man that he forgot to come out with the revolver in the first place and never even had a chance to use it. He was laughing and laughing, remembering the snap and wind of the rebel's pistol balls, the man next to him staring and then finally sliding a little away from him. "What's matter?" Tears were coming down his tanned cheeks.

"You come a pullen in heah and a laughen too. . . ." The man was Wilkinson, with a heavy black beard and a massive nose and forehead. He was sweating through his blue jacket and squinting up at the rebels and the men of the company running and jumping and dodging back down the hill. "A laughen like a sonofabitch," and that made Suttell laugh more, chokingly and like a hyena. "Whoowee," he said after a minute. "Whew, I ain't laughed like that in my life." He rolled over to look back up the slope. There were white puffs of smoke along the top of it from the rebels who were coming up, and there was fire from the right side too and down near the town, coming in on them.

But he was in a good ditch and could rest a minute. The company was scrambling down the slope, most of the men running and some of them tripping and falling headlong through the weeds and briars but getting up with welts and running cuts on their flesh and coming down again. They all had the same look on their faces, white and gleaming and frozen around the nose and mouth and eyes. They carried their carbines high and ran wildly, and their equipment jingled and flapped. Jones was walking down but he kept making quick shrugging motions, and kept looking backwards and holding up a cocked revolver. They were the last men down the ridge, Jones and Barr. Barr was holding out his sword and pistol and had found a washed place on the hillside and was sliding, one foot on top of the other, sliding with his boots pushing out the earth and then jumping out to the next place and sliding down more. The rebels were taking their time coming. Oh. I forget ol' Barr. Yessuh he a callen me while I was aimen at that rebel officer. Damn fool. If I had me a gun . . . he looked over at Wilkinson. "You goen use thet gun?"

"Damn right I am plannen to."

"All right, jest asken." He looked out around their ditch. The ground was reddish now. He looked back and suddenly saw they were right at the edge of town. Well now. He could see men in the town ravine, blue-coated soldiers running through rising fires and some of them forming a line at the edge of the ravine. He could tell they were Company E. He looked back around, his eyes narrow and quick. There was a blue body lying near the edge of the trail where it came into the ravine. He looked for a long time. Does that ol' boy have his carbeen on him? I jest shout over and ask. He giggled some at that, still filled up and drunken with laughing. Well I got to see. The man's hand was all he could detect, and it was curled back with the fingers up in the air and the wrist twisted. He saw the seams of yellow piping on the man's back. Well, git out there before the rebs come in for real. He got up and darted over to the man. He heard a bullet snap into the ground a few feet from him. He looked up and saw the rebel in the brown blouse, the pistol held vertically beside his head, peering through his smoke to see. Well now ol' boy if you can hit me at that range with that Navy six you got a right to shoot me dead. But he was nervous bending over the body. It was Jackson, the nest of stripes showing on his arm and blood all over his chest and coming out of his mouth. Ol' "Belly" Jackson. He moved him over on his back. The rebel fired again and the bullet hit close and he felt a sting from the thrown earth. Damn. Well now he was on top of his carbeen. Suttell pulled it out. There was blood on the wood and some on the metal, fresh in some places and drying in brownish circles in others. Suttell scrubbed at it with his thumb. Hell, it'll work. The rebel fired once more, Suttell seeing him carefully balancing the pistol in his crooked elbow. He smiled up at the man. He couldn't even tell where that bullet hit, but when the rebel was looking through the smoke again to see, Suttell smiled and showed his teeth and then stood up and thrust up his fist with his middle finger erect, and then ran back to the hole laughing again.

"Hell, I saw that rebel shooten at you."

"Why din't you take a crack at him? . . ."

"I figger a sharpshooter up yonder could lay me out easy in here. . . ."

"Naw, this is a good hole."

"Yeh, well I ain't taken the chance a reb knows better 'bout that than I do."

Suttell looked at him oddly. "You taken any shots all day?"

Wilkinson moved a little and shifted his eyes. "Not so far, no . . . a few."

"I thought ye said ye was plannen to use that thing."

"Gimme a good shot I will."

"You had a good shot, for Gawd's sake!"

"Aw let hit go. I ain't . . . say, is that blood on that thing?"

"Shore is . . . look, gimme that gun if you ain't goen to take a shot. . . ."

"Naw, I tell ye."

"Well, take a shot right now."

Wilkinson squinted nervously at the bluff. "I tolt ye the reb sharpshooters . . ."

"They ain't got settled in yet, take a shot."

"Well . . ." he squinted again. "Don't see anything to shoot. . . ."

"All right, see that where the ol' path crosses that ridge?"

"Naw."

"Right there, for Gawd's sake! There!!"

Wilkinson nodded, still squinting. "Take a shot at it, there is a rebel up yonder right at that place, you don't hit him you scare him to death."

"I don' see him."

"I know he is there! You only got to pull that ol' trigger. . . ."

"Naw, jest waste the shot. . . ."

Suttell ripped at the gun, furiously. Almost in a panic from the surprise Wilkinson hung on to it, holding it tight against his chest. Sweat on his face, Suttell yanked at it and moved him backwards a little. Then he let it go. "All right, all right you yaller belly. You watch."

Suttell stood up, one hand stinging from the cut he had gotten in the ditch on the crest. He was furiously angry. He slapped the gun to his shoulder, and despite the blood that rubbed onto his cheek he fired at the place on the ridge, standing after he had fired and reloading the gun, bracing it against his flat belly and shoving in the next cartridge and shooting that too, not sure where and getting the thickening, cooling blood on his face and hands.

Wilkinson, on his belly and stretching from the hole, was tugging at his trouser leg. "For God's sake," he was whispering. "Stop hit! Come in here. Stop hit!"

The third cartridge stuck in the breech of Suttell's gun. He fumbled with his fingers in the hot metal, and then began to pry with his clasp knife. The rebel sharpshooters along the bluff were firing at him, he could tell. The carbine was completely jammed. Wilkinson had wrapped his hand around Suttell's boot and was trying to trip him. Suttell swore and hammered down on his hand with the carbine. Wilkinson's face went white with the pain, and he drew his hand in.

Suttell dropped to one knee by the hole. "Gimme that carbeen."

"You busted my hand. . . ."

Suttell drew his pistol and cocked it. "An' I'm goen blow out chee brains with this ol' six gun, lessen you give me that gun."

Wilkinson threw it at him like a child in tears tossing a toy. Suttell uncocked the revolver and picked up the carbine. He looked around him, in the clayey flats with the rubbery brush and high weeds.

The Tennesseans were in a frenzy following his rapid three shots, and they were firing as fast as they could. The smoke jetted into the air and hung in the brush, and the men underneath the weedtops, their faces red-flushed or white and panicky, hammered the carbine breeches and stuffed in cartridges with the palm of their hands, and spilled caps all over the ground like pollen from burst pods. Barr was to his right, holding his revolver vertically, looking open-mouthed up at the ridge. He was kneeling on one leg and craning forward to try and see to either flank. Wilkinson was still snuffling. Suttell was glad again with a black gladness. Din't need his ol' gun lessen he's goen to use it. An' he sure wadn't. Nawsuh. Jackson's blood had stuck in thin lines to his face and shoulder and hand, particularly on his cheek. It smelled salty and he almost could taste the odor. He rubbed distractedly at his cheek with one palm. The rebels were keeping down, out of sight under the volleying fire from the company. No one in the depression had any clear idea of what to do. It was hot under the choking, arching powdersmoke, and they were sweating in their wool jackets. The grass was thick and juicy from the rain and it stained their pants and faces. They could not see the ridge through the layering of the smoke, but there was a steady fire coming from it and from the flanks, and behind them there was the sound of the fort's artillery pieces. A shell went over them and over the ridge in a dark line against their eyes, but again it did not burst. A bugle was being played somewhere down the line but the slamming of the carbines cut up the sound.

Suttell thought, well I better be goen out of this here place. Caint even get in a shot with all these damn ol' fools. He started to get up, but then he saw Barr, coat buttoned back and sweat-stained shirt, still studying the ridge intently with his revolver cocked. Oh yeh. Oh yeh. That ol' boy theh, I nearly forget.

There was open ground behind them to the wall of the fort if they went backwards and to their left. Right behind them and to their right was the town ravine but he could hear Company E fighting from around there, also evidently firing now pointlessly to make noise and smoke and hide the closing rebels behind a blanket. I will run over to the fo't. I may find an ol' rifle pit them niggers were diggen, all to mysef. Maybe Dan Stumps or somebody, but not no damn fool like Wilkinson. Or that Poyles. Find me somebody set on killen. So maybe this is the last ol' chaince I got to git in a shot on Barr. He done pretty well so far. He come over two ridges all right. I got to find me a place. He started looking around for a spot to his rear, in the reddish earth or the small grey and green clumps of weeds and brush and thorns. Hell, ain't no place. He glanced out of his eye at Wilkinson. He was rocking back and forth and holding his hand, and there were tears in his eyes. His big face was bent and curled. Hell, he won't see.

But then he looked back toward Barr, and the man was not kneeling any longer, he was up and walking behind them, behind the line of men, stopping at the holes and trying to get them to slow down the firing. He bent over one hole and his tie was dangling from his throat. And even while Suttell was watching in almost a paroxysm of despair and anger, well goddamn hit I been cheated agin don't nothen in this world ever work out, the rebels hit Barr. The young officer had turned and was looking back down the line in the other direction and he got hit by a ball right through the chest that sent him sprawling out across the dirt, legs spread. Suttell was up and running low over to him almost beside himself with joy. He got to the body and looked down and the man's shirt was already completely red in the v above the blouse and vest, red except for the bent and crumpled white collar. While Suttell bent over and pursed his lips Barr opened his eyes and made breathing motions through his mouth like a stranded fish and then arched his back once, and when his eyes fixed on Suttell's face with some statement clearly framed in them Suttell smiled. He grinned at him, handsome and biting and savage, and knew that he was the last thing Lieutenant Barr ever saw, in the very moment of his death.

The company had stopped firing and Smith was yelling at

them until he saw Barr and came over, trotting fifty yards through the brush and haze and hum of bullets. The men all turned their necks, straining in their ditches and holes. With sweat glistening on their faces they began to move out, keeping away from Barr's body. Some of them were throwing away their carbines and leather belts. Smith dropped to his knees beside Barr, his face streaked with earth and clay and grass stain. Then Smith realized with a clicking sound in his throat that the company was dissolving from this end, and he got up trying to clear his sword to whip them back into line. Isaiah Jones was hitting at the men with his revolver but he was in a panic too, his feet stumbling and his mouth wide and white around the edges. Then he pitched forward too, right into the ground, sledgehammered it seemed and bleeding from both his throat and his belly. Smith was shouldered by one man and lost his balance and toppled to the ground, coat tails flying and his boots in the air. Suttell stood up and laughed once and looked over to the right. The rebels were already down the shallow ridge and walking toward them, faint through the smoke layers but he could see the gleam on their rifles and the flashes of their gunshots. He stopped and arched himself around the iron and wood of the carbine, and fired at them not more than twenty yards away, and thought he hit one but the man might have just been falling to duck. Smith was pulling himself up and cursing and suddenly there was no one left between Suttell and the rebels. The Unionists were all running up the slope, stumbling from exhaustion and falling and getting up, running toward the fort in scattered clots of blue.

Suttell drew his revolver and ran back hard to his left, knowing he was closer to the rebels in that direction but the ground was more broken and the smoke had blown that way. I ain't no good with this here Navy six. I better keep down. He stopped behind a fallen tree and looked both ways. He didn't see anyone and kept on running to the next break, a flat ditch behind a low, reedy bank, and he dived there, facing the fort and still watching. Up to his left he could see his company running for the shelter of the fort, with the artillery pieces in the wall blasting out over them. Some of them, like weird blue sacks, would topple and fall, and wounded were crawling up the slope. He could tell the bullets hitting around them from the kicked-up earth and mud, and a lot of the men were slipping in their terror, and tripping one another.

Well now. He took a deep breath and got up and ran some more, angling up the slope in front of the fort. He dropped into one waist-high ravine and suddenly looked down it and saw standing in the shelter of the bank a party of rebels, yellow-faced and sallow with wide-brimmed hats and horse-stained clothes and long hair. They were laughing and nodding and not even looking in his direction, and some of them were trying out their rifles on the companies running for the fort. They fired and the smoke curled back over their shoulders.

Suttell got up and, scrambling out of the ravine, keeping low, he ran on a slant for the fort, thinking, they caint get a bead on me 'thout showen themselves to the fort. Hell of a lotta good them niggers caint shoot anyhow but maybe they don't know that. He crossed three more ravines, keeping low but not pausing any more. The ground was wet and spongy under his feet but he was feeling good. He was out of the smoke and noise and the air tasted good. He worked all the way over to the northeast side of the fort, after a time straightening up and not bothering to crouch. He had lost his cap, and his hair shone fair and blond. There was a rifle pit and he dropped into it amid twenty Tennesseans of A Company. They asked him questions about the fight and he borrowed a carbine and some cartridges from them and then began to answer, thinking, well hell, ol' Barr and that sombitch Jones both, that's more than I can ask for, really. Hell that is good. I got to git back to Comp'ny D now.

He got back through a sally port into the fort and started looking for his company amid the Negro soldiers and the sounds of the artillery and the smoke and confusion. Negroes passed him carrying boxes of artillery ammunition and officers were yelling to each other, and everything was heat and smoke and the steady thudding of the guns firing on the rebels. Squads passed with glinting bayonets and knots of Tennesseans were standing spitting tobacco juice near the firestep or carrying boards and timbers. Suttell, hatless and smiling, walked easily through all of the noise feeling confident now that he had a carbine again and a batch of cartridges. He smiled at all the bustle and confusion and said, "Whoa theh," when a gun's recoil tripped up one of the Negro cannoners at his feet. This has been a good ol' day so far. I killed me lessee six or sem rebels, and ol' Barr is dead and so is Jones and Jackson and Steward and Poyles, and I never cared for none of 'em. The rebels missed me clean. God damn, this is a good ol' fight now. I got to git me a hole somewhere and go at 'em again. He found his company, sprawling along the firestep and sitting hollow-eyed and confused. Some of them were snuffling and others were crying or pulling at canteens, their flecked throats gulping and tugging. He stood still and put the carbine down on the ground and grinned at them.

It was nine o'clock, Smith was noticing, only nine o'clock and it seemed like a damned eternity. Lieutenant Barr was dead and so was Wilson and E and D were piled back into the fort shot to pieces, and it was only nine o'clock. Ah God, he thought, will this day never end?

3

JONATHAN WAS STANDING ABOVE THE RIVER BANK, AT THE REAR
of the fort. The morning roll call was finished; to his right,
McClure was talking earnestly to Sergeant Weaver. Mist was
everywhere above the river, a steamy, wet mist that touched the
cheeks with pressing fingers. The Negro soldiers were standing
in line for breakfast among their tents, talking to each other
and holding plates and tin cups, their feet shuffling along to the
table where the coffee and thick bacon and hardtack were being
dished out with clinking sounds. The sun was a pool of yellow-
white light in the mist, and Seabury looked up at it for a time,
and then down at the *New Era* which was getting underway,
with whistles and bugle calls and blasts of white and black
smoke, and the clang of engine-room bells. Birds flew in circling,
falling arcs along the river front and Negro women padded
down the slope toward the water, carrying washing or water
pails. Jonathan felt irritable and somehow angry; the thick,
greasy stiffness of the morning routine, the sloppiness of the
bluff behind the river, the choking smells of the bacon and the
flat, grey birdcalls closed in a tight web around him. He angrily
opened the top button of his frock coat; his face stung from
shaving with an unsharpened razor, and Van Horn was still in
his bed in a pool of his clothing, the sallow bemoled chest rising
and falling spasmodically.

He could smell the river smells, mud and water and dead
fish and mist, and he could see the rippling glint of the water,
but the mist was too thick to see the Arkansas shore. He looked
over at McClure and Weaver; McClure nodded good morning

317

to him, and kept on talking to the sergeant, who was shaking his head. In the stained white tents behind him some of the Negroes were still asleep, or arguing or talking in rapid vowelless monosyllables, the words perceptibly a part of the thick and turgid and greasy morning, "Why man, yo ain' got no mo' sense said said why I done tol' ol' man."

So, so we spin out these days. Today I shall write home. I will write the dateline and then the first sentence will be, Pardon Mother for taking so long to write. . . . but then he thought, why even thinking about the letter exhausts me. Oh God, I will be happy to depart this place . . . and then they heard the pattering of the gunfire at the pickets. He turned and looked at McClure, feeling the slight impact of the shooting upon his eardrums. Everyone had stopped talking; the mist seemed to be rising and there was a milky-blue sky, but everyone was listening for the gunfire. It had stopped for a moment, and McClure who had walked some steps over toward Seabury said loudly, "Only the ol' sentries shooten at some rabbit, I warrant," but then it began again, and Seabury who when it had slackened had thought, oh dear God, let it continue, let it continue, almost jumped up feeling the surge of joy and release rushing through his chest. It could of course still have been nothing, but everyone in the fort turned and stopped. The Negroes dropped their plates and cups and the food was being carried off the tables, and the officers, gathering up their swords, were running across the parade toward the headquarters.

Seabury ran with his sash bobbing and his head down, smiling despite himself. He almost tripped over some of the shovels and picks laid out for the digging detail this morning, and he kicked at one of them and it fell over. The officers, their jackets purple and moist-looking in the mist, were in a muted, tight group around the headquarters tent, and there was a ripple along the tent wall where Booth obviously bumped into it rising from his desk. The gunfire was spreading and the officers looked at each other wordlessly. Jonathan ran up still smiling and his eyes sparkling, but the others were talking dully and pulling at their equipment. There was a spate of firing and they all stopped talking and then murmured again.

Somehow, because of the mist, it was like a dream to Jonathan, or rather something turning into a dream, and he leaned toward Epenter and Bischoff and John D. Hill, all of them murmuring but he could not hear what they were saying. He strained to but he could not, the words could not get past the pounding blood in his ears. He thought, my God I have to go to the latrine; he almost danced with the need to urinate. The officers had all been in at breakfast, and Epenter, adjusting his narrow spectacles, still had some egg on the edge of his coat.

The Negroes were out of their tents and gathering along the firestep in a dark swarm of purple and blue and black, or were standing on the parade at a distance from the officers, a line seeming to separate them, and they stood back behind it, dark and featureless and impassive in the mist; and the only light came from their buttons. Between the Negroes and the group of officers stood the white sergeants, in a second tight knot so close together their elbows and sides seemed fused together, their faces pale and silent and listening too at a respectful distance. The cannon gleamed wetly at the portholes. There was murmuring from each of the three groups, and beyond them in a fringe of bizarre, light colors stood the Negro women and children, talking in piping, high voices like crows, chattering and excited, around the edges of the wall of black soldiers.

Don't let them break it off, oh Lord. Don't let them run now. Let the rebels come on, and we will give them some shell. Seabury was almost beside himself, grinning and trembling. The other men were still silent and murmuring and some of them would look nervously back toward the Negro ranks. If we win 'twill be wonderful and if we lose then of course I will have my death. Perhaps, perhaps I need more time, though. This is a thing requiring a great deal of thought. Let me see. I should put my thoughts in some sort of order. There was too much noise and he could not find the perspective for his thinking. Will they not be quiet? Let us see, now. Suppose I die . . . well then, that damned gunfire . . . suppose I am killed (but of course I will not be killed, will I?) . . . well then it is either a life after death for the soul or it is blackness, and either way I have won, haven't I? What shall I miss . . . oh, that gunfire

The Battle of Fort Pillow 319

and the Negro women chattering! . . . will they not be quiet? Perhaps I should not think. What will be will be. Yes. I will not think. That has been my problem, I have thought too much. But today I need not, indeed I suppose I cannot, the blood is pounding so in my ears! That will be the beauty of it all. No more thinking and I will not have to push myself against these people white or black whose flesh I cannot stand. There will be a simple purgation, of course. A thoughtless purgation . . . is the gunfire halting? No, it mustn't! What now, what?

Booth was in the doorway, still somewhat disheveled with tangled hair, carrying his leather holster and scabbard in his hand. He appeared in a flush of light and then stepped out into the rising mist in front of the three congregate masses of men. Everyone was silent and Booth came a few more paces toward them and said without looking up, "Well, it sounds like an assault . . ." and then he looked up. He looked up and closed his mouth when he saw his officers, and walked into the middle of them. He was shorter than most of them, hatless and still struggling with his swordbelt, but he looked into them and whispered hoarsely, "Well now, gentlemen. Well now, this is what we are here for, is it not?" He was almost biting the words off and speaking in a flat, low, taut-jawed fashion. "What is this, gentlemen?" He looked around with his eyes flashing. "This is what you are being paid for, ain't it, ain't it? This is what you are eating your government bread for? You did expect to fight, didn't you? You did think a day would come when you would have to lead your troops, eh?"

Why is he speaking like this, Jonathan thought. Why? Oh. It is because they are afraid that the Negroes will not fight. They are scared. Well, this time he will see it at last, that at least I am not. That at least I am ready and indeed eager to lead these men, and that I trust them. Of all his officers. Jonathan looked hard at Booth while the others shielded their eyes by glancing down or at each other or turning their heads slightly to the side. Booth ran his glance over them. "I am sorry to have to wake y'all up to the realities, gentlemen. That we are fighting a war. And that we have to fight. If you have been good officers your men will follow you. If you have not, they will not and you will suffer. Eh?"

He turned away. Hill, who was post adjutant, stood right behind him with the roster books. Booth finished arming himself with his back to the officers, all the while the firing growing closer and heavier. Bradford came through the sally port, white-faced. The officers began to murmur again and Jonathan thought with rage, he did not even look at me, he would have seen, and perhaps did see, that I am ready out of all these men; but of course he would not give me that much credit, would he? Bradford was almost running across the parade, his feet jerking and then slowing and jerking again. Leaming was right behind him, sniggering. The officers of the Sixth loosened visibly when they saw Major Bradford. He was obviously more afraid than they themselves and even more distrustful and had come to hide in the fort. At least they trusted the white men if not their own niggers, but Bradford did not have the sense to. And too, Bradford was a major and they were frightened by what Booth had told them, so they were relieved and justified somehow and they slouched perceptibly. Booth turned around and his eyes squinted at them when he saw them smiling, and then he saw Bradford tripping and nearly breaking into a run. Bradford shouldered through the group of officers with a weak, apologetic grin, and Leaming smirked openly.

"Major Booth, Major Booth seh. . . ." Bradford was breathing through his mouth, with his jaw jerking slightly from the intake of breath. "I put two comp'nies D an' E out on the skirmish line . . . an' . . . 'en I put another'n in the ol' works on the eastern ridge . . . an' told the others to stay in the rifle pits around the fort. . . ."

"Major Bradford . . ."

"I don't know how many rebels they are, seh . . . but . . . but I heard 'twas considerable. Maybe two brigades, maybe more. Heard they was McCulloh's men and Chalmers with 'em. Now . . ." he gulped ". . . now I last heard that Forrest was up around . . ."

"Major Bradford." Booth did not raise his voice, or touch Bradford, but his eyes went steely cold. Bradford lost the rhythm of his speaking and then said, "Umm . . . well I heard . . ." and then he shut up, and looked white-faced at Booth, and licked his lips. He drew his head slightly to the side, and looked at the ground and then around at the other officers and then said, "Yesseh? Um, yesseh?"

"Major Bradford, I am about to make dispositions of the garrison of this federal post. Please be so kind, be so kind as to listen carefully, for if somethen happens to me, then command devolves upon you."

Bradford ran his sleeved arm over his mouth. "Yes seh."

"All right, then. Le's see." He looked down at the duty rosters, and then at the officers. Seabury met his glance defiantly but Booth still did not mark him out. "Now, then. Company A will take the north portholes with the six-pounders. Company B will take portholes three and four in the east face, with the twelve-pounders. . . . Is Captain Smith here?"

Hill looked at his roster while Booth looked squinting among the men. "Naw suh. He is in Memphis."

"Well then, we better put B out in the rifle pits. . . ." He looked at Jonathan, whose face turned angry and white. "No. All right, Seabury, all right, you take one section to porthole four, an' take over the howitzer there. Putcha other section under a white sergeant into the rifle pit nearest the bluff."

There was some stirring around Jonathan. I will show him. I shall show him that I can die in a way I could not live. He was not certain what he meant, but it was a noble sentiment and it made a lump come into his throat. In a way I could not live.

"Now, Lieutenant Hunter, take your section of the Second to porthole three, and handle the howitzer there." Unlike the other white officers still standing almost huddled together in the center of the huge semicircle of Negroes, Hunter immediately went off calling to his boys, the light-skinned boys in the shell jackets who were grinning broadly and already going toward the wooden gun platform. There was more murmuring. The white sergeants stood and spat and looked anxious. The Negroes were still silent, in the clear light now with the mist risen. "Sergeant Weaver and Lieutenant McClure, you two will take the ten-pounder Parrots and put 'em in portholes one and two. You got to make a platform for porthole two. Open on the rebels from the south as soon as you see 'em."

The firing increased loudly, freckled sound coming over

the south wall of the fort. All the men shifted their weight from one foot to the other and crossed their arms and looked over in that direction. Hunter and his section stood on top of the walls, straining to see, near their gunport. The Negroes of the Sixth, in their big heavy coats, were scared-looking now. They rolled their eyes at each other, and murmured in a hum, like the white officers in front of them. They saw the white men were anxious and worried and they rustled and twitched.

Booth looked up under his eyebrows from the roster and said, "The sections I told off git on with it." The officers looked at him blankly, still huddling together. "Git on with it!" They began to shift apart, talking to each other and walking in twos and threes until they had to separate to get to their sections, Epenter going to the northern face of the four, and McClure going with Weaver to his post. Jonathan walked alone to his men, wishing they were not packed in with the other Negroes. Gaylord fell in beside him, the white sergeant, to take the second section into the rifle pits. Gaylord was young and tall with blond, flopping hair which looked like silk, and a narrow face and body and very white teeth. He smelled of grease and body sweat already, and he looked very nervous. He said nothing to Jonathan but stayed right by his shoulder when he called out the sections.

Bischoff, pink-faced and fat with his wispy beard, was calling out his sections too. He grinned weakly at Jonathan and Seabury ignored him. He won't get his courage from me this day. They have treated me like a nigger, and now that I am ready for this and they are not, they look to me with weak faces. Jonathan drew himself up straight.

Booth told D Company off into the rifle pits, Delos Carson taking them out of the fort through the sally port with their rifles flashing in the sunlight. The Negroes were walking jerkily with their mouths hanging loose, and the white officers snapped orders at them, looking very frightened around their eyes. They were all scared and did not want to leave the fort.

Jonathan waited while his numbers five and six went to get the first ammunition chest, and saw that Gaylord was watching his men going out along the southern side of the fort and was staying as long as he could in the corner of the sally port. Seabury went over to him; Gaylord's face was pale and his stomach obviously working in his nervousness. The file of Negroes he had sent out were wandering around, looking back at the fort and standing at the lip of the headlogged and bunkered rifle pit, holding their rifles uncertainly and talking to each other. "Get on out there." Jonathan spoke stiffly.

Gaylord made a motion with his right hand. "Ah Lieutenant Seabur', I got no wish to git out there. . . ."

"You are as safe there as here."

"Nawsuh. All them niggers out there. Man caint tell what they fixen to do."

"They will do all right if you are strong with them and firm. Be just with them, and strong, and they will do everything you wish."

"How do you know that?"

"Hunh?" Jonathan was confident but the question jarred him.

"How do you know that? I caint hardly make 'em do a day's wuk, and now you 'spect me to make 'em fight?"

Jonathan recovered himself. "Yes. I expect it, the government expects it, your people expect it, you expect it. . . ."

"All I got is yo' word they'll fight, and I doubt you know, Lieutenant."

"Listen. Listen to me, Sergeant . . ." but then before he could say they would fight as well as white men and weren't they men and would not they be returned to slavery if they were captured, Booth yelled across the parade at them. "You two! Unh hunh! You two, why ain't you at your posts?" He took two steps over toward them, across the parade. "Git out there Gaylord, and you Seabury git over to your piece!" Gaylord pulled himself away from the wall and went out over the wooden footbridge across the moat, wordlessly. He held his rifle by the barrel, balancing it over his shoulder. Seabury was furious.

"I was only trying . . ."

"I don' care what you was tryen to do, you git over to your post! I had all the backtalk I want from you, young man!"

Seabury felt almost like crying; his face glistened with rage. He had been honestly trying to get Gaylord into a spirit for the coming ordeal, and Gaylord had needed what he could give him. Why, he was the best prepared of all the officers in the fort, was he not? He was the only one thirsty for the fight, with nothing to lose save his life which had become intolerable anyhow. He was right now the best and noblest, yes even noblest, of them all, and he did not deserve lecturing in front of the whole fort. He imagined as he trudged back to his post that all of the civilians and sutlers and farmers and Negro women crowding into the fort had formed an interested and amused and even vindictive audience to his insulting. Backtalk. That is what he said, the old, grey-toothed fool. Backtalk! I will show him backtalk of my own. When the rebels come, he shall see.

He was indeed almost crying by the time he got back to the Negroes at his gun. He stood behind them. They were crowding at the gunport and along the wall trying to see the fighting. He wrapped his arms around himself and stood tight and angry and almost crying, and furious at himself. Oh, I hope they tear off this flesh, this encumbering, encompassing, fleshy shell with all of its weaknesses! Let them tear me apart with bayonets and ball. I swear this, I swear that I will die here at this gun. All I shall have to do is stand here and wait with my sword in my hand. He felt the hilt of the sword. Just stand here hatless and wait for the rebels to come through the gunport, which of course they will. We will give them a full charge and then they will close in with their sabers and pistols forcing their horses through or maybe on foot, coming on over their dead and everyone in horror will draw back. And they will break. And I will stand here and plant my feet like this—and he stiffened the calves of his legs—and not move. That is all I will have to do. Smile faintly—he felt the working of the flesh around his mouth—smile faintly like this and hold myself rigid and the rebels will stop in their onrush for a second when this one man does not run, and then Booth will see. He will be turning to run and wondering why the rebels have halted, and he will see me alone confronting them, and he will then want to hold out his hand to me, but of course it will be too late. They will cut me down after a moment, perhaps after they first offer surrender and honorable terms to me and I will sadly and nobly refuse. Then they will cut me down and, having saved his life by the respite granted thus, Booth will see. Yes. And he will be contrite and there will be this pain in his throat for having treated me so. I wish I could be there. Perhaps, perhaps I can, grievously wounded but transferred and tended and spared by the rebels—no! no! do not defile your thoughts in this sacred moment by clinging to life. Bend your will and steel yourself in expectation—full expectation—of death.

He no longer felt like crying. When the Negroes saw there was nothing yet to tell about the fighting except confused motions in the brush, blue and grey and smoke, they turned back and found Jonathan behind them, wrapped up and smiling to himself in the midst of his thoughts. They straightened some. Ol' Lieutenant, he don't carry on like them others. He ain' so scaired. He too dumb to be scaired. Naw he ain't, he ain't dumb. Other ol' buckra they ready to break any minit. Not this heah white boy. Jonathan was very handsome, delicately featured with the fine, white bone almost showing through the flesh, and clear and large-eyed. The sunlight fell in a warm, early-morning wash over his shoulders. The Negroes could smell the rising odors of the earth, and a cool watery smell coming in over the dank river stench.

Bradford was dancing around Booth while he gave orders to his Negro orderlies and aides, and they ran off with them. All around them men worked or waited, the Negroes shoveling away and laying the timbers for the field piece at number two porthole, their jackets laid on the firestep while they worked. Weaver checked it intermittently with a level. Others were going back and forth to the embanked magazine and coming out with halting steps carrying the heavy ammunition chests, the white officers and sergeants yelling steadily at them in a nervous anxiety near the artillery pieces, "Naw, naw, you got the wrong one go back and tellum we need the shell for the Parrots, hustle up man!" Everyone gathered in the six tight knots around the cannon, or stood in a scattered line armed and watching along the firestep. The civilians, mostly in vests and shirtsleeves and work pants and jeans stood around morosely until Hill began to hand out rifles to them and tell them to find a place on the firing line, some of them going to the wall with the Negroes but most waiting and watching, and some slipping down below the bluff. The Negro women and children were shoved and herded and yelled at ferociously by the white sergeants, and gathered into splashes of color among the stained tents. They were wide-eyed and the babies were unanimously crying and squalling. Three orderlies gathered around Doctor Fitch while he was laying out his knives and scalpels and pans on a table made of a board between two stumps, near the river.

Bradford finally plucked at Booth's arm, ridiculously twitching at his sleeve and then jerking his hand back and staring speechlessly when Booth turned at him. "Yes, yes, what is it? What is it, Major?" Bradford jumped from one foot to the other and tried to put his mind on what he was going to say, and then just as Booth turned away with a deep sigh it came to him and he had to do it again, catch him by the sleeve and then put his hands behind him quickly.

"Well sir, I was thinken hadn't I better take care of . . . you know . . . of the bluff . . . you know, like we said with Marshall?"

"Hunh? What the hell are you talken about?" Booth glared at him, his blunt thumb marking his place on the sheet of names and duties he was holding.

"You know, put some cartridge cases and things down below the bluff . . . ?"

"Oh. All right, all right do whatever you want, only let me handle this list for a time."

"Yessir." This emboldened him. His black eyes were laced with red streaks, the only mark of color in his face. "An' don't you think it would be a good idea . . ." he paused, while Booth turned and glared ". . . a good idea to break out the sutler's liquor for the men . . . you know . . ."

Booth shouted and it startled him and he jumped. "No! No, I am not goen to have a lot of drunk niggers and whites in this place! No, an' you suggest such nonsense again and I will relieve you right here and now! Now git on with whatever you were asken about, and let me be for a while!"

Bradford tried to smile and then turned and left, again almost running, to the magazine. He got three Negro soldiers who were sitting in the shade of it to carry out the cartridge chests, six of them. They took them down the slope, Bradford listening to the firing behind him and watching their caps disappear down the bluff and then come back up. "Did you break in the tops? Hunh?"

"Yessuh, lak you tol' us."

"Awright, git these others down yonder."

Booth told Hill to take the women and children and the men from the sutler's stores and the farms who were obviously not going to fight down to the barges along the slips. When Hill and seven soldiers began to perform this amid renewed squalls and yells and whimperings, Booth went over to the second porthole and gave a supervising eye to the emplacement of the ten-pounder. And when that was done he then climbed painfully onto the firestep and shouldered his way through the men to watch the rebel advance through his glasses. When he had done that for a time he called for Captain Theodore Bradford, a slight, grinning boy who was Bradford's younger brother, and told him to get onto the bluff with the signal flags and when he gave the signal to tell the *New Era* to start putting shells into the number one ravine on the far side of the town ravine. Booth did these things one at a time and checked them off in the small, leather-backed book he carried in one hand, pausing between observing and giving orders to attempt to fasten his sword onto the belt and failing each time, so he walked as the scabbard whacked into the back of his boots, and the unfastened hasp tinkled against the metal loop.

Bradford scrambled noisily onto the firestep beside him and when Booth put his glasses onto the skirmishing again Bradford fumbled with his own and then got them to his eyes too. Booth dropped his binoculars for a moment and looked at Bradford, his chin knotted with muscles and his eyebrows drawn together. You puling coward. Major Booth had learned long ago, or rather had had beaten and baked into him that you performed in a certain military fashion; that you bore down upon yourself and did everything studiedly and calmly and with a straightforward and unshaken faith in yourself, with the sensation that all you had to do was will it hard enough and bite down into it and soon the world would begin to respond. He completely submerged the imagination, or whatever it is that prompts the hollow intuition of a man, behind the cold edge of his will and the steady, rhythmic fulfilment of his pattern in a sequence of carried-out orders; watching the orders carried out, the artillery piece now mounted and the sweating Negroes buttoning their coats again and picking up the spongestaffs and linstocks, the women and children no longer cluttering in tight, loud knots along the bluff amid the sinks and tents and coal piles but now on the barges where at least he did not have to hear them. By carefully giving the orders and then watching them carried out one by one, Booth had learned to completely trust his own ability to shape the world into a certain precise pattern and indeed make even the sequence of forthcoming events somehow subject to his will and his judgment; with the faith that the politician has because of his continual closeness to his own political machinery; every politician in some measure cannot conceive of his own defeat.

Not death; Booth accepted the edge of death as part of the deal he had made with the military service, but even in death Booth assumed all he would have to do was lean stern-faced and unyielding into the bite of the mortal swordstroke and so making of even that an image of his will. But when he looked over at Bradford, tightening his chin in anger and feeling for a moment the thrust of his submerged forgotten intuition or imagination, he was suddenly afraid. Suddenly in an ejaculated thought he realized or tasted that the world would not conform; that there was within the fort a hollowness and a mistrust and out there a fierce, relentless, implacable hatred, and that the fort would fall inevitably, the rebels having too many troops and not even trying to split his command by slicing off the Tennesseans but simply driving the Tennesseans back into the fort; not rushing but just penning them up for the kill. This was tangential of course to what Booth principally saw, simply the quick instantaneous realization that *there is this man too, this coward,* and in no way can I make him conform to the military demeanor his rank demands. This sudden helplessness in front of the rank human cowardice of the man beside him in the sweat-stained, pale-faced hunch over the field glasses, the sudden inability to in any way manifest his will over this man, threw him for a swirling moment into the fact that he was himself exposed and human, and that the simple teeth-gritting determination "they shall not win" meant nothing under the arching sky.

He looked back quickly to his field glasses, studying the rebel approach under the early-morning sunlight and wishing he had some coffee in his belly, clinging to the soldier's eternal wish that he had had just a little more time to have had some coffee and bacon. He felt helpless watching the process of the skirmish. The Tennesseans were being whipped much too easily; they were falling back on the right, down by the town ravine now. They ran out of the woods and the ravines and over the last ridge, small blue seeds spilling from a sack, running through the weeds and dropping down into the ditches and behind the fallen logs. He watched them hold silent and still for a moment except for some running for the shelter of the houses, and then they all began to fire as the rebels appeared, small puffs and jets of smoke marking their places in the blue-green shadow of the ridge.

Too fast, too fast, he thought. They ought to hold the rebels longer and punish them. Now is our chance to sting them. He licked his lips, aware of Bradford beside him, Bradford's mouth drawn into semicircles revealing teeth and gums at the corners while he squinted into the glasses. The soldiers around him on the step were beginning to whisper and talk among themselves again, "Ol' buckra he sho gitten whupped. Lookit him run outa thet bresh. Must be a passel uv rebels down theh. All acommen thisaway."

He swept his binoculars over the whole range of the fight, hoping for a second to find some place to make a thrust or a show of force or something, and shake the rebels loose. Immediately in front of the fort on all sides were men in the rifle pits, the Negroes with their backs to the fort huddling together and their kinky hair glistening with sweat in the clay slits, and the white troops sitting more apart, some of them in studied calm not even in the pits but on the edges, all of them watching. To the east was the long ridge with the scattered huts and shanties and the old earthworks, and Bradford had put in a company where he should have put in his whole battalion. Booth looked through his glasses at them there, knotted firing behind the corners of the earthworks or down in the huts and lean-tos, where they were looting the houses before the rebels got closer.

The ridge was closer than he had noticed and higher; he could look right into a section of the trench along the crest, and see the yellow stripes on the sleeve of one of the corporals, the man brown-bearded and looking back toward the fort while loading his carbine. The rebels were coming at them from due east all the way around to the riverbank at the south where the town ravine was. The firing was heaviest along the center, where the ravines and rises shallowed, between the town and the old trenches on the ridge crest. Smoke puffs and balls jumped and seemed to sparkle, somehow; more of the smoke, greying as it rose against the background of the trees, arched into the sky or swept back with the land breeze toward the river, weird, hairy columns, or trunks, drifting across the blue morning. He put his glasses down on the actual fighting; he could see jerking and squirming and darting things amid the foliage and thickets, and smoke licking around the southern edges of the ridge with the trenches along the top. The companies in the skirmish line were being outflanked.

Booth put his glasses down and thought for a moment, hand on chin. There was no way he could see to stop the rebels from getting into the ravines around the fort. He thought about putting more men into the trenches along the eastern ridge, but in the first place he could not do it without weakening his own position and in the second place it might be too late and would just be throwing them away. Obviously Bradford should have put his entire command into the works there.

He studied the situation again through his glasses. Now he could see the Tennesseans running back in the middle of his skirmish line; they came back over the ridge in groups, darting down the slope. Smoke rose from along the top of the shallow ridge, and more of them came down from it. The rebels were across the ridge, obviously. He tried to see the men as they ran back; their faces were pale and stained, and most of them were running hard. The gunfire was continuous and loud, a beady pattern. He looked through his glasses until he was certain that all of the blue skirmish line was back, driven against the town and the valley floor southeast of the fort. Bradford was still staring and breathing through the sides of his mouth with his canine teeth showing. "Major Bradford, tell your brother to signal the *New Era* to begin putting some shells into ravine number one."

Bradford dropped his jaw, looked frozen for a second, and then nodded and jumped off the firestep, running across the parade awkwardly, his big boots creaking. Booth spit and looked again, and then called down the wall toward gunport number one. "Mister McClure!"

McClure stepped back where he could see Booth. "Sir!"

"Open up on the first ravine. Try some shell."

I got to do something, he thought. The growing doubt was in him now. He felt helpless, and there was nothing he could do about the checkered fight out there. Maybe we can get some good artillery down on 'em, if the ground ain't too broke for it. The Parrot went off with a roar and a great rebound and a pall of whitish smoke bathing the Negro gunners to their knees. They all smiled like children at the noise, and we began to hop around the gunbreech with joy. "Oh we done hit ol' secesh now! Yessuh!" McClure stepped back from the parapet and shook his head to Booth. They handed him the next shell, and kneeling on the firestep he cut the fuse with his penknife. Everyone in the fort had jumped with the explosion, and now they were crowded to the parapet jabbering and yelling and weaving, trying to see. The gun fired and the Negroes all jumped and cheered again because of the loud noise. There was a cottony burst in the reddish, washed ground between the ridge and the town, but it was clearly short. The horses stabled in the town area were jerking and rearing, and the Tennessee company skirmishing there was running back up the slope for the fort. Booth ran along the thudding firestep, shouldering and bumping past second and third lines of the garrison flattened against each other watching and straining. He knelt near the gun. The company that had been fighting in the town was piling into the rifle pits or running, sucking in air, for the fort itself. The gunners sent off another shell, and McClure squinted and brushed away the smoke near him, and then cursed, "God damn it, it dint go off!" But the Negro gunners were all cheering and yelling anyway.

"Damn shells won't go off, Major."

"Well, you got the range down anyhow."

Booth got off the firestep and walked over toward the sally port. Bradford was right behind him every step. The Tennesseans from E Company were coming into the fort over one of the sally port footbridges; they staggered and wandered about and then sat down, breathing hard and their whole frames moving, their equipment tangled and high around their chests. Most of them had smears of blood and grease and mud across their flesh and their clothing, and one man with a beard mottled by black mud was holding a shattered arm, still breathing too hard to realize the pain but holding on to it with his good hand as if it would fall off. The smoke from the cannon fire threw drifting shadows over them, fragile, perceptibly cool touches along their cheeks. Booth tried to find out where Captain Poston was, yelling at the sergeant seated on the ground. The man rolled his eyes over at Booth and panted a moment before he could answer. Bradford was pacing up and down in nervous circles behind them. They heard the first salvo from the *New Era*, sounding ridiculously flat and helpless for some reason, and Bradford immediately ran over to the bluff to watch. Booth was glad he was gone.

"I think, I think ol' Poston got shot, seh."

The man beside the sergeant said, "Naw, he done stopped in a hole, I seed him. Lieutenant Wilson, though, he got shot, and Lieutenant Barr down to the other comp'ny."

"What happened? . . ." Booth had things to find out from them, but they were breathing so hard and stank of powder smoke and excrement and urine and sweat, and did not seem to be able to stir at all. He kept trying to hold on to the questions he had to ask them, but men kept running up with slips of paper and his orderlies had all come back and were standing around him, and he could not concentrate. Another artillery piece went off and Booth straightened with a jerk, his eyes crinkling in anger. Weaver's crew was running the gun back to the number two porthole through the smoke, all the Negroes with their caps off yelling and yelling along the wall. The firing was an incessant noise, tiny fingers pushing and pushing against his ears.

"Well seh," the man with blacked stumps of teeth was saying, feeling for a pipe the whole time in a spate of exhausted nervous reflex, "well seh, these rebels come outen the woods at dawn and druv us like hell. Ol' Sergeant Leonidas he helt us to the firen line but the rebels wuz ever'where. They was Mississippians, ones I seed, and I heard tell one of 'em . . . uh, one of our boys . . . saw McCulloh the rebel. Anyways, anyways, we fit 'em frum ridge to ridge, but they flanked us ever' time, and we got back to the ravine . . . the ravine—thankee suh— the ravine right in front of the town, and they shot Lieutenant Wilson minit he step up."

"Yes, yes, well how many were they?" The man drew at his pipe.

"I reckon I seed a brigade of 'em . . ." and then Bradford was at Booth's shoulder saying, "Ted says the riverboat is firen too high and do I have yo' permission," and he straightened up feeling his bones creak from weariness which had already drained him this morning and it not even eight-thirty. He straightened up and glared at Bradford and put his hand on his shoulder and half dragged him to the corner of the sally port.

"All right, Major Bradford, now you listen here! You shut up and stay away from me this mornen. Me I got work to be about, I ain't got time to fool and wetnurse you. Now you go and play with those signal flags or whatever the hell you want to do but stay out of my sight! You hear? You hear?"

Bradford shook himself trying to get out from Booth's hand, the hand digging and pushing the flesh of his shoulder. Finally he sank back against the wall, his eyes going from one of Booth's to the other, back and forth wildly, with their red veins standing out and his face pale-white. Then he was trying to say yes, the word not quite coming out but the lower lip drawing back again and again trying to form it, still hunched against the wall with his coat collar almost as high as his cowlick and the buttons pulled taut.

Booth went back shaking his head and confused and tired already, thinking, that man has drained me this day. That man. . . . But this time Hill was running toward him, stopping and saluting, his eyes earnest and almost pleading, "Sir, sir, they's rebels comen in on the nawth, you can almost see 'em from the fifth po'thole."

They walked side by side back across the parade to the northern face of the fort. The parade was covered with litter, a wheelbarrow on its side and shovels and picks spilled around it, a man's shirt clotted with mud and dirt, a spilled keg of nails. The garrison was packed along the south wall of the fort, the Negroes still yelling every time one of the artillery pieces went off, their caps waving frantically and outlined against the swirl of smoke. Weaver, his white face shining in concentration, was cutting the fuses of the shell while the Negroes in the wash of sunlight loaded the cannon, red piping flashing on their jackets and their faces shining and sweaty and happy. The Negro orderlies in a chattering monkey-like eagerness were step for step behind Hill and Booth. Booth was walking steadily, his head held up, and Hill was having to take a skip to keep up with him.

They crossed the planks of the platform and went to the fifth artillery piece. The Negroes were all itching and straining to see what was happening to the south. Bischoff, his tiny lip flecked with spit and sweat in his hair already, leaned over while Booth propped the field glasses on the rim of the cannon wheel. He balanced them and pushed them gently from side to side, straightening up and frowning and then bending again, Hill behind him trying to find the rebels again, and Bischoff beside him pointing them out and in a pet to push Booth's glasses and bring them to bear. "God damn it Bischoff, give me a . . . ah! Yeah, I see. Yeah. . . ." The rebels were visible coming up the creek bed in a constant glitter of metal and a vague sinuous motion, blanketed by the foliage. Glitter and sheen and weaving motion. He lost it and then found it again. He straightened up after a moment, with a crick in his back. He worked at the stiffness and thought and then said, "Well, we might as well wait. Wait till you get a clear shot when they cross that last hill," pointing to the breast-shaped rises, "and then cut loose at 'em. John, stay here and keep an eye sharp, and lemme know."

"Yessuh." Both of them remained frozen, watching the rebels coming through the creek bed on the north, while around them the Negro gunners at Bischoff's six-pounder fidgeted and stood on their tiptoes and swore softly, trying to see what was happening where the firing was.

They won't give me a chance to think, Booth thought, recrossing the parade. Give me five minutes and I will figure out something to do. But every time I look there is somethen new. They come pilen in here from the skirmish lines, and right away we get penned up in this fort. The rebels are coming in from each side, I reckon Forrest's whole army. He paused; the firing in the center was letting up and scattering, no longer the single beaded impact of sound but now stretching and pausing more. It sounds like we gave way in the middle. He turned and went straight to the firestep, and again had to force his way through the clustering Negro soldiers.

He could see the faces and chests of the men running up the slope; they scrambled over the rifle pits running hard, and their tongues were hanging out. One dropped to his knees from exhaustion and, propping a hand on the ground, was helped up by an officer, Captain Smith, who was shouting hoarsely at them. They were hatless and stumbling and their bones seemed disjointed and they could not make their limbs do the right things. They tripped and fell over logs, and slipped in the mud. Christ, they look worse than Poston's company.

Booth got the footbridge up to help them into the fort. He saw a company sergeant named Talley, stumbling, his feet weaving and his mouth open and pointing toward the sky. The rebels have killed most all of their sergeants and officers. Booth squinted at the men, their clothes stained and burned and their leather dirty, the straps across their chests and shoulders twisted and the breastplates dangling. A lot of them had stopped trying to run; they shuffled blankly toward the fort, carbine across the backs of their necks and their hands on them. Booth was leaning over trying to guide the bridge into position and then he saw a quick, flicking motion at the foot of one of the men coming in, and he thought in the same breath, what is that? and, a rebel bullet. He looked up quickly.

They are in the ravines along that side, and closing in along the edges of the eastern ridge. He could see the flashes of gunfire and the white puffs of smoke amid the tangle and thorns. He ducked as a ball thudded along the top of the parapet not far from him. A man near the footbridge suddenly went popeyed and threw his hand across the middle of his back, and fell forward into the dirt. Git some cannon onto the rebels. The falling minie balls jerked most of the Tennesseans into a run of sorts, shuffling for the bridge, and some of them jumping into the ditch at the base of the parapet. Booth squinted toward the brush, standing erect again and thinking, 'y God I don't aim to duck like that again. He felt for his glasses. He could see the writhing motion of men down in the brush and the tangles. He turned toward the third gun position. Seabury, staring up into the sunlight under one visored hand, was watching him. Damn it, would git this fool of a boy.

"Lieutenant Seabury!"

"Sir?"

"I got us some rebel sharpshooters spotted. Can you put down some shell on 'em?"

"Yessir."

"All right, cut a shell for two-hundred yards. . . ." A ball clicked going over his head. They seen me. All right. "Two hundred fifty, I make it."

Jonathan, with the blood pounding in him and thinking, well, this is not how I expected it but I can show Booth in this way, knelt at the open ammunition chest, the howitzer already loaded with powder. The ranges and fuse cuttings were set on a table pasted in the lid of the chest, and he used a knife, cutting toward him and bracing the shell with his hand and knee. He chopped out the top of the fuse, to the right setting. He handed it up to the number two man, a yellow-faced Negro boy named Cargo, handsome and well built. Cargo put the shell in and they rammed it down.

"See to the right of that ridge, Seabury?" Jonathan searched wildly. No, which one, find it! I got to find it myself. "See it? See it to the right . . . damnit. . . ." he started to come down off the firestep.

Oh. By the brown patch of ground. "Yessir, yessir, I got it. By the brown patch of ground, is it?"

"Yes. That is it. Good, good, now put that shell down onto it for me, boy!"

"Yessir!" He straddled the wooden prolongs of the gun, thinking, I did it right, now watch this, watch my shooting. He slapped the left side of the artillery piece to bring it into line. But the Negroes with the spikes didn't move. They were all gaping and rocking back and forth trying to see the spot. Oh no, they will not spoil it! "Move this thing! Quit looking and move this gun, niggers!" I have never called them that. Never. . . . "Now then, a bit more. A bit more. Too far, all right, too far, now then, now then. . . ." He held up his hands and stepped back. Something whirred past, chipping a piece of wood off the bracing at the port. So that is a bullet. Well, I flinched but I am not scared. No. Now then, let's get the barrel up, and he twisted the worm screw under the base of the howitzer, going the wrong way imperceptibly for a time and then realizing it and with great jerking pulls lowering the breech and raising the barrel. Booth had his glasses out, watching and waiting, and he fiddled with his fingers along them and looked down and said, "Well?"

"Yessir. A minute." I cannot make a mistake this time. This should be as close as any man in this fort can put that shell. He snapped the primer in place and stepped aside. Then he looked and saw that Cargo, still watching the rebels, had not moved so he slapped Cargo with his gloved hand and the man stepped back, and still feeling the warmth where his hand had struck the golden flesh he jerked the lanyard and there was choking smoke and a loud noise and one of the Negroes was knocked sprawling backwards because he had not gotten his spike clear of the trunion. Above the eye-stinging smoke and the yells and cheers of the Negroes Jonathan saw the quick rise of the shell, a black dot making a blurred line against the sky and then falling gone, and he stepped aside from the smoke. Lexington, the tall Negro with the head shaped like the head of a match, was watching beside him, leaning against the trail piece of the recoiled gun. Jonathan heard him breathing in the two seconds of waiting and then Booth was saying, "It did not go off. It was an excellent shot, but it did not go off." The Negroes were straining, yelling still and slapping each other on the back. Somehow it is my fault. It did not go off. Booth stepped down while they were swabbing the cannon. "Keep up the shooting on that patch there, and you will flush them out."

"How many more rounds, sir?"

Booth stared at him. "Till you do the job, man. Till you do the job. Don't anybody ever make decisions here except me?" Fretting with his sword belt, he turned on his heel and left. The Negroes were loading the gun again, and running it back into place. A rebel bullet hit the top of the parapet near them and sprayed fine dirt into Cargo's face. He turned with a grin. "Ol' massa he miss this boy thet time. I heard the bite, but he ain't tetched me. . . ." He grinned, his teeth bright. Everybody else was saying, "Heard the bite! Laws, heard the bite but ain't tetched me. . . ." Jonathan thought, they are doing well. They are doing well. 'Twas not my fault the shell was a poor one. We will hit them this time. The Negroes were dancing through the smoke to get the gun run out again and Jonathan cut the shell and gave it to them and then climbed on top of the firestep to watch, handing the lanyard to Gator after sighting in the gun again as best he could judge. He climbed up thinking, this will not be as good as the first shot. The first was precision. This will be low.

Another bullet clicked by in the air and he flinched again, his flesh jumping, but he still did not mind. There was a tingling thrill to the thought of being shot at. He took off his hat and placed it on the parapet, and stood letting the spring-morning wind play with his blond hair, fluting it into a wash of yellow in the sunlight. The Negroes, their eyes glittering, knelt or stood in the shadows beside the big brass howitzer, the gun glinting richly in the risen sun, like some proud trainers ready to loose a fierce animal into an arena, watching it with their lips folded under in suspense. Jonathan dropped his hand, and the gun blasted, bathing the Negro cannoneers in billowy white smoke while they jumped into the wooden-breeched porthole tugging the gun back to load it. They seemed disembodied and the smoke shadowed their features into deeper black, and swirled around their waists. They were cheering again, "Given it to the ol' secesh, lawsy. We done given hit to him, I reckon!" Jonathan could not mark the fall of the shell. Some passing Tennesseans, wounded and trying to find the hospital, sniggered at the Negroes.

4

BILLY GAYLORD STOOD IN THE MIDDLE OF THE TWENTY NEGRO soldiers in the rifle pit. They were a hundred yards from the fort and about fifty from the nearest row of cabins in the town, and the rebels had just driven the two companies of Tennesseans back from the skirmish lines and the ditches, right in front of them. They had run back past the rifle pit, faces pale and spittle hanging from the corners of their mouths. Gaylord had pleaded with some of them to get into the hole with his Negroes, but they would not do it. The Negroes were packed tightly into the pit, a large rectangular ditch with a headlog. They moved and rustled and talked to each other, and shoved against Gaylord, sometimes tripping him and making him bury his face in a Negro's back, smelling the leather of the crossbelt and the sweat-stained wool.

Gaylord was almost wild with fear; rebel bullets were coming over now that the skirmish lines had been stripped back, and the sharpshooters in the ridges and the thickets were working on the rifle pits and the Union troops still outside the fort. A bullet kicked into the ground, skipping a piece of earth at them. Immediately the Negroes began to fire, shoving and thrashing toward the edge, pushing their rifles over the headlog and shooting, and then trying to find room to load. The smoke choked Gaylord; the Negroes kept on firing blindly. He started yelling at them, "Stop hit, durn yore hides, stop hit!" He hit one or two nearest him with his free elbow or the barrel of his long revolver, but they only jerked and flinched and whimpered. He finally got two steps through them and caught one of the Negroes at the front of the pit by the shoulder and jerked him around, looking at the pock-marked black flesh two inches from his own face and shouting, "Stop hit, stop shooten! Stop shooten!" The smoke was spilling back over into the pit, holding close to the wet ground and it was too thick to see through. Gaylord almost went berserk, thrashing with the revolver barrel and with his free hand slapping at the black faces and once being hit in the face accidentally by a rifle butt. By the time he had stumbled and shoved and shouted his way to the front of the pit and had gotten them quieted his nose was bleeding brightly.

Then he made a space for himself by waving and thrusting with the heavy revolver, punching at their faces and bellies, until they pulled and shoved back, stuffing elbows in one another's chests and throats and having to stand on tiptoe to see at all. He looked at them for a second, his long, lank blond hair tousled and flopping, his head slightly ducked and hidden by his shoulder. The blood ran into his mouth and there was the blue pain in his nose from being hit by the musket butt. He looked like a surrounded, hunted animal. Then he ran a hand through his hair and straightened a little. All right, he breathed, closing his eyes. A bullet pattered into the log right behind him and he jumped, his head kicking up, but he pushed out the pistol barrel when one of the Negroes shoved his rifle across the log again. He waited until he calmed down, breathing through his mouth now and still tasting the salt of his blood. He turned then and waved feebly at the smoke with his free hand, trying to clear it. It was heavy and choking, and his throat was irritated by it and he coughed and gulped.

It finally rose enough to see down into the town. He had expected to see the ravine filled with rebels, but it wasn't. Ah Lawd Jesus. He was scared to death. I hope to hell to git out of this ol' pit. Feels like I been buried under a ton o' nigger flesh. He sucked at the air. Ol' Booth he says take 'em out theh and take care not to git captured. Ain't gone git captured cain I he'p it. If there was rebels down there I would be a runnen to the fort this minute. Another sharpshooter's bullet hit the headlog.

The Negroes were still holding back from him in a semicircle, their eyes white-ringed.

"Listen now. Listen. Keep your haids down the rebels caint git to you. Keep your haids down and wait for somethen to shoot at. Don't go burnen up powder like field hands." He scrubbed his sleeve across his nose, but the bleeding didn't stop. Another single bullet and then a volley spattered around the pit, and bits of earth were tossed over into them. Everyone was crouching from the waist down.

Billy Gaylord cautiously put his head up over the log again. He looked down into the town, where the horses of the Thirteenth Tennessee were still picketed. Rebels want them hosses, I reckon. He ducked down when the flesh couldn't stand it, but then looked up again after a minute. The Confederate sharpshooters were on the ridges; he could see the smoke puffs of their fire, but they were concentrating on another pit. We ain't firen so they don't mess with us. He kept watching the stained tents and brown shanties and the alleys and paths between them with boards over the places that turned swampy in the rain, watching for the rebels to make their rush on it. The horses were picketed on the other side of the town, threshing now at their curbs from the cannon fire which was rustling and exploding into the brush at the edges of the area. These goddamn niggers. Caint tell what they goen to do. There they are! There come the rebels. He jerked when he saw them.

Actually they had already gotten to the horses; he saw the greasy sheen off the leather crossbelts of one man, trying to cut through the picket ropes of the horses. The horse and another one, trailing their ropes, suddenly bolted from the picket, two rebels running alongside them. They were hairy-faced men with wide-brimmed, pointed hats. Mississippians, he thought. I be damn. Like ever' Mississippian I ever seen. He looked down into the town. There were more rebels, running crouched from the brush into the huts on the far side, and he could see them in the paths and streets between the shanties, with crossbelts and rifles kneeling at the corners.

Someone began firing from the rifle pit to his right, where

there was a platoon of white Tennesseans, and almost instantly rebel sharpshooters were hacking away at them. A bullet hit inside their pit, and everyone jerked, the Negroes wild-eyed again and some of them, out of Gaylord's reach, beginning to shoot again. He felt terribly exposed, all of a sudden knowing the rebels could fire into the pit. He looked around him at his men, shoved and packed together in the pit, sweating into their frock coats and their faces shiny and terrified, some of them trying to drop to their knees and others trying to get forward to get a shot over the headlog. They were all swaying and jerking at each other, some of them beginning to claw at one another in desperation, their mouths closed and their leather belts creaking. Some of them were firing their rifles almost straight up, now, their hands holding them up into the air and shooting them and the recoil twisting their wrists. Smoke was everywhere and terror and the thick smell of the Negroes and of urine and the cloying smell of the chopped earth, and drifting powder smoke. Then one of the men in the pit, a Negro named Anderson, was shot right through the chest. The bullet hit him in a split second of complete silence and every man in the pit heard the "pock" noise it made and saw the sweat jump from the man's face and his sudden mask of terror and pain and then he was dead but would not fall since the press held him up. "All right!" Gaylord realized he was screaming. It was as if he felt the shot himself; he wanted to shield them somehow and when it hit Anderson's flesh it was as though it had hit his own. "Let's go! Git to the fort! Git back to the fort!" He shoved at them and they began to clamber over the edge of the pit and pull and shove and then run for the fort. The white men on their right, rising seemingly out of the earth, were also running back to the fort. Billy Gaylord looked over the log once more, the air coming down to his sweating body as his men cleared out of the pit. Some rebel had put a battleflag against the huts, and it was blowing in the April wind, a touch of furious color against the brown huts and the green foliage.

Then the last Negro to climb out said, "Oh" and fell back with blood all over his shoulder. The hole was visible and even bone showed in it before the blood flooded, wine dark, all through the shot flesh. Gaylord shoved him with all his weight, supporting and then thrusting him up onto the top of the pit, and then the man was running in a dazed way but running anyhow, and Gaylord himself was up on top. Then he thought, get the rifle, get the man's rifle, and he reached back down and could not quite touch it on the floor of the pit. He reached for it until his armpit ached and then almost wild with fear and the slapping sound of the bullets hitting around him he clambered back into it and got the gun, and then was out and running weaving toward the fort. He jumped into the moat with the mob of men. He was still bleeding through his nose, and his jacket was stained with blood. He couldn't think for a moment. Why did I git this ol' rifle? Answer me that. Over his head one of the ten-pounders fired again and his eardrums stung.

He got around the corner of the ditch and into the fort through the rear, wandering with the others in a dazed shuffle through the tents, holding their carbines or rifles wearily, taking chest-aching breaths and feeling warm and safe behind the artillery pieces and the walls of noise and smoke and of the earth fort. Well, I made it. Ol' fool came through, I reckon; one more time. Never thought I would. Honest never did. Gitten shoved in a pit with twenty niggers. That is enough for a lifetime. I hope to Gawd I never have to smell one of 'em again. Hope to Gawd. They ain't done badly as I thought. Ol' white troops, ol' Tennesseans cut as soon's we did. Caint blame the niggers more 'en them.

He wandered through the confusion, the wounded and the shouting and the lines of sweating Negroes hoisting along ammunition cases, toward the second position where Weaver was directing his artillery piece. Weaver looked up from sighting the gun, stripped to the waist and his beard dark against the white chest. His Negroes were standing open-mouthed waiting for the next shot, the smoke still hanging around the spokes of the gun. The firestep was crowded with Negroes holding bayoneted rifles. The dejected and exhausted Tennesseans were lying under the step or sitting at the foot of it, still breathing and holding their hands slack across their knees.

Weaver stepped back from the smoke-haze and tension of

The Battle of Fort Pillow 345

his gun for a moment and said, "I saw you comen along, boy. Thought they got you way you went back into that pit."

"Went to git this," and he held up the rifle, a bit shame-facedly.

Weaver laughed. "You take good care of guvment property, boy."

"Hell, you ol' fool. You nearly took off my haid with thet cannon last shot. Still caint hear a damn thing."

"I tell you next time, boy. Good to git chee back in the fort."

Gaylord looked around and saw Seabury directing his piece and kneeling on the firestep near the gunport. He don't need me for a time, I will sit here and talk to ol' Weaver while he works that gun. It was quieter right behind the walls in the fort, the sound of the artillery spewing outward from the walls and the rebel sharpshooters' crackle masked by the thick earth. There was a hum of conversation, mostly the Negroes talking to each other and popping up to look over the walls and then back down breathlessly. One of them had been knocked dead by a hammered slug and was sprawled out in the clay, face down with his cartridges all around him like fat, grey worms. Blood was pooled near his split head. The others near Gaylord were all talking about him "Ol' Simon he never knew hit. Boy he is one daid nigger. Ol' secesh shooten mighty good." The Tennesseans were silent or murmuring to each other: "I never been so dog tired my whole life. We got all of Forrest's army out there. Shee-it. I want to git out of this ol' place. Le's wait and see."

Gaylord sprawled along the firestep to watch Weaver at work, some of the tightness and worry flowing out of him and his muscles and flesh easing as if he had gotten over a fever. He felt almost delirious he was so exhausted, and he enjoyed the sounds and faces and the comfort of being behind the walls next to Weaver, away from the rebel bullets. A Negro behind him popped up and a rebel bullet chopped a V into the parapet an inch behind his dropping face, and he went almost blank with terror. The others sucked in their breaths and said, "Woweee. Look it thet. Boy you nearly got hit up side the haid fo' good. I mean to say." Then while Gaylord was looking around from that and thinking, I reckon I got a piece more sense'n that, one of Weaver's Negro cannoneers was shot through the leg in the sally port. He was almost paralyzed with fright and shock, and tears were rolling down his cheeks. He had his hand splayed pressing the blue cloth down around the bullet hole. Weaver looked at him for a moment and started to step back from the sally port, and his crew ducked away from the embrasure too, going into the black shadows near the gun. Their eyes glinted and their tongues licked at their lips.

And then Booth was there, running the last few steps to the second porthole. "What is the matter here?" He looked from one to the other of the men. "Get this gun back into operation." Booth, red-haired and grizzled with his grey teeth and mottled flesh, put his hand on the trailspike of the Parrot, his palm upon the wood. And posed and framed in the open space between the earth walls, his buttons glinting in the light, he made a perfect target and a Mississippian in the Eighteenth Battalion, resting his rifle on a log, shot him dead. The man allowed perfectly for wind and had the sights on his good Enfield rifle set for three-hundred yards, and the bullet entered Booth's chest at almost precisely the same instant he put his hands upon the spike and it tore through the uniform and right into his heart. By the time he toppled onto the wooden edge of the platform and sliced open his face he was already dead, the tactile sensation of the wooden spike in his hands and the bemused concern with keeping the rebels pinned down the last thought, the sum and total of all of the dusty, dry years on the parade grounds of army posts.

Gaylord had heard the "pock" sound again and raised up thinking, my God, not Weaver! All of the men were standing in a dingy little group over Booth's body, the officers coming away from their posts to look squinting through the mass of people, the Negroes open-mouthed and dirty, their black flesh glinting with sweat. Some of them dropped down to pray, moaning and rocking backwards and forwards. The white men were more guarded, some of the Tennesseans even snickering and hardly bothering to roll out from under the firestep, cocking their heads over and sitting up or taking a couple of steps but instantly regaining not so much their composure as their easy contempt. The white officers were vaguely conscious of the poses that ought to be struck, even in the haze and smoke and deadly cloying fear all around them, over the body of the slain commander so they clasped their hands or became very solemn and tightened their chins, sober-eyed. Everything in the fort, spreading out like ripples from a thrown rock, became quiet.

Seabury stepped back from trying to clear the elevating screw of his gun, wiping his hands mechanically and thinking, Yes, yes ah. There was a blaze of freedom. But then he was lost, crying, injured. As if he had awakened from a dream, with that curious sense of having lost some precious opportunity. I never had the chance. I never had the chance. He was the one that had to be on the boat when I made the gesture. It was as if Booth had owned a part of him. He was stung with frustration, loss; he worked furiously at the elevating screw which had become bent. His fingers were too slender for the work and he bruised them trying to straighten the metal ridges with the tools in the limber chest. He was squinting furiously.

What? What was he to me, that his death should affect me in this manner? Oh, when a friend died, I would remember the thousand personal things, his way of brushing his teeth or of putting on his clothes, or of eating or talking. That was one thing. But I never saw Booth out of uniform! Why this horror? (This damned thing will not give, ouch! Suck the finger for a moment.)

He shared a terrible, irrational involvement, along with the Negroes of his section who still stood frozen, staring over at Booth's body even while the rebel bullets thudded and struck all about them. The fabric of Jonathan's dream fell away, unraveled. He still struggled, blindly now, with the elevating screw, but Booth's body—the blue, sack-like form, sprawled across the platform—Booth's body seemed to bear down with a palpable weight upon his thoughts. There was a terrible sad and hollow sense of loss; things could no longer be redeemed. (All right, try this thing then. Here, you boy, help me here for a moment. Press down, like that.)

He owned a part of me, and I was freed—but I wanted him

to like me. I wanted him to think well of me. When he died, he still thought of me as a young damn fool. I wanted him to think well of me. That thought rattled within the shell of loss, bewilderment, shock, that Jonathan actually felt; but it was impulse and catalyst. (Well now, see what elevation we can get. If that does not hold we shall have to use the piece as best we can.) Jonathan felt that he had never seen, touched death before. That he had never died himself before. He still stumbled with the brutal reality of death's cone-like thoroughness.

What am I doing here, beneath this pelting rebel fire, working with stinking Negroes and smeared whites? This is me, here, now. All around me, men are dying, flesh is being ripped and torn, and I am doing some of the ripping and tearing. This is me, that is a rebel bullet that just struck the wooden bastion, this day is real. All of this, this haze and the Negroes in their sodden uniforms and the high clouds and the rich blue sky and the noise. And men are trying to kill me. What a fool I am, indeed. What a fool.

He stood for a moment behind the gun. His life was suddenly on a different level, like the first time he had told himself, "I am," over and over again. He saw in a way what Booth had seen earlier that morning, that the world was so unanswerable to his desperately contrived pattern of things; and indeed that he was helpless and befouled and completely alone. He stood still while the Negroes rolled the gun back to the embrasure. The Negro Gator said, "Mistuh Se'bur', seh?" and he stepped forward almost blindly, trying to reason and re-establish some ordered pattern of thinking, thinking, well, I can't die now. No, I cannot. I have no reason to now. There are things I must look at first.

Gaylord helped a Negro carry Booth's body down below the bluff, his handhold at the armpit feeling the wetness and warmth there, thinking, this man sweated like a stuck pig, and saying, "Mmph," when the weight sagged against him. He and the Negro wrestled the body down the steep slope and they rolled it under a log, looking all the time for Bradford. The women and children on the barge and the wounded men were staring, suddenly silent. Gaylord got back to the top of the bluff, still remembering the clammy feeling of Booth's sweat. Even after he stone cold dead. And I mean he was dead. Well, I better git over to see Mr. Seabury.

He was walking toward the third porthole passing Captain Epenter's position and he looked at Epenter, with his square teacher's glasses, bending over his range table, and then Epenter was holding his face and there was spurting blood on the chart. He was shot through his jaws. There was blood and spattered broken teeth and the hot sense of pain. His men all bent over him. Epenter's whiskers were soaked and red, sopping up the blood and there were whiskers in his mouth now where the bluish hole was punched in the flesh. Some of the men began to help Epenter up, Negroes staring with the whites of their eyes like vast zeroes.

Gaylord leaned close, among the black shoulders and the "Let him be, all right I got 'em" that the Negro corporal was saying. He noticed something and bent down and picked it up. It was a whitish, stained tooth, with a green spot in the top and tobacco stains, and now cracked and red with bits of Epenter's gum hanging to it on the bottom. Epenter was trying to scream but the words would not form through the choking blood and hair in his mouth. They walked off with him like some strange six-legged creature, taking soft and precious steps and Epenter jerking now from the pain and thrashing and the black arms around him and supporting him. Well now, Gaylord thought. We ain't goen to have any damn officers left. Ol' Bradford must be in command now. Them Tennesseans lost two, three officers already, and now we lost two. Gawd, them rebs can shoot a rifle.

Bradford was standing beside his brother on the raised signal platform at the bluff. The *New Era,* bobbing under a slow wheel and fighting to keep position in the river, was amassing a huge pile of brown and white gunsmoke shelling the ravines south of the fort, and then, at the almost petulant demand of Major Bradford, plodding northward to shell the rebels coming through Coal Creek. William Bradford was desperately fascinated by the gunboat: by the creaking, huge fabric of metal and rivet and wood and cannon and human flesh, responding slowly but massively to the flicks of the signal flag, puffing and in a swirl of water changing position and belching away into the bright April morning.

The boat had touched once to take off the barges to the north, the women and children thrown into hysteria by the approach of the bolted and shuttered monster throwing steam and coal smoke into the air, and the voices from the echoing interior of the shield telling them over and over, "Take hold that rope, sharp nah, take hold that rope." *New Era* had nosed and towed the barges through a small storm of sharpshooting to a landing on a small upriver islet, there abandoning them amid the reeds and muck, the wounded men hollow-eyed and the women clutching at their children while the rebel bullets kicked up the water harmlessly about them at that range. The monster said, "Git up to the house; go on. Go on up to the house," the house being a small and abandoned shack in the midst of two dry acres of overgrown sedge and plum and muscadines green and seductive to the children, an event unforeseen by the captain, Marshall; but fortuitous enough, since it stopped their shrill and piping screams even if it did pose new problems and concerns for their mothers. I done tol' you, don' tech thet stuff, I done tol' you.

Bradford had stood in a torment of worry until the boat had come swinging out into the river, back to its north position and again settled under a slow wheel, thrashing and treading water and firing into the underbrush. The twenty-four-pound shot threw up chunks of mud and turned the flat sinks in the creek into dappled and chewed morasses, but the rebels ducked into the ravines and broken places and huddled there mud-spattered but untouched. Major William Bradford, though, had found respite, or at least peace from his fears, in the huge bank of noise the artillery was making to his rear; and his own furious sense of accomplishing much destruction by means of this iron monster on the river. The smoke from all of the cannon fire drifted south with the coming of mid-morning, changing from white to dull-brown.

Bradford got his brother to send the boat back down to the first ravine when the wave of Tennesseans and Negroes, driven in by the rebel sharpshooters, began to come around the edge trying to slip back into the fort. So that just as Marshall was beginning to have some effect, simply because the shifts in the river and the boat's position and his own gunnery were gradually saturating the Coal Creek area and the rebels were beginning to crawl higher into the underbrush and slow down their rifle fire, the water in the creek steaming and the banks swept by huge claws of grape, the gunboat had to plod responsively back down to the lower position. The sharpshooter that picked Epenter out ran back across the creek when the boat had gone and found a good niche and had undisturbed time to make that good shot at three-hundred yards.

Bradford, though, had found his own way of enforcing his will upon a segment of the fear-stung world. The gunboat, its sides glistening in the sunlight and smoke coming from its boilers and the number 7 bright on the pilot house, moved where he told it and presumably tried to shoot where he told it as well. The Negroes were reassured by the noise from the river since outside of trains the gunboats were unquestionably the most unfathomable and most impressive things the white man had brought, so when the Negroes straightened from carrying the ammunition chests or manning the guns or huddling under the parapets with their rifles, they could hear the thrashing and the broadsides and assumed the secesh were being chopped up. And the Tennesseans assumed the same things, insofar as they were now willing to see anything good at all in their situation, most of them drained and still broken-winded and frightened, sitting in blank and sweating and rancidly angry groups, despising everything and above all their white officers. And the officers of course had to depend upon the riverboat since they were not about to depend on their own men. They had clung too long to the fact that the rebels couldn't take a fort with adequate naval support, and they too were impressed with the noise.

Booth alone had not been impressed, but he had been too busy to pay attention to what Bradford was doing. He had put it away somewhere in his mind after searching his pockets for a pencil, that one of the things he would have to do was put a closer rein on the gunboat and try to work it more into the defense of the fort. But he had let that go in the immediate effort to burn the cabins in the town where the rebels were getting into good sharpshooting range, and to this end he had right before his death dispatched John Hill, his adjutant, with twenty wide-eyed Negroes and a promise of plenty of artillery to cover them. And then, in trying to get the second gun position back into operation in order to protect Hill, he had been killed.

Hill in his turn, his frock coat buttoned and his sash bright against it, eyes earnest and face twisted into deep sincerity, paused and then said, "Come awn," and led the Negroes out in a run around the end of the fort for the town. He got them into a rifle pit, packed shoulder to shoulder and sweating and panting without losing a man, and decided to wait for the cannon fire from the fort. Well, he thought, it ain't comen. He did not know that Booth was dead. He smiled for a minute showing a chipped front tooth to the Negroes and said, "Well boys, we got to do this alone." He looked very sincere with the flesh over his eyes slanting upward and wrinkling and his sandy hair brushed straight, bare-headed and very calm while rebel sharpshooters were ranging down on them and rebel cavalry in regiment size were at the outskirts of the cabins waiting for the order to rush. Hill had been told what to do and he figured the Negroes would thereby follow unlike almost every one of his fellow officers except Hunter and perhaps Booth, but Booth by this time was dead. Why wouldn't they follow? Sandy Addison, a square-faced, yellow Negro with a roll of fat over the back of his neck, had been out in the pit with Gaylord and knew this white man was different. Gaylord was more afraid of them than of the rebels. He expected them to run and since they did more or less what the white man told them to do with as much prevarication and evasion as they could get away with they had packed in around Gaylord, frightened too. And when he fidgeted in the middle of them they were almost close to panic and when he had slapped them with the pistol barrel they had cowed and whimpered. They had been ready to run. But this was different and Sandy knew it, different principally because Hill was very calm and steady and they all liked Mist' Hill who didn't put on in front of them and punched their shoulders and grinned at

The Battle of Fort Pillow 353

them. And Hill wasn't afraid and dint act like there was anything to be afraid about.

Hill said, "All right, Corporal Addison, take ten men and
go round that side, and I take the rest. You got matches? All
right, here some. Move fast now." Hill was up and running and
they were step by step with him, dodging the logs and sometimes tripping and falling amid clattering equipment. On the
last few yards they were shielded from the rebels by the cabins,
and they got there only three men short, those three as a matter
of fact still back in the rifle pit refusing to go out since as they
had climbed to the top of the pit a rebel minie ball had hit right
among them.

The soldiers dodged around the dank and stinking houses
and shanties and tents, some of the Negroes going through the
trunks and saddle bags with quick, furtive hands looking for
anything bright, but most of them trying to make the matches
work. Addison's men got fires started in three of the huts in the
row nearest the fort. One man stayed in each hut throwing
things into the fires but after a minute of wild exertion the
impetus was gone. With the bright sunlight and the burning
huts and the rebels' bullets humming and kicking all around
them, the woods in front of them a mass of Confederates under
flags and firing steadily and rebel sharpshooters in some of the
outermost huts shooting at them, hairy men jumping out to fire
and the balls chopping through the wooden walls, Addison lost
his nerve. He didn't see Hill and figured Hill being a white man
had gone over to the white men for some reason, a fancy taken
whole from a dream Addison had had a couple of nights before
and had invested importance in, wherein they were working in
slavery now for their white officers. He saw rifle-fire down one
twisted and narrow path between the huts. He thought, Hill he
is shooten at us. Secesh catch us they kill us, we ain't suppose' to
bust white man's truck, and he cut and ran. His men sensed the
terror and ran too, only three huts ablaze and the men exhausted by the spate of quick and nervous action. The Negroes
were accustomed to slow and laborious and endless movements
and they were nervous and unready for the quick, dodging,
reflex-demanding actions of the job of both firing at the rebels

and burning the huts. All of the other Negroes, trying to make the wet blankets or the leather burn in the huts, looked up and saw the others running and cut from their own positions.

Hill as a matter of fact was trying out his revolver on the rebels in the nearest house, and had seen one ball hit an earthen pitcher in a window and smash it satisfactorily. With his mouth open in concentration he heard his men running, and looked back. His face clouded in disbelief, but he thought, well I got work to do then. He methodically stood amid the flames in one hut, feeling them pressing like warm and then scalding irons against his flesh, until he found a suitable torch. Then he ran from one hut to another trying to get the fires started. Most of the huts in the first row fired easily enough and then he ducked into the last house in the second row, but the flames would not catch there. He broke a lantern but it was empty, and the wood was wet and the bedclothes damp. He kept thrusting the torch in, his genitals throbbing with fear and his back twitching, until the rag and wood torch was snuffed out. He bent over in the middle of the earth floor, sweat all over his face, and tried to get another torch going, and then used up his matches one by one in studied deliberation trying to set a fire. He knew the rebels had seen him go into the hut, and he heard their footsteps slapping across the board footbridges and the hard-packed earth, coming closer. Through the wall in front of him he heard a man saying, "I think the sombitch's in yonder," so he finally cut and ran, feeling disgusted and sick and hoping Booth would let him try again, and maybe they could do it with artillery. Just as he was remembering simultaneously that the artillery would not depress enough to reach the huts and was thinking to duck to the right to avoid the rebels, he was shot in the arm. His arm stung and then the pain was bluish and aching. He dodged furiously through the last row of huts and ran back up the slope for the rifle pits. The Negroes had run back to the fort, and he did not have any protective fire. He got to the rifle pit and jumped in, still not even thinking about cursing the Negroes, breathing hard and checking his wound. It was not too severe and his arm was not broken. Well, twenty-five more yards and I am there. He got up and dodged to his left coming out of the pit, and then ran to the right, running head down, his uniform flapping around him and his red sash unwinding. A Mississippi trooper with a long, narrow face knelt at a window in one of the far huts and led him just enough and put a minie ball right into his temple. Hill toppled face down, dead instantly with half of his head blown out. Lieutenant McClure saw him fall, and went to tell Bradford that too.

So by the time Bradford received the news of Booth's death and walked stonily across the parade ground to assume a command that he assuredly did not want, the *New Era* was dangerously low on ammunition and her crew, shuttered inside the iron plate, was choking and exhausted. And the post adjutant, Johnny Hill, was dead on the slope with his brains spattered over the shiny leaves of an oak sprig. Bradford, when he was told that Booth was dead, had gone completely limp in the knees, and his face had turned even more white.

William Bradford at one time had had, if not courage, sufficient enterprise to raise and recruit a battalion of loyal troopers out of a region where nine-tenths of the population were staunchly rebel. He had come at the age of twenty-six into West Tennessee with three wagons of Sharp's breechloading carbines and twenty-two federal troopers from a Pennsylvania regiment, and had within him or within the wagons sufficient inducement and enterprise to raise some two-hundred-odd men for the federal service. Even if history and the course of the war helped him in no small way, he nevertheless had been able to assert his will, which is a much rarer thing, especially in war, than is recognized.

But during the subsequent years of the war that enterprise of willingness had dissipated, largely because it had not gotten him what he wanted. It had not gotten him into the positions of authority and respect he had set out to achieve, and instead there was a new, continual jutting fear in his throat, a fear growing when he saw the barns flare into flame against the winter night and heard the yells of the women and the pistol shots. A sense that what he was doing was wrong and that of course the balance of things would move against him, against William Bradford, just as certainly as it turned the tide again to the beach. Every day dressing for his pilgrimage to the fort and the cannon and shiny-faced Negro soldiers, he had buckled on the sash and thought, if I can just make it a little further, the war will be over. Perhaps I will go out west. Just a few more days though. The rebels are collapsing. Just a little longer. And while he patted the buckle smooth he would suddenly consider the shadow in the back of his mind, the shadow of the arching vengeance.

He was eroded by fear; going up the hill each day for the month during which the Negroes had been at Fort Pillow he had spent more and more time in Booth's quarters, reading and rereading the reports and looking at the maps, letting his troopers carry out the patrols and the orders of the day unsupervised, even keeping Leaming, who could have controlled them, by his side; Leaming who was strong and certain of himself became a sort of glorified personal bodyguard. Every morning he had spent some time looking out at the gunboat in the river, looking at it as a child looks at a Christmas present the week after he receives it, wanting to touch it and reassure himself of its presence, thinking there, there, there it is and it is for me and it is mine.

He had been frenzied all that morning until Booth had told him to go wherever he wanted, at which point something in him had said, oh yes, of course, go to the riverboat. He had spent an hour and more obliviously watching his gunboat lob shells and grape and canister by twenty-four-pound loads into Western Tennessee, taking it for granted that it was doing great execution and marveling at the fire-breathing, smoking, noisy complexity of the thing. He had been completely absorbed in the ritual of its movements, the gradual loss of position in the current and the working back to the station, the broadsides and the rammer staffs and the bells and steam.

Then the Negro orderly, like a doll with chocolate skin and bright eyes and a shell jacket, came running up saying, "Majuh Booth he done been kilt, come quick," and he had at that moment lost the absorption and felt his legs give way under him. They walked back across the parade, McClure telling him in passing that Hill was dead too and maybe Epenter. And the world curved in like a hurled rock upon William Bradford.

He walked across the depth of Fort Pillow, his coat swinging around his legs. His face was pale and deep with worry, and his eyes were glazed. There was an aching in his head, something that would not leave. Why am I here with these niggers and this white trash, why caint I be out there with those rebel boys? He walked on. The Tennesseans in his regiment were all sitting on or under the firesteps, dirty and worn and scared too, their eyes rimmed in red and darting from one side to the other and their faces pallid. They sat with their hands dangling from their wrists or leaning talking in small groups together, whispering behind raised hands and exuding panting short laughs and quick stares. They won't fight. God knows they won't. They got to. The rebels won't take me alive, I know it. The Negroes were together too, bent underneath the level of the parapet in friezes of blue cloth and black flesh, holding their bayoneted rifles and huddling against the earth, or standing in the shadows of the portholes, regarding the ports like furnaces and pressing against the reassuring wood at their backs. Their officers paced and did not look at each other. It was a weird, nightmarish walk, the men all silent and looking at Bradford and him feeling feverish and ill and like his legs and knees and back were water. The only sounds were the continual and now audible rustling approach of the rebels and the skirmishing fire around the zigzag trenches where the Tennesseans were still hunkered down and desperately waiting for the Confederate rush so they could bolt for the fort, and the whine and spit of sharpshooters' bullets.

Bradford got to the middle of the fort not knowing what to do or even why he was there, just having walked there because the Negro orderly had gone in that direction. But now with the officers and men all looking at him, he stood in front of them all, straggly-bearded and white-faced, sweating into his big frock coat. I got to make the Negroes fight. My own men are wuthless, I got to make the niggers fight.

The Tennesseans were fought out and dispirited, afraid now too and feeling the sense of their own guilt and coming punishment out there, and most of them thinking of a way to get out of the fort once it surrendered or once the rebels took it. While Booth had been in command they had not been too worried; they sat slouched and out of the fight, listening to the Negroes and watching artillery firing and laughing and making small comments to each other, figuring, let the niggers do the dyen a spell. They had figured this was a stronghold, this was a place to run hide when the rebels came after them and no rebels could take a place like this. Not with Booth and the niggers. But Booth was shot dead and the niggers and the cannon were suren hell not stoppen the rebels. They had not been allowed to run hide, they had been made to go out and fight for a time and the rebels had been too good for them and they knew it, and now suddenly it wasn't any place to hide at all, it was just a trap. A trap with niggers and Bradford who was a durn fool and a coward to boot. Bradford who with his good carbines had gotten them into this mess in the first damn place and dint trust 'em or know 'em a damn sight. They had been shot up badly outside during the skirmishing and in the rifle pits and now they huddled in contemptuous despair, thinking, well now, I ain't taken no part in this, we are goen to git cut to pieces by ol' Forrest. Watching the Negroes sweat and work and thinking I got to git out of here. I ain't goen to git killed on account of no nigger. They spat tobacco juice and ridiculed the white officers and laughed at the Negroes. "Hell, a lot of noise won't stop them rebel boys, let me tell ye. And you niggers better watch out, they comen in here after some ol' black meat," then looking at each other and grinning flat and hard, their own fear exculpated in the Negroes' murmurings and terror. "Them rebels is too good fer this ol' place, we caint hold 'em. Me I aim to git out of here; you ol' black boys better git too." And then examining a fingernail quizzically while the Negroes looked at each other open-mouthed and rolled their eyes. Yessuh, y'all better git on back to ol' Massa. They could make the Negroes afraid anyhow; they had been so terrified they had wet in their pants and had run and wasted ammunition and shot each other and ignored their officers, so now they could sit while the fear gradually subsided like the panting and the debilitating tenseness, and let the fear pump itself out in laughing at the Negroes, murmuring so they had to lean forward to hear and saying over and over, "Yessir, this ol' place won't stop them boys. They looken for someone, and 'tain't us. Ain't that so, Ben? Yessuh, had us dead thutty, fotty times, let us go. 'Tell them niggers they what we want,' they said."

Now Bradford stood in the center of the fort and they shut up, save for laughing a little at him. The Negroes were afraid enough as it was, because it was painfully obvious their own officers were glazed with sweat and terror too. They were left in groups along the walls, silent and desperate, no one telling them where to go or what to do, surrounded and blinded by the noise and not even sure where ol' secesh was comen from. Their officers were wandering in groups of two and three or standing alone and apart from the men, faces nervous and tense and the muscles working all the time around their jaws. Booth had been more than a father to the Negroes, not because of personal contact but just the opposite; because he came from the North where there was Mistuh Linkum and he had Lincoln's picture on his wall, Lincoln the man who evidently owned all of the panting, noisy machinery and the shells and who had reversed the patent order of things and given them their freedom, which they did not understand but which they did appreciate. To the nigger from the field with the rifle in his hand, Booth standing in front of them had seemed a god; the man invested obviously with the respect of, and the power over, men. Therefore, because Booth never spoke to them any more than he would have taken upon himself the personal problems of a man of his infantry regiment before the war, he had immured himself even more in his legend of dark puissance and omniscience and power, not splayed out but controlled and centralized and vast, the sense of the man's authority stamped and credentialed, of course, by the picture of Lincoln on the wall and the gunboat snorting into the slip when he told it to. He was their Goliath.

On the other hand there were just enough house Negroes from before the war to sufficiently depreciate Bradford; house Negroes who were learned in the recognition of "quality," the "quality" folks you announced in the echoing, tiled front hall and the folks you merely let in and the ones you shooed to the back door. Bradford with his sweaty palms and the ready money did not act like quality but he acted like the buckra desperately wanting to be taken for quality, paying off the Negroes at the one place where they had more than enough pride as it was. Caint fool us, nawsuh. We seen quality. By the second morning Bradford had tipped the sentinels coming through the porthole the word was around that Bradford was just white trash and that Bench from A Company had worked for him before the war and the man was white trash and nothing more. They took the money, even tussling and flashing their teeth and knives in their dank shanties for the place at the gate where he came through. But it was not just for the money, but for the enjoyment and the relish of taking the money just as money; for reducing, by their contempt and their certain knowledge of Bradford as white trash, his tipping to a demeaning public action unwittingly committed each day. It delighted them.

So while Bradford stood in front of them they watched afraid now out of their ignorance and their officers' own fear, and what the Tennesseans told them. Bradford knew that he could not get his own men to fight. They won't. They are yellow trash. They know I know it, and they hate me for bein' better because of knowen it. But the Negroes, I always got along with the Negroes. I always got along. They will fight. But when he looked along the frieze of them he did not see their respect or willingness to fight. All he saw was the staring white eyes, scared colored men crouching under the wall all along the parapet. So, thinking, they are just a little afraid I can cure that, he turned to an orderly and said, "Son, get me the sutlers. Let's git some beer for these men. This is goen to be a hot day's work, stopping the rebels." And he turned and smiled at them.

5

THE NEGROES CLUSTERED AROUND THE KEGS WHILE THEY WERE
being prized open with bayonets. They were sweaty and stinking and they pressed in close around the cursing sutlers working at the tops of the kegs and trying to pass out the dippers.
The Negroes laughed and shouted, "Hey man don't git in mah
way I aim to git some beeah, I tell ye." Their poll heads glistened
with sweat and plastered red mud from the earth rampart, and
they dropped canteens into the beer and ale and used the dippers, dribbling it over their chins and down the front of their
uniforms, blackening the red piping. Their officers paced back
and forth with swords under their arms, sending the Negroes in
groups or letting them go at will, grins cracking at their faces.
The Negroes drank with the dippers and when others tugged
to get the cups or spoons they cursed and drank more. The
groups dissolved into struggling, tussling, laughing knots of
men, with more and more of them filing away from the wall,
leaving their caps and leather equipment and rifles against the
firestep and going for the beer. They drank principally because
the stuff was there; they had learned not discipline during their
slavery, sufficient discipline and more having been beaten down
upon them in the hot Alabama cashcrop fields, but they had
learned to take animal and quick advantage of any situation;
they had learned how to completely drop any vestige of discipline for the allowed five minutes or the day or the week. And
their military service, chopping out the bunkers and the earthworks and unloading the ships and building roads, all under

the supervision of careless, hot-tempered and fretting officers and white sergeants, had not only not inculcated discipline into them but as a matter of fact—through what they had seen of white soldiers off duty and the peculiar and new circumscriptions the military had made upon their lives—had made them less disciplined than ever. So while the beer was there they would drink it. They would drink it with a ritualistic desperate abandonment, throwing back their heads and pouring it into their throats, feeling it surge choking down and fill their noses, and spewing and laughing. The beer was homebrewed by the sutlers at the post and it was thick and cloudy and had an apple flavor when it was good. The sutlers stood back scowling and the officers were laughing and still pacing and keeping a sharp eye out for the rebels.

The Tennesseans sat in bony silence or snickered to each other and did not go near the beer. The Negroes clapped each other on the back and tussled over the dippers and danced away with full canteens.

They were also drinking because of the fear in the fort, the fear that came in upon them from outside. From the spitting noise of the rebel sharpshooters and the wounded men and the red, red blood when they were shot, and from white troopers whispering in their ears and their officers sweating too freely and looking at them sideways and cursing. And now Bradford too, Bradford completed their fear by walking up and down around the five kegs of beer, talking to them and slapping them on the back, a flurry of pale-white in the middle of the dark-blue and the black flesh, slapping them and saying, "Well now, we whip them rebels, boys," and, "Git the ol' courage up, boys, and we teach the rebs a thing or two." He smiled effusively and paced between the kegs, the smile aching the folded ridges of flesh in his jaw; walking among them under the hot sun and the drifting breezes, patting the Negroes and cajoling and praising them.

The Tennesseans were not drinking. They were sitting in their diffuse knots too afraid to drink, thinking each of them individually, I got to find me a way out of this place, I got to find me a way. These niggers caint stop the rebels, we got to git out of here. Them rebels will be madder'n wet cats, yessuh. We got to git out.

Seabury sat with his legs folded under him beside his twelve-pounder, watching the Negroes at the keg. Sounds came through the porthole to him, popping sounds of skirmishing around the outer works on the eastern ridge, gunfire from the riverboat thudding ponderously against his ears, and the rustling of the rebels' advance. He was looking at the tall figure of Lexington, the trail man, standing in the middle of the knot around the keg getting his canteen filled. They had all laid down their staffs and linstocks and trails and gone over to the keg, following Gator, who walked on the sides of his feet. Some of them were coming back, pausing to sip off some of the beer in their tin cups or running to jump up onto the firestep and nurse their full canteens. They should not be allowed to drink, he was thinking. No, they should not be allowed to drink. But I am surfeited with watching all of this. I have been under fire now for how long? Four hours, I have crouched here behind these earth walls listening to the gunfire and seeing men hit and fall and die. And what of it?

For a time he had been afraid, and had crouched away from the ports and the top of the parapet like a man on a cliff hangs back from the edge, but he had found where he could walk in safety, the walls and ground taking on a new aspect of depth and safety, and he stayed in the bounds. If the rebels take the eastern ridge I will just have to be a little more careful, that is all. For all he knew, the cannon had been utterly ineffective, the shells refusing to burst because of the fuses, either falling perfectly placed or thrown blindly, but crashing into the brush where the rebels were too spread out to be hit anyhow. I have been waiting for this for so long, and what does it turn out to be? Not the Armageddon I had expected, but a lurking and a hiding, keeping well behind brush or walls or protection, making ineffectual noises, and all of it boring and deadly only along the edges. But along the edges, it is very deadly indeed.

In that instant the rebels attacked. In the fort they thought the rebels were making a rush on them. Really they were not; Forrest had just come up and they were straightening their lines by taking the cabins in the town once and for all, and by driving the Yankees out of the rifle pits along the east ridge. But instead of working in short rushes with sharpshooters picking off the Federals they came with bugles blowing and in an open rush for the cabins and for the ridge.

Jonathan was up instantly, peering over the top of the parapet along with the Negroes and Tennesseans, hearing the "Yaaaa Yaaaa," gabbling scream over and over and the brassy sound of the bugles, and the flurry of aroused gunfire. Jonathan saw the eastern ridge right in his face, covered with gunfire along the crest. The zigzag scars of trenches were now clothed with puffs and banks of smoke; and bolting out from the smoke came the Tennesseans put there by Bradford. They ran fast down the river side of the ridge, running down the old paths and slipping and tumbling and running again, having waited in abject fear for the final rebel rush and now that it was come firing once and panicking. Bradford was walking behind the line on the parapet, his huge boots creaking. "Fire, fire! They are comen! They are comen! Everybody up and fire!"

Jonathan turned to the howitzer. They rolled it to the porthole and he cut the fuse and they rammed the shell in, and he jerked the lanyard himself. They were bathed in smoke and the gun jumped back out of it. They loaded it again, the Negroes working desperately and glittering with sweat, some of them taking off their coats. The wheels rumbled across the wooden planks and then he jerked the lanyard and the gun blasted back again, his ears aching and the heat from the muzzle forced and baffled back in upon his face. He stepped to the breech while they were loading and wrenched the elevating screw up, lowering the barrel to bring it to bear now on the top of the ridge ahead instead of firing over it. Bradford stood by his shoulder now saying, "Pump hit into the ridge. The rebels on that ridge, pump hit into them." The whole fort was turned into a fleecy roar of noise, the guns and rifles and carbines all spitting and shooting blindly into the growing bank of smoke. Jonathan squinted and cut the fuse to fire another round. A Negro toppling back from the parapet right behind him lay dying on the wooden planks. They dragged the struggling man away in an ecstasy of movement and anger and contempt and fear, shoving the gun out and firing it again and jumping to reload it, sponge, load powder ram shell ram kick at the elevating screw again run it out fire. And all around them the Negroes stood along the firestep shooting into West Tennessee, the rifles jumping back into their shoulders and roaring and flashing, sometimes shooting almost straight up and packed together along the walls in a wild, jerking mass of black skin and blue cloth and thrusting ramrods and glinting bayonets. One man, one of the yellow-faced, slender orderlies Booth had used, pumped two loads into his Springfield instead of one in his panic and it went off into his face, ripped his nose and lip and teeth out and he fell to his knees in a slobbering, choking, bloody wallow; no one noticed. The Tennesseans shot blindly and the clustering civilians and extra-duty soldiers and sutlers all were loading and shoving the rifles over the parapet as fast as they could. The smoke and heat boiled back over their shoulders and into the fort and it was choking and noisy and stifling in the portholes, and rebel sharpshooters were riddling them, knocking them back into the parade or falling around their howitzers.

But then the yelling stopped, the rebel yelling and bugling which none of them had thought of but which had always been right there above the other noises and had flecked their lips and made their eyes desperate and furious. The rebels stopped because they had gotten into the pits and the huts and along the ridge. They raised the battle flag of the Eighteenth Mississippi Battalion over the eastern ridge on the zigzag trenches and moved the flank companies with the sharpshooters into them. In the fort everyone stopped firing and then started cheering and yelling, the Tennesseans waving their hats in the air and the Negroes with the beer now impacted in them by the pumping excitement, sucking more of it from their canteens and hugging each other and yelling too, "We done it, we whupped 'em, yahoo, we done it!" over and over; white men masked with powder and red-eyed from the smoke and the Negroes dancing wildly around their cannon. Bradford ran around among them clapping them on the back, trying to get his hand on each of them, shaking them by the shoulder and whooping, saying, "That is the way, boy. That is the way. We whupped 'em."

Seabury stood holding a shell in his hand thinking, is it over, did we whip them? The fury in him was subsiding, and he blinked. The cheering was dying down, with the drifting away and clearing of the smoke. The sunlight cast shadows of powder smoke over the ground of the parade, dappling it. They could hear the popping of the rebel sharpshooters again, and the company that had been in the trenches staggered in from the rear of the fort, dirt-covered and weary and most of them without weapons or cartridge pouches. The peak of their emotions had diffused with the smoke, and the rebel sharpshooters could see clearly into the fort again and a Negro down near the fourth porthole was kicked back into his howitzer by a minie ball.

Also when the smoke cleared from the ground around the fort, they fully expected to see the earth covered with struggling, squealing rebels, dead and shattered and maimed and wounded; because of the fierce impress of their own noise and gunfire and the hail of minie balls they had surrounded the fort with, and, because they were still stifled and choking and red-eyed and their shoulders ached from the musket recoil, it seemed incredible that the rebels were not dead in stinking, gory heaps. But there were no dead, and the Confederates were not even on the slopes near the fort. Now that their yelling had died down they could be seen clambering among the trenches on the east ridge and darting between the houses and shanties in the town, but they had not even tried to rush the fort. The garrison began to step blankly down from the parapet, and the fear and disgust came into the faces of the Tennesseans again like a yellow cast; and the civilians settled back in their knots of dun and jean cloth and put their muskets down, and the Negroes in nervous groups looked at each other and held their lips pursed, and then remembered their canteens of beer and ale and drank from them or grouped again around the kegs. The white officers drifted apart again, back to fumble around with their artillery pieces or pretend to examine sections of the firestep. The haze of smoke seemed to cut off the air, and it was choking in the fort, not stifling with heat but with a kind of humid dankness, like in the summer cellar of a long-abandoned house.

Seabury felt his flesh jerk and quiver in reaction to his own spent ferocity. He wiped his glove across his eyes and instantly they stung of powder. That was a stupid thing to do. He crushed his eyes tight and took off his gloves and searched for some water, and one of the Negroes came over and said, "Somethen wrong is it, Mistuh Seabur'?"

"No, no nothing. Just got some powder in my eyes."

"Lemme take a look."

"No, that's all right. I will find some water. . . ."

"Better lemme take a look. . . ."

"No, damnit!" All he could see was the blackness and he felt trapped. "Get away, I will be all right." He felt humiliated, and kept thinking, is that the other side of war, the side beyond sitting here in safety behind these walls? To react like an insane animal? Spurting out shells and bullets into nothing? He gently washed around his eyes with some water from a canteen. When he could blinkingly see again and the white pain of the eyesting was over, he sat down on the firestep near the howitzer and tried to bury himself again in his detachment, reaching for the grey, thick sense of disgust and anger and disappointment and folding it around him, sitting head down looking at the lay of the cloth across his thighs.

But things did not return to the same pattern as before. The rebels could see clearly into the fort now. The guns could not depress enough to reach the cabins, something Booth had foreseen but which Bradford had to be shown, by yelling and fretting around a gun until a Negro cannoneer was shot dead and another wounded and he finally had seen that they could not rake the ground with canister as he had originally ordered. The rebel sharpshooters put a swarm of ball and buck through the portholes in the south face whenever they tried to run one of the howitzers out to fire it.

The rebel sharpshooters had taken their time getting settled into the east ridge, but once there they probed the whole parade with fire. Seabury watched the Tennesseans jerk and flinch when the balls came clicking and whining into the fort. His own guncrew huddled against the earth, some of them still drinking beer from their canteens covertly, twisting their wrists sharply to get the last of it out. They held onto the wall and would not cross the planks around the howitzer. The other Negroes of his company were behind him on the firestep with Gaylord among them, all of them lying on their sides or buttocks, still drinking the apple-tasting beer, and sweating and getting fresh layers of dirt and mud and dust on their uniforms, yanking with their throats at the beer or scrambling across to the keg to get more. It had been, he thought, that I could not step out into the breech there without being shot. Now it has pushed farther into the fort. Now I cannot cross behind the gun to a depth of, oh say ten feet, without being shot. It is like an incoming tide, or the setting sun. Soon we will be pinned down behind our segment of the wall, safe huddling behind it but unable to move from it, we will blend into the wall with the Negroes and press our mouths and lips up against it.

The Negroes, though, were beginning to twist and raise up and jerk and thrash, no longer shoved tight against the wall. The beer was pressing into their thoughts, cloudily and sweetly, impacted by the thrill of the fusillade and the dankness and stifling moistness of the earth under the pall of smoke, and the danger, tickling in their genitals, of the rebels outside. The white soldiers sat in desperate gloom and disgust, but the Negroes found things golden and new and strange. Gaylord struggled with Sam Camper, yelling at him, "Stay back, damn it, stay back!" Camper said thickly, "Goen to git a secesh" in a spate of single consonants, and pushed himself up the mud wall. He got to the top and stood swaying upright and fired his rifle, and then dropped with his face splintered into laughter, whooping and saying, "Got ol' secesh, yessuh." Then the others began to do the same, scuttling up and firing their pieces and dropping convulsed with laughter. Gaylord began to pull at them, hanging on to their jerseys and arms, saying, "Stop hit, stop now," but they shrugged away.

Gaylord looked over at Seabury. Jonathan was staring over his shoulder at them, still seated and thinking, the fools, the poor fools. The Negroes dissolved; they hopped up and shot wildly and then fell back down in ludicrous tangles of arms and legs, reloading their rifles with their lips open in laughter and their teeth flashing. Rebel balls went over them with clicking noises and they all laughed and gabbled and Jonathan could not understand what they were saying. Two of them got up and fired, one shooting quickly but the other swaying and trying to draw a bead, the beer and excitement and fear swirling in him and the hate too, and the sense that ol' white man make nigger pay fo' this, fo' drinken all the likker and shooten he gun, and then while he was aiming down at a figure on a horse and trying to squeeze his eyes to see the man better a rebel ball went right through the bridge of his nose, and he toppled back dead. All of the dead, Jonathan thought, fall the same way; if the ball catches them high enough it just topples them over, but if it hits low they rock into the parapet and then either slump or pitch backwards.

All around the fort the Negroes were shooting, maddened by the beer and the dankness and the thrill of their fusillade and the rebels' silence. Their officers and sergeants swore and lashed at them and tried to tackle and hold them back, but they kept popping up. And the rebel sharpshooters were knocking them down. Jonathan saw Bischoff claw at one man and turn for another and then the man jumped up to shoot and was killed, leaving Bischoff with a fistful of shirt cloth and a dead body. It was a weird nightmare, the Negroes rising in something coming toward battle fury, prompted and frightened and goaded by the beer and the silence and doomed sense of it all to shoot and fill up their ears with their own sounds, firing and dropping to load and firing again until they were hit in turn. It spread like a wave of an epidemic, from one porthole to another. The Tenneseeans sat in the dirt and watched sullenly.

What do I care, either? The poor, poor fools. He looked into their faces, the ones nearest him. They were sobbing or laughing or, cunning stamped in their faces, trying to coax the cartridges into the rifle barrels with sloppy fingers. But there was a thread-like pattern of correctness to it all, to the Negroes. Even to their officers cursing or simply indifferent, trying to

make them quit. That was something they knew too. The ol'
buckra comen into the fields to make them work, cursing or
indifferent. Or maken them stop drinken or whippen them.
They were fighten. Fighten the secesh, shooten and getting shot
by the handful but immersed in the assumption that if the
rebels were hitting so many of them with so little noise they
must be killing the secesh by the houseful. They kept on jumping up and shooting and there was a ring of them, a fringe of
black, dead bodies in stained blue uniforms, spattered and salted
with red, brown-drying red and bright-red, around the edge of
the firestep. The Tennesseans drew back their feet from the
bodies. The Negroes were whooping now, yelling in blurred,
thudding sounds at the rebels and waving their rifles and their
caps in the air and shooting, and all the time the rebel sharpshooters were riddling them. They would be hit twice or three
times and other bullets would kick up earth around them. The
wounded were herded back toward the bluff in weaving, blind
steps.

Seabury felt his stomach turn, watching them. Gaylord had
given up trying to hold them and was sitting, eyes cast down, in
the middle of them, while they loaded and capped their pieces
and then jumped erect. I ought to be doing something. What?
What can I do? This is like a nightmare. This is suicide, of
course. Gradually satiation came to the Negroes, satiation and
increased fear and the beer worked through and out of them
with the sweat and exertion. They stopped firing, after fifteen
minutes, and collapsed, panting through their mouths like dogs.
They huddled together, or bent over the bodies looking at the
hacked flesh, or went over to refill their canteens. They began to
nestle again into the clay of the fort walls, to hug their rifles and
look at each other. Nothing had come out of it. Ol' buckra had
got a lot of them, he bound to git more.

Their own officers looked at them in fear and disgust and
cleared their throats, and the Negroes clustered below the wall
and drew their feet in. White man he mad. Nigger done wrong.
Don't he know hit now. The fifteen minutes were as suddenly
gone as come, the emotion drained out of them. They began
working at the beer again, throwing it down. They were

covered with sweat and it stained their armpits and backs in great purple circles through the blue cloth. Their faces shone and their eyes were dull and worn. They ran their tongues over their lips and felt for their canteens, and slipped between the white officers to get to the kegs of beer.

The rebels had stopped firing too. The gunboat was still thrashing and shooting, and every now and again McClure would touch off his ten-pounder, or Bischoff or Hunter. Now they could hear, in the interstices of silence, the rebels' voices rising and falling into and below what they could hear. "Ovuh this way down now le's move how much we got." The rebels were moving around them, they could tell. They could hear rattling and scraping and clattering equipment and the drone of modulated voices and a bugle call. The minutes drained, the men frozen in tight fear or absorption, waiting.

One of the Negroes had fallen off the firestep onto the gun platform near Seabury. He was shot through the face at the cheek, a ragged, bluish hole in the black skin. He had been a tall boy, with a bony, high-cheeked face and dull black flesh, and now with his eyes askew he made scrabbling motions in the dirt at the edge of the gun platform. He was not dead but he seemed to be dying. Bloody bubbles rose and exploded sound-lessly in his mouth, a red, mottled skein forming and then expanding into tinged transparency and then bursting. One eye showed white and the other was closed. His hand kept moving and pushing into the dust, mindlessly.

He will die soon. I should help him. No, I cannot. I am too rooted to this spot. My flesh feels as though it is melted against this wood. It is not fear. I am not afraid. I just cannot move. I could not move to help him if he had fallen onto the parade instead of in the breech. I simply could not. Nor can I take my eyes away from him. He looked over the whole body, still squirming slightly. He has a torn place on his knee where the pants are ripped. He must have slipped and fallen against a board-end this morning. The skin on the man's knee was slightly covered with wisps of hair, and there was a crosshatch mark of red. Did he drink beer? Probably, to dull the pain of the scratch on his knee. When will he die? Why doesn't he go ahead with it? Jonathan sat still and warm inside the tight ball of his little world, contemplating one thing and fighting back the other thoughts and sensations.

This is not the purgation of this country. No. It is boredom, with a deadly cutting edge not the less boring because of the possibility of the death. I never expected to one day sit like this and watch the last moments of a man, at my feet, and feel nothing but contempt and irritation that he is so long at dying. I had expected a great engulfment of blood-red light, a glittering, quick tournament, I suppose, with names and ideals on flagstaffs and the death of the brave ones in hallowed glory and the crushing of the ungodly with the fierce steel and the revelation of the weak and the cowardly. Instead we have this, a thick mound of earth at my back with the noon sun overhead, a haze of smoke, beady sounds of gunfire. It is the fools and the unwary who die, and death is not at all selective or supernatural. It takes the ones it can get at. The Tennesseans sit and sulk and brood in their rancid hatreds and thin-blooded fears. The Negroes cluster around the kegs with their crossbelts askew and drink the beer, even though it is going flat and stale. No one says anything. The bullets skip and bite and whirr and clip, and every now and then like over there by the sixth porthole a poor drunk Negro climbs to his feet and shoots out into the distance. Bradford worries at one of the gunports and Bischoff, sweat showing even from here, is bending over the gun—yes, he is going to shoot. He jerks the lanyard but the crew is too afraid to push the gun into the breech, so they cannot know where the shell falls. Perhaps I shall set off my howitzer soon. My crew are there, beer running down their chins, the ones I had once meant to tutor and to teach, by precept and example.

Gator, hatless now and his eyes yellow and cunning, sits among the stacked rope in the niche of the gunport, a study in shadow and black flesh and leather and blue cloth. And Lexington and Cargo flattened out against the wood braces, Lexington stripped to the waist and his face grinning and whispering and Cargo nodding and laughing too and sharing the wooden canteen. Telling their lascivious monosyllabic tales punctuated by incomprehensible "yehmans" and "sed seds" and all the paraphernalia of inter-negroid speech. Oh, Mr. Higginson had much to write about their poems and indeed about the ways they say "de" instead of "the" (which by the way is not true, really, since they say "dhe"). But he did not mention the fact that when they talk among themselves they can lapse into an incomprehensible sequence of plosive sounds and rattling, accented vowels and you cannot understand them. The boy who made such fun of me is now dead with his face burst in. So is Booth. Booth is dead too.

We see each other as it were through haloes, small encircling clusters of thoughts and emotions and remembrances. But we look at these Negroes whom I have known as long as I have known Booth or Van Horn, and I do not see them through that halo. I only see the outside, the run of the flesh, the moustache on Cargo's lip or the flat, rounded head of Lexington or the yellow eyes of Gator.

I did not know Colonel Shaw at all well, but I did know Mr. Higginson, and he was not a saint, he was not a man among men capable of performing miracles by himself. We did not account him unusual, we merely accounted him lucky. He was always brusque and quick and large and they said he was hard to know, that was it, he was hard to know, and perhaps because he was hard to know among us 'twas easier for him to know and be known among his Negroes.

I do not know the difference, what the key difference is. Except this is not it. This waiting under a mound of earth knowing I could step out easily with a certain muscular combination and be instantly sent into eternity by a man I have never met and feel not even idealistic animosity towards any more.

I could take that step but I will not, not because of cowardice but simply because I do not care, and it is easier to sit here than to walk out there. I do not care. Caring about such things has only led to hurt. So I will not care. 'Tis easier to sit here like this, feeling the simple, warm spread of the sunlight on my back, wrapped up in a grey shawl of isolation.

Leaming stood in the middle of the parade near the flagpole, cleaning his revolver. Bradford talked to him for a moment energetically and then sought out and talked to Delos

Carson in the shadow of the magazine, Carson working there and having stepped out for a time to wipe off the sweat. Bradford looked over his shoulder at Jonathan, and then turned to look more at him. He began to walk in Seabury's direction, turning to talk and nod several times at Carson. Jonathan did not get up, and Bradford with sweat in a thick sheen over his face looked down at him.

"Well now, why ain't you firing at the rebels?"

Jonathan had to squint when he looked up, because the sun was clustering right around Bradford's head. "I cannot see any targets worth . . ." thinking, the question is so preposterous I cannot really think of an answer. Bradford cut him off, dark and dripping sweat above him.

"Well, I don't see you looking, for that matter. I see you here on your ass taking in the weather. If you was up in that porthole you might see some targets. . . ."

Jonathan studied his thumbs, the sudden thrill of defiance running through him like a cold, sweet shock. "Well sir, seems rather foolish to me. The rebels will kill ten of my gunners to any one of their men I might . . ."

"So you are scared. So you are scared and that is it."

"No sir, I don't think I am scared. It just seems pointless. . . ."

Bradford was now in an ecstasy of rage leaning over and grappling into his collar and pulling at it and saying thickly into his ear, "You goddamned yellow-belly dog. You yellow-belly dog. Git to that gun before I shoot you where you sit on your rosy soft ass. Git to it and start shooting at the rebels."

Jonathan made several motions to get loose, and finally grinning and looking up he said, "Yes sir. Anything you say, sir."

Bradford let go and stood straight again, breathing loudly and flexing his hands, and finally turned and walked off, the big cavalry boots creaking.

Jonathan got up stiffly and stretched and then got his crew up, most of them having seen the talk and already in place and holding their poles. They ran the gun halfway to the gunport and Jonathan jerked the lanyard, not even bothering to look at

The Battle of Fort Pillow   375

the fall of the shell, looking instead over his shoulder at the back of Bradford. The hot smoke gathered around the gun and they loaded it, swabbing and wordlessly loading powder and then the fused shell and ramming and running the gun halfway out, and Jonathan fired it again. The howitzer fired and recoiled and fired and recoiled into the deepening smoke, the Negroes moving like wraiths through the cottony thick smoke, losing their feet and knees beneath it.

The steady thud of the gun roused some of the Negroes at the parapet and they began to jump up and shoot and yell again. The rebel sharpshooters were prodded into action, and while Jonathan bent to take off his jacket from the heat one of the Negroes at the gunport was shot through both hips, and had to be dragged clear while thrashing and screaming. They had fired twenty rounds of shell and canister away, spewing the iron and metal and powder over the faceted, befoliaged eastern ridge, ripping away the small ferns and spreading the green stain of the leaves over rocks and logs. Then Cargo stepped into the breach to swab the gun and a rebel shot him squarely through the neck and his head swiveled to a weird angle and he fell out of the porthole, tripping and sprawling outside on the ledge. That is what Bradford wants. All right, I can shoot up all of the shell and powder he can give me, and I can kill off every man of this crew. They kept up the rhythmic patterns of loading, threading the lanyard and cutting the fuse in a ritualistic and meaningless act since they had nothing to shoot at but the expanse of West Tennessee.

Bradford walked along the walls from one gun to the next, and at each position the white officers dripped sweat and swore and fired their artillery pieces, the smoke pluming and then rising and hanging over Fort Pillow. The riverboat kept on shelling the ravines below the fort and the creek beds above it, the shells thrown away into the faceless, warm moistness of spring, rustling through the leaves and the iron biting into the creeks and muddying the streams and ripping off branches, but the rebels hunkered and grinned and wormed through the underbrush all but untouched. The rebel sharpshooters kept the walls swept clear, drawing their beads from the huts in the town ravine or the abandoned trenches on the east ridge or the clumps and thickets and ditches along the periphery of the fort. The shells chopped logs into golden spills of wood chips, and rang off the lichen-pinked rock, and hacked palm-sized chunks out of the scrub oak and evergreen. The rebel horseholders eating captured hardtack for lunch grinned around their mouthfuls and said, "Ol' Yank really putten on the show, ain't he?" and washed down the bread with spring water and calmed the horses. The regiments and battalions packed semicircularly through the ravines and gullies and ditches around the fort, closing in continually in short rushes to new protection, hugged the ground shoulder to shoulder and buttock to buttock and listened to the pitching whine and rattle of the shells and the canister going futilely and continually over them and smiled through stubbled beards at each other, waiting for the next command.

In the fort, there was an hour of desultory shelling. Three more of Jonathan's company had been shot down at the gunport. They were all killed in the same slot, the number one position on the gun crew where the cannoneer had to stand in front of the muzzle of the cannon to swab it after the shot, to feed in the new shell and to ram down the charge. Evidently some rebel sharpshooters along the eastern slope had a perfect angle, for they had hit each of the men—a tall, sullen, facet-skulled man named Arnold, a short blue-black Negro named Black, and last, North, who had been one of the corporals— while the gun was being loaded and while they were standing with their heads turned waiting for Jonathan to pass them the next shell for loading.

Jonathan had had them drag the bodies away to the side among the emptied ammunition boxes, satisfied somehow and even pleased, looking at the pile of emptied boxes and the woolen sacks of dead flesh, colored with sprays of blood, thinking, well, that is five men dead at this one gun and we have used up three chests, and Bradford next time he passes will doubtless be pleased. His own judgment had been vindicated: the fact that the Negroes had been no more than shells of men to his knowledge—that for all he knew (or cared) they had had no aspirations, no emotions, desires, any more than had animals—cushioned him away from the fact of their death. They had not owned a part of him, as had Booth. That was his personal dividend, he thought.

He considered the Negroes around him. They were all silent, now, one or two of them at each of the kegs, the rest hollow-faced and silent, sitting or slumping or lying along the firesteps in tangles of caps and crossbelts and rifles, faces wild-eyed and attenuated with exhaustion, their nerves riddled. When he knelt to cut one of the fuses, his arm brushed against North's foot. Jonathan looked down at North's socks, black government socks a shade deeper than the flesh of a man's leg. The socks had slipped down during the fight, folding into the soles of his shoes and coming up only to his ankles. Did he feel the socks and think about pulling them up before he died? When he put the socks on did he think he might die in them? It was a curious irrelevance, but it seemed important, as when he had noticed the crosshatch of scars on the knee of the young Negro who had died at his feet. It was not an appeal; the dead bodies carried no appeal, no remonstrance. Jonathan passed the shell up and the Negro in the number one position took it and fitted it to the mouth of the cannon, and pulled the rammer pole free and rammed the shell down. Jonathan waited for him to die.

They are performing with amazing courage, he thought. Perhaps they are drunk. They are certainly stepping up to the breach into the number one position and I would not do that. We wondered about their courage (not wondered; we denied it and wondered how they would act in the absence of it). But it had been sufficient to the point of madness. Is it courage? He looked up from cutting the fuse of the next shell, at the Negro in the embrasure, waiting for him; he was white-eyed with fear, his flesh was quivering spasmodically, his hands wiped at his sides and he held them out again.

Jonathan felt a surge of terror and responsibility, a blued, mingled series of questions and doubts. What came to his mind fell short of his sudden terror: Do they know what they are doing? Have we taught them enough? Would we be putting white men up there so easily?

With seeming irrelevance, he was suddenly glad that the walls of the fort were so thick and high; that these Negroes were sheltered. But Bradford is eating this garrison hollow. I hope that the rebels do not realize that one rush would carry the walls. Easily. But surely they will not rush these thick walls. They must see that they cannot carry walls this high or this thick, and while he paused he rammed the penknife into the palm of his hand. The quick red pain made him curse, "God damn," and then he began to chop at the fuse, anxious that the young Negro at the number one position would not die while he fumbled. His hand left scimitar-shaped prints upon the shell.

Then the rebels made their next concerted rush, with bugles and sporadic yelling and clumps of men running through the brush at the northern flank of the fort. It was an effort by Forrest to align the regiments of Bell's brigade with Barteau's regiment on their right, which was very close to the fort and protected by the Coal Creek Ravine, and with McCulloh's brigade on their left, also close and investing the eastern ridge and the town and the ditches and creekbeds between the two. The ground the two regiments had to cross was broken into small, barrow-like mounds and thickets and fallen timber and scattered, reedy creeks. They moved forward company by company in rushes, Wilson and Russell waving each company forward in surges to the next hollow or thicket or ditch while the sharpshooters tried to keep the defenders' heads down.

In the fort, of course, it seemed like the second major assault of the day. Hunter and Bischoff were standing away from the trails of their guns and yelling, "Here they come! Here they come!" down the line toward the other portholes. Officers were running up and down the firesteps yelling incoherently. Bradford stopped in midstride and lurched and then ran hard for the fourth porthole. All along the firestep the Negroes were being prodded up by the officers and by each other, rising shakily and loading their rifles with their tongues caught between their teeth and squinting. Everyone in the garrison cut loose. The

The Battle of Fort Pillow 379

Tennesseans were jumping up to the firestep and the civilians were running over to the walls again too, their beards jerking.

Smoke rolled back over the walls from the sheets of musketry and rifle fire, and the cannon recoiled again and again. They could hear the rebel bugles now and the short spasmodic yells, "Yaaay Yaaay," coming over the walls from the north side. The rebel sharpshooters were firing steadily from the huts and old rifle pits and trenches and the trees and ditches. Jonathan could hear above him the lick and whistle of their crisscrossing shots. The walls of the fort were covering with smoke from the rifles and the rebels could not see as well through the white blankets. Seabury fired his howitzer twice straight out of the port; then Bradford was at his shoulder saying over and over "The north! The north! The north side of the fort! Get your piece over that way!" and small flecks of spit were jumping in Jonathan's face. He said "All right" loudly because of the roar of artillery and musket firing and the hoarse yelling the Negroes were doing, a hoarse "Aaiii Aaaiii" over and over. Smoke was all around them. He had to slap his crew on the shoulders to get their attention, all of them looking at him now with bloodshot eyes and anxious and angry faces.

He slapped them and pointed over to the left and finally they did not understand but just stepped back and he picked up the handspike to show them. He shoved at the trail of the howitzer and finally they came in around him with the spikes and poles. He leaned over the breech of the gun again and kept on slapping the right side of the trail until it was skewed as far to the left as it would go, the muzzle almost resting against the wooden bracing of the porthole. He then removed the lanyard so none of them would fire the cannon. Amazed at his own calm he stepped up to the breach and got the numbers one and two to stand aside and holding the lanyard he leaned forward to try and see what they were shooting at. He leaned over and finally knelt right in the breach in the wall, near Cargo's body which was still sprawled outside the porthole. He could see under the smoke and the glinting flashes of the discharges.

The rebels were making rushes down around the creekbed, he could see. There were small movements of men, and he could see the leather shining on their chests and shoulders and the glint of their rifles and he even saw the feather in one man's cap. Outside it was green instead of the dull clay-color inside the fort, green and yellowish and watery and full and faceted with leaves and brush. He could see the rebels in it, running and dashing from a ditch in a stringing clump of men to a bank and going flat at the bank, another group rushing to an open spot to the right of the bank and going flat too and an officer slapping at them with his sword and they getting up and rushing again and vanishing nearer the fort in another shallow place in the ground. He thought, so those are rebels, coming this way to kill me, and he thought, why they look so human. Why should they want to kill me? They do not know me, and he was simultaneously reflecting rather than thinking, I had forgotten this was the spring, I had forgotten this was April and of course everything would be green since it is April. They are at the base of my sycamore. The sycamore used to be much farther away than that, but that man standing underneath it makes it seem so close. He is an officer. I can see his beard and he is holding his sword and it is glinting.

Then something hot cracked past his ear, turning it into a blue ache, into the side of the wall. He jerked and scrambled back into the fort. The guncrew was still there but the trail man was lying on his side thrashing at the ground and they were trying to clear him away from the gun. His whole chest was torn away and there was a thin tissue of lung exposed. Jonathan rethreaded the lanyard absently. He was bemused by it all, by the lush greenness of the world on the other side of the clay-colored wall, and the sweet adventure out there and the death and routine and smell of sweat and beer on the inside and the roaring and the powder smoke. He remembered the men rushing from one point to another and the officer under the sycamore tree. They would kill me if they had the chance, he said to himself, but he instantly could not believe it. With their leather cross-belts and their feathers they looked vaguely like illustrations in a children's book about Robin Hood he had once had read to him.

He jerked the lanyard and the gun fired and the recoil

The Battle of Fort Pillow 381

kicked one of the wheels off the wood platform. They struggled to get it reset, while on the walls all around them the Negroes and Tennesseans fired and fired and fired as fast as they could stuff the cartridges in and ram them home and cap the rifle or as fast as they could snap open the breech of their carbine. Some of the Negroes stabbed themselves in the wrist with their bayonets as they rammed their guns, and the Tennesseans occasionally chipped off the end of a thumb in the sharp metal blocks of the carbine breeches in their haste; the men did not even notice what they had done and bled on their equipment.

Jonathan got another man for the trail of the gun, a tall Negro with liver spots on his face. He kept firing the howitzer over to the north, curious and wanting to go and look out again but afraid to, not only because of the rebel sharpshooters but because he thought, my will has been corroded enough today by all of this. I cannot be confused by child-like reveries any more. I must mind my work here. They fired the howitzer over and over until they had to wait for a new chest of ammunition to be brought forward, Seabury stamping and fretting and pacing while the gunfire still echoed and blasted as furiously as ever and the rebels still yelled above the noise and their sharpshooters still riddled the fort. The carriers set the new chest down and opened the straps and began to pass out the charges, the sweating Negro who brought it saying, "Mis' Cahson he say to say tha's awl."

"What, what did he say?"

The Negro froze for a second at Seabury's expression and then went on, "Mis' Cahson he say to say tha's awl th' twe'eve-poun' stuff we got."

Jonathan let the man's collar go and stood up, in the middle of the guncrew bent and clustered over the ammunition. He looked up in the weaving turmoil of the smoke overhead, and listened to the savage fire all around them. So that is it. So we are running out of ammunition. That damned Bradford, he has had us shoot away box after box, and now the rebels are rushing us and we are running out. He turned back now, furious and cold and not sweating any longer. The Negroes looked at each other and then squinted up at him, still with their hands cradling the shot and powder. "Well, load the thing. Load the thing." I am through. He felt helpless, exhausted, furious. I would throw away my sword; his train of thought was interrupted because in the cooling of the metal the elevating screw was jammed again.

He went to work on it, the Negroes dripping sweat on the metal and scratching at their cheeks and watching. A dead calm came over him, and he felt himself bearing down into the moment. He concentrated on what his hands were doing, on the play of the fingers over the metal of the gun, probing and searching for the swollen place in the metal ridges. Around him there was turmoil and sound and heat and pelting death, but he bore down furiously into the work at hand, and everything around him was as a shadow and an echo in his ears. The metal responded to his hands, he pounded a few times and then dropped the hammer and twisted the screw again and it slid perfectly, and he stood aside, cold and handsome and clear-eyed, and began to fire the shells to the north again.

What is it all? All of this? A weird, cynical game, and the only fools are those who take it seriously. I am educated enough in the classical tragedies and in all the ironies of history to recognize them in the flesh. This is a poorly done drama, a weird and endless play, and that is all it is. The Negroes, the poor fools, are involved in it because they do not have the benefit of an education. They don't see how farcical all of this is. Why should a man's life, any man's life, depend upon how many boxes of ammunition are stored away—no, don't say ammunition, say boxes of charcoal and metal and urine products probably—are stored away in a place in Tennessee? The howitzer blasted again and the crew, weary now, moved through the smoke of the discharge to reload it.

6

THEN THE BUGLING AND THE YELLING STOPPED AND THE REBELS
stopped their advance and the firing gradually slackened. The
officers walked down the firesteps hitting at the men and making
them stop firing, but this time everyone stayed at the walls.
The guncrews huddled around their artillery pieces, and men
drank at canteens and waited for the smoke to drift away.
Bradford was howling, "We done it again, we stopped 'em
again!" and some of the men were yelling too, the Negroes along
the northern walls mostly, but again there were no piles of
rebel dead and the rebels had gone to ground nearer to the
fort than before and with the clearing smoke their sharpshooters
began to knock men down again.

Everyone ducked and stayed down along the wall while
Bradford patted men on the back and walked up and down the
line in jerking little skips to see through the portholes.

One of the Tennesseans on the southern face saw a flag of
truce and yelled out, and Bradford turned and ran over to the
place beside the fourth porthole. He scrambled clumsily onto
the step and stood up cautiously. There was no fire, and out in
front of them three Confederate officers and a man with a white
flag were placidly sitting their horses. All of the garrison gulped
and stretched like men awakening from a bad dream, and stood
up, breathing the air still tainted with smoke but unbelievably
fresher than that below the level of the parapet, and stared out
at the countryside. It should have been mangled and torn, but
except for one or two small fires glowing and twinkling orange
in the huts and some whittled and hacked scrub oak in front of

the fort, the earth was still green and full of water and spring. There were no dead rebel bodies anywhere except a cluster of them barely visible down by Coal Creek, three or four at most and those were being dragged away even as they watched.

The rebels with the flag came closer, and everyone stood bare-headed, watching.

The rebel officers were halted by a shout about a hundred and fifty yards south of the fort, three captains sitting their mounts very calmly and watching while the gunboat was signaled to stop firing. Seabury went over to the second porthole to look at the rebels. One of them had a spade beard and wavy, thick, dark hair, and he kept running his hand through it, and the other two were younger and clean-shaven and bony-faced. They all had capes and wide-brimmed hats and all you could see were their boots below the hang of their capes. Bradford climbed back down off the wall, into the silence and the expentancy of the fort. The men were all along the walls and in the portholes, standing up straight now and watching Bradford and the rebels. They swabbed at their faces with their sleeves and handkerchiefs, wiping off the dust and the sweat and the powder stains, and they drew their jackets and blouses closed at the throat. They had forgotten the chillness in the spring air.

Bradford called Leaming over to him, "Mack, Mack come here," and Leaming with his long arms swinging came over. John Young was with him, an open-faced man who had been stopping over at the fort. They talked and then Bradford returned their salutes and they started out to parley with the rebels, and then suddenly Bradford said, "Wait, wait a minute," and they stopped, looking over their shoulders. Bradford shouted to his brother Ted and he climbed down from the wooden signal platform and came over wiping his hands on the seat of his pants, and then he went out with Leaming and Young. While the six officers were talking in the grass and scrub on the south of the fort, saluting and introducing each other with handshakes and then producing the formal sealed envelope with the surrender demand in it, one of the signalmen on the bluff came up to Bradford and told him that there was a steamer coming downriver.

The Battle of Fort Pillow 385

Bradford had been standing near the sally port waiting for the surrender demand in not really indecisiveness, since he knew or thought he knew that he personally could not and would not be allowed to surrender, but thinking maybe I can see some of those Tennessee boys, maybe I can see and talk to some of them and change something. The signal man came and told him and he turned immediately away from the sally port and ran, holding the sword against his side so it would not clatter, over to the bluff. He got the telescope with the brass rings off the stand and looked upriver and saw the boat coming, the plume of smoke from it. It might be a gunboat, and then while he watched across the freckling, steely water he could make out the blue along the decks, the massed and packed purple-blue of uniforms. He turned back with his lips open, looking at the sally port where the men were coming in with the letter from Forrest.

Time now, just time to hold them for a while and we can get some support here. Some more men. He turned and ran back across the parade with his boots creaking. The men standing all around the walls watched Bradford jogging clumsily, almost tripping on his spurs and then running again. He got the letter and opened it, surrounded by the three officers who were looking at each other in some little consternation. He shook the letter out of the envelope. The spidery writing was across a yellowed piece of army requisition paper.

> Headquarters Forrest's Cavalry,
> Before Fort Pillow, April 12, 1864
> Major Booth, Commanding United States Forces, Fort Pillow:

The introduction was a surprise. In the eternity since the death of Booth and his own succession to the command it seemed that surely no one in the world could not know that Booth was dead. But then of course the rebels did not know! He smiled. It seemed somehow a tremendous secret, one advantage which he had over the rebels. Of course, they think that Booth is still alive! They will not know that he is dead and that I am in command, and in the instant of that sudden burst of pride and cunning there were other ramifications opened to him. Then they do not know that I am responsible here. They do not know that either, and that seemed terribly important, that the rebels—who of course would have benefited in no way from knowing of the death of Booth and indeed who would not even have cared by this point—be kept out of the secret. But then he read on, treasuring and stroking the secret that he now had, that the rebels did not know that Booth was dead.

Major—The conduct of the officers and men garrisoning Fort Pillow has been such as to entitle them to being treated as prisoners of war. I demand the unconditional surrender of this garrison, promising you that you shall be treated as prisoners of war. My men have received a fresh supply of ammunition, and from their present position can easily assault and capture the Fort. Should my demand be refused, I cannot be responsible for the fate of your command.

> *Respectfully,*
> N. B. Forrest,
> Major General Commanding

Then the signalman was there again at Bradford's elbow and said there were two steamers coming upriver now, coming upriver and in view and carrying federal troops as well. Bradford smiled and skipped and slapped the letter against his thigh. Well now, well now. The rebels do not know how weak we are. The weakness somehow involved in the death of Booth; Booth in two weeks had come to stand not only for Fort Pillow but, in Bradford's mind, for his own personal safety; since that safety was involved in Booth's post and in his niggers and in his cannon and certainly not in the ragtag whites of his own command. So with Booth's death something that remained in Bradford had snapped, the one exterior person who even in his contempt seemed to indicate safety had gone; and in the rest of the day, in the defense of the fort from nine o'clock until now at three in the afternoon Bradford had wandered from one place to another in a frantic and pathetic attempt not to defend or to direct but simply to shore up what he assumed Booth had left. To slap the men on the back and tell them to keep on firing and firing, to yell and cheer and walk back and forth behind the howitzers telling them to shoot and keep on shooting, in an agony of desperation and fear and hope that by putting enough noise and smoke and firing enough iron into West Tennessee he could stop the rebels.

But now then, now then the rebels, he thought, do not know that Booth is dead, they think he is still alive, and somehow he thought, well then, the post is as strong as ever. We can stop them, and there are the steamers coming upriver. We can stop them until the steamers get here, and I will not be involved personally at all because they do not know I am in command. They still think Booth is alive. We can stop them now. They cannot cross that wall because they will not be let to cross it, not with Booth and the men on those riverboats. So he turned and handed the note back to Leaming and said, "Tell General Forrest that this does not produce the desired effect," thinking, he will not scare me out of this position. If he knew Booth was dead he would know how weak we are, but he does not know that so he is just trying to bluff us out of here, and he will not frighten us.

Leaming looked startled and started to say something but Bradford had looked away, and was twitching and straining and looking upriver. Leaming thought, he looks like a child that had to go teetee too bad. In a spate of anger and frustration he turned and went out of the fort between Ted Bradford and Young, down the short distance to where the rebel captains were waiting, lighting cigars and sitting their horses. Leaming saluted and they seemed friendly enough, putting their hands on their pommels and leaning forward. Leaming said, "I am instructed to say that this does not produce the desired effect." They looked at each other, rising a little in their stirrups and looking darkly and questioningly. This answer and the return of the surrender notice was jarringly out of keeping with even their enthusiastically amateur knowledge of military procedure. Without returning the salute but leaving the sergeant still holding the flag of truce and picking his teeth, they went to find Forrest.

Forrest was to the north now. He had been told of the riverboats and his side hurt and he was tired and angry. He had

had a horse shot under him as soon as he had reached the outskirts of the fort and he had fallen from the horse and hurt his side, the pain and the blue bruises masked under the long dull cloak which came to the tops of his boots.

His side hurt in a dull, bluish pain, and he twitched from time to time from the stabs of pain along his ribs. He had lost a good horse, and he had lost good men. It was mid-afternoon and he had gotten the military equation by now to perfection. He could not lose, he could not even be stopped for a moment. His men were within thirty yards of the fort at many points, so close that in one almost reflexive move like the stretching of an arm he could take it. There would be a score of men killed and that score was too many because by this time there was no question about the situation. His side throbbed and the man came telling him about the boat coming downriver and he set out immediately with the jolting pain coming to him over and over again, through the winding, circuitous route behind the rebel lines, over the chopped and overgrown ridges and through the thickets and past the breast-shaped hills, to get to where he could watch the Yankee boats for himself. He had to see them for himself. He watched the upriver boat coming closer with the packed blue uniforms along the lower deck and the striped flag a spot of color against the green of the Arkansas shore. He looked at it for a long moment through his glasses. The gunboat he could tell was standing off, silent, but it was making no move to signal the boat off, and neither was the fort. Well, he could stop the boat if he had to. He knew he could stop any boat that was not an ironclad, just by putting enough riflemen in the ditches and old rifle pits along the banks near the fort to riddle the men on board, exposed on the deck or at best behind a few inches of thin wood and cotton. That would be no problem. His jaw twitched from the pain of his side.

It had been a long day for Forrest, already; tedious, time- and ammunition-consuming patterns had eaten at his patience. But it was the patience of a stalking hunter, and he had solved every problem and had closed the situation so that just the thrust, the lancing, was all that was necessary now.

His subordinates, McCulloh and Chalmers, had invested

the fort at dawn, expertly, before the Yankees anywhere in the district knew of his presence. He had let Chalmers direct the investment along the south side, driving the Unionists into the pocket of the fort itself, so they would not be able to cut and run for Memphis. He had awaited the arrival of his wagonloads of ammunition; then he had directed the movements against the north side of the fort himself, since there was no town ravine there, and no eastern ridge (Forrest knew all about the dispositions and topography of the fort; a Mr. Shaw who had been a prisoner there until a day ago had told him all that he needed to know, during the night ride to Pillow). He moved up with Bell's brigade to plug the center of the encirclement, and moved his men expertly and with a minimum of loss, ridge by ridge and gully by gully. The hail of gunfire from the fort and the gunboat had been annoying but not effective; he had put two entire brigades into positions as close as thirty yards to the fort walls. He had sharpshooters in position who could command the entire position except for the few feet behind the wall itself. The Negroes and Tories in the fort were trapped and invested and he knew they were shot to pieces; they must be, by this time, aware that the fort was doomed.

So this was the time to send in the courteously phrased military demand for surrender, with just enough praise and formality to satisfy Booth's regular army background, and the precision of expression which a young staff officer writing on a Tennessee stump under shellfire could cull up from a year at La-Grange Military Academy and three books on Frederick the Great and Marlborough. They had sent the note in, the courteous military note with the formality barely masking the threat of bloodshed. It was the same note sent in a hundred times and more to all of the post and garrison commanders Forrest had attacked or invested or just bluffed, sometimes sent in when there were only thirty smirking rebels in the brush and sometimes after a full day of hard fighting. He had sent Goodman and the other two captains with the note and then heard of the federal steamboats, and he had made the long and arduous trip to inspect the situation for himself. Now he sat weary of the whole thing and anxious simply for a quick resolution, for the

Yankees to see the hopelessness of it all and surrender in which case he would gain the horses and the guns and would eliminate this post. Or failing that, the equally simple rush, like the quick and expert lancing of the boil, which doubtless would cost lives needlessly but which would be a cheap victory for the price, in view of the strength of the position. Just one way or the other, just one way or the other, by this time.

While the meticulousness and the precision and emotion of the operation were in jeopardy and he had to make dispositions to deal with the oncoming boats which would not weaken his storming party but would be sufficient to turn away the boats, while anger at this delay was going through his mind and pain was coming up from the twisted and bruised bone and flesh in his side and he was trying at the same time to plot his withdrawal and his movements for perhaps the next week, the answer came from the fort, that the note did not produce the desired effect.

His eyes instantly darkened and his face became brazen and the battle blood was up in Forrest. He jerked his head to look at Goodman, and for a moment Goodman was deadly afraid thinking, did I fail to specify that that was the answer from the fort, and starting to move his lips to explain it again. Then Forrest with his large jawbone barely moving said tightly, "This will not do. Nossuh. This will not do. Go up," and here he pointed at the mound of pierced and parapeted earth up on the bluff, "go up there and get me an ainswer!" He sat his horse darkly and scowling now with the bronze cast in his face, the flesh not seeming white and mottled and flushed but hewed out of metal or made of moulded and poured and long-since cooled metal. He turned to two aides, and they kicked their horses through the underbrush and rattled against each other's sides to get to him. The one with the bugle slung across his back he told to go down to the south side of the fort. "Tell Captain—le's see, Captain Anderson of my staff, he's down there, to come up here."

Anderson came up, benevolent-looking with a spade beard and a large nose and sheltered eyes. "Captain, call off two-hunnerd men from McCulloh's brigade and go down yonder to the south side of that fo't and Captain, shoot ever'thing between

The Battle of Fort Pillow　　*391*

water and wind that comes yo' way." Anderson dropped his smile and saluted and turned off clattering through the April woods. Forrest turned to the other aide who was sitting his horse holding his breath in fear and adulation. "You, boy. Go down to Barteau's brigade and tell him to put two-hunnerd men along thet river bluff, and shoot up ennything he sees twixt wind and water," and the boy whipped and lashed his horse down through the twinkling and gurgling black-bottomed Coal Creek to find Colonel Barteau, the horse's hoofs spewing up the water and mud.

Forrest sat his mount, surrounded by the silent and stock-still aides and bodyguards and buglers, all of them wearing the long grey cloaks. Barteau, wizened and mud-spattered, sent two-hundred men with Springfield and Enfield rifles down to the scrub brush and the logs and driftwood and scows along the river bank. They dug in and huddled and drew their beads across the water, at the cavernous and smoke-bubbling boat rocking in the crosscurrents and still coming downriver.

Captain Goodman guided his horse over the broken ground toward the fort, still under the flag of truce. He squinted up at the fort; there was a dead Negro outside one of the gunports, spreadeagled in the red earth, and there were heads and torsos of men standing watching all along the walls, and packed into the portholes. Goodman looked around him, at the ravines and the creeks filled with grinning, dirty rebel soldiers, sitting or standing up and loosening their crossbelts for a time. We can run right over them, he thought. We can run right over them.

Goodman dismounted again and stood for a while in the open space between the town ravine and the fort, near the flapping white flag. Behind him Captain Anderson was moving with his two-hundred riflemen from the Second Missouri Cavalry down toward the bluff. They were getting up out of the trenches and the cabins and half-burnt shanties, stretching like the Tories and the Negroes in the fort in the cessation of firing and the sudden safety, and walking across the moist, wet earth in single file, carrying their rifles loosely and grinning up at the fort. Looking over his shoulder, Goodman could see Anderson still mounted, in fine Confederate grey cloth with yellow cuffs and collar and all the spangling sleeve-marks of rank, in the middle of them. Anderson waved to him. No one seemed to know what to do. Goodman nodded to Anderson and Frank Rodgers. Rodgers was smoking a cigar. "We mought as well wait for them to show again. They still respecten our flag."

Leaming stood at the sally port nervously. The clump of rebel officers were back. He went out to see what they wanted. Goodman rode over a few paces toward him. "Forrest says to tell Major Booth that answer won't do. Says to say one way or t'other yes or no."

Leaming nodded and went back into the fort. The garrison were confused and still standing upright. The Negroes were beginning to gather around the kegs of beer again and refill their canteens and the Tennesseans were spitting tobacco juice and making cracks. They were walking around in tight, nervous groups with their hands in their hip pockets. Nothing was happening, and Bradford was standing watching those boats and Leaming walked up to him and said something and he did not hear him the first time. Bradford was still watching the steamers, the two coming upriver and the one down, the steamers converging on the fort now and the gunboat making no signal to them, the ones downstream stopping in a great spilling of smoke and noise and closing together. He could see the blue uniforms on board through the glass. He did not know what to do. He wanted to wait for the boats, but he did not want to go on with the fighting. Somehow, this close, things might slip out of hand. His men might run for the bluff all of a sudden. He did not want the fight to go on. Leaming told him the rebel officers were still out there, waiting. "Dint I tell them? Dint I tell them we weren't scaired into surrendering?"

Leaming slanted his head and looked at him, frowning. "Sir, when they send in a written note, you got to send out one."

Bradford snorted and looked back again at the riverboats. Leaming looked at him and then turned away and shook his head. All of the Tennesseans crowded into tight knots like curdling sour milk, talking. "Ol' Bradford he is gone in the haid." "He caint git us out of here. He ought to give up." "He knows hit. They ain't talken about taken ol' Bradford alive." "Ain't none of my fault. I live to fight another day, I reckon." They spit tobacco juice again through their teeth. Leaming paused and then went out through the sally port and heard the rebels again say they wanted some word.

The Negroes were not paying any attention to the white officers any more. They had stopped the rebels twice, they thought. Bradford had told them they had stopped the rebels twice, the ol' white major had walked down slapping their shoulders and their rumps and said, "We done it, we stopped the rebels twicet." There was still the guilt and the nagging thought that ol' buckra heah in this fo't he is a Yankee man, he is from the Nawth, he gwine leave after a while an' old white cap'n out yonder he come back and he whup us good. He whup us fo' drinken his stuff and shooten at him. He kill ol' nigger. Bradford an' these no-count po' white trash, they standen around scairt to death. They gwine leave, they gwine stan' up and say all right y'all come in heah, y'awl, we is white too. They gwine leave ol' nigger heah. That thought had bothered them from the precise moment they had individually and collectively stolen away from a hundred plantations in Alabama and had been culled and seduced and dragooned and persuaded into joining this regiment, called a host of names and finally the Sixth Heavy Artillery. Every time they stood provost duty in Memphis they had learned that ol' white mans stood together, that ol' Yankee was still a white man. They had learned that their officers would not stand up for them except maybe Booth, and now Booth was dead and the rest of their officers were no-count white trash anyhow. They knew and had known by hearing and the perceptions of their flesh under the knife and the belt buckle that the white Tennesseans in the town hated and were as much afraid of them as they were of the rebels. Instinctively there was a time, they knew, for playing and for acten big and for shooten the guns down at buckra and for dressen up in the blue cloth and for drinken the white man's beer, but just as on the plantation there had been the time for foolishness, giddiness, there had also been the moment they had been caught and had been punished not by one white man as a man but by one white man in all of his whiteness with even the law behind him. And they knew that down there, in the ravines and valleys and creek bottoms were the white men anxious and ready and a step away from reasserting the old authority over their flesh and mind. So in that moment left, acutely perceived as a moment left before the whole dream came to an end and the white man came and took out his punishment in their blood, they would have to have their victory and their moment.

If at any moment enough of their officers or the white troops they had been garrisoned with had taken the pain to establish them as brothers in arms or at least as soldiers in arms this process might have been reversed, or halted. But they of course had not, since they did not believe in them, the Yankee boys from the Midwest hating them and having come down to hold the nation together and fight for the Union; and the white officers afraid and contemptuous of them and always under the stigma themselves of being "black officers"; and the Tennesseans of course the worst of all, the rednecks seeing in the Negroes the perpetual mark and badge of their own shame since they did not own them, and the instrument indeed of that shame, since in the not owning they were not wealthy and could not become wealthy, the Tennesseans not even so much afraid of them as just hating them as some sort of animal, some species allied against them and their family and kin.

The result of all of this being that now, in the breathing space and moment of this truce, the most sensitive and polite and formal thing in the military world, when man's basic instinct toward the outright destruction of his fellow has been allowed full rein and then and only then after some indulgence is halted and bridled for a moment, when every man is mistrusting every other man on the other side and always has a finger on the trigger or the hilt, into this space the Negroes, bareheaded, refilled their canteens and began to jump onto the walls.

Bradford, white-faced and stinking of sweat and still looking at the tantalizingly close boats filled with blue-coated men, reconsidered and puzzled out a response. He fingered and dampened the paper with his hand and worked at the answer with a wetted pencil nub and raised his head repeatedly to watch the steamers. Leaming stood near him, snorting now and folding the side of his mouth into his cheek in irritation and contempt. The white officers stood silent and waiting and rocking on their heels, and the Tennesseans cursed and stood in their tight knots watching everything with cat eyes. And the Negroes having learned that one lesson from slavery, that inevitably you will be returned and censored, so in the harsh and sinful and guilt- and terror-filled act take your victory in the moment of the committing and by overindulgence; by searching for insensibility and the triumph of forgetting ol' buckra for a moment through drunkenness or the lungings of the woman underneath or the anger and wetness of the knife-fight. The Negroes put this into practice and drank the flat, stale beer, staining their leather and wool with lathered foam and drinking it, pouring it down. Then climbing up onto the parapets, driven by the flat and impacted terror and fear they had magnificently channeled and hidden all during the morning of indecision and death, driven now by this terror and all of the memories of the slave cabins and the whip and the easy coming of death, they stood on the walls and yelled and taunted the rebel soldiers. Drunk on the beer and the blood all around them and the vacuity and desperation of their officers and the hatred of their fellows in the garrison, driven by all of this and their slave-bred sense of the inevitability of the retribution ol' buckra down there was on the verge of taking, they yelled and screamed and laughed. There was a white-hot and swirling moment of victory for the soldiers of the First Battalion of the Sixth United States Colored Heavy Artillery.

Bradford was in his own fear, immersed and trapped and desperately entwining himself in indecision, sending out the reply to Goodman after interminably licking the pencil and staring downriver and putting the words down. Goodman took the sealed and slippery, wet envelope and turned his horse back to find Forrest. All around him the rebel soldiers were sitting up in their holes with their eyes narrowing in hatred and coming fury. The Negroes were standing on the wall and some of them were even pulling their pants down and urinating or showing themselves and their black pelts and private parts, yelling and shouting and waving their hands making insulting gestures at the Confederates. "Hey man, hey man, we gon to take yo' sistuh! Un hunh!" "Yeah man, we stop yo heah and now!" Over and over the vile and hidden and heretofore even in slave-cabin conclaves unspoken obscenities, rude because unpracticed and unused, doing rude and obscene dances on the walls. Some of them even setting off their rifles and all of them yelling, a piercing, piping yell. "Hey white bo, hey white bo, you got a wife? You got a wife? We gon git her! Ol' Yankee he say he he'p. Mis' Linkum he say he he'p. We gon fuck her." "We kill you, white bo, we kill you and cut you up. You heah? We kill you and we cut off yo' balls." "Hey bo, you like that? Dis nigger he gon take yo' sister! Hey bo, hey white bo, you like that? Hey, watcha say 'bout that, hey? Hey watcha say? We gon kill you. You know hit!"

Seabury tried to control his men, pulling at their belts and blouses, but he could not keep them from jumping up onto the wall, or from yelling at the rebels. He clutched at them from a terrible pity, thinking, the poor, poor fools. He had sat, stunned and indifferent, while the rebel sharpshooters had decimated his company and Gaylord had struggled with them; but this splayed, terrible, pathetic moment, this had a terrible urgency which the actual bite of the minie balls had not carried. But now Jonathan's hands could not keep them back, they threw their elbows at him and pushed him away.

He looked from side to side. The other white officers were smiling and nodding to one another. "They got spirit. Yessuh. They got some spirit left." They were smiling weakly; the concern over what the Negroes would do in a fight had come to assume the whole of their burden, the whole of their attention. The fact that the Negroes were screaming obscenities at the rebels seemed to resolve that central concern, and for the better. They had for so long feared the moment when the Negroes would break and run, leaving them alone, that all of their fears were soothed by the weird, vicious, childish scene. If we can trust the Negroes, had been their doubt; since it seemed the Negroes would fight, they struggled toward a confidence that still eluded them.

But Jonathan kept thinking, we should not be letting them do this. This is vile and obscene, and he looked up at their gesticulations, the proffered fingers and the circles of thumb and forefinger. This is obscene and we must stop them. It seemed more terrible than that; it seemed to threaten a remorseless destruction; it seemed to challenge patterns and powers and hatreds. All of the pity which Jonathan had assumed lay in the world now seemed bound up only in himself. He was not afraid for himself, but for the Negroes. He sensed that he could not protect them; he was the only fleck of compassion, of desperate sanity, under the arching sky.

Jonathan was concerned because no one else was; he sensed the wall of assimilating, accreting hatred and destruction which was a part of the land, and the day—the fleecy sky, the battle smoke, the spring moisture. He felt chillingly alone and exposed, he began to see what the Negroes had felt. He quit trying to hold them back; he stood beside the wall, looking at the rebels between their legs, his eyes glowing. Gaylord sat near him, large, shiny black circles beneath his eyes, his blond beard smeared with dirt and blood. Gaylord seemed to share a conspiratorial glee, contempt, with Jonathan; he shook his head and leered. Jonathan looked at him coldly, and looked back, and the hot spray of urine fell near him, but he did not move or flinch.

7

ALL AROUND FORT PILLOW ON THREE SIDES, OVER A THOUSAND rebel soldiers stood stock still and watched the Negroes with their eyes narrowing. They had climbed out of the holes and the ditches and from behind the thickets and put their tobacco out in front of them and loaded their pipes and taken the air above the ground level to which they had been limited all day. They knew what to expect of a truce, a time when they would climb out of the holes and loosen their straps and grin and wave at the Yankees and joke with their officers, smoking and chewing and studying the numerous cuts and scratches, from the briars and twigs, that now coated their wrists and palms. And they had proceeded to do that, up until the Negroes, with a consistent unanimity, lined the earthen walls of the fort with their weird and hideously obscene show. It was not only offensive and frightening; it was like a nightmare which was coming true. Worse than that, it was a victory for the Negroes, their kind of victory; momentary and with a hinging retribution, but it was a victory because it embarrassed and stung the rebels, and they had no reply in kind. The Negroes were doing things to them that they could not do to the Negroes; in this, they were un-approachable, and the rebels knew it. They stood open-mouthed with their tobacco still spread on shiny paper in front of them and untouched, and they watched with astonished hatred.

All of them were from Union-occupied regions except the Texans, and the thought of their exposed womenfolk, and the things that the Negroes might do to them, was the point that did not bear thinking about. Now here it was thrown up to them. This was the age when a woman showed no more of herself than her face and the rest of her figure was a masked and delicately fashionable roundness beneath the dress; sex was a desert cherished away from society and even from God; this yelling and this screeching humiliated them and it unmanned them because it embarrassed them, it seemed to tell aloud a secret about each of the rebels.

Most of them were very young, unwilling conscripts and recruits, and they hated the war and being away from home, and the only thing that made it bearable at all was their perceptible strength; they were Bedford Forrest's men and they hadn't lost a fight. And when this was thrown up to them—the humiliation, the display which showed how actually helpless, how chained, pent, helpless, exposed, they all were—they burned with terror and hatred and unmanning humiliation. Most of them had never owned a Negro but now they had ridden forty miles cheerfully and with a young man's sense of mission, because Fort Pillow stood for a reversal, a challenge, that could not be permitted. Part of that crusading sense had been worn out of them by a day of crawling through brush with death inches above them; tension and exhaustion, and the fact that they had proved so able, so capable and certain, had satiated them. They had invested the fort, and had gotten within yards of it; that reconfirmed their ability. Bradford and the garrison were as close to safety as they had ever been, when Forrest had sent in the flag of truce. 'Y God, their goddamn artirry and their goddamn boat caint stop us; I reckon they know they ain't safe, 'y God. They had stood up and stretched and thought, we busted this fort and the Yankees ull stick to a white man's way of fighten; now this came, this cold water and searing heat across their exposed and screaming and stifled, retrammeled nerves. This war was not supportable any more. The age-old sense of helplessness came back to them, the sense of being robbed of ability and strength when they would surely need it. They had no reply.

The hatred congealed on them as they sank back into the holes or folded up the tobacco without even seeing it, the hatred congealing and forming in the lines of their faces, the frozen young flesh, in the lines around the nose and mouth. They did not talk to each other, and their eyes went hollow and cold and tinged with snake-like steel concentration. And their officers, the ones at least who were not affected as much as their men by the specter of the Negroes' dark bodies raping their women and the humiliating ability of this capering black creature to embarrass and to wound and shame them with this show, the officers untouched by this thought, well yes, it will make the boys fight the harder. But now no one wanted the fort to surrender. One way or the other, I aim to do me some nigger killen this afternoon. I am a Christian an' I ain't really hated no man black ner white but this afternoon I aim to do me some head busten.

Forrest looked at the scrawled and sweat-smudged note, still sitting in the greenish light on his horse behind the trees.

General Forrest, Commanding C.S. Forces:

Sir—I respectfully ask for one hour for consultation with my officers and the officers of the gunboat. In the meantime no preparations to be made on either side.

Very respectfully,

L. F. Booth,

Major Commanding

Forrest, his face still in the brazen and moulded cast, looked up after reading the note and knew full well that Booth had written that last line knowing that the boats were there and hoping and indeed counting upon the steamers to land more men; knowing this but not knowing of course that Booth was dead and that Bradford had signed his name.

Forrest said, "I will give 'em twenty minutes. I don't want the boat." This was in turn translated by the young staff officer, writing this time on the trunk of a blackjack oak.

Major L. F. Booth, Commanding U.S. Forces, Fort Pillow:

Sir—I have the honor to acknowledge the receipt of your note, asking one hour to consider my demand for your surrender. Your request cannot be granted. I will allow you twenty minutes from the receipt of this note for consideration; if at the expiration of that time the Fort is not surrendered, I shall assault it. I do not demand the surrender of the gunboat.

Very respectfully,

N. B. Forrest,

Major General

Goodman took the note back to the place south of the fort and handed it to Leaming who took it in to Bradford, who opened the envelope and read it, all of this beneath and masked by the gibbering, yelling, hysterical Negro soldiers. Their noise was like a piping Greek chorus as they stood silhouetted along the walls, while around them the white soldiers peered out at the rebels and the officers smiled weakly at each other. The Negroes were standing and rocking with laughter along the wall, one man in four bent forward in a crouching yell making signs with his hands and with his lower jaw jutting and working, and the others around him squeezing shut their eyes from the laughing and their mouths thrown open and their tongues quivering. Groups of rebels near the wall began to get up and walk solemnly to even closer holes and ditches, stonily watching the Negroes along the walls. We got us a job to do, this time.

In the fort Bradford read the letter twice, still standing near the signal platform balanced in his big boots and watching the steamers. The one above the fort came down closer and closer. He smiled and thought, yes, yes, now put her over for the slip, watching the wake churning as the sidewheels thrashed into the water with clunking sounds and she built up speed. The gunboat was making some signals to her and Bradford looked around for a signal officer to tell him what the flutter of flags were; the boat came on, the signboard above the cavernous lower deck reading "Liberty" and smoke pouring back and the water folding away from her bows. She passed by the bluff at Coal Creek and the rebels there burst into a flecked roar of gunfire, the tattered white gunsmoke clotting and rising above the bluff. No, no, leave her be, leave her be. Bradford frowned. What do those signals mean? The water around the *Liberty* burst into a white, pocked flurry of spouts from the rifle balls. Then she was in midstream and obviously not going to turn for the fort, and Bradford squinted and frowned and the whole thing was a hideous joke of some vast sort, of course she had to come back and land those men. Of course. He watched dry-mouthed and with the flesh bunched around his eyes. The steamer, the large one below the fort, swung out into the middle of the stream now heading for the one from upriver, with a clanging of bells and much dark smoke and puffs of white smoke. He put his glasses on the large boat and he could see blue uniforms covering the lower deck and all along the gangways and around the pilot house. Well now, that one will have to stop. Yes.

Bradford watched and mused and worried, and his officers crowded around him, and the truce still held; and Bradford made no effort to signal the boats. The help they offered was dubious, in truth: as soon as signal flags had fluttered on the walls and the boats had made for the shore, the rebels would have assaulted the fort, and riddled the boats with rifle fire. None of the three steamers offered Bradford substantial help. But it did not seem so to him. All of them; three boats; the fact that there were so many seemed to mean not only support, but rescue. He stood and looked back and forth, from the upriver to the downriver boats. The truce forbade any reinforcements but that did not deter him. His own white-blinding fear, his own corroded will and helpless cunning, did.

Everyone in the world, he thought, knows this fort is about to fall. The sense of the massive and arching judgment which was falling upon himself sucked the whole world into his thoughts and equations; of course everyone knows the fort is about to fall. How could they help but know it, how could they fail to see that here the whirling earth itself was plunging upon this time and this small and tiny position in West Tennessee? Of course they knew, Hurlbut and Lincoln even, and certainly the men on the river. Else why have they sent the boats (not one but three)? Bradford stood on the bank clutching the surrender note and staring at the nearest riverboat and around him the officers formed in a curious semicircle, and he waited for the boats to put in to the landing. Those men on the boats had to be reinforcements for the post, else why should they be here?

But he was waiting in an agony and an expectation that was in no way communicated to the boats, even to Marshall, who had been on station all day. Bradford might assume the boats were other pieces of the universe falling into place, assistance for him and his command; but for that very reason and the magnitude of his desire and his fear, he never told them. It never occurred to him to ask or tell or even query; he watched in spates of anxiety, and cunning, and fear. But everyone in the world was not absorbed in Bradford's fight.

On the *Olive Branch,* a steamer in the passenger service from St. Louis to New Orleans, General Shepley stood in the pilot house and argued with Captain Pegram. Shepley, a courteous and efficient officer, who by his own request was being relieved of duty in New Orleans, was trying to get Pegram to run past the fort. In Memphis General Brayman as an afterthought had put two complete batteries on board, the gun carriages and caissons and leather and the gunners taking up every inch of space around the boilers and on the lower deck. But they were artillery-men in red-piped shell jackets and they did not have a firearm among them and there was no room to work the artillery pieces on the lower deck; even when they had had to land at coaling stations Shepley, in a half-hearted gesture against guerrillas, had put some of the Ohio boys ashore with tree branches, standing whistling nervously while behind them the roustabouts loaded the coal and wood. They were worse than helpless because they constituted a fat military prize and Shepley knew this; but there was a fight and Shepley wanted to lend a hand in the fight. But Pegram had women and children aboard and they even now were gathered in a fascinated, gabbling group along the boat deck gesturing toward the fort where the guerrillas were, and Shepley said yes, that was true. Besides, the rebels, word was, wanted to seize some boats to get across to the Arkansas shore. Maybe they would try to seize the *Olive Branch.*

Shepley, his white sideburns bristling, went back with hammering footsteps along the deck and made the men signal the second boat, the *Cheek,* to come alongside. The *Cheek* was a nondescript trading sternwheeler with bales of cotton on the decks and two coal barges alongside, and he decided to put some guns onto it and run up to the fort in that. While he was terrorizing her captain, bellowing at him from the towering Texas deck of the *Olive Branch* with his uniform glittering in the sunlight, down below the gunners were scrambling over and under and around the box-like caissons and the limbers and their Napoleons, trying to get the cordage loosened and sweating in the tight, tangled places at their work. The *Cheek* in the meantime began the arduous process of throwing the cotton over the side and getting rid of the coal barges. Shepley was dealing with the difficulties of transferring the dead weight of two-ton cannon from one bobbing steamer to another, when a messenger came up to him and said a boat was coming past the fort.

He went back to the pilot house and joined the knot of uniformed men looking anxiously at the boat, which at this distance could well have been covered with rebels. "That is all right, General," Pegram was saying, "if the rebels try to take us in that thing I can run right over them in the *Branch*." They let go the *Cheek* and bells rang and the *Olive Branch* swung back into midstream to gain room and headway if needed, and then they saw the clustering blue uniforms on the *Liberty*. She kept away from them. The soldiers on her stood with their long rifles looking up at the big passenger steamer, and her captain hailed, "All right, you can go by up there; the gunboat is lying off the fort!" Shepley nodded and Pegram rang for speed and the boat swung up past the fort. Shepley stood near the ornate windows in the pilot house watching the fort. He could see flags of truce, and above it the drifting haze of smoke clearing away in the air, and he did not pay any more attention to it. Some stragglers or guerrillas fired at them from below the fort, shooting at the pilot house. Shepley looked at the jetting and scattered scarf of white smoke contemptuously.

They reported to the gunboat, which was lying away from the fort with her portholes open and smoke and steam rising from them. The women and children who had run gabbling to look at the fort and then had raced back from the scattered firing to the other side made all sorts of noises about the gunboat. Shepley frowned in anger and irritation. The gunboat was a tinclad with a big number 7 on the sides of the pilot house in red. The sides were pockmarked and dented and there was a lot of smoke, and from the look of the bare-chested sailors in the ports and on deck they had been at work all day. A small boat with a very young naval officer in a pillbox cap came over, the officer pulling up the ladder expertly and saluting Shepley. He was very officious and eager and this was his world, and Shepley had to play the interested and benevolent grandee trying to be of assistance. The officer said, "Mister Marshall don't want any boats to stop. Go on to Cairo, he says, and ask the man on station there to send down four-hundred rounds of ammunition, please sir." Shepley said, of course, of course, and was that all they could do? and the young man said everything was in hand on the gunboat. Then he went back over to it and the *Olive Branch* picked up steam and went through another flurry of rebel sniping and then was clear again upriver. Shepley looked at the water sliding past and felt a moment of doubt and concern and worry about it all, but then he thought, why that is Fort Pillow, one of our strongest positions, and I know that it is in constant communication with Memphis. Captain Pegram looked at the fort too, and then said to Shepley, "They say in Memphis that place can be held for forty-eight hours 'gainst any number of rebels; that is what they say." Shepley nodded, and thought, Hurlbut would know what is going on up there better than I.

Captain Marshall stood on the gundeck of the *New Era,* looking around him. The deck was foul and stinking, with the eddying smoke and steam still hanging under the battle lanterns, with black scars and cuts in the polished deck, and powder and shot spilled all around. The seamen, shirtless and red-eyed, were at the ports gasping at the fresh air. The shot lockers were mostly empty and the guns were all so befouled that accurate shelling was impossible.

Marshall placed both hands above his hips and rocked back, stretching; he had spent the whole day squinting through a slit in the pilot house. Two of the sailors, stumbling over cordage, bandages and tangled shirts at their feet, were trying to force open one of the jammed sideports, to let in more air. The sailors had spent all day in the back-breaking rhythms of loading and firing; and in working the engines and the wheel, trying to keep the light tinclad in place against the current of the river. The twenty-four-pounders were blackened with smoke, and some of them were scored with the impact of rifle balls. Poles and rammerstaffs and sponges and chains lay all around the deck.

Marshall had had no word from the fort, other than the flurry of signal flags all day, ordering him up and back and up again; the firing instructions had been so rapid and confused that he had stopped trying to respond to them, and had just laid his fire down around the fort at random. He went outside the shield on the riveted metal ladder. Some of his crew were stretched out in the niches around the armor plating, sleeping or panting and vomiting. It had been hot, furious, choking during the steady firing. Lack of headway had pressed the gunsmoke back in upon the deck, and men had passed out there, and in the engine room where Marshall had had to keep constant steam pressure to hold his position at all.

But he—they all—figured that they had done well. There were no more signal flags from the fort for the moment. All of the men were impressed with the big howitzers and the rate of their fire; they assumed they had cut the rebels up pretty bad, since they heard nothing at all from Booth up in the fort. Well, we done our best for a while. Let us rest, Marshall thought, and we will be able to give a hand again, but we are beat out right now. I reckon we just about tied the record for throwing shell and canister; heard tell ol' Swift at gun four tol' 'em to skip the swabbing between the rounds. Time that that ol' gun blows up in his face, he will learn; but we really laid the fire into the rebels, I warrant.

Of course, he thought, they should not have much trouble holding for a while longer—maybe they've druv the rebels off already. I bet that is it. I bet the rebels are taken in their wounded now and withdrawen, under a flag of truce. With all our fire, we must have cut 'em up pretty bad. He looked around; no hurry, I will give these men another half-hour before getting under way again. He squinted up at the fort. Booth will let us know, time he needs help again.

8

THE WHITE SOLDIERS OF THE GARRISON, LOOKING OUT OF THE portholes or between the feet of the shrilling, yelling Negroes, saw the rebels moving. They could see them down in the town ravines, ones who had slipped out of the loose discipline of the Mississippi battalions and were now looting the stores, coming out of the half-burned quartermasters' and sutlers' stores drinking hard liquor with adam's apples bobbing, and carrying clothes over their arms. On the eastern face, one of the Tennesseans from B Company looked out over the rampart and saw a party of twenty rebel soldiers, stone-faced and solemn, rise from their ditch and walk toward the fort. They stared straight at the walls of the fort and came on, walking in quick, easy strides. They got to within twenty yards of the fort, a tall and sunburnt officer in the middle of them with his pants stuffed into the boot tops. "What are you doing there?"

They kept on, not hearing because of the piping yells and a sudden spurt of laughter from the Negroes at one of their number who had slipped and fallen off the parapet into the moat. "Hey, hey rebs!" They looked up, their faces stiff masks with the corners of their mouths turned down. "What chee doen here?"

The officer looked at him. "We know our business." His voice was hoarse. They shifted their weapons easily and jumped down into one of the rifle pits right outside the fort. The Tennessean thought about telling his lieutenant and started to, but the officers were all in conference and he thought, what the hell, what I know I know. I got to find me some other ol' boys

408

and plan on getten out of here alive. Johnny rebs are goen to come over that wall any minute, I aim to git out of here alive.

Bradford, surrounded by all of the officers of the garrison, was standing on the bluff. He looked after the *Olive Branch*, which had just run by. He had seen the artillery pieces on the deck and the men crammed in among the equipment looking up at the bluff with pale faces, and then he had seen the boat put in toward the gunboat, and he had seen the officer from *New Era* go aboard her. And the big steamer stood off with its wheels turning and lifting water and its smoke pluming into the air, and Bradford had thought, of course, of course she will put in to the slip and land those guns. Of course they are for this post. They must be for this post, and Marshall (thinking of tall, sure Marshall saying yes, yes, to Booth, yes we can shell those rebels out of any ravine around here), Marshall will be giving them the orders to land or telling them how to land or something. Then the boat had stood off with a jangling of engine-room bells and for a second lost headway against the current of the river and he had thought, they are coming, they are coming now. And without any change or rhythm or signal to the fort the steamer had put over and bitten into the current and slid close to the Arkansas side and was gone up the river, the wheels lifting huge chunks of water and leaving a bubbling, thick wake and the soldiers wandering aft looking up at Fort Pillow and leaning against the stanchions. There had been no signal from her and Bradford could not understand it, could not understand at all. Perhaps, perhaps they are going to turn the thing around up yonder and then come back. He could see some of the Confederate snipers under the north bluff standing out in the water firing their rifles toward the boat. Bradford could not understand it. Why had the boat not stopped? Did they not know?

It had never occurred to his officers that Bradford expected help from the boats: or that he had forgotten to signal them. They assumed that he had properly obeyed the truce; hell of a time for it, but it was the right thing, they reckoned.

But the passage of the boats—unrelenting, uncaring—had crushed all of Bradford's spirit, or potential, or ability. The universe itself leaned down for his betrayal and his destruction. He struck his gloved hands together; he was past taking any action, and so he was past indecisiveness. He clung to the shield of earth and to the Negroes; *I cannot assert myself, no. They will see me if I do.* The patterns he had been following were those of his nightmare cunning. *Fall back to the fort. They will not cross the walls. If they do, fall below the bluff.* Death was outside; he had to keep men, walls, paths for escape between himself and it. Even surrender, even betraying the truce, were beyond him.

Bradford had reached for his power, and he had put out all of his self-assertion and his will power and his ability, when he had raised the companies of the Thirteenth. But power and authority had eluded him; he was a victim, powerless, and the *Olive Branch* mocked him, churning upstream at six knots. Power had not perpetrated itself, it had perpetrated guilt and responsibility and then helplessness.

I am goen to stay behind this fort and wait, and if we lose here, in the anonymity of all my men and my nigras we will run down to the bank and the gunboat will shell the rebels and they will go away. They will not find me. They think Booth is still alive and I will sign his name so they will not know it is me. Bradford watched the boat and his lips worked trying to call it back, but then he reread the note from Forrest. The world seemed to cluster in a haze over his will—*if we surrender,* he thought, *they will see me and mark me.*

Bradford turned around toward his officers. He smiled wanly at them, Bischoff with the pink jowls, Seabury still handsome and now very, very remote behind the collar of his jacket, Francis Smith with his bandaged hand, and William Cleary of the Thirteenth, Hunter, black-haired and stained with powder and frowning, Bradford's brother Ted grinning and naively holding the signal flag. Van Horn was scratching his cheek and looking very blank, and he stank of sweat, and Leaming was scowling at him openly, looking at Bradford and twisting the side of his mouth and looking at the others and shrugging; Young, the Missourian, was minutely examining his pistol, Delos Carson with his big, brown, mutton-chop whiskers and pink, shiny lower lip smoking a cigar, and a few others; middle-aged men and young men with beards and face whiskers and stinking through their soaked and splotched shirts and frock coats, some of them still with black neckties and with blue vests buttoned all the way, with their shoulder straps and askew sashes and small black hats and pistols, standing with their hands on their hips or looking at their bandages or pistols, all of them silent and waiting. A lot of them had been killed, out in front of the fort or behind the walls by the snipers, and others like Epenter were now down in the tents or under the bluff surrounded by bandages and cotton rolls and their own bright blood and hours of dazzling pain. They stood in front of Bradford, and behind them the Tennesseans congregated in their tight knots, worrying and complaining and swearing, and the Negroes still in a frieze against the sky along the parapet, their noise now no longer really thought of as human but rather as a weird, natural, piping gabble, imprinted on the officers' ears and accepted and now forgotten.

"Well boys, the rebels give us twenty minutes to give up." Bradford looked around him with a smile. "Now I reckon we ought to take a vote."

Leaming snorted and folded his arms and looked at Young.

"For myself," Bradford went on, "I think we can whip them. I think with the gunboat we can stop them cold. But I want to hear what you think."

There was a moment of silence and in that moment Bradford had the wild sense of sinking, of plunging uncontrollably down and down. Then Leaming said, "Forgit this shit. We can stop 'em, you all know it."

They did not know it. Leaming looked at them and scowled his contempt, and they frowned and shuffled and played with the toes of their boots in the sand, but they did not know it. They had had no commitment to anything other than their own fears and their own desires, since they had enlisted in the Negro regiment and taken the insults and with them the pay increase. They had no stomach for the fighting and they sensed that they ought to surrender now. But they had lived so long in the fear that their Negroes would break, that alone they would have to face the rebels, that the rebels would have some terrible ven-

geance for them all. They did not know how frightened Bradford was—I wonder where ol' Bradford got the heart for this
fight, I woulda thought he'd hev curled up an' died—but as with
Bradford, the walls of the fort still seemed sheltering, the ranks
of their Negroes seemed like walls for them to crouch beneath.
They had always seen themselves as individual white men looking out for themselves, doing a job with good-for-nothen niggers. Now they did not want to be caught amid their troops. It
was hot, dangerous, painful behind the walls; but they could
not imagine that the rebels would let them march out of their
fort and into the relative security of surrender. They had hollow, indistinct fears of what might happen to them on the other
side of the walls. But still, they were not quick to turn loose the
chance of surrender.

Leaming was offended and weary and he knew the rebels
were going to make their rush and he wanted them to come
ahead with it. To get it over with at the point of cold steel and
no more of this huddling and getting picked off. He turned
away from the group of officers and rocked on his heels. Hunter
had already gone down the line to his own section, his face stiff
with anger; Jonathan watched them all, coldly, steadily. Ted
Bradford said, "I vote we fight," and smiled at his brother. He
was so obviously not even aware of the meaning of the Negroes'
hooting, much less the strained and chilled silence of the white
troops, that everybody almost looked down out of embarrassment.

But then Delos Carson, who was known primarily for
whoring among the Negro women and for playing cards, spoke
up and said, "Well, the nigs will fight, that was what bothered
me all along. Look at 'em. The nigs will fight, so we ought to let
em." The question of the Negroes had been with them so long
they all suddenly thought, yes, why of course, and the moment
of pause had gradually dissipated some of their fears about the
security of the fort. The sweat dried on them and they grew
more confident. Yes, now the niggers would fight, and my Lord,
my Aunt Minnie could hold these walls! They nodded to each
other. Boats on the river showed them they were not alone. All
right, we give it a try.

Delos Carson dragged at his cigar and Van Horn and Bischoff and Leaming immediately nodded yes, let's fight. "We caint surrender now," Bischoff said, and pointed toward the Negroes on the parapet, now making the signs with their hands and yelling, "Come own, come own, white bo, we kill you, you know hit!" Young said, "Well, as a visitin' officer, I think you got a chaince to win," and they all turned then, some making quick motions of voting with their hands, and they went back to their positions. None of them had seen the rebels, or had seen how close they were to the walls. They were all too busy watching Bradford and commenting militarily on the exchange of notes and looking at the steamboats and disassociating themselves from the yelling and pirouetting Negroes.

None of them realized how easy it would be for the Confederates to take the fort, and they all thought, well, the niggers are ready to fight now, so we ought to stop the rebels; not realizing how close the rebels were or how the Negroes were on the point of breaking or how the Tennesseans were in open defiance and rebellion themselves from eight hours of strain. The officers went back to their men certain they could win, and the Negroes were thoroughly certain that in a minute the whole pattern of the universe that Linkum and Booth had reversed would come back and punish them and in that moment they were living in wild and skyrocketing joy and rebellion themselves because they knew that horror was just outside the walls. Ol' buckra was comen in to put the cold steel and the whip to their flesh. And the Tennesseans were scared and looking for a way out, in tight groups talking about how to surrender to the rebels or maybe work out with a skiff into the river.

The officers went back suddenly secure in their strength and not even knowing where the rebels were. No one could cross the massive walls; that equation was and always had been with them. The moat and the huge walls. No one could cross them. And the nigs will fight. They suddenly assumed they had proof of that. They were confident now, and Bradford alone among them was miserable in his fear and, standing in the middle of the parade, was looking behind him for a way to run down to the bluff without getting tangled in the tent stays of the Negro quarters. He told Ted Bradford to signal with the blue flag to the gunboat and Ted said, "Sure Bill," and grinned. He got out the blue flag and climbed to the little platform and signaled the boat, but Marshall had made up his mind and did not answer. Bradford watched his brother wave the flag and then took out his pad and wrote his reply to Forrest, this time writing it quickly and not smudging it.

General—I will not surrender.
Very respectfully, your obedient servant,
L. F. Booth, Major Commanding

Booth now, he thought, takes all the responsibility. He watched Leaming running to get the note to the rebels.

The Negroes saw the flags of truce going down, and they were ordered off the walls. The fort braced. The whole garrison were on their feet, holding their weapons. Bradford stood in the center of the parade and watched them. The civilians in jean cloth and broadcloth and tan suits were coming up to get muskets and rifles again from the orderly sergeants. There were shuffling sounds, and feet splattered in the mud in the parade. The running and the jarring of the cannon fire had shaken and hacked the parade and there were pools of water. Bradford stood amid the soldiers and thought, oh yes, oh yes I had better tell them, I had better tell them of the plan to drop below the bluff if the rebels get into the fort. The Negroes were bleary-eyed now. Some of them stumbled against each other and tangled up their arms putting their leather crossbelts back on. Bradford smiled at them weakly and stepped forward and said, "Men," and then had to clear his throat to shout louder, "Men!"

Everyone in the garrison turned and looked, the Tennesseans cursing under their hands and turning to see what Bradford wanted, and the Negroes turning with slightly askew eyes and dull, open mouths, drunken in varying degrees and masked into silence. The officers handled their sashes and sword hilts and looked down. "Men, I want you to know we officers just voted unanimously to defend this fort!!" The Negroes cheered and cheered with their eyes still dull and askew, deep-chested cheers that shook the water on the ground. The Tennesseans looked at each other and swore. "Men, I want you to take an oath, here and now." Bradford when he had their attention was coming more and more to himself, or to the self that had wrenched, with the aid of the three wagonloads of breech-loading carbines, a battalion out of West Tennessee. "I want you to take an oath to me, to Major Bradford, that you will never surrender, that you will defend this post to the death!" Again the Negroes cheered, and the officers raised their fists or made motions with their hands on their uniforms. The Negroes held their heads at an angle and cheered hoarsely. "Men. Men, I will never desert you!" and they cheered that too. Then he stepped forward smiling and said, "Listen, now. Listen. I made a plan with Marshall on the gunboat. Listen. If the rebels get into the fort," he propped his foot on a board and leaned forward with his arms crossed on his thigh, "when they git into this fort, retreat below the bluff. Foller me below the bluff. We put six cases of ammunition below the bluff, dint we, Charles? Hey, Charles?" And the Negro Charles, a corporal of the Second, stepped forward and said, "Yessuh, Majuh! We sho did!"

"Foller me below the bluff and we will keep up the fight there, an' ol' Marshall will chop the rebels down with grape."

Bradford smiled and leaned forward and the Tennesseans spit tobacco juice and swore and grinned nervously at each other, ol' Bradford he is a durn fool, he git us all kilt. The officers looked at each other with their foreheads bunching over their noses in worry. The Negroes did not know what to do; they looked and cheered sporadically and thought it was an order, and some of them went back toward the bluff but were stopped by their white sergeants with rifles pressed across their breasts. Bradford was among all of them now, among the Negroes and the Tennesseans, walking among them and slapping their buttocks and their backs and shaking hands with them, smiling and saying over and over, "We goen stop 'em, ain't we? Yessir, we goen to stop the rebels and whip 'em, ain't we?"

The men stood below the wall and loaded their guns, while Bradford was walking among them patting and slapping and smiling, the Negroes occasionally dropping their cartridges from between thick fingers to the mud, and clumsily ramming down the charges. The Tennesseans loaded their carbines at their hips and they loaded their pistols, looking covertly and almost guiltily over their shoulders at each other and at the Negroes and their officers. They all of them had extra revolvers in their blouses and their waistbelts and they checked the loads in them too. The officers were loading their own pistols and getting the cannon doubleshotted. No, man, put in another load, that is it, that is the way; now then, roll it out; now hold it, hold it. Everyone was loading and getting onto the firing step, the wood creaking under the weight of men pressed shoulder to shoulder and putting their boots onto the kicked and marred and chipped wood. The civilians loaded their guns quickly and judiciously, measuring out the shot like bird hunters and thumbing down the ramrods and then stepping with squinting, narrow faces up beside the white Tennesseans. Everyone kept down, below the level of the parapet. Some of the Negroes jerked upright to fire but their officers and sergeants were nervous and slapped at them with sword flats and they whimpered and stayed down. The Negroes, sweating and smelling of the sweet beer, were laughing now, slapping each other on the back and laughing, choking back the noise with lined and streaming faces, sobbing with the laughing and squeezing their guns tight.

Jonathan stood behind his twelve-pounder looking along the line at the firestep, at the Negroes with the thick leather belts over their shoulders and their kinky hair and sweat-stained caps and the pallid Tennesseans in yellow-piped cavalry jackets, and the civilians. Well, he thought, well it will soon enough come. Of course the rebels will not come over that wall. The wall is too big and too thick and the ditch is too deep. Of course they cannot. He looked around, and looked up then and saw the sun in the pure April sky. He smelled the moist and surging odors of spring. My Lord, but 'tis a beautiful day! He raised the hat back off his forehead to look up at the sky, and the thick clouds floating over. The clouds were fleecy and round and white against the pure, deep-blue sky. He smelled it all and thought, there is a life to be lived like this, in the pure enjoyment of this sort of thing, in the relish of the soul. But even with—even despite—the perfect touch of the fingers of wind upon my flesh, there is no mercy beneath this sky. He was glad, thankful, that the rebels could not cross the moat and the walls. The rebels seemed a part of the day itself, to him. There is no delicacy or mercy out there, or beneath this arching sky; we only delude ourselves. He was close to the sense of completing horror that the Negroes shared; they had learned long, long ago not to expect mercy or compassion; they had lived this day all of their lives, and all of their fathers' lives, the day when the white man came for them. Jonathan dimly sensed this spurting fear and expectancy; it chilled him. Well then.

9

AND THEN THE REBEL BUGLE BLEW. GOODMAN HAD NEGOTIATED
the ground with the sealed envelope while the rebels ducked
into their ditches and their holes again and checked their equipment. Goodman found Forrest and Forrest opened the letter
and read the note and crumpled it into a ball and frowned, his
eyes flashing. He had made the preparations and told even the
company commanders what to do, during the long hours of the
approach. He had told them where to go and when to move and
he had told them what to do if they had to rush the fort. So in
each hole and in each company the encircling twelve-hundred
men were confident and sure and filled with an intense desire to
get over that wall and into the fort and on with the now pre-
dominant business of the killing and the busting of heads. They
cradled their polished revolver butts and they waited, looking
at each other with their eyebrows drawn up.

Forrest rode his horse with a consciousness of the expiration of each minute, through the delicate, blossoming April
woods, through the yet untrampled ferns and the lichen green
and pink across the rock, and the sedge in clumps green again
after the purple fall and the dun winter, and the dogwood
blossoming through the woods like incandescent fire, white and
purple; and through the light sifting through the thin leaves
which could discolor and throw their green gentleness over
everything but could not cut out the sun. Forrest sent off two
aides with his orders, to Bell that he didn't want to hear of
Tennessee being left behind, and to McCulloh that he didn't
want to hear of Missouri being left behind. At his shoulder

Gaus unslung his bugle and held it on his leg, waiting for the order. They rode and the earth around the fort was spongy. They could hear the pipe and twitter of birds in a pleasant undercurrent of sound. Chalmers in his red-lined cloak was thinking of the operation, but Forrest was not. Forrest rode with his face in a mask of anger and weary resignation and hatred, and the mood of the Tennessee woods, which had absorbed all of the Yankee cannonading without mark, was upon him. They were in a gentle dell, of green and gold and the colors of an April afternoon, and the tragedy of the thing gave the moment a depth and a horror and an identity. The fact that this afternoon and under this sky young men would die, and needlessly. Well then, if there is to be blood let it be theirs. They reached the knoll and looked out over the fort, four hundred yards away, a knot of men in featureless grey cloaks hanging to their boot-tops. They looked around, Forrest the hawk-faced man in their middle, impassive and staring at the fort. Then Forrest dropped his hand and Gaus blew the charge, the notes fierce and fluted from the bullet holes in the horn, burbled as if running under water.

And all around the fort in a wild and yelling release of the stored, chest-aching air in their breasts twelve-hundred young men jumped out of the ground with their knees and thighs and calves driving them bent forward in a great, curving grey and dun scythe under fluttering red flags for the fort; with their bursting lungs relieved and pumping out the yell, the "Yaaaaaaay Yaaaaaaaaaaaaaaaay Yaaaaaaaaaaaaaay," while their lithe bodies dodged and skipped and swerved for the fort and the quivering, shiny spring leaves danced or snapped off as they ran by. Their feet drummed and splattered against the slippery earth and their mouths ringed with stubble or silky, adolescent beards were thrown back and howling into the sky. "YAAAAY YAAAAAAAAAAY YAAAAAAAAAAY!" They sprinted hard and the tops of the walls of the fort exploded at them in grey forms and jetting and puffing smoke and the flat flame of rifle fire. The air hummed and whined and some of them fell toppling and still thrusting forward, suspended in the yell and not knowing they were hit and dying until somehow the charge spun away from them up the hill. The rebels ran flat, hurtling, and

The Battle of Fort Pillow 419

dived into the ditch at the foot of the wall, clattering amid their leather and equipment and breathless and gulping and still with hatred in their eyes, and they gathered to scale the wall not even pausing to check who was still alive or to look at themselves or their equipment. They flooded into the muddy, watery bottom of the ditch amid the scattered dead Union bodies and drowned, white-bellied squirrels and green slush and black scum, their feet drumming whiteness out of the water and they clustering for the final leap with the blood still so high in them they could not hear anything and ached to be killing.

In the fort they heard the bugle and then the yell and the rustle and splattering footsteps. Jonathan was standing holding the lanyard of his howitzer, and with the unexpected, nerve-wracking yell he jerked it immediately, the gun rocking back sharply with smoke and noise and everyone stepping forward mechanically to reload. Jonathan looked up at the mass of men packed along the parapet. There was smoke all around them and they had jumped up too and fired, but a lot of them were lying backwards now with wounds in their faces and hands, horrible purple and blue holes with the blood dripping out on the wooden firestep. They were still firing their rifles, the ones that had not fired pressing forward to do so, and more and more of them were hit in the face and collapsing. The top of the wall seemed to be jerking and jumping, and bits of earth were flying off of it and there were miniature furrows ploughed in it, and rifles left lying across it when the Negroes were hit. Jonathan did not know what was making the top of the wall jerk until suddenly he realized that the rebel sharpshooters were pouring in the fire, and when he looked behind him he could see the minie balls going over the wall and splashing into the water on the parade.

The Negroes were making a weird and mindless gabbling noise now, still trying to fire their rifles, to climb to the parapet and shoot down at the rebels, but the sharpshooters were picking them off steadily; they would get one leg on top of the wall and then topple backwards dying or with their faces broken in, and Gaylord kept clawing and grabbing at them to keep them down. Jonathan looked down the line at the Tennesseans and the civilians, and they were all panic-stricken and pressed flat against the wall of the parapet, clinging to it with their fingers and their officers were walking up and down prodding at them and trying to get them to stand up and fire.

And then Jonathan heard the rebels, he could hear them splashing in the water and the mud outside in the moat and he could hear them climbing the wall, with grunts and curses and the rattle of equipment. He thought, my God, they are there, they are there on the other side of the wall. He stared at the wall as if it were crawling or diseased, thinking, they are there, they are right on the other side. He looked around wildly at the shell boxes and the dead, sprawled bodies of the Negroes and the sponges and rammers and did not see anything to get rid of the rebels with. He rolled his eyes up to the sky and it was still there and that was a mistake somehow, the rebels on the other side of the wall making no noise at all except for the clink and scrape of their equipment as they edged closer and closer and here, here, the Negroes babbling and trying to load their rifles and the whites doing nothing, huddling in confusion against the wall and pressing their faces against it with their eyes like those of a trapped animal rolling and looking sideways and their officers prodding and cursing them. Jonathan felt the noiseless impact of the sun, and felt the sheer terror of the rebels coming closer, their equipment perceptibly scraping against the hard earth wall and them clawing up and getting ready.

Gaylord was among the Negroes saying, load your rifles, load your rifles, and the Negroes were trying to. They looked up at him with dulled eyes, all of the drunken fire in them broken and gone, and then they said, yes, and fumbled trying to find their cartridges, fumbling and then trying to fit the cartridges into the muzzles of the guns. Jonathan stood right behind them open-mouthed and feeling the wind and the air against his exposed and pumping chest. He looked at one of them sitting with his back against the parapet, making hollow noises in his throat with his mouth open wide and pulled back against his chin in myriad folds of flesh, and the tongue winking pinkly, and the man's eyes seeming to fill up with blood. Then he realized, that is Gator and he has been shot through the back of the neck or something because there was blood everywhere and Gator kept working with his mouth trying to bring up something from the back of his throat. Jonathan looked wildly down the line, the live Negroes sitting among the dead ones, still trying to load their guns, and then there was less light somehow and Jonathan was thinking how helpless he was; this is too horrible to be true, I cannot believe this. He could hear Bradford yelling.

He wondered in the midst of all of the horror and the bloody, torn Negroes and the drunken ones and the scraping of the rebel equipment and the noise of their breathing on the other side of the wall, why there was less light and then he looked up and the rebels were atop the parapet. He turned and he had to yell to someone, "They are there, they are there!" He took some running backwards steps but no words would come to his mouth. Some of the Negroes and the whites around the perimeter of the walls had shot off the first rebel heads to appear but for the most part they were still huddled against the wall in terror or trying to load their rifles in the impacted fear and terror and haste with the world plunging around them like a mad, wild horse.

The rebels were there, in a series all along the wall like some emanation from the earth itself which had suddenly grown in profusion. While the Negroes and the whites even were trying to struggle to their feet and keep their heads down and hold out their rifles in a tangle of leather and woolen blue and rifle metal the rebels were right above them, on their knees and balancing on one hand and holding the pistols with the blinding sunlight pouring all over them. Jonathan thought, they cannot have crossed the wall, no, and then, they are so young. The one in front of him was kneeling and balancing on the knuckles of one hand and holding a revolver pressed down right against a young Negro's head, only the Negro did not realize what the weight of the metal was and he kept pushing with his hands to get up, and then while Jonathan watched and noticed the feather in the rebel's hatband the man pressed the trigger and the Negro sank in a red spray of blood.

The rebels all along the wall were leaning over and firing

their pistols, leaning over and shooting down at the Negroes and the whites along the firestep, and Jonathan was standing still and watching in horror. The Negroes trying to rise were being cut down and torn apart, the long, heavy pistols making roaring blasts and triangular jets of smoke and powder burns in the Negroes' uniforms they were so close. The Negroes now were getting down in a blind terror from the firestep and trying to turn and look up at the rebels on the wall like a man trying to get rid of a wasp on his neck. They stumbled away from the wall still holding onto their rifles, and stood there in front of the rebels and the rebels were grinning now; Jonathan could see their grins, shooting the Negroes as fast as they could thumb back the hammers of their revolvers. The rebels were jumping down onto the firestep and the Negroes stood in one long line in front of them all around the circuit of the fort, standing there holding their rifles and staring now with terror while the pistols were chopping away great chunks of their faces and bodies and uniforms. Jonathan was standing behind them still staring at the rebels and looking at their brown and grey uniforms and the yellow collars and cuffs and the wide-brimmed hats with the twigs and feathers stuck in them, and at the rebel officers with the yellow facings on their uniforms and their collars with the rank-bars. All of them were excited and even scared but all of them had thin smiles on their faces, firing into the wavering moaning and terrified line of the Negroes, standing in the mud of the parade and being blown apart. Jonathan had never seen the effect of heavy pistol balls up close; the bullets chewed and tore and hacked away at the Negro bodies all along the line. There were bits and pieces of flesh and cloth still burning from the powder which were kicked and flung back about his feet as he stood behind them. He looked at the Negroes in this moment which was somehow ripped out of context from the rest of the world and they were trying to fire their rifles or standing with their mouths open or huddling and screaming behind raised, pink palms, and the rebels were shooting them all down. The bullets were slapping amid them and Jonathan could hear the sounds and he could hear the Negroes screaming and moaning and he saw some of them throw down

The Battle of Fort Pillow *423*

their rifles, lift them and actually throw them down, and step forward with their hands clasped. He saw one rebel look down at the Negro as he came toward him hands clasped and the rebel put his pistol to the man's forehead and fired at a range so close it spattered blood all over his grey sleeve.

There was a second line of rebels on the walls and Jonathan, feeling the shift and the terror in the Negroes and hearing the smothering roar of the rebels' carbines and rifles along the wall, stumbled backwards himself. He saw Gaylord take a step behind the line of the Negroes and then pitch down into the dirt holding his ankle, his face twisted in clear, white-skinned lines of pain, and then he heard Bradford yelling, "Boys, save your lives!" Bischoff grabbed Bradford by the front of his coat and yelled, "We kin hold 'em!" and Bradford clubbed Bischoff away with his fist. "Run, run, save your lives! Git below the bluff!"

Everything dissolved. Jonathan had his sword out and was stepping forward, prompted by something he was hardly aware of in the screaming and the roaring of the guns. But then the press of the Negroes was upon him and there was black, kinky hair in his face and blue, thrusting shoulders in his belly and leather straps and rifles and terrified, blind faces and the Negroes and some of the whites were breaking behind Bradford, breaking and running in blind, complete and shrieking terror. They ran and Seabury was jostled and kicked once to his knees and then picked up. He stumbled with the rest of them in a blind wave for the bluff, the Negroes pressing their hands into each other's backs and shoulder to shoulder running and stumbling and tripping over each other, their eyes rolling up to the sky or looking down at the ground or squeezed shut. Everything was wild yelling and terror, "Run run run git away git git," and the hoarse roar like the surf of the rebels' revolvers and guns behind them and among their bodies like rain came the "pock! pock!" sounds of the balls and the buckshot tearing into the flesh. Negroes sank in pools of blood, their faces screaming and trying to get clawing hands on the sudden burning wound. Others toppled and tripped over them and before they could get up the balls chopped into them. They ran crazed in a tangle of bodies and blue cloth and sweat and blood through the tents, stumbling and tripping and packing together amid the sudden complex web of tents and poles and cords and straps. Jonathan slipped again amid the tents trying somehow to get control of his body. His knee hit a tent pole and he fell into the roof of the tent and it collapsed and more Negroes fell on him, so as he turned his head to look up everything went into a plunging dark mass of bodies and yelling and wetness and stench on top of him. He struggled for a moment, drowning in a pile of wool and tent cloth and the strong, acrid smell of sweat and urine, and he kicked from sheer terror, striking out at the flesh and clawing with his hands. Finally the flesh was giving above, lifting and giving except for one man between his legs and in terror he kept clawing at that man over and over and kicking at him with his heels until suddenly he could see and breathe again and he looked down and the man was dead, a very young Negro with a bullet hole in his temple and Jonathan's claw marks all over his face, blue against the yellow skin.

Then Jonathan was clawing up and he looked and there was only a running and sinking and falling fringe of Negroes between him and the rebels. The rebels were walking in a packed line with their revolvers firing constantly, just walking next to each other through the sweetish, moist smoke of their last shot and cocking the revolvers and firing again. The Negroes right in front of them sank clawing at the holes in their backs and tried to turn and the rebels, even while they lifted their empty hands, shot them down. Jonathan dodged between the tents and dropped his sword and ran and ran and then the bluff dropped between his feet. With the rest of Bradford's men he tumbled over the bluff with his stomach lurching in sudden terror and his feet kicking, trying to find the ground. Then running down and down and down and down, past the sinks and the paths and the shanties and the logs and the wounded and crawling and dying men, down the bluff with his feet never quite catching up with his falling. Bradford's men spilled on all sides of him over the bluff like sheep, bundles of woolen clothing and sweat and leather and vast terror and drunkenness, all of them piling over the bluff so fast they tripped and plummeted and fell, and all that could ran hard to the left. They spilled over the bluff and bolted to the left, running along the hillside with difficulty, swinging their arms for balance and some of them were shoved aside and pitched down farther tearing their flesh against briars and small scrub trees. They all ran through the dust and the mud and the smoke from burning huts along the bluff with the sun cartwheeling over them.

The Negroes were packed together tighter and tighter and they had no courage left. This was the white man's world and the white man's sky and the white man's sun above them and the white man was killing them all. This was Tennessee where they died and in the past had been and now were being killed in blubbering, whimpering masses. They ran and ran, screaming or sobbing or silent, some of them vomiting and all of them packed together and fleeing along the hillside and running down the bluff trying to get out from under the spiraling falling sky and the white man's bullets which lashed their communal flesh and, hit or not, they all felt the impact and the sting and the print of death upon the black flesh. Just like drinking and yelling at the rebels back along the walls, this too was part of it, was part of what had been instilled and inherited in them and they knew it would come and here it was and they pelted in terror over the bluff, through the briars and down the clay-slick ground, blindly, trying to hide from the white man who hovered over them, lunging, who killed them at his own will and with his own malevolent caprice; he brought death down on them, gave them death despite the hundreds of human dreams and emotions and desires and fears invested in the running mob of men, stampeding down the bluff in the Tennessee afternoon. Hunten the nigger down, hunten him down and killen him and watchen his blood flow and his flesh break and burst, Negroes in the tight mass screaming hysterically along with the rebels, "Die nigger! die!" They pelted and stumbled blindly, instinctively down the river bank along the slanting bluff, and then the earth rose up and smashed them in the face.

The earth in the form of Captain Anderson and his men, who had seen the mob of men come hurtling out of the fort and over the bluff, running down toward them with their rifles and with the flag still flying on the pole up there. A few of Anderson's men were startled into fear, we gon be run over by the niggers; but most of them were only grinning and looking up at the flag and thinking, that is reason ample enough, that is excuse. They were invisible to the Negroes, the two-hundred rebels in their jerseys and clay-brown jackets standing in the open, holding up their Enfields ready to volley, bending their thin, corded bodies around their rifle stocks and watching the Negroes pelt toward them, close enough now to see the spittle on their lips and their wild eyes and the government "US" on their breastplates, and terror as perceptible in the air above them as the gunsmoke. Then the two-hundred rebels packed in a double line from the rifle pit to the edge of the water fired the buck and ball into their faces.

It seemed to them the earth itself had come up, the earth that had always been the white man's itself flew into their faces and chests and forearms and genitals. The volley was hot and blinding and stinking; they stood frozen, blinking into the banked powder smoke, dots of burning powder on their uniforms, and then the live ones who could turned and ran in double terror, and almost half sank dead and dazed and wounded and stunned in bleeding heaps, sprawled across each other in the scrub growth and the oak and fern and rock, lying wounded and squirming with the thorns and briars digging even more into the blue-torn and bleeding flesh; face down and thick lips still biting the earth.

When the wall of smoke was blown away in front of the rebels, there was only one Negro still standing amid the squirming and dying piles at their feet. A corporal stood in front of them looking at his belly, which was torn wide open, and shaking his head, putting his fingers up against his kinky head in parody of every puzzled minstrel-show Negro, his mouth moving in surprise and his eyes blank with puzzling and his fingers moving the kinky hair. And then he toppled forward when the sudden shock of the pain tore into him, he toppled forward and began to sob and scream and twitch and thrash, arching his body off of the ground and yelling until a rebel lieutenant with tears, real tears, in his eyes stepped forward and shot him deftly, right under the ear.

After Anderson's fusillade some of the Negroes pelted the other way, upriver, ran with their tongues hanging out and almost collapsing, stumbling and grabbing for each other and falling over the logs and bodies and second-growth trees. But they reached the upper edge of the bluff in scatterings only to find Barteau and his men, still with the federal flag flying on the bluff above, coming out of their holes and confronted with the twos and threes and half-dozens of the Negroes, who did not yet know they were trapped and were still panting in the rising dust toward what they thought was safety. Barteau's men shot them down as they ran toward the rebel lines, even the ones that were unarmed and screaming for surrender and waving the white handkerchiefs, because they were tangled and mixed with the ones firing and still desperate. But after a ten-minute hysteria centered around the northern end of the bluff, the Negroes quit and abandoned themselves.

There were rebels above on the bluff firing steadily, no longer with revolvers but with rifles and carbines now, rebels vaguely seen through the thin smoke of the rifle-fire but picking out their targets and yelling, "Yaaahooo," and shooting down the Negroes under the bluff.

The Tennesseans were hiding themselves under the logs and even under bodies, or were cached in small groups in every ditch and hole and sink on the face of the bluff. They hung into the holes face down and huddled their bodies against the earth while the bullets spit and wheeeed around them, pressed together and moaning but not running. They were waiting, safe and waiting for the killing to be over. When the Negroes came looking for holes and holding their bleeding heads and hands, the Tennesseans kicked at them viciously and drove them out. Jonathan had been deposited at the foot of the bluff by the first panic; he could see the white troopers under the growth of weeds and in the tangle of drift wood in the river, clinging and hanging with one arm and just their heads out of water, and keeping hidden.

But the Negroes, crazed by the liquor and fear, were

wandering now or even staggering up the slope, snuffling through their lips and holding on to the trees for support. They climbed up the slope, waving their white handkerchiefs and rags and some even still carrying their rifles, and they were all begging for surrender. Not speaking the words but moaning through their lips and holding their hands palm up. The rebels grinned along the top of the bluff and closed in from either side, shooting through the palms and into the faces, and when the Negroes, staggering and holding their heads down, were close to them, beating them to the ground with musket butts.

It was incredibly tangled, sodden. Jonathan, with the pain in his legs and belly from smashing into brush and trees on the wild run downhill, catching his breath with strong gulps that lifted his whole frame, gulped and shook his head saying, "No, no, don't do that, no." Talking not to the rebels but to the Negroes, the ones down around the water's edge who with their eyes lighted into an animal cunning were still loading and shooting the rifles, the big government issue Springfields which almost all of them had carried over the bluff as Bradford had told them to, and which they still carried, crazed and blind, even while they were trying to surrender. The ones down around the water stood in tight groups looking up the bluff and loading the rifles. They were barely strong enough with their wounds and their exhaustion and panic to lift the heavy, long rifles but they pointed them vaguely up the bluff and fired anyhow, laboriously, painfully. And the rebel minie ball and buck whistled down the slope and chopped them backwards into the water or knocked their jaws off or tore their wrists into loose rags of fresh and smashed bone. And Jonathan thought, no, no. "No, no, this is all wrong. Do not fire, do not fire back." The poor dumb fools.

He walked among them and for a hideous moment everyone of them he touched and dragged the rifle away from was hit and died: a small boy in the uniform of the Second giving up his rifle with tears all over his face and then hit straight in the heart and dying, and a bigger man with enormous lips and wounded already letting Jonathan take the rifle and then doubling over and dying in lurches and twistings at his feet, and then a corporal of Jonathan's own company dying with a minie ball through his skull. But then he was hacking at the others and sobbing too, with them, sobbing and looking around, and there were no other whites, there was only him and these hysterical poor men lost under the Tennessee sky and dying and no one telling them what to do, firing their rifles hopelessly or shaking and crying in their fear and exhaustion or running and trying to get to the rebels for mercy and not even knowing enough to drop their rifles.

He looked around him and the sunlight was upon them all, upon them standing in the new green foliage of the river bank, the ferns and the small oak trees and the yellow and brown vines, standing there under a deep and beautiful sky and around them the rebel bullets still kicking white out of a dull slate river. The Negroes stumbled and cried and were killed, and no one, no one at all of all their officers was among them except Seabury and Hunter. Hunter was already up to his waist in the river among them trying to save some of the wounded from drowning. And Jonathan, who was trying to make them quit firing and to huddle down, making them kneel in the water like the whites with the thought that came only from instinct, the killing will not last long, the bloodletting will be over and then if they will just kneel here they will be allowed to live; knowing this because he was white and knew the exhaustion that would come to the other white men on top of the bluff firing and expending energy and, more important than that, will power in killing until the glutting of it would flood over them and they would stop because of a leaden exhaustion. He was certain of this as he made them stop firing and crushed them under him into the water and forced them with his hands pressing their sides and knees to kneel there in a small, cut place on the bank, grabbing and tackling them one after the other. Not paying any attention at all to the whispering and snarling bullets thrashing the water and making the vines writhe and hitting the flesh all around him. Just getting to one after the other of them and knocking the rifle out of their hands and forcing them with his own palms to kneel. Saying over and over, "Just keep down. Just keep down for a time. Just keep down," and grabbing the wounded, his own hands getting more and more discolored from their blood, coughing with his own sobs from exhaustion and the impossibility of sheltering them all and from the exasperation, why don't they see, why do they wander up the bluff, why don't they see?

But he knew why they did not see (sensations and fears and perceptions darted through his brain faster than ever in his life, but his lips kept forming the words, over and over, just keep down, just keep down for a while). All of their reasoning is gone. It is the color of their flesh. The white men can hide, they can mingle, they are still crouched and cunning and will survive. They will drift away and blend. But these men cannot change the color of their flesh, it indicts them and dooms them.

His task was endless. The bank was thick, clustered with the Negro soldiers, sobbing, wounded, their eyes glazed. They tried to climb up the bluff, pleading, and they tried to escape into the river. Jonathan stumbled into the water, splashed back along the bank, pulling at them, pushing them down into the shelter of the stumps and brush and earth. His boots chewed at the ground and it slipped and spilled him over and over into the river.

The Negroes seemed caught up, in some part of an inexorable ritual. A fulfilment, a completion; I alone am not part of this. (Why am I here? Images and patterns and sensations of his youth and his life and the North came to him randomly, all clear and clean as porcelain against the heat and tangle and panic: gaslights and pipes and Greek, the crimped days of spring and the smell of lavender and starched white collars. . . . What led me here?) He knew that all of the mercy and all of the compassion in the world was within himself. He was dazed with exhaustion and death, and he seemed to crawl and plead along the face of time. The rebel fire slanted down from his left, a part of the afternoon, and the world was a hollowed cone spiraling up the bluff where the heat and noise of their guns seemed sun-like and eternal, could not be looked at.

He scrambled out of the river, away from a dead man whose blood was staining the steel-grey water. He surged to his knees, out of the water, and scrambled to the side of a wounded soldier who was trying to climb up toward the rebels with his Springfield still in his hand. When Jonathan touched him, the young Negro stared at him with fear-blinded eyes, and tried to pull away. His eyes rolled in pain and fear, and he was afraid of everything he saw; the earth and sky and river were his enemies. "Hide yourself, hide yourself!" (But he cannot, he is black.) "Lie down, man!" Jonathan did not know whether his voice was audible, he seemed to have to push the words at the man. Then someone kicked him in the side and he looked to see who and saw he was wounded. He rose, with one hand kept gently on the shoulder of the Negro boy, who was sobbing and calming down under the soft white flesh laid against him where the metal had torn it. Jonathan probed his own wound, and saw that he had been shot in the side, and wondered, how serious is it? I would have thought it would hurt more. And then another ball hissed close to the Negro. It laid open a green vine near his face. Jonathan looked up into the sunlight and the smoke haze. The rebels were coming down the slope now, still firing and closing in on the Negroes from both sides. He saw the man shooting at him, a very young rebel with a squirrel's tail in the side of his cap, loading his rifle, his face pinched across the bridge of the nose with hatred. Jonathan watched the buttons bobbing as he worked to load the rifle and then he was aiming again, aiming at the Negro. He fired from twenty paces, balancing on a fallen log, and he missed and he cursed and began to load again, shouting at Jonathan, "Hey ol' white man! Hey ah don't want you! Ah want that nigger! Hey shove aside!"

Jonathan thought, where is my pistol, and he looked down and was shocked at how filthy his uniform was, how dirty it was. His belt was ripped off. He did not have his gun and he thought, I would not have used it anyhow. I am too tired now for that sort of thing. I have been dragging at these Negroes all afternoon and now I am too tired. He looked up and the boy was jerking the gun to his shoulder and he thought, ah yes, ah yes I see. He moved his body forward across the Negro who was beginning to thrash again, and then the rebel shot him and he felt the bullet and he thought, so this is what it is like to die, and, I have no regrets. I have always thought I would have re-

432   *The Falling Hills*

grets, at least a last-second twinge, but I have none. Even as he felt the electric shock and the sense of himself at the center of a whitish explosion and the quick spurt of pain, there was a picture of his house in the summer, with the bay windows and bees buzzing among the boxwoods around the small windows and the sunlight drifting through the tinted-green small panes, and then Lieutenant Jonathan Seabury was dead.

10

HAMILTON LEROY ACOX HAD GONE ACROSS THE WALL IN THE FIRST wave and now stood atop the bluff with his right sleeve covered with blood, and his sword blood-spattered as well and dangling from his hand: the crust and sheen of the still-wet blood covered his glove and the hilt of the sword, and the sword seemed an extension of his arm. He was watching the target-practice his company was making upon the Negroes, the ones coming up the almost vertical slope at his feet with their hands raised and fluttering bits of handkerchief and rag in front of them, and getting shot down by his men. He felt satiated and weary and disillusioned all at the same time. The Negroes were being killed right in front of him in the dazzling, rich April sunlight, against the background of the slate-grey river and the thick new green. Powder smoke clung web-like between the saplings and bushes of the bank. The Negroes were being shot down and all around him they were being dragged out of the tents, even the wounded, and being beaten and shot dead. He could hear them moaning behind him but he was suddenly weary and it was not even quick, much less clean.

He had thought, in the instant of pushing himself across the earth wall and into the fort, at last, at last we are getting to the underbelly and the killing. The fort had stood above them, on the slight bluff, all day; the long morning of skirmishing and fighting had been like fighting a man and hitting his elbows and his back and bony forearm, and now at last sinking the fist into his underbelly. And as he pushed over the wall and the earth cartwheeled he had thought it would be fast and clean. But of course it was neither.

They had lost one man all day, Van Nest, killed by a river-boat shell at a twinkling creekbed which suddenly turned into steam and noise and confusion, leaving him face down in the subsiding water. But Acox had lost no one else; he had worked the company up the slope, from hole to hole, painstaking, cautious, experienced. He had put his hard-earned lessons to use, and his instinct, and once he had carefully avoided a slight ravine which he suspected was exposed to the river and right after they slid by it a Yankee shell clawed it up like a furious rooting animal. They completed the tactical rituals and patterns, crawling, lunging, advancing in stages, bodies slanting with exertion; they had waited with their faces pressed into the roots and twigs and ferns while companies moved past them or the line was straightened.

Until at last, after the Negro obscenities during the truce when they had become once more hungry, not just to bust the fort, but to kill. During the truce they had been close enough to count the buttons on the Negroes' blouses, and read the brass numerals on their caps. Then they rushed the fort, and plunged into the ditch; then up and flattened against the face of the fort, panting, standing on the narrow path between the wall and the ditch. They had waited while over them like fierce bees their sharpshooters put the lead and the balls into the Yankees. Then they had wrestled themselves up the wall and they were on top of it and then, still feeling the hands pushing them on the rump to get them onto the wall, they had been leaning over the six feet of earth and getting their revolvers into the faces of the Negroes and whites. Then Acox had exulted. They let out a yell, the Negroes standing there dumbly and with their faces crowded with fear while they began to blow them apart.

Acox had thought it was going to be swift and clean, the swift lancing of the boil; but it had become almost in that instant a drunken sort of bloodletting. They had stood on the wall or the firestep and started killing the Negroes, and it grew in them because it was so bloody and so easy. Acox thought, we got drunk on the blood, like hunting dogs.

They had stood and fired and fired as fast as they could pull and draw back the hammer and pull again and then fish out the next big Navy six and draw back the hammer and pull. They could see the impact of the big slugs against the bewildered, terrified wall of Negroes in front of them. It was that easy, Acox thought, and there was not even any danger, we just stood there in front of the Negroes watching the bullets chop them down. The Negroes had stood there cringing behind their palms against the shock, still holding their rifles; above them in the air was a continual pitched mass of flakes of cloth and flesh kicked off them. Even while the wall of Negroes had been breaking the air was full of those flakes, like ashes swirling from a burning house.

It was such a sense of power. Acox had never before seen the power which he wielded, which wielded itself; nor had the others. They killed with incredible, detached fury, stunned, awed, infused by their power. The Negroes had broken and run, and the killing of them had been so easy. Just find one and look at him and get the revolver down and he is dead and then find another. Every time you found one, you killed him without thought, without pause, instinctively. It was not like killing white men when you saw their faces and you stopped after they broke and looked after their wounded. The Negroes' faces mirrored the horror, as did the faces of the white soldiers he had fought; but the mirror was dark, distorted, grotesque. The Negro faces were different and were not only drunk but had an expression you never saw on the white faces, an expression of complete and whining terror which caused the contempt to kick up alongside the hatred, which seemed to confirm the hatred. Yelling, they had clubbed down the sinking, pleading wounded.

The power and hatred and contempt surged over them, like their yell. The Negroes in front of them packed into the aisles between the tents and fell in knots over the ropes. Acox had emptied his first revolver in the plunge across the wall, and he emptied his second into a thrashing pile caught in the web of tents and ropes; he watched his bullets knock the feet out from under them, but he had not killed all of them when his gun was empty. That had annoyed him, pure, lucid annoyance, so he drew the big cavalry saber and suddenly it had not been too heavy for him. He strode toward the tangle sensing only that he must complete this, feeling himself lifted and coursed by his power and the annoyance that his gun had not killed all of them. He had thrown all of his weight behind the saber and kicked right in among them, right among that animal-like fear that was so different from the white fear he had seen for three years. He was cracking the big saber down, smashing it down into the faces and the heads, right through the raised fingers and slicing the raised palms in half and chopping through to the heads and faces; he was in a frenzy just to complete this, to kill every one of them and then get on. Their blood splashed up on his arm, over the gold braid on the grey sleeve and splattering over his gauntlet and even into his beard and his face as he swung the saber and burst the skulls and flesh and teeth and hands and chests, spilling them into the dirt and sand. Then he was tracking them and hacking down at the crawling wounded and ripping the tents off to find the huddling ones, the wounded and even the dying, swinging and swinging and crying even, until his arm had ached so much and the sleeve was so stiff with gore and blood that he woke up.

He woke up beating at a Negro that somehow never caught the edge of the sword. He had beaten the brown skin purple all over, but the man would not die, and while he was sobbing and cutting, it came to him, the weight of the sword and the wetness over his sleeve and his face, and he stopped. He stopped and straightened. Orrison, standing beside him, turned from shooting the Negroes down the bluff and put the muzzle of his carbine against the squirming and now blinded Negro and shot him dead. Orrison nodded as if to say "you're welcome" at Acox and loaded the carbine, squinting again at the Negroes down the bluff.

Standing there feeling the blood and his weariness, listening now to the screams and the yells from down the bluff, Acox felt a great horror and a great guilt. What have I done to these? But then he looked around guiltily and everyone was doing the same thing, men still going through the tents and killing the wounded Negroes on the ground and a few men standing back frowning but doing nothing more. Then he looked down and some of the Negroes by the water were still firing up, he could see them through the drifting powder smoke, still loading and firing and waving their guns, and he thought, thank God, thank God they were still trying to fight. There was sudden expiation. They were still fighting.

He was standing just behind the line of rebels along the river bluff; men from his company were packed in with men from all of the other commands that had swarmed across the bluff. They were all reloading their weapons with frenzied movements, forcing the cartridges into the chambers, swearing, glancing back down the slope through the shifting curtains of powder smoke. The noise of firing, from down the bluff and behind him on the parade, did not let up. The men all around Acox suddenly stiffened and grinned with expectation and cunning. A line of Negroes, herded and disarmed by Captain Anderson, was making its way toward the top of the bluff, just now visible, twenty yards below them and climbing painfully through the smoke. Their hands were raised palm out, as if they were trying to ward off rain. Individual shots still pocked into them but most of the rebels waited in masks of glee and hatred, their mouths frozen in calculating, spit-flecked smiles. When Acox looked among them, he felt embarrassed, as though he were intruding on intensely private moments in all their lives. The Negroes seemed to rise up the bluff in painstaking silence, afraid to look up at the line of rebels. Their knees rose and fell, their eyes rolled from side to side: their faces he could see were wet with vomit and blood and tears, and they held bandages and fluttering bits of soiled white rag over their heads. They were without guile or reason. Acox watched one of them in shirt sleeves, the side of his face mangled, as he slipped, fell, rose wearily and climbed on towards them; Acox felt the momentary urge to encourage him, as you encourage any man who visibly, painfully, struggles against the steepness of a slope.

Then the rebels to each side of Acox began to shoot the Negroes down, with sharp accuracy and humor. Fire lowered his pistol deliberately, and knocked down the Negro in shirt sleeves. Acox did not notice the new wall of roaring gunfire; the man seemed to fall silently, and topple beneath the level of the brush and green scrub. The line of Negroes paused, as the smoke blotted them in grey and brown. They stood terrified, falling, and then began to stumble back down the bluff, the men still carefully, slowly, picking their way. Most of them were dead or dying in front of the line of rebels. Some of the soldiers leaped forward with their bowie knives and began to hack at the Negro wounded who still moaned and crawled. And down the slope, Anderson was painstakingly, compassionately disarming another mob, lining them up, sending them up the slope where he thought, masked as they were by smoke and the volleying rifle-fire, they were being taken to safety.

Acox knew that they were wrong to shoot the ones that had surrendered. But it seemed a part of the afternoon, an extension of his own surging blood-lusts. He had no thought of trying to stop them; they crumpled up another line of Negroes, this one smaller than the one before. Perhaps I should stop this? Or withdraw my own men?

But he felt very tired. His arm ached and he was sick at his stomach and his legs quivered and braced. He leaned on the sword and watched. The rebels began to drift apart along the bluff, after the last line of Negroes had been shot down. Smoke still hung and gun-fire rattled and broke; shadows of smoke moved across the face of the sun. Some of the rebels, satiated, were beginning to wave to the huddling Negroes still alive on the face of the bluff, come on, come on in. But the caprice of the moment shifted and stung: Acox saw three Negroes rise from behind a log and move uncertainly toward the rebel line, and then Johnny Tell stood up with a pistol he had just finished re-loading, and shot each one of them, drawing a bead and even tracking the third who broke and ran down the hill and drop-ping him with a very good pistol shot. Acox's own men, turning away from the bluff and holstering or slinging their guns, turned back; " 'Y God that Johnny is a tiger, ain't he? Got yo' share, Johnny boy?" They grinned: he was the pet of the com-pany.

Then Clark, with his face smeared with dirt and powder smoke, was right in front of Acox. What does he want, why is he yelling in my face? Clark kept saying, "Captain, Captain, stop this! Stop this killen!" He pointed back down the bluff where groups of the rebels, some from Acox's own company, were still prodding among the dead and bleeding Negroes and killing the live ones, going down the hillside getting the whites out of their holes, killing some of them, but shooting all the Negroes. As they watched, Orrison and three other men dragged a wounded Negro from behind a pile of ammunition boxes and bayoneted him and laughed as he twisted around the steel shaft. Clark's face twisted in horror. "Stop 'em, Captain, make 'em stop!"

Acox looked at Clark, and all he wanted to do was sit down. He smiled weakly and said, "It is Forrest's orders that we kill them all," and then turned and sat on a straw pallet near the edge of the bluff, wondering why he had said that and then thinking, well, I suppose because it might as well have been true. We killed them as if it had. Acox sat and watched them chase the Negroes down, and Clark stood near him looking down the slope in horror. Acox noticed that every time someone fired a gun in the haze he flinched and his face jerked.

Acox looked out into the river. There were bodies floating there, floating and packed all along the edge, and some of the rebels were standing along the edges of the river firing at the Negroes still out in the water. The bodies were blue-black humps, rocking in the wash of the river. The rebels prodded them and walked along the shore loading their rifles and laughing to each other and firing at the swimming, wading Negroes, the bullets kicking up high sprays of water around them. In the hot sunlight and the fresh smells of the river and the April afternoon, it looked like the mud from the bluff was running into the river. The water was discolored and filmy and red, all among the rocking bodies where the leather straps still gleamed wetly across the soaked wool.

The organized killing had stopped, the rebels taking prisoners in some places now and turning to loot or wander around the fort. But down the bluff they were still shooting the Negroes, and there was still firing down in the ravines or in the ditches, groups of privates walking together and shooting the Negroes out of hand. It was all caprice, and chance; Acox watched as the prowling boys with the jay feathers in their hatbands walked up and down and jabbered to each other when they found a live Negro and he could see the upraised black hand, and then the gun firing down. Some of the officers within the fort itself were protecting the wounded and captured whites and Negroes; one of the white men asked for water and a rebel handed him a canteen. But none of the officers moved to stop the slaughter down in the ravines, or along the bluff. They were satiated, filled, with death, but with exhaustion and indifference as well.

For Acox, the hatred and fury of it had washed out in that moment he had stood and realized that it would not be quick or clean. His shoulder ached. There were still a lot of wounded men in the fort, white men who had not been allowed to surrender next to the wall, and Negroes who had been shot down in the slaughter. They lay under logs, moving feebly and moaning and trying to keep quiet. Acox had not noticed them before, but now he looked and they were everywhere around him, most of them with hideous head wounds, bullet and sword holes in heads and faces, bleeding and the flesh shiny and raised around the wound. Their terror was palpable and urgent; Acox was so exhausted he could not understand their urgency, but they were too scared to even ask for water. Most of the Negroes who had been killed or wounded down the bluff had fallen below the level of the second growth and the scrub, and it was odd, he thought, looking down and seeing only an elbow or a knee where they had shot so many of them.

Someone had taken down the flag and raised a Confederate flag. Forrest, wearing the grey cloak, rode over the wall and into the fort and ordered the firing to stop and the officers to re-assemble their commands. The moment of fury was over and past, and Acox got to his feet and went to find Russell while Bowles and Clark, who was white-faced and silent, gathered the company. There were still shots out in the underbrush and down on the bluff, but no one jerked now. They were filled with death and slaughter, and they did not care any more. It had all been let out of them, and now the Negroes were dead by the dozens on the parade and all along the bluff and out in the river.

It was an hour and more after the fort had fallen. The energy and drive of the men was ebbing, the sense of urgency and power was fading from them. They had been sustained all through the orgy of blood and violence and extreme exertion, through the concentration needed to wield and load and swing their weapons, by a furious and pounding drive that hit most of them in their bellies and throats; the presence of every emotion from fear to lust to anger and even to love; they could have gone on fighting a regular battle of maneuver and skill and response all day—indeed, at Okolona, they had—but from this, their minds and nerves were quickly worn out. They had been driven like soulless bodies in uniform, plunging into the slaughter, caught up with power and urgency and hatred and contempt and filled with a roaring surge like the hollow, sheeting roar above a forest fire. The pace did not come from them or from the pattern of their lives in the army; they were mentally exhausted. They slumped and wiped sleeves across their foreheads and pulled their fingers across their lips, and jiggled their canteens for water. They wandered, or looted, or watched idly while a few of the men under Forrest's eye worked the captured artillery pieces on the gunboat until it finally left.

Some of them looked for whiskey or beer; Bell had put guards over the kegs of beer but they winked at the men they knew and they filled up their canteens. Others wandered down into the town, but the stores had already been looted, the liquor and clothes and leather and weapons had all been taken, mostly by the Texas Rangers who had occupied them during the fight, and had been more interested in looting than in slaughtering the Negroes. Some of the rebels made the white Tennesseans show them through the sutlers' stores, but the only things left to take were shabby clothes, paper, quills.

Out in the river, Negroes were still drowning. The ones left alive in the water were just too tired to even be afraid any longer, mouths tasting the blood in the water, their arms weary and chests aching and their clothes pulling them under. Most of them did not have the energy to swim back; the mad rush and the plunge downhill and the furious spate of fear had exhausted them at the same time it left them out in the cold, blood-salty, steel-grey water, and they drowned with the water closing over them and pouring in through their mouths and nostrils.

I I

SOMEHOW THE GLORIOUS APRIL AFTERNOON WITH THE FLARING OF the sunlight had been the time for the killing and the slaughtering. Now that the sunlight was gone and the officers were there and everything was chill and soft, the air fresh and from the west now and full of sweetness and birdsong and there were even lightning bugs in the blue light; now that everything was murky, men spoke softly and laughed at each other's jokes and whistled "Lorena" to themselves and smoked pipes and cigars and stood in groups among the piled and mangled dead, listening to the rise and fall of each other's voices and glad there were no orders and no more massed firing.

Down in the ravines and along the bluff there were still the flat reports of revolvers, and the eighteen- and seventeen-year-old boys from the Mississippi battalions down there and some Tennesseans as well, wandering too by this time among the foliage with the garish feathers in their caps and trying out the new breechloading carbines on the wounded and the dying Negroes they found; standing a group of Negroes and whites up who had been hiding in an old shanty and making a military thing out of it all their own, laughing to each other and giving the orders like their officers and shooting the prisoners or not giving them a drink of water or cursing them and marching them around a while. But there were only a few of the rebel soldiers standing in the dusk and still firing their weapons into the Negroes, a few of the boys and some of the tight-faced men with the hate still burning in them walking around making the ferns rustle in their thirsty search for more Negroes to kill. Most of the Confederate troopers were in the fort in tight knots with

443

their officers, waiting for orders and just taking the air and silent and weary, and letting the air wash over them and remove the sweat from their arms and crotches and backs and straightening the uniforms. It was a time of softness and quiet and a few ebbing pistol shots from the growing darkness, somehow unrelated to the men congregating amid the piled dead in the fort.

Acox in the gathering darkness listened to the single shots while Tom Morse silently moved next to him, and looked down and realized he was carrying the cavalry saber, still holding on to it. It was heavy and very bulky, and the weight was not enough in the hilt for easy handling. He wondered vaguely why he had carried it. The thing was big enough, that was the reason. He looked at the long length of heavy plate metal which was now covered and flecked with blood and bits of white sticking in the blood and hairs, the blood thin and browned at some places and caked in others. So that is what they call gore. This ol' thing really does hit hard, though. It shears the flesh properly when it hits. I can see why Forrest carries one, but I reckon it is too much for me. My shoulder aches something fierce. He held the sword for a minute, made a motion to throw it down, held it and balanced it again, and finally tossed it away, near four sprawled Negro bodies with the sightless faces crossed by knees and thrown-out arms.

Morse coughed and was trying to draw his pipe. The men of their two companies were gathered around them, and Acox looked at them in the dark and realized he could recognize every man near them, looking at them in their faded grey jackets and waist-length coats, and feeling very happy and warm somehow that, wordlessly, they were clustering around himself and Morse. McCulloh was over at the other end of the fort, calling out his regimental officers and the interminable names of the Mississippi battalion commanders, and the detachments over there were falling in one by one and leaving the fort. Forrest, on horseback with his staff and his bodyguard, was leaning over talking to Bell and Russell and Wilson. We will get our orders in a minute. Hmmm. I am very tired. 'Twill not take long to fall asleep this even'. I must see that the cooks get some of the federal rations. We could use some good coffee and bacon and hardtack. He started to look for Tell and some of the other cooks but then Morse made another coughing sound and he realized he wanted to talk a while with him, so he asked, "Lose many men, Tom?"

"Naw." Morse was obviously grateful and smiling around his pipe. "Naw, we lost three all told. One kilt and two wounded. . . . Linn boy, you know him?"

"Tall, red-haired boy. . . ."

"Mmm. Got shot crossen the wall. Kilt dead before he hit the ground. Did yore comp'ny get hit bad?"

"No, we came through all right. We lost Van Nest going across the creek."

"Mmm. You know, I heard some of those Mississippi companies lost heavy, down thar in the huts. I heard some of 'em lost ten, twe've apiece."

"That right?" They both fell silent, looking out across the river, broad and white-looking in the darkness.

"Say," Morse said suddenly and grinned and patted him on the shoulder, "say, you best take it a bit easier next fight. . . ." He was grinning hugely, like a bear, at Acox, and Acox was suddenly afraid and sort of guilty and a twinge which he could not quite fathom made him shift. I know what he is going to say now. He shifted.

"What you mean?" He grinned back in the darkness, uncomfortably.

"I saw ye take that ol' sword and go right into a whole pack of 'em duren the fight. Scared me half to death, you goen alone right into 'em. I thought you were out of your mind, way you went after 'em."

Out of your mind. Acox snapped somehow and felt cruel.

" ' 'Em?' What do you mean ' 'em,' Tom?" Make him say it, make him say it.

"You know, the nigras." He said it and smiled and did not flinch at all. Then it did not seem so bad and Acox shook himself and grinned too. It did not seem too bad at all now. Yes, the Negroes. "Oh, I did get overwrought, I think. . . ."

"Overwrought!" Morse laughed hard and then shyly, suddenly afraid of making him mad, Acox noticed. "Well, I got to say next time you git overwrought, come on over to ol' D Comp'ny, I kin use a hellcat like you. You tore the hell out of 'em. I was afraid for you and next thing I notice I was afraid for the nigras!" He laughed again.

Acox smiled, and the two officers stood together now, and he took Morse's elbow and squeezed it. "Thanks for noticen, Tom. Thanks. I do appreciate it. If something ever happens 'twill do me good to know that you will notice. . . ."

Morse smiled and took the pipe out of his mouth, boyishly. He was very embarrassed. Acox was older than he was and he always looked up to Acox and was afraid Lee looked down on his Bible reading and so on. He was embarrassed and he blushed and was grateful for the darkness. Acox was the most popular and best-liked officer in the regiment. Everybody in the brigade knew and respected him, he was so quiet and so sincere and they all knew little Amanda, his wife, too and liked them both. Acox still had his hand on Morse's shoulder, but he was looking away now with his face sad. Morse cleared his throat a little, worried and still embarrassed, and Acox looked up again and smiled and took his hand away and turned a little and looked away again. Morse could see that he was looking at the piled and scattered dead Negroes and whites. They made sort of a carpet across the strewn sand and the mud and the earth of the fort, dark and featureless lumps now. Some of the bodies along the wall were beginning to swell and to stink, the ones that had been dead since early in the fighting.

Bell and Russell came over to them. They all four talked for a while, Bell saying "good job" over and over and Russell saying, "It's boys like this," and putting his hand on Morse and Acox, "boys like this who did it. They tore the Yankees up, 'tween 'em." And they all grinned and shuffled and then decided to move the men out of the fort. Each of the companies was told to detail two men to gather up the equipment in the fort and tend to the Yankee wounded and dead. Morse looked around. Acox said, "I will send Sergeant Clark," saying it immediately out of the remembrance, coming to him clearer than any others, of Clark standing there with his face streaked and broken and saying, "Captain, Captain, make them stop," over and over.

During the walk back down the hill, the men carrying their weapons loosely and still talking in small groups and everyone quiet and comfortably weary, Acox thought about Clark. It had shocked him and he suddenly knew that it had been nagging at him, Clark standing there. It was somehow as though no one else had seen him in that way. When he raised up from the killing and the hacking of that one Negro he had looked around and thought with such a flow of relief that no one was paying him mind and that they were still firing, the Negroes were, from down by the river. Well, they had noticed, and Morse had and so had Russell, noticed his fury and his anger. But what he had done, what they had seen him do, was tear into a still-fighting enemy. They called him a wildcat and he was proud of that, proud of it like he was proud of the stiffened, blood-soaked cloth of his right sleeve which was somehow like a badge, the sleeve feeling weighted and sheathed, and he felt proud of the gore on it. But Clark standing there blond and desperate and saying, "Make them stop, make them stop," was somehow penetrating. It was a moment that he wished had not been. He remembered then the talk on the ride and Clark alone of all of them saying, no, no he did not want to fight at Fort Pillow any more than they had to and he did not want to teach the Negroes a lesson. He remembered that and he thought, no, no he cannot hold that against me. He will put that together with this afternoon and he will think what is wrong. He cannot put those two things together. And after all, after all I was standing there only, I was not encouraging or still firing. I was just standing there. I was not stopping them but I was not still killing myself. I wish of course that I had not said 'twas Forrest's orders. I should not have said that. That is the only thing I am ashamed of, saying that it was Forrest's orders where it was not. That was not necessary and it sounded as though I were making an excuse for myself. I was, but I should not have been.

They got to the camp in the darkness and ate the captured

Yankee rations, the coffee tasting rich and good and the bacon sizzling and filling up their noses with the fat, thick smell. They ate wrapped in cloaks and blankets and everyone was talking to each other in the darkness, feeling very good and warm and filled now and tired. Acox finished eating, talking to Bowles and grinning and laughing for a time with the rest of the men, even talking to Orrison about farming for a while without getting angry at the man. He gathered his blankets around him and smelled the fires and the last of the food odors and the smell of the horses in the picket lines, and listened to some of the men telling the horseholders again about Cap'n Acox goen in like a ol' wildcat into them niggers. That was my error, telling him that Forrest ordered it. It made me sound guilty and indeed I did feel guilty in that instant of Clark standing there horrified and with the smears of earth and mud on his face. I did feel guilty and I will say it again, I did feel guilty then. It seemed good to say it, and he nodded for emphasis to himself in the darkness.

But that was in the moment. He got me at the moment I had turned away and seen how messy it all was and how drawn out, he got me when I was offended too and he stood for some part of me I reckon. Yes, he stood for something in me, that was in me even while I was fighting them. So that was why I felt guilty in that minute. And perhaps now. Perhaps now. We should not have killed them while they were coming up the bluff to surrender. The poor, drunk fools. We should not. But then the Yankees should not have plied the nigras with liquor, they should have known better than that. And yes, the Yankees should not have kept on fighting, they should have surrendered the fort. Yes. So the blood is really on their hands. They should not have let the nigras drink and then they should not have let them behave so during the truce. There are men in these brigades, especially the Mississippi ones, who cannot take that sort of thing and it enrages them. They should not, indeed, have started using the Negroes. I do hope that this will prove to the Yankee powers that be that the nigra straight from slavery is not a good warrior and cannot stand up to us. I hope this is lesson enough and the fault of arming them will not have to be shown by the blood of white women and children killed with the disruption of the order of things. That is what it stood for, the arming of the Negroes, and I hope that this lesson will be enough and that they will be disbanded. Yes. The cooler military minds on the other side must prevail and disband them. I hope we horrified them enough, the military men over there, so that they will see this and send the nigra regiments down, before the violence that will follow their freeing and their arming begins. It is better that the Northerner learn the lesson this way, on a purely military term of complete defeat, than that he learn it when the Negroes are emboldened enough to start their rampage of destruction and rapine.

Acox leaned back and looked up. The sky was lightened now and like washed silk, and the fragile and delicate spring buds on all of the tree branches were like gentle lacework against it. Black and grey and the palest of white. He sighed. There was an odor of pine needles close to the ground, and above that an elusive odor of springtime, of the trees and the moisture and the moving in the land, and Acox held the odors gently and did not breathe too hard because that would dissipate them. His flesh felt tired and comfortable and warm beneath the blankets, and the odors were so nostalgic and so filled with memories and with melancholia that he choked on them and tears came to his eyes. He rolled over on his belly and smelled the pine needles, closer to the ground, lost in a reverie not of memory but of the sensation of the whole pressure of his past and even of his heritage pressing upon him softly and nobly. This ability of the senses, he thought, this ability of the senses to trace and begin from the gentlest of odors or of colors and make perceptible a whole realm of memory and of sweetness, this is one of the things that makes life worthwhile.

He thought again about the fort. Well, Lord, I am sorry that I killed some of the wounded and that I did not try to stop some of the firing sooner. But thank You, dear God, thank You. You gave us, You gave me this victory, this battle. Thank You. I hope that what we have done is not hideous in Your sight but is acceptable. I swear this, dear God, that every day I shall attempt to remember and serve You. Perhaps, he thought, I should say

Thee. We had to have this, dear God, to continue our fighting, and to live even in this land. We had to have this day, this afternoon of blood. Thank You for giving it us.

The sense of the praying washed over him like the air. He smiled and did not think anything for long minutes. Then he thought, well, I do not feel guilty. And I am not fleeing from the sense of guilt. No. To be honest, there is an edge that guilt, a certain portion of guilt, gives to living, and I am searching for that. But I do not feel it. No. Not at all. Perhaps I should, I do not know. All that I do know is that I feel free now. We have destroyed something that I think is abominable, or was abominable. That fort stood for something and we destroyed it. It needed the destroying. . . . It stood for all of the things that would if they prospered and won and were imposed upon us, all of the things that would turn the South anarchist and bloody and dead, a land of weeping and fire and death in the night. And we exorcised the fort. I cannot feel the pity or the remorse or even the guilt. I am sorry that I did not stop the firing sooner but the price of that is small to pay for the utter destruction of the fort. I am more sorry that I did not tell the truth and that I said 'twas Forrest's orders. I am more sorry for that. For the nigras were drunk, and they would not have spared us had the positions been reversed. And I think because of what we did today the positions will never be reversed. No.

The thought of the utter and complete destruction of Fort Pillow was a good, warm thought, and it was at the base of his mind continually and it made him smile. He rolled the thought of the fort's destruction over, pictured the dead and sprawled bodies and the Negroes climbing the bank to surrender and the cannon being hauled out of the gunports. Somehow there was a pressure removed, 'tis like a man with a headache awaking and finding it no longer there. No. 'Tis more like a man with a throat sore with cold, the soreness that makes it an agony to swallow and to cough, and then awaking to find that soreness gone. When the throat feels somehow like silk and there is no pain. You did not notice the throat before the illness but now it feels good. That is how the elimination of the fort feels to me. And now, now I can begin trying to rebuild what has been shattered. I can attempt to establish a distance of culture once more between Amanda and the world and the demands of the world. Now that the threat has been removed.

Acox went to sleep hearing a bird singing in the darkness, and the flat gunshots down by the bluff did not bother him. He slept dreamlessly and deeply.

12

SUTTELL OF COURSE ESCAPED. WHEN THE REBELS CROSSED THE wall he dropped his rifle immediately and threw down the pistol in his belt and stepped back and under the firestep, huddling on his knees next to Corporal Dollins who was wounded in the shoulder. He could hear the footsteps on the wood above them and, looking up through the slats, could see the rebels coming over the wall and still shooting and the lines in their faces filled with blood and their cheeks white. The Negroes stood for a minute in the hail of fire and then collapsed and everyone was running for the bluff in a tangle of blue in the sunlight, and Suttell huddled under the firestep in the gummed spit and the mud and spilled percussion caps watching cat-eyed. 'Y God, got too much sense to get out there and git killed. Them ol' rebel boys they are comen, and I am goen to stay here and wait. He huddled. Dollins was moaning and his face was feverish, cut by the lines of sunlight through the slats. Hesh up, man, hesh up. Suttell knelt looking out at the parade. He could see the boots of the rebels who were firing their rifles into the running Negroes and whites. Then they ran after them, the whole fort filled with firing and screaming, and their boots kicked up water and jerked off disembodied.

Two more lines of rebels crossed the wall, their boots crashing on the boards of the firestep right above Suttell's head, shaking down powdery dirt and splinters as they jumped down. Quick groups of them clustered near his hiding place, around one of the beer kegs. He could see the beer splash over their boots and bare feet, as they dipped their canteens into it before running off toward the tents and the bluff. I want no truck with them, not for a time. I saw as soon as the rebels was in the ditch, we wuz done for. I got to wait here a while. He was trying to sense when it would be safest for him to come out from under the firestep. Suttell had agreed with Sergeant Stephens, right before the truce, that the best place to hide was beneath the firestep; they had known, instinctively, that the Negroes would not have the cunning to duck under the boards, and they had known too that the rebels would be after the Negroes first off. But Stephens had been shot right through his mouth by a rebel officer as they crossed the wall, and he now lay in his socks about three yards from Suttell; a rebel had paused interminably, tugging at Stephens' boots, while Suttell had pushed his mouth down against the earth in fear..

Dollins shoved and moaned, and began to babble. Suttell felt the pistol tucked away inside his blouse and thought, well, I can bust him side the haid and shet him up; but then he lapsed into silence. Suttell looked around the parade; the firestep was so low that all he could see were the boots and feet of all of the men between him and the tents. But he could see the rebels still hacking at the Negro wounded, on the parade and in the tent lines.

Suttell sensed that the rebels were mainly after the Negroes; the white officers and the Tennesseans were sometimes shot down, but sometimes they were disarmed and herded to one side. The rebels seemed to have tired of killing the white men, but they were still after the niggers. Still, hit won't do no harm to wait a spell. Groups of rebels still wandered around the horseshoe of earth, beating the Negroes with their rifle stocks, and sometimes shooting down the white officers as well. Suttell saw them pull Captain Carson away from the wall and say something to him, and him smile weakly and start to shake his head, and then one of the rebels shot him right through the chest, and the others put minie balls into him as he lay on the ground, flicking their big revolvers down toward his twitching body.

It was, Suttell sensed, a matter of luck whether the whites were being killed or not. Near him he saw a rebel with a silky beard under his chin shoot Sergeant Gwalteney through the head; and he saw a whole group of rebels shoot Ted Bradford off his platform, as he started to climb down to surrender. But ol' Leaming, he noticed, who had been crawling in a mindless circle of agony after a ball had carried almost halfway from his shoulder to his hip, ol' Leaming that Texas cap'n done helped away.

The waves of rebels had gone by quickly; the mean uns, Suttell thought, the mean uns and the ones without no stomach for the killen, are the ones lef' on the parade. Fear dazzled his eyes, flecked the air above him and the fetid smell of the ground; but his eyes still watched with cunning. He felt a bitter contempt for the white men he saw shot down, and envy for the ones who were being sheltered in groups of prisoners. He saw them take Pennell over toward a knot of prisoners, and he thought, thet ol' sombitch Pennell. And Billy Gaylord, him too. An' him a nigger officer. Well now. He hated Pennell and Gaylord. Individual shots pattered and rang around the parade but he could not tell what they meant. He flinched, and tried to guess, at each one. The niggers, he thought, now the niggers ain't got no sense ner no chaince; but I aim to keep low here a while.

But he sensed, too, that that was dangerous as well; he saw Dan Rankin crawl out from under a tent, right at the feet of a rebel who was watching the slaughter down the slope; and the man turned and shot him out of anger and surprise. Don't do, he thought, to surprise these rebs. Or to make 'em mad because they missed ye the first time.

His eyes still roamed, back and forth, watching, estimating; he knew that he had better try to get into one of the groups of prisoners soon, before some rebel came across him by chance. There was a group of rebels not far away that he figured were officers. Maybe they had enough; he sensed he had a better chance with officers. There were two big pairs of hip-boots, and smaller, fine-looking yellow and brown ones around them. Ain't no rebel soldier gonna have boots that good. He could see, too, a cluster of blue pants over to the left, blue pants spotted with mud and dirt and the knees flexing every so often. They done took those boys prisoners.

He thought. I got to git out of here and over there with

those other Tennessee boys they leaven alone. Caint see nothen here, and they likely to see me when they turn some of these bodies over to loot. He looked around. Well now, if I move out they like to shoot me right off. He studied Dollins, a big fleshy man with a wiry beard. Dollins's wounded shoulder was up and he could see the rent in the sleeve and the greasy wound underneath. I push ol' Dollins out yonder and let 'em git their fill of him; then come out if they don't shoot. He moved over through the dried white spittle and brown-stinking urine and percussion caps and put his hands on Dollins and began to move him. Dollins groaned and shrugged nervously and feverishly. God damn it, come on man. It was hard to get leverage under the firestep but he pushed and prodded and Dollins kept on moaning. The cloth was hot and sticky with sweat and blood and Suttell had to wipe his hands.

Finally Dollins moved enough and, half delirious, even pushed himself a bit, moving out from under the boards and into the streaming sunlight. The light dazzled Suttell and a rebel was saying something and then Suttell could hear the click of cocking pistols and he leaned back away from Dollins, back under the boards. He did not know what they were going to do; he stiffened with fear.

The shoes around the two pairs of hip-boots had moved back and were facing Dollins, half out from under the firestep. Then they were lowering their pistols and coming to help, and one of them knelt on the ground and looked under the step and saw Suttell crouching there and his eyes widened. He was a young man with wide brown eyes shadowed under a grey hat, and he motioned Suttell out, jerking his pistol barrel. Suttell crawled out and blinked helplessly into the sunlight and, squinting, held up his hands. They were all officers, standing in a knot keeping the men away from the liquor and not wanting to go to the bluff. One of the men in hip-boots was long-faced with a weary kind of smile and small-lidded eyes, flesh wrinkled and thick and brown, and he said, "Come on, boy. We won't hurt ye."

Suttell stood up grinning slightly, and looked around and wiped the palms of his hands on his hips. His jacket was unbuttoned and he looked very young and helpless with his blond hair in his face. The man who had told him that they would not hurt him was a major, or a captain—Suttell did not know which. There were three lieutenants, one of them in big boots, handsome except for a bulbous nose and a scar on his throat, and they all wore grey jackets and stand-up yellow collars. They looked at Suttell silently, while the lieutenant who had motioned him out tended to Dollins. The officers shifted against the sound of firing from the bluff; then the man with the long face said, "All right, boy, git over with the other prisoners."

Suttell nodded and walked over to the group he had seen; he passed two rebels who were bending over a pile of bodies going through the pockets, and they bared their teeth at him, out of stubble faces. The other prisoners stood frozen in fear with their eyes darting and their bellies pulled in. A young rebel with yellow teeth and a straw hat stood over them with a shotgun, standing on tiptoe to see what was happening over by the bluff. Suttell looked back over at the rebel officers. They were standing together talking, the major in hip-boots looking over at him and smiling.

The prisoners were all from the Thirteenth. Suttell knew a big sergeant named Craig, who was the first sergeant of A Company. They shifted every time the boy pointed the shotgun at them, and they were frowning and not talking. Rebels passing in groups rubbed their rifles and grinned, and the loyalists shifted from foot to foot and looked down at the ground. In front of them, at points on the parade ground, they could still see some of their own men being killed out of hand. The rebels who were not at the bluff seemed to have nothing to do; they roamed, went through the pockets of the dead, shot men out of hand. The knot of prisoners ached with fear.

Suttell was easier, now that he had gotten into the prisoners; but he was still wary. Thet ol' captain, he thought, meaning the major in hip-boots, thet ol' rebel captain he keeps on looken this way. I got to git with that man, er someone like him, if I want to git out of here.

A young rebel with a bluejay feather stuck in his kepi and big brown suspenders walked purposefully over toward the prisoners from the direction of the bluff. They all huddled and frowned, trying to make themselves smaller. That ol' boy looks mean, don't he? The rebel reached out toward Pennell, slowly, grinning with arrogance: Pennell shuddered, his hands raised and his belly sucked in. The Confederate reached out and took off the little box of his percussion caps and grinned almost conspiratorially and said, "I been killen niggers so fast I need some more caps, I run out." Pennell whimpered with relief; the others caught the shifted sense of companionship and began to breathe with a little more ease. Them niggers sure air taken hit, ain't they? 'Y God, they sure are. They don't fight wuth a damn. But the boy with the shotgun shifted his feet and looked at them, and they froze in fear again, like rabbits.

Then three Confederates came toward them, back from the fighting along the bluff and putting their pistols back into the holsters. The boy looked at them querulously. "Whut's goen on ovuh yonduh?" He spoke with a nasal whine.

A big rebel corporal with tarnished yellow stripes looked at the prisoners. "We're killen the niggers and the home-made Yankees faster'n you kin shake a stick. You got a good bunch here." He winked at them and Craig made a fluttering sound in the back of his throat. "This ol' battalion taken any prisoners I dint see it." He was sizing up the Tennesseans in front of him. They were shifting now and looking worried and some of them glanced at each other for the first time. Suttell stood slightly away from them, putting his palms down on the firestep. Don't let 'em kill me the first time, that ol' captain will step in an' stop 'em. The corporal reached out suddenly and grabbed Craig by the collar and Craig's face went white as a sheet. The corporal had big teeth and a big moustache and a stubble beard. "You got any greenbacks?" Craig shook his head desperately. "Naw?" He pulled out his revolver again, big and shining and he put it against Craig's chest. "You sure now?"

Craig nodded. The sweat was standing out all over his face. The boy began to whine, holding the shotgun, "Major Perry is over yonduh looken this away. He is looken." The corporal grinned in Craig's face and said, "I got me some private business with these Yankees. I don't think I got to hurt 'em any."

He shoved the pistol hard in Craig's chest and then shifted immediately to the next man. He went down the line and got in the greenbacks, the men that still had them handing the money over to the corporal. The rebels behind him, lean and tall and yellow-faced, were all grinning and snickering. Major Perry was leaning between the other officers and looking on with his face solemn.

Suttell suddenly remembered and felt, almost like a live thing, the revolver still in his blouse. Oh, my God. He find that he kill me. He fished in his pocket and didn't have any money. The corporal was closer to him now, at the man next to him, and shoving the pistol into his chest and the man was fumbling with a purse and then the corporal grabbed the whole purse, and Suttell felt the heavy weight of the gun and then the corporal was standing right in his face smelling of tobacco and sweat and saying, "You got some greenbacks too, sonny. Don't chee now?" Then Suttell's heart was pounding and he thought, Gawd, he is goen to shoot and everything was centered on the face of the man and his own flesh was quivering with fear, quivering, and he had never been that afraid in his life; his flesh actually shaking and then he urinated in his pants, feeling the hot, quick flow down his leg, his buttocks pressed against the wooden firestep, edging back from the man in terror and the man reaching forward with his eyes flat and light-blue and not grinning like his mouth. Then the rebel major was yelling, "Corporal, Corporal Beckwith! God damn it, Beckwith," and striding over with a snapping of the leather in his boots and his face set, saying, "You leave this boy alone, you hear? You leave all these men alone and git back to yo' company, you hear!" The flesh in the major's face was curled around his forehead in anger and fury. He was cold-faced and pointing back to the bluff; the corporal looked quickly at him coming closer and then looked back at Suttell, looked down at him and then shifted the revolver back into the palm of his hand and turned and said, "Yesseh." He slouched back to his company swearing down at the mud, and the rebel officer was standing by the boy with the shotgun and looking at him going, still with his face set and his mouth in a tight line.

The major turned away after a while and all of the prisoners were beginning to murmur and shift into the life they felt they had been given, shifting now and saying softly to Suttell as the major drifted away, "What you got, boy? Why dint he git your money too? You know somethen 'bout that reb officer?" The boy with the shotgun said, "Shet up, shet up," with his voice piping, but the men were gabbling with relief. Suttell felt weaker than ever in his life, weaker far than the time his mother had nursed him back into some semblance of health after the typhoid before he had to go out into the fields again. He breathed and his whole body eased down. He felt the stickiness itching along the side of his leg. Gawd. Gawd. And then his cat instinct came back and while the rest of the men murmured and talked and shifted and began to even reach for tobacco he thought, that ol' corpral ain't through. Naw he ain't.

He stared into the haze and the glare of the firing lines along the bluff and into the lines and triangles and ropes of the tents, and he saw the rebel. The man was there and his eyes met Suttell's like eyes hollowed out of the whole world, so quick was Suttell's instinct. He saw the man crouching in the corner of the tent and he ducked, ducking wildly and with all of his senses quivering again, while the other men unaware now and relaxing were moving together and reaching for tobacco and even smiling tentatively. He did not hear the bullet but by that time he was squarely behind the man nearest him, an old man with a grizzled grey head and clean-shaven, floppy skin. He heard the bullet hit the man right beside his own head, his ear practically pressed into the man's back and the bullet going thwack into the flesh, and he even heard the snap of a bone under it and the man pitching forward now into the muddy parade ground. Suttell went on his hands and knees, away from the sudden sunlight after the old man fell, into the shadow again behind Craig, and Craig's eyes were focusing and he was saying, "Whut's matter, Johnson?" and then he was hit in the belly and went down gagging. Suttell was crouching behind Craig who was on his elbows and knees choking and making gurgling efforts to scream, Suttell crawling now and thinking, he is goen to have to kill us all to git me. Then the rebel major was there again, squinting over toward the tents and all of the prisoners were now huddling in a tight, wide-eyed group, pressing together against the firestep and some even going under it. And the boy with the shotgun turning and turning in confusion now and bubbling, "Whut whut whut?" and the rebel major standing right over them all.

The rebel major reached down for Suttell, and Suttell, again on pure instinct, rose and put his head near the man's knee and knelt almost like a dog and the man put his large hands on his head and smiled down at him. The hands were large and gentle and they folded around his ears and through his blond hair and they sort of lifted him up, rising like a soft helmet and he rose too, and then the rebel major dropped his hands and smiled at the boy. Suttell looked terrified and smiled and then looked around nervously again, the thin, clear skin on his face shifting quickly and easily into the emotions. The major reached out again and put his large, moist hands on his shoulder and said, "All right, boy, all right now," and smiled at him, and then nodded toward the rebel officers who were standing in a group still looking over at the tents.

"Go over yonder. Go over yonder and find Lieutenant Tarkenton and tell him I said you was to go down with him, an' show him where to find him a new frock coat in the town. All right, boy?" Suttell nodded again and wiped at his nose with his sleeve, not even trusting himself to have any thoughts and hoping the big pistol would not show while he walked. The major patted him on the back and then turned to look after the other prisoners. The firing was still intense on the bluff, a roar against the ear. Suttell was nervous and he walked splay-footed across to the other officers, looking all the time in the direction of the tents. I don't trust thet ol' corpral. I hope this ol' gun ain't showen. Hit feels like a brick.

He got over to the officers and lowered his head and grinned at them up through his hair. Most of them looked at him angrily. "I was tol' to come an' fin' Captin Tarkenton." He snuffled again and wiped his sleeve across his nose. Tarkenton was the one with the big nose and the scar, the only one who was grinning at him. "Here." He smiled at Suttell and put his hand on his shoulder too, looking down at him because Suttell who was at least the same height had ducked his head into his shoulders deferentially. "The officer over there say I am to take you down to town and show you whar to git a ol' new frock coat," and he said it softly and with the flesh above his eyes bent into a V of worry. Tarkenton still with his hands on his shoulder looked over at Major Perry and nodded and smiled broadly and said, "All right, lead on, boy," and said, "I see you men," to the other officers, who were standing with their faces still set and hard and their spade beards lifted.

They went out of the fort through the second porthole, climbing through the embrasure and across wooden slats the rebels had stretched over the moat. Suttell kept his head down and his chest and belly held in to hollow around the revolver so the rebel officer would not see it under his blouse. The moat was filled with cartridge boxes, flecks of percussion caps, hats, cord and some artillery leather scattered over the green scum. They walked down the path leading to the town ravine, the rebel officer saying how odd it was that they could now walk across this open ground which had been so hotly contested before. Unh huh. Suttell looked around him, considering making a quick run for the forest, but it was obviously too far away and the area was covered with rebels, moving with blankets and stretchers among the wounded. There was one boy lying on his back near the path, his whole chest torn out as if by a giant shotgun, Suttell thought. There was a squirrel's tail still in the brim of his cap, and a stubble of beard on his chin. He had very blue eyes. The rebel captain was now in front of him walking along talking steadily, about how strange it was too that the two of them should be walking along like this in the late afternoon when earlier during the morning they would have tried to kill each other on sight.

Unh huh, Suttell thought again. Now that the man's back was turned the revolver did not seem so heavy at all. Unh huh, you ol' reb officer, you git high an' mighty with me and we see about that mess. I shore am glad to be shet of them ol' Mississippi officers. I sweah, they soon kill you as look at chee. There

The Battle of Fort Pillow   461

were dead men still scattered along the slope and some of them were from his company. Barr's body was still there he noticed as they came down into the clayey place after the grass and fallen logs. Barr was turned over onto his back now, and his pockets were all reversed. His sword was gone and his belt buckle had been snapped off. One eye was open, and one eye closed. His flesh which had been very swarthy was green now, and there were flies around his mouth, quick black flecks on the skin. The rebel captain cursed and flicked his boot toe at them and they rose. He said something about flies making war horrible, some funny thing, and Suttell grinned in appreciation but he was really thinking, uh rebel, don't you go maken any fun of me, naw. Not when I got this here Navy six which I can grab holt of lot sooner you can git out thet ol' sword. He looked down as they passed some more dead men of his own company and of E Company. The rebel officer paused at a cluster of four sprawled bodies and wanted to talk. "Was this battalion of yours a good one, Private?"

That is a hell of a question. "Naw. Naw, hit warnt no good atall." He started to go on, to show the man where the dry goods store was. He was nervous with all of the lean Mississippians, a lot of them wounded and pallid, walking around with their big rifles and stringy beards. "Why wasn't it good?" The rebel captain was still looking down at the body of one of the men, face down in the dirt.

He shuffled and looked at the man, thinking quickly, is he maken a fool of me? and then said, "Well to tell the truth, I reckon it were because ol' Bradford wuz a yellow-belly coward in the first place. Dint have no good officers at all, 'cept for maybe Leamin' and he was a strict un. Not much in the way of good men neither, not out of West Tennessee this time in the war." He was circumspect, looking at the rebel captain all the time.

The man looked down at the body and toed it slightly and then said, "Umm, that is what I would have thought. That is what I would have thought," and nodded his head again. Well now. Suttell grinned suddenly. That is the first time one of 'em ever said howdedo to a Suttell I reckon. Well. He grinned warmly at the man and then remembered the pistol and slouched again. He prized the rebel officer's agreement and treasured it in his mind.

"Well, we better be getting on to the store." The man winked at him over the big nose. "Before it gets too late and they start putting sentinels around, you know what I mean." Suttell was confused but led him to the shanty where the dry goods were kept. All around them were burning huts, burning desultorily and in flickering swarms of black ash. There were wounded men being put in the huts and rebels with sad faces and bloodied sleeves going into some of them and tending to the wounded. He even saw a wounded nigger, a young one with very light skin, being taken into one of the huts and smearing blood from a torn leg over the doorsill. There were hoarse yells from some of the other huts and rebels coming out carrying the clocks and spoons and picture frames the Tennesseans had looted from West Tennessee, and hats and gunbelts and clothes, drawers long and white and obscene-looking and men's clawhammer coats some of the Union Tennesseans had owned or stolen. They were whooping and yelling and a lot of them were drunk. Men were shouldering into each other in the streets between the huts and laughing and every now and then a rebel with a grey jacket and stained cuffs would shoot off his revolver and raise his grizzled chin in the air and whoop. The cries and the way they looked at him made Suttell's blood run cold. *I got to git this ol' jacket off, and in a place where this captain won't see my Navy.*

They went into the store and there were four rebels there, Texas rangers with big spurs and red cuffs and collars, all of them drunk on the floor with their big pistols still in their hands, trying with infinite cunning to open a metal box. They were swearing and the biggest of them, a blond-haired man with lantern jaws, was turning the box over and over like a bear trying to get into it. Suttell was instantly afraid, the instinct then flooding back over the fear and he suddenly felt very capable and lithe and quick again, his eyes going everywhere and his mind rehearsing the steps to getting the big revolver out of his blouse while jumping behind the counter. *I can do hit, too, if* they go fer me. The captain in hip-boots and yellow sash was standing over the Texans now and his face was hard. They looked up hostilely and then at each other. "All right," the captain said, "get up and back to your companies."

The four looked at each other, their big spurs jingling slightly and their eyes close-set and cunning. "Naw. Cap'n Jonas he say we can take off fer a time."

"Get out of here and get back to your companies, I am telling you."

"Who be you?"

"Captain Tarkenton of Forrest's personal staff."

The youngest of the four, red-haired and with a spattering of freckles between wide eyes, grinned up and said, "Come out from behind thet nose, I kin see yer eyes sticken out." Suttell was standing in the shadow of the doorway, his hand playing with the button of his blouse. They goen to shoot that ol' captain. You don't talk that way to a captain lessen you goen to shoot him. And then they comen after me. His instinct was flooding and he had pressed his back to the wall and his eyes were glittering, and he knew that in the time it took to draw a breath, if he had that long, he could be on the floor behind the counter with his gun out and a pile of cheap leather spilled all over the Texans on the floor. His hair seemed to rise on the back of his neck and his face was not young and clean-cut, it was set and hard and fierce with the eyes cold and brutal.

But he was wrong. Tarkenton smiled and the four Texans were looking at each other now and embarrassed about the remark. One of them in the spate of silence, to fill it up more than anything, cuffed at the red-haired one. "Hesh up, Tony. You drunker'n a skunk." They were sitting up on their knees now and smiling self-consciously, and then getting up, still embarrassed and now cold-headed. Tony was querulous and said, "I ain't no more drunk'n you, Tom Sandridge," but they were pressing him and moving on out of the door, the big one still with the tin box in his hand.

Tarkenton kept on smiling at them and then turned without looking at Suttell and said, "Now then, I want to find me some good leather stuff for my horse, and a good frock coat for me." He did not look at Suttell and that probably kept him from being shot right then, since Suttell was still frozen and his instinct was still pumping desperation and quickness into him and he even had his hand on the polished pistol butt inside his coat. The captain, had he looked, would have seen the sheer animal anger and quickness in his eyes and in seeing it of course would have reacted with surprise if nothing else and Suttell would have killed him. But he did not look, he kept putting his hands on the leather and picking up one piece and then holding it and shaking it easily for balance and feel and looking over the rest. It took him twenty minutes to find the right bridle and then he asked Suttell where the coats were and Suttell by that time was thinking clearly again and he dropped his head to one side deferentially and was standing away from the wall. He indicated the next room. The captain said, "Well now, I will see about that. I will be gone a while. The woods are not far off, are they?" and smiled at him and went through the hanging blanket to where the frock coats were kept. Suttell stood staring blankly now, suddenly and for the first time in his twenty-one years honestly amazed with an amazement which he had inured and steeled himself against ever feeling. There it was on him.

He stood in the middle of the floor with his mouth open and thinking, of course hit is a trap. Of course hit is. He wants a chaince to shoot me in the back. . . . Of course he does. He stood there while the captain was rustling around in the next room and he felt the revolver and this time he drew it out. He cocked it, muffling the sound with the palm of his hand. He was thinking, I can slip up and shoot him in the back and he won't never know a thing and if he does I got my gun out and he will be dead before he gits to his'n.

He turned and looked out of the door and there were the woods, very close, and no rebels in sight. He suddenly felt very exposed in his blue jacket and he took it off, burying the pistol under some of the blankets on the counter and taking the jacket off and tossing it away and pulling on a tan coat. He found a wide-brimmed hat with a flat crown and he put it on, a little too big for him but better than being bare-headed when all of the rebels had hats. There. There, I look like a rebel, you caint tell

The Battle of Fort Pillow   *465*

the difference. He pulled out the pistol again and felt its heft. He checked the caps and they were all in place. He looked over his shoulder, feeling the tingle coming into his genitals. *All I got to do is step through that door and shoot and then run. And I am clear.* The gunfire from the fort was coming in a speckled roar. *I can get into the woods in twenty good strides and the only ones around caint even tell I ain't a rebel.* He felt the gun and stroked it with his hand, musing and feeling the tingle and wanting to preserve it as long as he could.

Ol' rebel they done sho nuff humiliated me this day. The thigh of his britches still chafed him where he had urinated when that corporal had come up to him. *This here might be a trap too. Prob'ly is, I never knew any ol' planter with this much given nature. Prob'ly is, least I can do is take that ol' captain with me.* The sunlight was going fast. He still stood immobile, trying to remember enough of the hatred from before to make him shoot the captain down, calling the litany out from before. *Law, I remember the time they done come ariden into our ol' yard and took out Pa;* all the time holding the gun in his hand *take that step, take that step* and push the curtain aside and shoot that ol' rebel and then cut out; *I remember the time ol' deLacey dint even git the name right, dint worry about it, just stood his horse in the road and shouted down to Pa sayen Mistuh Suttle if you please;* but it would not come. The hatred would not come and he still felt very flat inside and dulled and cold. The instinctive flood which had filled him before the Texans had embarrassed themselves had drained out and had left him feeling dry inside. He shook the gun and then he thought, *that ol' sombitch an' I kin walk right out and into them woods and I do kill him an' somebody hears the shot and I got to shoot my way out. So I got to go.*

John Arness Suttell opened the door of the shanty still in some confusion, having been stopped for the first and only time in his life by his conscience, or anything approaching his conscience; by his inability to work himself into a rage, after the sustained fear and anger and glee of the combat, which had satiated him for the first time in his life as well. For the first time, his hatred let him down. He went out and walked quickly across the stretch of open ground to where the ridges began, not even looking at the dead bodies of the men killed that morning in the skirmish, and then he was gone into the trees. There, that clustering hatred came back to him, and he was alone and afraid no more. He was mad that he had not killed Tarkenton. The fact that he had extended beneficence to him made him better, made him think he was better than Suttell, most likely; he thought, I should have gotten me a ol' Springfield, there were enough of 'em around, and waited and set out and gotten him and that ol' Mississippi major too, I reckon. Him too.

When he left the room and Tarkenton heard him go he stepped out from behind the curtain with two coats over his arm and watched the sunlight falling across the man's back as he crossed the open, and thought, good ol' boy. Would not mind haven him beside me in a fight. No. He tried on the coats in front of the mirror, looking at the hang of the cloth and still smarting from the young Texan's remark. I am glad, he thought, turning in the fading light to see the back of the coat, I am glad Major Perry picked him out. I am glad we did something Christian this afternoon, in the midst of bloodshed. Were it not for doing things like that we would be no better than the Yankees; this war would be hideous. And that boy would not have lasted a minute, way that corporal was looking at him. This coat will do, he thought. It will do for the time. We will get to Memphis one day, I bet, and I will pick out a better one from Hurlbut's own closet. He grinned at the thought, and left the sutler's store in the falling light, a man in a yellow sash and brushed grey cloth a little stained now and big hip-boots, carrying the black frock coat over his arm.

Later that night, south of the fort, Suttell was walking down a moonwashed road and the moon splashes were like spots of leprosy. He passed a plantation, one of the houses worked by Yankee overseers with Negro labor, and the Yankee was in the door, lighted by the lantern inside and standing in the door with a shotgun saying, "Who is out there, who is outchyonder?" Laughing, Suttell pulled out his pistol and shot at him twice. He ducked into a ditch when the shotgun went off, and carefully fired a third time himself, the bullet carrying too high and to the left at fifty yards to hit anything. But the man ran into the house with a clattering and a yell of pain anyhow and it delighted Suttell.

He got up smiling, and a little later, still walking in the moonlight, he laughed and laughed coldly, alone on the road. Some Negroes run off from the plantation out of fear heard him through the trees; the white man walking down the road laughing, and it filled them with a cold, thick fear. They looked at each other and the woods around them were suddenly populous with terror, the one man in the moonlight walking and laughing hollowly.